PRAISE FOR *HOMECOMING*

"Gripping . . . It keeps the reader in a thoroughly satisfying state of anxiety."
  —Dean Koontz, bestselling author of *Hideaway*

"This is Matt Costello's strongest book yet—a gasp-a-minute thriller that is also a powerful novel of character."
  —Ed Gorman, editor, *Mystery Scene*

"This is the real thing . . . There were spots where I was forced to turn my head and read out of the corner of my eye. I haven't had to do that since *Misery*."
  —F. Paul Wilson, bestselling author of
  The Keep and *Reprisal*

"Simply put, *Homecoming* is an incredible book. It's more than just a 'good, fast read'; it takes you into dark and dangerous places—inside the twisted mind of a psychopath; into the life of a tormented woman and the miseries of her husband, a former hostage; through the worst fears a parent may ever have to face; and—even more dangerously—into the darkest corners of the human heart, where life and love are *still* very potent forces. This is powerful stuff!"
  —Rick Hautala, bestselling author of *Cold Whispers*

"A highly suspenseful story . . . keeps the reader turning the pages."
  —Don D'Ammassa, *Midnight Zoo*

HOMECOMING

MATTHEW J. COSTELLO

BERKLEY BOOKS, NEW YORK

HOMECOMING

A Berkley Book / published by arrangement with
the author

PRINTING HISTORY
Berkley edition / November 1992

ISBN: 0-425-13503-9

A BERKLEY BOOK ® TM 757,375
Berkley Books are published by The Berkley Publishing Group,
200 Madison Avenue, New York, New York 10016.
The name "BERKLEY" and the "B" logo
are trademarks belonging to Berkley Publishing Corporation.

PRINTED IN THE UNITED STATES OF AMERICA

10 9 8 7 6 5 4 3 2 1

DEDICATION

*To Ginjer Buchanan—who
helped bring this one home . . .*

PART ONE

HOSTAGES

Fear of punishment in humans may be much more stressful than actual punishment.

—Ian Gregory and Ephraim Rosen, *Abnormal Psychology*

1

He heard steps. Simon Farrell did a quick check, asking himself: What is that sound? Is it real or is it merely in my head? Is it like the other sounds that I hear . . . that I think that I hear?

What is it?

No, these were definitely footsteps, definitely someone coming here, coming down to him, to this room, his hole of a room filled with his stink. The stench of urine and dried feces and bits of food too disgusting to eat. After all this time there was still food too disgusting to eat.

Simon could always tell when the food was too bad, even when he couldn't see it. When he sat in the darkness or lay down—the only two choices—and he chewed on something—crumbly dry cheese or tasteless, rock-hard bread.

He knew the food was bad when he bit down and something moved, scurrying away from his tongue, the oh-so-hungry pressure of his lips, the chewing—frozen at once by something living on his food.

And then those bits of food, thrown or spat away, stayed there, dotting the floor, becoming a home for whatever had been moving on them. Or maybe becoming food for something else, something larger.

The footsteps, close now, nearly to the bottom of the stairs . . .

He reached up and checked his blindfold, thinking, I have to keep it in place so that I can't see anything. They have to know that I can't see anything.

The footsteps reached the top of the stairs. Simon felt his hand shake. He moved, and his chain rattled sluggishly. He heard the key in the lock. Someone fiddling around, sticking a key in the lock and . . .

3

Simon tried to suppress the fantasy. But it wouldn't go away. It was always there, no matter how many times he heard that sound. He'd get an excited feeling in his stomach. Butterflies. An almost sexual thrill.

They'll open the door, the fantasy went. They'll open the door and say, "It's over. You can go now. We don't need you or want you. You can go home, Mr. Farrell. You can go home to baseball and opera and dinners with your wife and your little girl whom you can't see inside your mind anymore. You can go home."

The fantasy hurt. It was evil, this fantasy, something that cut his mind, a horrible torture. And he couldn't stop it.

The door opened, banging hard against the wall of the room. There was laughter and someone talking loud. A tiny breeze brought other smells into the room, fresher smells—the hallway and real food, what his captors ate. The smell of a strong cigarette.

All of it so wonderful.

There were three of them coming down. All three of them at once. That was odd; that wasn't what usually happened. Simon's hand shook more. He chewed his lip, sucking at it for comfort.

They were talking. And though Simon couldn't understand any of the words, slowly he did understand that something was about to change. Is this good? he wondered, as if he might possibly have the resources to answer. Could this *possibly* be good? Or is it that other thing? Is this bad? Is this the end?

He felt his chain being moved, picked up, and then he heard the lock that kept him chained to the radiator being undone, the chain suddenly sliding free.

And he guessed: I'm being moved.

He had been moved once before.

It was early on, during the first year, back when he had still expected to be freed any day. Such a stupid expectation. Stupid, unrealistic. They'll swap hostages and I'll go free, he'd thought. Or Jesse Jackson—the Reverend Jesse Jackson—will come swooping down in a helicopter and get me released. There will be parades and big state dinners that will make me sick. And there will be Lizbeth—

He stopped.

He didn't let himself think about Lizbeth. It was too . . . unseemly.

Hands grabbed him. More words were spat at his face. Then the loud clank as someone pulled him to a standing position, and the rest of the chain fell to the floor.

Normally, he stood only once a day, when they took him to the toilet. Once a day. And when he'd had some virus, so sick he had to go all the time, they had just let him lie here, sick as a dog, stinking in his own filth.

They pulled him to his feet. He knew his captors by his own pet names for them. One he named Garlic Breath. His strong mouth odor was a welcome relief, a break from the other smells. Simon caught himself sucking the aroma in deep.

Then there was Big Shoes, because Simon could look down through the tiny gap at the bottom of his blindfold and see that one of the guards wore these black army shoes, giant shoes, scuffed, spotted with mud and bits of red—maybe food, maybe blood.

Big Shoes had a strong grip. He liked to clamp his hands around Simon's arms. Real tight, causing pain, a little squeak. He was into pain.

Then there was the Smoker.

It was hard to tell where the Smoker was standing. The room filled with his blessed cigarette smoke, wonderful smoke. The Smoker gave the orders to the others, snapping at them, barking in his gravelly voice as if they were dangerous imbeciles handling a precious cargo.

The Smoker also spoke English. Simon was not supposed to answer back, even when asked a question.

Simon knew that. He'd been hit in the gut enough times in those first days so that he learned that lesson real well.

"You okay?"

It was more of a statement than a question. Simon nodded. He felt his blindfold slip a bit. It was loose. That wasn't good. If it was loose, if it slipped off, if he ever saw them—

They'd kill me.

The Smoker laughed. "You okay. You move . . . to new friends." The Smoker laughed again. Simon nodded.

Big Shoes clamped his hands around Simon's arms, right where he used to have muscles. His hands closed real tight. Simon felt hands squeeze his flabby arm meat against his bones. His eyes teared.

The bottom of the blindfold tickled his nose.

Please, no, he thought. Don't let me lose my blindfold.

The Smoker said more words. "A new home," he said. Then he laughed. He gave orders to the two men, and they dragged Simon out of the room, his chains rattling, an unwilling Marley visiting Scrooge.

Simon tried to walk, but they dragged him. His feet banged against steps, steps that he had come down—what? two, maybe three years ago?

Now they hauled him up, and his feet, shod in thin slippers, banged against every step.

They're going to let me go, he thought. No. They're going to kill me. Yes, they're going to kill me.

No. They're just moving me. It's moving day again. Taking me to another house, someplace safer, deeper into the Bekaa Valley, deeper into the mountain valley.

Like the last time.

No, they're going to let me go.

And on and on, and around and around . . . inside his brain.

His feet banged against the stone steps like chunks of dead meat.

They're going to kill me.

He felt the bottom of his blindfold graze the top of his lip, pushing against the tight bristly hairs of the bushy beard that covered the lower half of his face.

On and on and . . . *They're only moving me.*

He heard the front door being kicked open. Cool—no, cold air attacked his sweat, letting him feel how drenched he was. He heard an engine . . . a truck.

Moving me . . . to a new home.

Simon was thrown into the truck. He felt slimy, slippery things under him, wet and cold things. The back door slammed behind him. And then the truck pulled forward, its engine sounding muffled and distant. His cheek rubbed against some of the slimy stuff.

And he thought, I'm beyond being grossed out. How bad could it be? Whatever it is I'm touching, almost tasting. How can it be worse than what I've already tasted and touched?

His hands were cuffed behind him. He would have liked to raise the blindfold, taking the risk that there was no one there, no one who could see him look.

And see what the hell the stuff was.

The truck plunged into a hole, and he rolled over, his face flat against the floor, his lips pressed into the slimy stuff. He felt a texture, something he remembered.

It was lettuce or some other leafy vegetable, but old, left here until it had started to turn all soupy and brown.

And yes, Simon was tempted to taste it. To snake out his tongue, just to taste it. Maybe it wasn't so bad. Maybe it wasn't all rotten.

Could be my lucky day, he thought. My lucky goddamn day— *Lucky. Oh, God*—he caught himself.

Now I have to be careful here, he thought, real careful. Can't be asking for help, for a favor from God. *If* there is a God. Can't be asking for something and talking like that.

That won't do. Because the magic won't work. It never works.

And then he fell, swinging, clutching a bizarre pendulum taking him from one ideological polarity . . .

It's stupid. *There is no God.* And if something doesn't happen soon, I'm going to die. Maybe I even want to die.

To another polarity . . .

If I keep my spirits up, if I just hang in there, well, maybe with God's help I'll get out.

Back and forth, until Simon imagined each swing of the pendulum cutting a groove into his brain, slicing his sanity into little pieces.

The truck rolled again and then tilted back, going uphill. Simon rolled against the door.

Hope it's bolted, he thought. There were more big bumps, and he wondered where the hell they were taking him.

Why are they moving me? Did someone track me down? Did the CIA find me? Or the Mossad? Or the Mickey Mouse Club?

He smiled at that.

An expensive expression, that smile—his lips cracked anew. His tongue snaked out and he tasted one—no, two thin rivulets of blood. Smiles weren't good things.

His head rattled against the back door. He inched forward, away from the back of the truck. But each lurch, each desert pothole, sent him rolling back again.

Until, like the rest of his existence, he recognized that he couldn't care if he smashed against the door or not. No, because like everything else in his life he couldn't do anything about it.

The truck leveled off and picked up a rhythm, less violent now. Time passed. Minutes. Hours . . .

It was dark, doubly dark because of the blindfold, now touching his lip, slipping down.

And Simon slept. . . .

He woke up.

The rumbling of the truck had stopped. And there was a thin

line of light at the top of his blindfold, which was slipping down over his eyes. His heart started thumping away; he was always so scared about losing the blindfold. There was no moisture in his mouth. Now he smelled the vegetables, the soupy, decaying vegetables. He asked himself, Did I eat them? Did I eat any of them last night?

My face was down, touching them, my lips . . .

He demanded that his brain give him an answer.

Did I fucking eat them?

He shook his head. No. I'm hungry, very hungry. Hungrier than normal. And my stomach is empty, not filled with some rotten tomatoes, peppers.

The blindfold, the goddamn blindfold was slipping off.

He arched around. He felt the back door of the truck behind his head. He pressed against it, eyes facing it, and then dragged his face down, scraping it against the splintery wood door, trying to push the blindfold up.

He heard voices laughing, growing louder, then closer. It was morning.

The blindfold didn't move. But he felt the wood chew at his face. Splinters jabbed into his cheek.

"Ow," he said.

He wondered if he'd made the sound too loud, if it would draw their attention. Simon had known someone who was caught without his blindfold.

Simon hadn't seen what happened. No, but he'd heard the poor man's grunts. He was a minister. Reverend Trevor Cale, Church of England. He had come to lecture at the American University at Beirut on historical evidence in the Acts of the Apostles.

Reverend Cale prayed a lot. He tried to get Simon to pray, and he talked of God in a tiny whisper that he was sure no one would hear.

Cale liked to keep his blindfold off. He put his trust in God. But once, the guards came in, and Cale didn't have time to slip it back on.

Cale saw them, saw the guards' faces.

Then Simon heard his moans, the sound of something hitting Cale's flesh. They did it right there, right in front of Simon, so he could hear. They beat the poor man. So Simon would know.

Then, as if by magic, Cale had disappeared. Simon had never asked what happened to him.

He scraped his face against the door again.

Thinking: If I had a free hand I could fix the blindfold.

Another splinter, a long spike plunged into the not-so-soft meat of his cheek. The sudden pain made little white stars, mini-novas, explode behind the perpetual gloom of the blindfold.

He kept rubbing his face against the door, like a slave dragging great chunks of stone for the pyramids, oblivious to the risk of death, and to the pain.

He felt the blindfold catch.

But then Simon heard the rattle of the door behind him, that and laughter. The blindfold rolled up from the bottom, now threatening to come off completely. It was loose, and then it slipped down.

And he couldn't get it back in place.

Simon's lips moved soundlessly. Please. He tried to picture someone he could beg for help, for mercy: It was a mistake. I didn't want it to come off.

Then the blindfold stopped rolling, caught by the small hook of his nose. He started rubbing his head against the wooden wall of the truck.

And then, blessed moment, a wonderful event—Make it a holiday, let everyone celebrate!—he was able to push the blindfold up, just a few centimeters, but enough to completely blot out the light and the terrible forbidden faces of his captors.

The latch on the outside of the door rattled. He tried to squirm away.

But the door popped open suddenly, letting icy air rush in. Without support, Simon's head fell down and then back. He heard one of the men laugh, then smelled a familiar smell. It was Garlic Breath. He caught Simon's head before it cantilevered against the back of the truck.

Big Shoes grabbed him and roughly pulled him out of the truck.

Simon paid close attention to his first impressions. They were precious, these new sensations. This was a smaller house. Simon knew that because as they drag-walked him inside he immediately started going downstairs.

So, he thought, it's a small house, probably still in the Bekaa Valley. Or maybe—maybe I'm not even in Lebanon anymore.

My value is low.

Unlike other hostages, Simon guessed that he'd had the misfortune to be taken by free-lancers. His captors had taken him to be sold to whatever sect or group would pay the most.

But business had turned bad. The Smoker told him, "We hold you. You a spy. We trade for our brothers in Kuwait."

That was about all Simon knew. No trade had occurred. I guess, he thought, because their brethren in Kuwait aren't about to be released.

Which means *I'll* never be released.

I can't do this forever, he thought. There's a limit. And I've got to be getting real close to mine. I can't take too much more. I can't . . .

They dragged him down the stairs. There were more new smells, bad, foul smells . . . but different. There was the smell of old food, and there were human odors.

And there was something else. Simon sniffed at the air. Once, then again, another deep draft.

Big Shoes threw him down. Simon's bones, unprotected by his wobbly, pasty flesh, smashed against the ground. It was a dirt floor. His fingernails dug into the dirt.

He heard a chain being wrapped around something, then the familiar click of a lock. Someone jerked him up to a sitting position and opened his handcuffs.

Simon's arms sprung free. He flexed his fingers.

":There's water," the Smoker said. "In front of you." Simon nodded.

I've got to look like Ray Charles. Nodding my head to the air. Pointing my ears, savoring every sound, every cue.

He heard their footsteps as they left.

A door slammed, and there was the sound of a lock clicking into place. Simon sat there.

I'll wait, he thought. I'll wait a few minutes before lifting up my blindfold and looking.

Check out my new digs.

He coughed. It was cold. He felt around, but he didn't feel any blankets. There had been two blankets back in his last place. It was colder in this new place. And he had no blankets.

He waited, sitting there, shivering. He sat quietly just to make sure. Never could tell, but somebody might be standing there watching, waiting for him to raise his blindfold.

Peek-a-boo. I see you. You see me? *You lose.*

He waited. Simon thought he heard something squeak. It didn't quite sound like an animal. But then . . . maybe it was a rat. Do they have rats here? Are there rats?

Got to be. It sounded like a rat. He couldn't wait any longer. He was too damn curious, and too thirsty.

He raised his hands to his blindfold. The motion caused his legs to move. The chains rattled softly, like slithering snakes. Rattle, clank, rattle, clank, his constant companions.

He pushed the blindfold up. The room was dark.

He looked to his left. There was a window, painted black, but glowing with a constellation of stars made by scratches and nicks in the paint. It was close. Easy to get out . . . if he could get there.

The chain rattled again.

He turned forward, looking into the gloom of the basement, the dungeon, in front of him. There was a bucket. A strip of metal hanging from the lip, inside. He crawled a bit forward and saw water. He grabbed the curved end of the metal strip and pulled it up. He saw, even in the dull gloom, the sparkle, the blackish shimmer of water.

He lifted the ladle out. So thirsty, he thought. I'm so thirsty. . . .

He brought the water close to his lips. He saw something familiar.

An oily swirl on top of the water. Oily, like a slick in some abused harbor where the water made the herring gulls puke up their hot dog buns, made the bluefish go belly up, bloated, floating on the water.

It will probably make me sick again. I'll get the runs.

He raised the bowl of the ladle close to his lips. He extended his lips. His mustache hairs touched the water. He felt it before he tasted it. He sucked at it tentatively, then deeply, knowing it was best to get past the taste and the feel of the water.

And he was looking straight ahead, past the pail, into the darkness on the other side of the room. Then Simon Farrell saw what was making that smell, what was making the squeaking noise.

Right there. Just feet away.

He dropped the ladle. Water splashed onto his clothes, his rags. The spilled water made a muddy smear in front of him.

''No,'' he whispered, ever conscious of making noise, of doing anything to upset anyone.

He shook his head. And though he tried to fight it, really tried, he couldn't stop the tears that somehow started dripping from his eyes. . . .

2

Lizbeth Farrell pushed aside two thin venetian blinds. Noisy rain spattered against the bathroom window, the drops catching the eerie glow from a streetlight.

She chewed her lower lip. A habit. A new habit. No, she thought, not that new.

She leaned closer to the window, looking for a sign of a car coming down Gaheney Drive.

It should be snowing, Lizbeth thought. There should be inches of snow outside, making everything white and pure. Making everything look clean. Now it looked dark and wet and dirty.

The lake behind the house had barely frozen before the top layer of ice started to melt and turn slushy. Erin wanted to skate. Lizbeth had told her no.

"Don't ever go on the lake without my permission," she'd said. "Please, baby," she had begged.

The wind gusted, and she heard the tick of the raindrops hitting the glass hard.

Where was she? Lizbeth wondered. Where was Mrs. Martin? She was never late. Were the roads bad? Lizbeth pulled away from the window.

She heard Erin downstairs, laughing at a sitcom, the laugh track raucous, hysterical, out of control. Everything was *so* funny. What night was it? Friday night. Then Erin must be watching "Full House."

That was another strange family. Three men and three young girls. Lizbeth never did understand what had happened to the mother in *that* program. Another peculiar television family.

Like us.

We're peculiar.

She looked at the mirror. Her eyes looked back, dull, stranger's eyes. She opened her lipstick and covered her lips with an orange-red that, under the fluorescent light, didn't seem attractive or natural. She ran a brush through her long auburn hair, hair that looked washed out in the light.

Downstairs Erin laughed again, joining the canned audience.

Lizbeth heard a sound. She went back to the window and saw Mrs. Martin's car stop on the street slowly, cautiously, and then turn carefully into the driveway, next to Lizbeth's car. The woman was only a few minutes late. It was no big deal, nothing to mention.

She went back to the mirror. She licked her lips, wetting them. She didn't put on perfume.

That would be too obvious.

Then she took a breath and went downstairs.

On the TV screen a little blond girl, cute as a button, was crying. She sat on her father's lap as he stroked her hair and gently spoke to her, explaining something with all the patience in the world.

For a second Lizbeth stopped there on the stairs and watched Erin, glued to the TV screen. Their Christmas tree, a five-foot baby spruce, blinked on and off, filling the living room with a rainbow of colors. A few gifts left-over around the base of the tree. This year half of the gifts had come from Santa, and half had come from Mom.

From the beginning, she had fought the urge to write ''From Dad'' on a few. But she had made the mistake, from the start, of being honest with her daughter.

Honesty. Funny word, that. Honesty. Who the hell needed honesty?

''Lots of kids don't see their fathers,'' she had told Erin. ''It's nothing to be ashamed of. You just have to stop thinking about it.''

It was hard for Erin, though, seeing the other girls on the soccer team with their burly, exuberant dads cheering them on. Some of them took time to smile and be nice to Erin.

Some of them acted real nice to Lizbeth . . . interested in being more than nice.

The doorbell rang. Erin turned around, her eyes flashing concern.

''That's Mrs. Martin, honey.''

Erin nodded and then turned back to the show. Lizbeth went and opened the front door.

Mrs. Martin stood there, dressed in a tan rain hat and matching raincoat, dripping wet. The woman stepped into the house and shook herself like an overgrown collie. Lizbeth closed the front door, shutting the night out.

"Whoa, it's terrible out there, Lizbeth. Very nasty. Some Christmas week." She shook her head in disapproval.

Lizbeth helped her out of her coat, feeling the icy rain. "Here," she said.

Lizbeth had this feeling. She hadn't recognized it at first. But now she knew she didn't want to go out tonight.

Mrs. Martin's coat was sopping wet after only a few seconds in the downpour. Her glasses were speckled with water. She took them off. "Can't see a thing," she said. "Driving was horrible. There was an accident, right after Briarcliff, before the first Harley turnoff." Mrs. Martin wiped the glasses on her blouse. "You've got a bad night for your makeup class. Stay off Route Nine-A if you can."

Lizbeth smiled. She liked this woman, so much like a stock character from a sitcom. The nice just-past-middle-aged woman who watched yuppies' children while the parents led exciting lives.

"And darn slippery, too. You know, I think it's getting colder. It might be starting to freeze." Mrs. Martin laughed. "Maybe we'll get a winter after all."

Lizbeth nodded. "I hope so." She hung the sitter's coat in the closet and put the rain hat on a top shelf next to some wrapping paper and on top of the old videotapes of Erin when she was a baby.

She shut the door and led Mrs. Martin out to the living room.

The little blond girl on TV who had been crying was now laughing, playing with a doll. One of the three men on the show was talking like a cartoon character.

Erin laughed.

The man was talking like Bullwinkle: "Gee, Rocky, do you think Santa has anything for me?"

The cute-as-a-button little girl answered. "Yes! A great big bag of coal."

"Erin," Lizbeth said, "Mrs. Martin is here."

Erin turned and smiled. Then she went on watching the show.

I have to go, Lizbeth thought. Because if I don't go now, I might not go at all. And maybe that would be a good thing. A way out. At least for tonight.

"Erin . . . are you being rude?"

Mrs. Martin touched Erin's arm and smiled at Lizbeth. "Don't worry. She's watching her program. I'll sit with her."

Lizbeth opened her mouth to say something. But Mrs. Martin moved quickly to the couch, sat beside Erin, and gave her a hug.

The two of them were together. All was well here, Lizbeth saw. *All was well here. . . .*

She stood there a second.

Then she put on her coat and left.

The left rear wheel spun, screaming on the wet asphalt as she backed up.

Lizbeth hit the brake, locking the car halfway up the driveway.

It was turning icy. She chewed her lip and thought, I'll have to put fresh lipstick on. She started backing up again, slowly now, to the top of the driveway. She stopped.

Then, making sure that no one was coming down the dead-end block from the newer ranch houses shrouded by tall hedges and stands of oak trees and pines, she pulled out into the street.

Right next to the curb.

Right next to the yellow ribbon.

It had been there for years, tied around the tree about six feet above the ground.

Wet, tied tight. No one had touched it since Halloween two years ago when some kids had slid it down the tree to the ground and covered it with whipped cream.

The neighbors acted as if the kids had committed some kind of horrible sacrilege.

Lizbeth felt nothing. It was only a big plastic ribbon. It wasn't her husband. In the wet gloom it didn't even look yellow. Not at all . . .

She put the car in gear and drove away.

Lizbeth took 9A to avoid threading her way south on Route 9 through the river towns, the stoplights.

She went slowly, driving the used Taurus wagon carefully past suburban neighborhoods dotted with colored Christmas lights, plastic Santas, reindeer with glowing noses—all of it out of place in a too-warm holiday season. Christmas had come and gone with record-breaking highs. Santa had brought global warming this year.

The windshield wipers flailed at the rain, but they left streaks. They're worn out, Lizbeth thought.

The rain smeared, and the taillights of the cars in front of her were a blur. She found herself leaning closer and closer to the windshield, as if that would help her see.

The radio was off. She didn't want to hear anything. Not tonight, when she had important things to think about.

Things like guilt. That was a fun one to think about.

I'm a bad mom, she thought.

Leaving Erin with a sitter, letting her think I'm taking a course at Hudson College. Going to a makeup class. No one questions it. Who am I hurting? It's no big deal; it's nothing at all.

Still—she said the words aloud: "I'm a bad mom."

She laughed at self-chastisement. But then the real thing was there. The true thing, the thing that couldn't be laughed away.

I'm a bad wife.

Sure. That's true, now, isn't it? I've seen the pictures of other hostages' wives, sitting on their living room couches, their hands in their laps, tying napkins into tattered, hopeless knots. "I'll wait forever, Johnny," they said. "However long it takes, I'll be here for you."

I've seen the heartwarming profiles on "Today." "One woman's lonely vigil for her husband . . . coming up next."

And then there were women like Sis Levin. She went over there, over to Syria, met with people, worked in the Syrian schools, the hospitals, all to convince whoever held her husband that she was a good woman, that her husband was a good man, that—please, God—he should be let go.

I could have done that, too, she thought. But I didn't. At first she had told herself she couldn't go because of Erin. A small child needed a parent. Leaving her was too great a risk.

But there was this: She was scared of what might happen to her. She hated flying, hated the idea of going to a strange country.

I'm a coward.

And . . . and . . . what if Simon was already dead? No one had seen him alive. None of the official groups had ever claimed responsibility for him. He had just vanished.

Part of her thought he was dead.

And—maybe—part of her wanted it that way, so that all this could all end. The newscasters, the reporters calling once a year for their hostage roundup. The sooty yellow ribbon on the tree, never going away, a permanent mark, a scar.

There was another thought.

She and Simon had been in trouble before this happened. They'd had some bad fights. Parenting didn't come easily. Perhaps they hadn't known each other well enough. And then Erin had come along, and then this.

My life as a hostage's wife.

She looked up to her rearview mirror. She saw a car, two brilliant white eyes looking at her, the light glaring. Two smaller yellow lights to either side, little accent marks. The car came up behind her, close, closer . . . as if following her.

Lizbeth grabbed the wheel tightly.

She tasted no lipstick on her lower lip. No matter.

The car behind her inched closer. Lizbeth kept looking from the mirror to the windshield.

There was a turnoff ahead for the Saw Mill Parkway. Hudson College, her supposed destination, was miles back the other way. She put on her blinker. The car behind her followed suit.

This is crazy, she thought. What am I scared of? What's wrong with the nut behind me?

She was at the turnoff, a wide ramp leading up to the parkway. A state trooper barracks was conveniently located to the right. There were some red and green lights on the door: "*Happy Holidays*." The building looked quiet, the parking lot filled with blue and white patrol cars.

All of a sudden the car behind her came to life.

A bubble light on the roof of the car flashed on, spinning around, sending shafts of red and white light at Lizbeth, filling the inside of her car.

She moaned, startled by the sudden appearance. And then—a reflex—she hit the brake. I've been doing something wrong, she thought. He wants to see my license, my registration.

She quickly looked at the stickers on her window. At the inspection sticker: 1992. She looked for the month punched out on the sticker.

It wasn't December. December wasn't punched. And it wasn't a month anywhere near the end of the year. It was September. The damn thing's *expired*.

She grabbed the wheel even tighter. The siren screamed from behind her.

Lizbeth slowed.

The patrol car gunned past, the siren wailing, rising in frequency, then falling, the shafts of light from the bubble quickly cutting into Lizbeth's car, blinding her with brilliant light for a second before disappearing, fading.

The patrol car went flying past her, after someone else. Maybe to an accident or after some drunk weaving down the road, now turning icy and slick.

Over the slap of the wipers, Lizbeth heard a horn beep. She looked in the mirror. Someone else was right on her tail.

Lizbeth had slowed almost to a stop. She shook off her paranoid feeling and hit the gas pedal. Too hard! The rear wheels—tires probably a bit bald, got to get new tires—spun around, screeching. The driver behind her hit the horn. Lizbeth imagined the guy cursing at her, his face twisted and angry.

She didn't go anywhere. She eased up, and then her car crawled forward, onto the parkway, farther away from Harley, farther away from home.

The rain turned to something else, an icy slush that gathered in piles at both ends of the wipers' arcs. The wipers worked hard.

But still it got more difficult to see. And what Lizbeth could see of the road didn't look good.

Her car now made a different sound, not that sleek, slick noise of rubber on a wet road, but something with a bit of a crunch.

She went even slower. I should have stayed home, she told herself. I should have curled up with Erin, watched some dumb TV shows. Cooked us up some popcorn. Let her fall asleep on the couch, watching her dirty blond hair reflect the Christmas tree lights. On and off, on and off.

She spoke to herself. "But I guess, girl, that's not what you needed."

She looked to her left. The exit was close, right here. She watched for the green highway sign. If she saw the other sign, the neon sign, the one with big block letters that read Motor Coach Inn, she would have already passed the exit. It was so hard to see . . .

"No . . . scratch that," she said, still talking to herself. "Not needed. But wanted. Want—"

Her lights picked up a greenish white blur ahead. A big letter E. The rest was lost to the icy flakes that stuck to the windshield.

That's it. Elmsford. That's the exit. And far enough away, she thought. Far enough.

But maybe you can never be far enough.

She toyed with the brakes gingerly, just a light tap, but she felt her tires slide sickeningly. They were so bald. If I had the money I'd get new ones, she thought.

She made a promise to some relentless bookkeeper who kept accounts, who watched when you cut corners. Maybe he'd let her go this time. And the next, and the next . . .

But she knew that sooner or later promises all come due.

There's no free lunch, her father had always said. No five-cent cigars on this planet.

The car kept sliding. There would be no more postponing the tires.

She felt the car glide—just a bit. Jelly formed around her kneecaps and then spread down and up. Her dinner—a bit of fried chicken, some green beans—suddenly seemed to come alive in her stomach. She felt her bowels go tight.

She was still headed in the right direction, up the off ramp, moving at a very safe speed.

But the tires were floating, sliding. What was it called?

Hydroplaning.

Reluctantly she took her foot completely off the brake. There was a curve ahead, a sharp curve that she knew well . . . too well. Why do I know that curve so well? Well, Your Honor, here's the reason. You see, for the past three months, I—

She turned into the curve, still hydroplaning, still feeling that horrible lack of control, her legs useless, her arms locked, hopelessly locked, to the steering wheel.

The car curved around.

She almost made a promise.

Almost thought: Let me off the hook this time, and it will be the last time. Honest.

Liar. You lie.

And that's why I'm going to send your car smashing against the metal divider. Bang it up real good. Have the police come, the insurance people with all their questions.

So you can explain what you were doing down here. So it can be in the papers, the local paper that *everyone* on Gaheney Drive reads.

So your neighbors will wave to you when you drive Erin to the Brownies, to ballet, to school when you oversleep. Wave at you while you know what they're thinking: We read about *you,* Mrs. Farrell. We read what a poor excuse for a wife you are. What a—

The car slid.

"C'mon, c'mon, c'mon," she said.

A tire hit the concrete curb. She felt it. Then a rear tire hit the curb, too, and the car straightened. And, feeling the car slow ever so slightly, Lizbeth gave it a touch of gas, just the tiniest bit of pressure on the accelerator. The car moved forward. Bald tires or no, it moved through the gathering slush, away from the divider, out of the skid.

Blood returned to her legs.

She breathed. She hadn't breathed in the past half hour. She brought the car around to the exit onto Route 119.

The sign was across the way: The Motor Coach Inn.

She looked left and right, thinking, as always, Is there anyone here to see me? Is this really a town filled with strangers? Or is someone from Harley here, going out to dinner in the little Italian place up the road or coming back from returning unwanted Christmas gifts?

Will somebody drive by, see my car, turn and look, see me pull up the driveway to the motel.

Past the small white sign that said: Have Your Next Affair with Us!

But she saw no one on Route 119. It was a bad night.

And she crossed the road.

The room had to be around the back. That was a must, she had said. Even though only two cars were parked back there, Lizbeth felt naked, exposed.

She pulled her car into an empty place and killed the engine, the lights. She waited. The sleet built up fast on the front and back windshields. It dripped down the side windows, sealing her in. She heard the engine click, cooling. . . .

Another bad thought: What if it doesn't start when I come out? What if I have to call someone?

She dug in her purse and pulled out her lipstick. She tilted the rearview mirror down so she could see her mouth, her eyes.

A very strange person looked back. She no longer heard the sleet hit. The glass was covered by a muffling layer of slush.

She pushed the mirror away, sending the scary—*scared*—lady back where she came from. She grabbed the door handle and, after taking a breath, yanked it up.

Wet swirls hit her legs, her stockings. She grabbed her purse and an umbrella with her other hand.

She stepped out ready with her umbrella. Sluggishly the Totes slid open, in no rush. A few spokes had popped free of the fabric. They jutted out dangerously.

It's screwed up, she thought. Like everything else in my life.

She ran to the motel building.

Thankful now for the bad weather. Who could see me? Even if anyone was here, someone out to do something nasty, how could they see me? In the wet slush, under the umbrella . . .

She walked to the door. Always the same room. A bit of uniformity in the arrangement, a bit of safety.

Even through the curtains, the window was bright with light. She knocked.

Almost hoping that there would be no one at home.

Little Red Riding Hood knocking on Grandma's door.

No one at home. So I can just turn and leave.

But the door, too quickly, opened.

3

The blue car pulled up a hill along a winding single-lane road shrouded by full maple trees, with no lights anywhere. Tall grass, completely out of control, grew up to the edge of the road, waved at the car as it drove by, lost, forlorn. The headlights seemed swallowed by so much darkness.

It was supposed to be a country road in northern Westchester.

The scene changed, and now there was a young woman's face, pretty, all of twenty, catching the pale light from the instrument panel, filled with confusion, concern.

She was lost. And there were no streetlights here, no streets, just this road, slowly waving its way through the woods. The blackness outside the window was total.

The radio was on. Music. Classic rock from 92.3, K-Rock. The Beach Boys were singing beautiful harmonies. *La-da-da-da-da-da–a-a-a . . . da-da-da—da.*

Good, good, good vi-brations.

But the sound didn't fit. It made the scene that much more bizarre, and dangerous. There were no good vibrations here. The woman's face, leaning close to the windshield of her compact car—a Toyota, a Nissan, a Hyundai, a Mitsubishi, a Japanese something—showed no sign that she heard the music.

The headlights picked up an animal by the side of the road, a burly raccoon waddling out to the street, eyes glistening like jewels. The woman gasped, and the raccoon turned and waddled away, back into the tall grass, back into the blackness.

And the road kept curving. There were only woods now.

The song ended, and the deejay came on. A woman said

something about the Mets, about the 1986 World Series. The last game was being played, and the Mets were behind.

The woman, still leaning into the steering wheel, bent ever closer to the windshield and frowned. Lost. So lost.

"Damn," she said. The voice sounded low. The only sounds were the car engine and her thin, young woman's voice.

That was when she saw them.

The lights in her rearview mirror. Blinding, glaring, bouncing right off the mirror into her eyes. She shielded her eyes with her hands . . . and nearly swerved off the road, slicing into the grass. She cut the steering wheel hard, and the rear tires screeched. A new sound.

Now, with the other car on her tail, impatient with her being lost, obviously knowing where it wanted to go, she heard the sound of its engine.

Snapping at her heels.

Her eyes were wide, showing even more confusion, more fear. She looked down at the gas gauge, already creeping into the red, into Empty.

There didn't seem to be any pit stops on this planet.

"Oh, damn," she said again.

And at that moment, so conveniently, the trees parted and the road opened up. She got to the top of a hill, and there was a flat area, like a pull-off. A place where she could stop.

She could look at a map . . . if she had one. She checked the rearview mirror.

She spoke her thoughts, sounding artificial, theatrical: "I guess I could ask him for help. He sure as hell seems to know where he's going."

She slowed her car. The lights of the car behind her swelled in the mirror and then slid away as she pulled off to the side of the road.

She looked again in the mirror, and then she turned around. Perhaps the car would pass her, in too much of a hurry to lend a hand to someone lost. But no, the car came up behind. It slowed. Stopped.

She left her car engine running. And she opened the door and got out.

The air was cool up here. The wind whipped her long black hair back and away, off her face. Leaves were flying in the air, dancing in swirls. She looked at the other car.

But she could see only the lights, the blinding headlights. She covered her eyes, to no avail.

She waited for the driver to get out of the car, or at least to open the window. Then on her face there was a new concern.

There was a fear, at last, beyond getting lost, beyond running out of gas. A new awareness was visible first in her eyes, and then in her whole face, the tension of the skin.

She let one hand trail back to the open door of her car, touching it for security.

"Hey!" she shouted. "Could you help me?" A shallow laugh. "I'm kinda lost."

Nothing—for a second. Then a door opened in answer. Someone got out. She masked her eyes again. A dark shape. A man, perhaps. Or . . .

She held on to her car door, squinting against the light.

The shape walked up to her. A man.

"I took a turn off Six Eighty-four. I kept on going and—God, I don't know where—"

The man kept moving. Her words died on her lips.

Her feet slid back a bit, scratching the sand.

She made a mark in the sand that would join the other marks. Marks that would still be there in the morning.

With the tire marks . . . the other impressions.

There was indecision on her face now. Should she ask for help again—overcome the fear, the silly fear of darkness and strangers?

Or should she get the fuck back in the car?

And then it was clear that there was only one sensible thing to do.

The man hadn't said anything, he just kept walking toward her.

It's already—

Presto!

Too late.

A hand grabbed her throat, a hand covered by a latex glove. The glove caught the light, looking like strange skin.

She jumped away, a cat stepping on a high-tension wire. But the other gloved hand cupped the back of her head.

For a second he held her there like a bowling ball, suspended in space. Held her too long.

What happened next didn't happen right away. The experience wasn't to be rushed. She looked down, her eyes doing a terrible death dance, a sad hopeless dance in her imprisoned skull, at a leg kicking her behind her ankles.

And then he threw her to the ground and he was there, on top of her.

More marks in the soil, a small tuft of grass pressed flat, flattened still the next day.

A silvery blade appeared. The hand left her throat, and in its place an elbow was pressed across her neck. She could scream now.

She screamed. He didn't stop her. It didn't matter.

This was nowhere world. Empty Land. A real bad wrong turn.

The blade floated in slow motion toward her face. She screamed. Then begged, the tears oozing out of her eyes. It almost seemed real.

Nothing was hurried here. The blade played on her face sickly. There was *so much time*. Then it trailed down to the soft white skin just under her jaw. The point rested there. It made her stop screaming. If she moved her mouth, she would drive the point in. She could see that.

Then there were only her eyes, screaming eyes, completely wild. Terrified.

Terrifying . . .

And then, off to one side, away from this scene, another man walked out of the field, the dark meadow, looking out, talking. . . .

It was Leslie Nielsen. The actor who was in *Airplane!* and *The Naked Gun.* A funny actor. But here he looks so serious, so very serious.

"The murderer of Gail Tompkins is still at large." He says the words with genuine sadness, as if he knew her, knew this woman who was about to eat the knife. "The newspapers called him the Meatman. He killed five people, and the only clues were—"

The woman was gone, and her attacker. Her car remained.

"—the tire marks in the sand, the impressions of her struggling body. Because the bizarre case of the Meatman is another Unsolved Murder."

Electronic music jangled noisily. A hyper sound track. Time to get a beer and some Twinkies and enjoy the rest of the show.

"Shit," Lieutenant Jack Friedman said. He hit the stop button, cutting off the music, wiping away Leslie Nielsen and the magenta words, "Unsolved Murders." Brought to you by Bud Light!

Friedman shook his head. Outside One Police Plaza he heard the steady stream of Manhattan traffic. The sound was muffled, a bit different now. More rain, maybe something else.

No, it wouldn't be so bad if they got the damn story straight. But then, this was TV. This was entertainment. Facts shouldn't get in the way of entertainment.

Like the fact that Gail Tompkins wasn't alone. She had her son with her, her little boy, a cute kid with sandy blond hair and an all-American toothy smile.

Some of the state police had started puking when they saw his body. God, was America ready to see that on TV?

Whoever got Gail Tompkins also got her son. The network had decided that not all of the facts had to be part of the show. The victim had a sister and a father still alive somewhere, trying to live a life after their personal holocaust.

And that wasn't really *how* Gail Tompkins was murdered. It wasn't that fast. But the American public didn't really need to see how the murder was done.

Who could stomach the details?

Friedman got up from the green Leatherette chair. The chair had a tear right in the center of the seat, and a small tuft of yellow padding, genuine who-knows-what, had leaked out. A little fanny duster.

As soon as Friedman stood up, his knee ached. Despite what Dr. Perle said, the ache, the pain, was not getting better. I'm goddamn hobbled, he thought. Limping around the office.

If anything, his leg seemed worse.

He had to force himself to keep a smile on his face as he moved through the office. "Feeling okay," Friedman said. He smiled at the people who asked him, "Hey, Jack, how's things going?"

Just great.

No problem. Except, well, my kneecap is still a goddamn mess. The fucking thing may never work right. No, sir, and Captain Ramirez is still pushing me to take a disability leave.

The captain's proposal sounded very reasonable: "It's no problem, Jack. Take the damn money—and the time—and *run.*"

Wrong. Friedman was getting a bit desperate. He could see that the door was about to be closed. He'd seen other guys get pushed into retirement. It happened. He'd seen what it did to them.

Friedman hadn't come right out and told Ramirez that it was damned important to him to keep working. No, that wouldn't have helped.

The NYPD wasn't interested in personal problems. There were shrinks who specialized in helping cops who drank too much, cops who liked to sample the blow they confiscated, cops who beat their wives, beat their kids. You could get help. But you had to keep it under your hat.

The force had bigger problems. The city had no money. More crime, fewer cops, and less and less money. It was not a nice situation.

They didn't need a hobbled detective, especially one who was pushing retirement age anyway. There were enough Young Turks waiting in the wings.

You've done good work, Jack. An excellent record. Ramirez kept pushing. Even though the bastard was about Friedman's age. Take the money and run, he said. Hang it up.

Friedman didn't tell the captain that he couldn't do that. No, that was out of the question. He couldn't do that.

Now that Elaine was gone.

Friedman limped over the window and looked down at the street, glistening under the city slush. . . .

Cops made bad husbands. That was the story, and Friedman knew it was no myth. But somehow he had made the marriage work. He and Elaine were good together, even though she hated his job.

She made him change his clothes in the garage, in a little alcove, because she said she could *smell* it on him—the dives he went into, the bodies he saw, the blood, the stench of death.

She wouldn't have *that* in her house.

And she said that he drank too much. Which he did. Not as much as a lot of cops, but still too much. And some nights he couldn't sleep. Bad pictures came into his head and he ended up in front of the TV, playing roulette with the cable remote.

But he and Elaine still went to the movies. They still held hands. She looked beautiful to him. He loved the way she felt, he loved tasting her. She was a gift to him.

The other stuff was good, too. They loved talking about their two kids—Melanie, a teacher in Tucson, married, ready to start her own family, and Jeffrey, so serious, a lawyer in the San Francisco D.A.'s office. Good kids.

They'd had a nice family. Then Elaine got sick. Ovarian cancer that attacked their life together from within, invisible, insidious. There was nothing Friedman could do. The doctors were helpless.

The disease metastasized so quickly, there was nothing to be done.

The doctor actually said those words: ''There's nothing to be done.''

Then one day Elaine was gone, as if by magic. And he was alone. Which might be why he got sloppy.

Call it a lack of attention. He wasn't being observant enough. No, he was thinking about how he was going to live alone, wondering just how the *hell* he was going to get through each goddamn day without Elaine.

How could he live when Elaine—who laughed so wonderfully, who could get downright sexy after a single glass of white wine—was in a box. In the ground. He dreamed of her there. Dreamed of her alive, her eyes open, calling for him.

He had returned to work, but his mind chased those dreams. And that was how cops got hurt.

He and Brian Carty, a second-generation mick cop, were interrogating some green-card desperadoes about a bad-blood killing in a Colombian social club. It was no big deal.

But they had it all wrong. Friedman should have seen that. He would have smelled it—if he hadn't been lost to his dreams. The killing had to do with drugs and lots of money. And when he and Carty blundered into the after-hours club to ask questions, they didn't cover each other.

The petty drug entrepreneur was coked up on his own goods, flying real high on the paranoia express. His eyes were saucers—a comic-book villain—and he blasted at Friedman with an MP5 submachine gun that roared like a cannon in the low-ceilinged club.

Friedman felt his leg kick away. It wouldn't hold him up anymore. He melted to the floor, like the witch in *The Wizard of Oz*.

Carty quickly blew the guy away. Drilled a hole right in his fried brain. And Friedman, curled up on the floor, said those bad words, ignoring the pain, the blood, the bits of white that dotted the floor: "Shit, I can't walk, Brian. I can't move my fucking leg!"

Carty knelt down close to him, and they waited for the police, for the sirens and the ambulance. . . .

Friedman shut the TV off and then the VCR. He still heard the slush hitting the window, the wet ice slapping against it, sliding down the glass.

He had an idea, something that might get Ramirez off his back. Something that would let him work.

He left the tape in the machine; he might want to see it again.

He looked at his desk. So empty and clean, as if he was gone already, already retired. No investigation reports to be filled out, no court-appearance summaries, no expenses to file. A big gray desk, an empty sea.

I have to fill it. God, I have to fill it.

He had an idea, and the tape would help. He'd talk to Ramirez in the morning. The stupid TV show might help.

Friedman stood up. His leg hurt. Damn, it hurt. He took a step. An old man's limp.

Another step, into the outer office. Quiet now, everyone gone home. He walked carefully. He'd talk to Ramirez, convince him. Then he could start working. He'd have something to do, to keep the nightmares away.

Another step, the pain familiar.

And he walked out of the dark office to the elevators.

4

"It's about time, young lady."

Erin slid off the couch, away from Mrs. Martin's arm. It had felt comfortable—so cozy—sitting with her on the couch. She was just like a grandma.

"I have a grandma," Erin had once told her. "Except—she lives in Florida, in a *home,* and I don't get to see her too much."

And that was when Mrs. Martin said, "Well, then I'll be your grandma. Your New York grandma." Erin had liked the sound of that.

Now she shut the TV off and turned to face Mrs. Martin. "Can we play a game?" She saw Mrs. Martin started to shake her head, a tired look in her eyes. "A real *quick* game? Then right to bed. I promise."

The woman's tired look turned into a smile. "Yes. All right, a quick game, Erin. Your mom won't invite me back if I let you stay up till all hours. You wouldn't want that, now would you?"

Erin smiled and said no. Then, "You wait here. I'll get the game."

She ran upstairs to her room, to her closet, ignoring the dark hallway and her dark room and her spooky thoughts. She was too excited to let her fears stop her, too excited to let herself think what she always thought in the dark.

Something will get me.

Kids at school told her about the movies they saw—Freddy, Jason, living dead guys. Movies about ugly guys who liked to grab little kids.

They were only movies. That was all . . . but Erin believed

30

those things could happen. She believed because they got her dad, didn't they?

I once had a daddy. And now I don't.

She turned on her desk lamp. Humpty-Dumpty was holding a handful of balloons, each glowing a different lollipop color. The lamp just covered her small desk and one corner of her bed with a thin blanket of yellow light. She knelt before the dark closet.

The game should have been right here on the floor. She pushed aside stray shoes, old sneakers, a church pump, shiny and new-looking but much too small. A sleeping bag she played with, pretending to camp out in the playroom.

Then she saw the game. It was called Memory. And she was the absolute best at it.

She grabbed the box, squeezing it tight in her hands, and ran downstairs. She could hear that the TV was on again. Mrs. Martin was watching TV, waiting for her.

"I—I've got it," she said breathlessly, hurrying, wanting as much playtime as she could get. On the TV a man was holding a knife to someone's neck, and speaking closely into the person's ear.

It was a movie. Maybe HBO. Erin stopped, looking at the knife, at the man whispering.

Mrs. Martin looked around and shut the TV off with the remote control.

The knife was gone, and Erin smiled. "It's a great game. You'll love it." She guessed that Mrs. Martin would rather be watching her show, the movie about the man with the knife, hissing into someone's ear.

I wouldn't watch that, she thought.

Erin quickly squatted on the other side of the coffee table. She opened the box and set the board up.

"You have to move around the board and remember what the cards are," she said, putting the cards down. "If you match them, you get to take them." Erin looked up at the woman. Mrs. Martin seemed to be studying the board carefully.

Erin grinned. "You won't be able to beat me," she said. "I'm *very* good. I beat my mom all the time. And none of my friends—"

"Let's play," Mrs. Martin said. She sounded tired. Erin wondered if maybe it *was* too late for a game.

Mrs. Martin went first. She moved her piece one space and then tried to find the matching card. It was luck now, Erin knew. You had to see a few cards before you could go anywhere. It was all just luck in the beginning.

Erin picked a card and guessed. And it matched the space. She clapped and laughed. "I'm pretty lucky," she said.

Mrs. Martin smiled and ran a hand through Erin's hair. It felt so good. She said, "Yes, Erin, I guess you are."

Mrs. Martin pulled the covers up. But she didn't pull them tight against Erin's chest, the way Erin liked, tucking them so snug under the mattress.

"Say your prayers?" Mrs. Martin asked. Erin nodded.

Mrs. Martin opened her mouth, hesitated, and then said, "Did you pray for your daddy?"

Erin nodded. Then: "The newspaper's coming tomorrow to interview my mommy."

Mrs. Martin nodded. "Oh, really? That's nice."

"They'll ask her about my daddy and how much we miss him."

Mrs. Martin's hand, cool and smooth, slid across Erin's forehead. "And you do miss him."

Erin nodded, though in truth she was a bit scared. He was her daddy. She had his picture right there on her desk. A picture of this man holding her when she was only a baby. A man with a mustache and blue eyes. He was smiling, holding the baby— holding Erin—up to the camera.

Her daddy. But it was as if he was dead. Or he never was. She didn't remember him. Not really. She remembered a trip to the zoo and losing her ice-cream cone, watching it plop on the ground. And crying because she wanted a stuffed bear. She thought she remembered that. And . . .

There was one other thing. Daddy . . . She remembered him yelling at Mommy. Something had happened, and he wasn't happy.

And Erin was scared. She remembered that. . . .

Mrs. Martin leaned closer. "You're a good girl, Erin Farrell. Very smart and good."

Erin nodded, rubbing her head against her soft pillow.

Mrs. Martin kissed her. "And I'm your friend. If you ever need a friend"—she squeezed Erin's shoulder—"that's me. Okay?"

Erin nodded again and smiled.

Mrs. Martin stood up and reached for the light. "Sleep tight," she said.

Erin thought of saying "I love you." But she didn't. That was for very special people. The light went out, and Mrs. Martin moved out to the hall.

Erin clutched her blanket close, tight, listening for the sound of the TV, the noise of screeching tires and guns and loud music.

I don't like movies about that stuff, she thought.

I don't like that stuff. . . .

5

Simon spoke to it. His chin rattled as he crawled closer to the thing hanging there, swinging.

"Hey," he said, but he knew it couldn't answer. It was so dark over there, black, just the smallest bit of light catching the outline of the *thing*. . . .

He sniffed the air. He smelled it, and his stomach clutched tight. He gagged and coughed at the dirt and the wet slime in front of him. He stopped, catching himself, listening for them. They might come. They might see him with his blindfold up.

But there was nothing, no sound at all. So he inched forward as far as he could, to get closer to the thing.

Skre-e-e-k. A draft, nothing he could feel, made it move. It spun just a bit. Enough so that the face came into view.

The eyes were open. Simon saw the open mouth, the tongue protruding, looking too large, as if something had been jammed into the mouth.

Skre-e-e-k! It moved again. And the hanging man, bored, jaded with life here, spun away, showing his back to Simon.

Now Simon slid back, recoiling. The man's been hanged, he thought. They hanged him.

Simon wasn't sure, but the dead man seemed to be wearing a uniform. There were stripes, maybe, and buttons on his vest. Simon could now smell death in the air, taste it. The smell filled the room, a dead-meat smell, rotten. Worse, far worse than the food they served him, the moving food.

He pushed up to a sitting position, back against the radiator that he was chained to. The radiator wasn't on. It probably wouldn't ever go on. It was cold, and it would probably get colder.

Skre-e-e-e-k! The dead man spun again.

What's moving it? he wondered. God, what's making it spin like a kid's pinwheel blowing in the wind? What the fuck is making—

The dead man looked at him. Simon didn't know whether his eyes were getting used to the darkness or more light was sneaking in through the pinhole openings and scratches on the glass, but now—yes, now he could really see the man's face.

The eyes were like glass. Dry and dead, they stared around at the room. A dopey open-mouthed grimace. The tongue lolling out, as if the man had tried to spit it out. The rope hidden in the neck.

How long had he been here? Then—a more horrible thought. How long will they leave him here?

Simon pulled down his blindfold, covering his eyes, ending the show. He closed his eyes, thinking, Maybe I can sleep. But there was no way he could close his nostrils, no way to block out that smell, sweet and foul at the same time.

He huddled close to the cold radiator.

Somebody hit the soles of his bare feet, and he felt the sharp sting. Simon's eyes popped open to more blackness. The smell was there. The smell, the stench was on him. Another whack on his feet, and he cried out.

He heard his chain being undone. "You go piss," a man said. Simon longed for his familiars, for Big Shoes, the Smoker, Garlic Breath—all his old pals.

New voices meant new rules. The new voices had hanged someone.

My feet are bare, Simon thought. They took my slippers, my pathetic shoes. Already his feet ached from the cold.

The chain rattled behind him. "My shoes," he risked saying. "I need my—"

Whack. The answer came quickly, out of the black, a painful thumping right on the curve of his arch. Amazingly painful. Wondrously painful.

He moaned and curled on the floor, yielding to the pain. Hands grabbed him.

"You piss *now*," the voice said.

Simon tried to walk, to help the hands dragging him. But they moved too fast, and his feet stung every time he put his weight on them.

How could this happen? he wondered. How could things get

worse? Others had died at his last home. He knew that. He had heard their screams. But somehow it never touched him.

I won't die, he thought. I'll live.

Now death was here, in the room with him, hanging close by, waiting for him. He felt his tongue in his mouth. Would his tongue stick out like that, like a piece of meat, a tender morsel of veal, lodged there by mistake?

They let go of him. A door was shut. He smelled the sharp odor of urine.

He was never told that he could lift his blindfold to see the toilet, but the door was shut. . . .

Simon raised his blindfold. He saw tiny bugs swirling around the room, doing sluggish loops and circles over a hole in the ground. They were chilled, too.

He fingered the drawstring of his pajamalike pants.

His captors never gave him much time. He muttered to himself, fiddling with the simple knot that now seemed so difficult. His feet stung and throbbed, so icy on the cold ground. A few toes touched something wet, in the darkness below. He didn't look down.

He got the string loose. He brought out his penis. It felt foreign, alien in his hands. He waited, feeling a tremendous pressure. But he wasn't able to relax, to let it go.

A voice laughed outside the door. Were they standing by the dead man? Maybe looking at him and making jokes? How could they stand the smell? No, maybe they liked the smell, and . . .

He looked down at the shriveled, dark thing in his hand.

C'mon, c'mon, c'mon, he thought.

If they took him back and he hadn't urinated, he would have to wait another day. And the pressure would build. The cramps would be terrible. He'd feel an irresistible urge to do it right there, where he lay.

It came.

He looked up, feeling thankful. It was a wonderful gift, a blessed gift. He laughed, a pitiful, crazed laugh.

This is my world. This is my life. Where peeing into a stink hole during two minutes of privacy is a gift.

He heard the door handle rattle, then a few words in Lebanese. He quickly pulled down his blindfold. One foot moved farther into the wetness, into something slimy.

He tucked himself away and pulled up his pants. The door opened. The hands grabbed him, the voices talking to each other, laughing. They dragged him back and threw him on the ground.

His head banged against the radiator. The loud clank made them laugh some more.

He heard the chains being wrapped around his legs and looped through the collars on his ankles.

Then the voices receded, fading away up the stairs, until he heard only his own heavy breathing.

Once this would have had him crying for hours. He'd have cried for himself, felt terribly sorry for himself. But not now.

He pushed up the blindfold. He looked at his dead friend . . . who was looking right back at him.

There was no food. Simon waited. He was used to being hungry.

Simon prided himself on how little he could eat and still stay alive. It was a nice accomplishment, something to tell the folks back home.

Back . . . *home*. There, I thought it. Now, *that* was a mistake. That was a stupid thing to do. He had one hard and fast rule, only one. He could think of anything—list all the characters in Puccini's *Madame Butterfly*, go through the roster of the 1986 World Championship Mets, play Name the States and Name the Countries. All that was fine.

But there was one thing he couldn't allow himself to do. He couldn't let himself think of home.

And now it was there—the word, the images, the painful sound of it. And now, he thought, just because I'm upset, just because I'm sharing the basement with a dead man, I let myself think it.

Simon looked away from the body, but still felt the man staring at him. He thought of something he had seen on a tombstone once: "As you are now, so once was I. As I am now, so you must be."

No. He shook his head. Not me. I'm going to live. I'm going to make it. He moved his feet, and the chain rattled. No. They have no reason to kill me. Why would they want to kill me? I may still be worth something. People want me. My government, my family. I'm worth something alive, aren't I?

Sure I am.

His hands touched the cool metal of the dead radiator. He traced the curve of the radiator, not minding the cold, enjoying the bumps and grooves where the paint had flecked off. His hands moved up and down, pressing the curve. He was not able now to chase that word away.

Home. He opened his mouth. He could howl, bay at the room, at his captors. He could scream, demand, beg. Please. End this. It's all a mistake. Please. Let me go.

Then he laughed. He actually giggled. It was so silly, so dumb and stupid. What was he doing?

Around and around the curves of the radiator his hands moved. Around and around.

He brought his head close to the radiator and leaned into it. He felt the cold metal on his forehead. He pulled away just a few inches, then he bumped his head against the radiator. Slowly, but hard. He heard the thud. And—somewhere—he felt it. But not really. He brought his head back again, farther away, then slammed it down again as hard as he could.

Now the sound was more satisfying, a more complete thump. It echoed soundly in the room. And then again, and again. Now he felt it, Simon felt the rude smack on his forehead, the almost sweet sting as his skin split, tore.

Driving those thoughts away.

He thought, I'm playing the radiator with my head. A dull human carillon.

Bong, bong.

He turned and looked at his audience. The dead man wasn't moving. The body wasn't catching any breezes.

How do you like it? Simon thought. Then he said it aloud. "How do you like it?"

Simon paused and waited for an answer. The upstairs door rattled. He pulled down the blindfold.

They were coming again, and maybe they were bringing food. . . .

They didn't notice the cuts on his head. He kept it tucked down, curled into himself. They might get upset. He didn't want to do anything to irritate them.

They talked among themselves, jabbering away in Lebanese. Until someone said something in English, something Simon missed the first time.

The guard kicked him. "You hungry?"

Keeping his face hidden, Simon nodded. He guessed he was. But, he thought proudly, I bet I could go longer without food. Yes, sir, I bet I could do even better.

The guard laughed. "We give you food."

Simon waited. He heard a cutting sound, then a breaking noise.

It's not bread, he thought. There was more cutting and then a sharp snap. Maybe it's some chewy meat. Meat. That would be good, Simon thought. They're giving me meat because maybe they want to trade me. There's a deal in the works, and they know it won't be so good to have a human skeleton, not that I look that bad, but still, an extra few pounds. Maybe they'll give me meat and—

The guards talked among themselves, then laughed and made rude, coarse sounds. Simon smiled to himself, wanting to join in the fun.

He heard the sound of a plate being slapped to the ground, and then things falling onto the plate. One of the guards came closer. "Good food. You'll like."

Simon heard the plate slide up next to him, making a small clatter on the dirt floor. He waited. The guards muttered to each other. Usually they left after feeding; that was what Big Shoes used to do. Feed the zoo animal and leave it in peace.

So why are they hanging around? Simon wondered.

Then he knew the answer.

The plate. They didn't want him to have the plate. Maybe they thought he'd do something with it, fashion it into a weapon. Something . . .

That was it.

"Go ahead," a guard said.

Simon reached out, still keeping his head turned away. Don't want them to see the cut on my head. I just had a few bad moments there. Just a bad moment and it passed. They always pass. But it wouldn't be a good thing if they saw the cut. Not if a trade was in the offing. Not if I might get—

He stopped the thought. He *stepped* on it as if it were a plump, sluggish rat too interested in food. He'd squeeze it until it popped.

His fingers searched for the plate. He heard the plate slide, probably being kicked a bit closer by a guard.

Yes. Something was definitely up.

I'm getting out. Oh, God. *I'm getting out.*

His fingers touched the edge of the plate. Now he felt his hunger. It was there, so strong. How amazing that he hadn't felt the ache, the bowling ball–sized wad of pain.

His fingers moved on top of the plate, crawling spiderlike. Feeling the food now. Not hot but cold. And dry. No. A bit wet at one end. His hand closed around a piece.

He heard a guard snicker.

6

Friedman hobbled out of the elevator clutching a stack of folders under his arm. Two young cops were standing by the door watching the gathering sleet. They turned and stepped aside as Friedman approached the doors.

"Evening, Lieutenant," one of them said.

They know me, Friedman thought. They know what I do . . . and what I don't do.

Friedman nodded and pulled his coat tight, fingering one of the buttons, forcing it into a hole.

He went outside, down the steps. The sleet made his steps unsure. It was going to be a bitch driving to Bay Ridge. He thought of getting a room, something cheap, up on Thirty-fourth Street. The Milwood, maybe. He got to the sidewalk. The wet slush fell against his face like icy spit. No, he didn't want a hotel room tonight. He was in a bad enough mood as it was. No hotel room.

He clutched the folders tightly. He had only brought the case summaries of the last five Meatman killings. It was homework, before seeing Ramirez in the A.M. There were these five and at least seven other possibles, not officially attributed to the Meatman.

And there were other files for murders that didn't quite fit the pattern. They were called related cases, but who the hell knew whether they were related or not?

I'll get to them all, if Ramirez lets me run with this. It's all shit-canned stuff, but now it's new, fresh—thanks to TV. I'll get to them. I've got the time now, haven't I?

He hurried to his car, a black Celica covered with slush. He dug out his key and unlocked the door and slid in, grunting. His coat caught on the seat. He yanked it free and slammed the door shut.

He put the folders on the seat next to him. The top folder was wet, the manila cardboard was puckered from the wet blotches.

Friedman put the key in and started the engine. His knee throbbed. His knee didn't like it when he did something really far out, something really crazy—like sitting down.

I'd better let her warm up, he thought. He reached down and turned the heat on high. It had felt like fall when he came to Manhattan that morning. Now at last it looked as if winter had arrived.

He looked at the top folder. He flipped it open to see if the pages were wet, the copies of the photos, the reports.

He saw a picture of the star of the show, Gail Tompkins before she met the Meatman.

The small photo, a family snapshot of a pretty girl, so wholesome-looking, was attached to the top of the first page of the report from the Westchester County Police crime scene unit.

The report was a fair job, though not up to New York City homicide standards, Friedman thought. But then we got the experience. We get lots of bodies. *Lots.*

The car's heating system started pumping warmish air at Friedman's face.

The name Gail Tompkins was typed neatly on a label affixed to the folder's edge. He flipped through the pages. It was damn slim. There were no witnesses on that deserted road. The medical examiner's report was brief but graphic.

Multiple ligatures marked the woman's neck and hands, hard, purplish furrows where ropes had been tied very tight. The Meatman was a good Boy Scout; he knew all the right knots. The girl's circulation had been cut off. There were telltale black marks where the ropes had been tied.

The M.E. wrote that the victim struggled to breathe in her last minutes of life. He didn't say what Friedman thought: that maybe she lived long enough to see it all.

The report on the boy, Tommy Tompkins, came next. There was a before picture—a school photo, perhaps—at the top of the report.

There were large, tire-sized bruises on the boy's chest, caused, the report suggested, by pressure of some kind. Perhaps the perpetrator's knee, the M.E. wrote. Friedman nodded at that. The sick bastard knelt on the kid while he cut him.

Friedman looked up. He saw a car pull up beside him. He couldn't see who was inside. I should go, Friedman thought, get moving.

He looked back to the open folder. The boy, Tommy, had smaller bruises and marks around his mouth and face, all indicative of the struggle to tape the mouth. The boy's face—Friedman flipped to the crime scene photo, the after shot—was covered by a thick black adhesive. A wide strip of electrical tape had been placed there.

Just in case anyone heard? To keep the boy from biting?

He was naked. The boy had been given the complete treatment. The full Meatman experience. Friedman looked at the photograph again. The face was bloated to the size and puffy consistency of a decaying pumpkin. The eyes were like golf balls, wide with terror.

It was a goddamn hard photo to look at, a color photograph no less. It showed the rainbow effect of so many bruises, the sick purple-blue streaks surrounding the cuts.

One of the two main cuts started on the left side of the boy's neck. The other mirrored it symmetrically at the right. Both slashes trailed down the boy's lanky body, meandering—now narrow, now wide—the marks of a calligrapher adding flourishes to a capital letter. Friedman imagined the blade tilting this way and that, making its slow incision.

While the boy chewed at the tape.

While his mother, unable to breathe, watched. She had kicked at the sand. There were marks. *She had watched.*

Then there was the blood—here sneaking out in a thin stream, there gushing from the big incisions. The boy had been awake and aware through it all.

Friedman imagined the pain, the terror. His stomach went tight. He felt the remains of the jelly cruller sitting there, eager to come out.

When the work was finally done. When the killer stood back, the boy probably tried to move, not realizing that you *can't* move when you've lost that much blood. He probably flopped on the ground like a flounder while the killer watched before turning to the woman. Of course by then she might have been dead. Or he might have killed her first. But Friedman didn't think so. . . .

Someone tapped on his window. Friedman turned, startled, and a page slid to the wet floor of his car. He rolled down the window.

It was another detective, Anthony D'Orio.

"What's the matter, Friedman? Car trouble?"

Friedman shook his head. The cold air, the ice, was getting into his car. "No. I'm just letting the car warm up."

D'Orio nodded. "Take care, Chief."

"You too," Friedman said. He rolled up the window.

It was time to go home.

The apartment was too big—three bedrooms, a big living room. It was too damn big for only him, but he couldn't leave it. All their stuff was here, all of Elaine's stuff. She used to say that in the spring, when they finally opened the windows, she could smell the ocean, even though it was several blocks away.

She said she could smell the salt air, the promise of summer, of dinners at Sheepshead Bay, watching the fishing boats come in with the catch of the day.

Friedman went straight to the kitchen, which was small and comfortable. The kitchen was always safe. His eyes ached from the night driving, from peering through the windshield. He grabbed a beer out of the fridge and sat down with the folder, rehearsing what he was going to say to Ramirez.

Friedman looked at Gail Tompkins's body. She didn't get the same careful treatment as the boy. It must have been fast for her, perfunctory. The Meatman was done, finished with whatever sick transaction he had going. There was a drop of semen by the boy. Just one drop.

The mother might have been dead already from suffocation. If she was lucky, she missed the show.

But if she wasn't, she saw the killer sink a blade—identical in size to the one that he used on her son—just below her rib cage and then rip it upward fast, no artwork here, undoubtedly hitting bone on the way. The autopsy found deep nicks in the lower ribs.

The M.E. listed pierced lung and internal bleeding as probable causes of death. That, Friedman thought, and madness. The cuts on the mother were quick and nasty. Almost merciful in the light of things.

The Meatman was done. Killing the girl was just a matter of tidying up.

The homicide detectives had given the Meatman his nickname. It was a secret name at first, a bit of gallows humor by the cops on the case. It wasn't supposed to leak out, but soon the name was in all the papers. The Meatman. Like Darkman. Batman. A super-villain. The Meatman . . . It was pretty fucking appropriate.

Friedman took a deep slug of his beer and continued his homework.

7

Lizbeth sat up in bed, holding the sheet tight to her breasts, feeling the absurdity of this sudden demureness.

The motel room was dark and, exactly as in the movies, headlights kept slicing through the room. The occasional flickering light of a car leaving or arriving, had been exciting when they were making love, seedy and romantic and sexy.

Now, as she'd feared, the whole scene was tawdry—like me, Lizbeth thought. She imagined a headline: "Hostage's Wife Caught in Tawdry Love Nest." Or maybe it could be a "Geraldo" segment." "Hostage Wives Who Cheat! On the next Her-ahl-dough!"

She grinned at that one. Then she felt a hand snake up from the bed, fingers touching her spine. The fingers thoughtfully hurried over the puffy area near her waist. I've gained a little weight. But screw it. I've got a little roll there . . . but I don't mind. And neither does he.

She turned to look at him. Walt Schneider's eyes were glistening in the dark room. He blinked in the darkness.

Suddenly she was angry. No, she thought, this can't be as hard for him as it is for me. Walt was divorced, impoverished by an ex-wife and two kids. He lived in a small apartment in a two-family house. Which was why they had to come to the motel.

"What are you thinking about?" he said smiling.

She smiled back, a slim smile, faint and unenthusiastic. She wanted to say "Us." Or, rather, "Me." I'm thinking about me and about what a shitty job I'm doing at holding the fort and keeping the home fires burning.

She wondered how many other hostage wives had lost it.

45

Do they wake up in the middle of the night crying not for a lost husband so much as for a lost life?

Or is it only me?

She shrugged. "I don't know. This . . ." She gestured at the dark motel room. "It's so depressing."

Walt Schneider sat up. He was thin—too thin for her taste. Downright bony, actually. But he was smart, and he listened to her.

For a while he makes me forget everything.

He reached out and caressed one of her breasts through the sheet. He laughed. "You're right. It makes me feel positively adolescent."

She nodded. His hand stayed there. She felt her response, her nipple turning hard, a mind of its own. And once again she remembered how this had come to pass. . . .

Lizbeth needed to get a job. She simply had to get work. Simon Farrell wasn't a government employee. There was no generous stipend while he was a hostage. A State Department functionary had informed her that he was engaged in private business—free enterprise in a dangerous region. There had been warnings. The officious-sounding undersecretary had not tried to keep the disapproval out of his voice.

Her husband's business—he was an agent for commodities traders–had included one oil account. Only one.

The oil company was based in Beirut. Lizbeth had never been to Beirut, but Simon had. He called it "the Paris of the Middle East." He said it was a beautiful city on the Mediterranean, with grand boulevards, just like the ones in the cities on the Riviera. Beirut had cafés, wonderful hotels, and charming restaurants. It was an old city filled with two millennia of history and ambience.

Then Beirut was torn by civil war.

The Muslims—both the moderate Sunnis and the fanatical Shiites—were locked in a death struggle with the Maronite Christians, and they were all willing to destroy the city in their bid for control, for power. And there were the secretive Druze, a Muslim sect nobody knew much about. Their powerful Druze militia hid in the hills of Lebanon and launched sporadic attacks and raids on Christian strongholds.

Then Simon disappeared. All of the Muslim groups—the Druze, the Shiites, and the Sunnis—denied that they had Simon.

For all Lizbeth knew, he was dead. Sometimes, holding Erin

close, patting her head while she fell asleep in the darkness, she let herself think, I wish I knew. Let him be dead, let him be alive. I just wish I knew.

In time he seemed like an old friend, almost forgotten. Someone from old photographs, someone she looked at in pictures and said, Yes, I remember him. I wonder where he is today.

The money had run out. A home equity loan was quickly gobbled up. Lizbeth had to snap out of her torpor. She went looking for a job, something involving numbers. She had once been an accountant, so she was able to get mindless numbers work that kept her hunched over a screen, playing tag with a keyboard and mindless work ignoring the stares and hushed whispers of her co-workers. ''That's the hostage's wife,'' she could imagine them saying, their lips moving soundlessly. ''Poor thing . . .''

Hudson College had hired her. The assistant registrar, a young woman who radiated stylishness and chic, had made no attempt to hide her joy, her positive *excitement*, that Lizbeth Farrell—''our own Lizbeth Farrell''—would be working there.

Lizbeth had smiled and asked about medical benefits, dental insurance. When was payday? She was given a cubicle, an IBM clone, and enough student records and bills to keep her busy for months.

And if someone had said she was looking for a man had that she might be in the market for an affair, she would have laughed.

It was the furthest thing from her mind.

She worked there for a year. Then two. Keeping to herself. People seemed uncomfortable around her.

But one day, just before the Thanksgiving break, a man had walked into the business office. He was thin, scarecrow-thin. He wore blue jeans, a tweed jacket, and a dark blue madras shirt—an outfit that screamed teacher, junior grade.

Here was someone not on the tenure track to publish-or-perish land.

She was sitting alone. Everyone else was at lunch while Lizbeth finished some work. Keeping to herself.

He smiled at her and said, ''Are you in charge?'' And she knew then that he didn't know who she was; he didn't know that she was ''the hostage's wife.''

He casually sat on the corner of her desk.

She smiled back, uncomfortable with his sudden close presence, but enjoying the odd thrill, not seeing it for what it was. ''No. I'm not in charge. Everyone else is out to lunch.''

"You're telling me! 'Out to lunch' is right." He dug in his shirt pocket. "They can't get the damn deductions straight on my check."

Lizbeth held up a hand. "That's not my department. I deal with students." She cocked her head. "And you're not a student, are you?"

He laughed. It was a pleasant, open sound. She cherished laughs these days—Erin's giggles, the audience roaring on the laugh track of some idiotic sitcom. She had forgotten what her own laughter sounded like.

"Walt Schneider, English Department," he said. "Associate professor of American literature. I'm the new kid on the block."

She saw him look down at her hands on the keyboard, then at her nameplate: Lizbeth Farrell. Then he was looking at her wedding ring.

He slid off the desk. And she felt this sudden, terrible sense of loss. He scratched his head. "Well, I guess I could use some lunch, too." He turned. "I'll check back later when the real hounds return." He shook his head.

He took a step.

The sense of loss—a strange thing—washed over her. For a few seconds he had talked with her, so relaxed. It had felt good. She didn't want it to end.

She smiled, too broadly. Damn, what is wrong with me? "It was nice . . . meeting you . . . Walt."

He stopped and looked at her for a second. And then she guessed he was good at reading people, because he cocked his head and grinned back at her. His mustache was not neatly trimmed, and he looked like a young, reedy Kurt Vonnegut.

"Yeah," he said. "I'll see you around."

He walked out of the registrar's office.

Lizbeth was left with a strange feeling. I was flirting, she realized. I was flirting with him. And—

She shook her head. No, it will end here. I've spent too much time alone, too many hours in a big bed, hugging a lifeless pillow.

It will end here.

But it didn't. Although he didn't come back the next day or the day after that, he did wander in a week after Thanksgiving. There were only a few other people in the office—it was lunchtime again—but Lizbeth's desk tucked in her cubicle was shielded from theirs.

And Walt Schneider, dressed in the same clothes, sauntered over. He had a different look on his face. Lizbeth guessed he must have asked people about her.

Don't you know? That's the hostage's wife, they'd told him. Simon Farrell, her husband, is in Beirut somewhere. Or maybe he's dead. She has a kid.

He had a different look in his eye, a more serious look, minus some of the sparkle. She found herself breathing faster as he walked through the maze of cubicles to her area.

She hurried, speaking first, "Oh, hi. Did you get your problem sorted out?"

He nodded. Then he smiled. "They blamed the computer. Always the computer, never the human behind the machine."

She smiled. Walt looked up and around.

There were some voices in the distance. Two other women, chatting, eating in, getting caught up on the latest gossip.

He looked around. It took an eternity.

Because she knew what would happen next.

He turned and looked back at her. The air felt cold, dangerous. . . .

"You know, I was thinking . . . I haven't had lunch yet. Maybe you'd like to grab a burger somewhere."

He scratched his head.

She froze.

"But I see . . . you've got a lot of work. Yeah, well . . ."

She pushed her chair away from her desk. She didn't think about the consequences at all. "No, not a lot. I was going to break for lunch. So—sure."

She smiled. A tiny part of her mind demanded, in no uncertain terms, an explanation for her behavior. She questioned her ability to pull off this schoolgirl routine.

I'm thirty-something and so the hell is he. What are we up to here? Just what the hell are we up to?

Lunch, that's all. Someone to talk to. And maybe I can avoid talking about the *subject* for the next hour. No more retelling how Simon vanished. No more discussion of the news coverage, the interviews, the media circus, the government neglect, and then the slow slide to hopelessness and oblivion—colored by the admission that she wasn't one of those strong women who could go out and fight for their husbands.

It's just lunch, she thought. That's all it is.

"Great," he said, smiling.

She stood up.

Just lunch. And he never said a word about her husband.

Now she heard a police siren in the distance, out on the icy-wet streets. She felt as if it were coming for her.

The road was probably turning slippery. She thought of the drive home . . . and the expired sticker.

I'm not out of the woods yet, Lizbeth thought.

She imagined a patrol car pulling her over, the cop shining his flashlight into the car. "Now, where did you say you were coming from, ma'am?"

She got out of bed, letting the sheet pull away from her naked body.

"I've got to go."

Walt stood up. "Hey, it's early." She watched him turn to the nightstand and pick up the half-full bottle of red wine. "Let's—"

She turned on a light, dashing his hopes of prolonging her stay. He looked funny, standing there nude, holding the bottle of wine. The image splashed icy water on what remained of her libido. She got dressed.

"It's still raining, slushy. And I'm tired."

Walt nodded. "Okay."

He never pushed. She liked that. He was happy to take what she offered. He didn't want more . . . though she suspected it was because he didn't have a hell of a lot to offer. His alimony and child-support payments kept him on a real short leash.

Why, I'm the perfect find for him, she thought.

She pulled on her slacks. Then she snapped on her bra and squirmed into a navy blue turtleneck. When her head popped out of the sweater, she saw Walt pouring himself another glass of wine. He enjoyed drinking, she'd noticed. Maybe too much.

She tugged her boots on and grabbed her coat, a faded blue parka that was on its last legs. She ran a comb through her hair.

She'd have to check her lipstick before she walked into the house and faced the inspection of Mrs. Martin. Who, Lizbeth suspected, would one day soon come straight out and say it: "You're not coming back from some college class, now, are you, Mrs. Farrell? You're leaving your beautiful sweet daughter with me to go off and get screwed by someone. Isn't that the truth?"

She would almost welcome it.

Better that than this horrible fear of discovery.

Walt came over to her, still naked. Devoid of eroticism, he was all bones and absurdity, Bordeaux and swinging male genitalia.

"Good night," he said, leaning over, kissing her cheek. It was a sweet gesture. She smiled at him and then kissed him back.

He never pressed her about the next time, which let her know that there *might* be a next time.

"Good night" she said. Then, after peeking to see that there were no cars pulling into the lot, no chance of discovery, Lizbeth opened the door and went outside.

"Mom? Mommee?"

Lizbeth was halfway up the stairs when she heard Erin call. Looking out the stairway window, she saw the car lights as Mrs. Martin pulled out of the driveway.

She thought that slamming the door behind Mrs. Martin might have awakened Erin, or maybe the child had not been asleep.

"Mom!"

Mrs. Martin had reported Erin asleep, sound asleep. Dead to the world. Not too dead, Lizbeth realized when Erin appeared at the top of the stairs.

"I thought you were asleep, young lady."

Erin stood there, waiting for her. "I was, honest! But I heard something. I got scared." Lizbeth reached the top of the stairs, and Erin leaped into her arms, jumping, pulled up by Lizbeth with effort. Erin was no light bundle. Still, the girl fit snugly, clinging to her shoulder, resting her warm cheek against Lizbeth's neck.

Lizbeth kept walking back to Erin's bedroom.

"I had a bad dream."

"Uh-huh." She was a heavy load to carry. My little girl is growing up.

"It scared me," Erin went on.

Did she really have a dream or was she making up tales? It was hard to tell. She carried Erin back into her own room.

Erin turned her head a bit, and Lizbeth felt some wetness. A tear, lingering in the girl's eye. At Erin's bed, she let the child slip down. But Erin's hand traveled down her arm. Lizbeth felt her grab her hand.

"Stay with me, Mommy. Pat my back. Stay." Lizbeth sat on the bed. I'm in another dark room, she thought. Now, which is the real Lizbeth Farrell? Loving mother or town sleep-around?

God, I need a shower, she thought.

She felt alien in her daughter's room, like a betrayer of all that was holy and decent about parents and children.

Erin clutched her hand hard. "Mommy, the dream scared me."

With her free hand, Lizbeth brushed Erin's hair off her forehead and then smoothed her brow. The girl's eyes—two big shiny pools—remained open, unblinking.

I shouldn't ask this, Lizbeth thought. I really shouldn't. But Erin isn't letting go, I have to hear about the boogey-monster and put it to rest. She leaned close to Erin, conscious of the wine and the love on her breath. She whispered, "What was the dream, sweetheart? What was your nightmare?"

Erin squeezed her hand hard. Then she spoke, slowly, falteringly. . . .

And Lizbeth felt chilled, frightened by her daughter, frightened to be in the house, just the two of them, lights off, in the dark. The slushy rain made spattering sounds on the roof.

I don't feel safe here, she thought.

"What was it, Erin?"

Now the child blinked. "I dreamed . . . I dreamed that something was in the house, Mommy. It was going to get me—and it scared me."

There were more rain sounds, heavier, as if the wind was slapping the rain against the roof, slamming it down hard. Lizbeth—stunned, ready for monsters, dragons, and robbers—didn't know what to say. So she leaned close, and whispered, "That's okay, sweetheart. It's okay. Go to sleep. Go to sleep."

Lizbeth held her daughter close until she heard the calm, steady, reassuring rise and fall of the deep breathing of sleep.

8

Simon grabbed the food. But the laughter, the odd laughter, punctuated his movement.

These men were not like the others. No, he thought. These men sounded dangerous. No, worse, unpredictable.

Predictability was important in this world, he knew. He could stay sane if he could predict what they would do. But without that . . .

He felt a cold pit in his stomach, an aching emptiness. He brought the food up to his mouth.

One of his captors barked out, laughing.

Simon's lips brushed against something wet, and then—God, the texture, the feel of it. It was all something he almost remembered, some primal taste.

Until—like a balloon bursting in an explosion of color, confetti, jagged fireworks in his brain.

He knew what it was. He didn't let it go.

Instead, Simon held it, shaking, his hand waving in the air, unable to let the food go, but waving back and forth, violently shaking.

He gagged, hacking. The men laughed harder. They said things to him. The words were foreign, alien, as if he had landed on some planet where people got hanged all the time.

Yes, and then—and *then* they chopped off their victim's fingers, the dead, dry fingers, and served them to the others.

The taste, the texture. *It was primal.* An ancient memory of thumb-sucking, of walking around with a doughy, soggy finger lodged in one's mouth until the teachers, the good sisters of the demented poor, threatened him with whacks if he didn't stop sucking this instant.

"You'll get whacks," they'd said, showing their teeth that matched their white bat costumes from sisterly hell. "It's a sick, dangerous habit, sucking your thumb. A nasty habit, and you're a nasty boy for doing it. *You'll get whacks!*"

An ancient taste from childhood.

He started crying. He bawled out loud, howling, crying to the air, to the men. "No . . . Noooo!"

Now the guards laughed even harder. The spell was broken, and he could throw the finger away, toss it to the ground. His tongue lapped at his lips, tracing a course around and around, trying to chase the sense away, the taste.

He had a terrible thought as the tears poured out, as he sat curled up like a chained animal, choking and crying. *I knew it.* I knew what it was.

I knew it was a finger. Yes.

And I was going to try to trick myself, to get myself to eat it because I was so damn hungry.

It almost worked. I almost ate a whole plate of them.

He rubbed at his eyes. No. That can't be true. I didn't know. I'm not an animal. I'm not—

Someone kicked him. Completely unsuspected, a boot rammed into his midsection, knocking the air and any thoughts out of him. Simon curled around quickly to protect his stomach and his genitals from a second blow.

A boot crashed into his neck, just below his skull. The pain was intense, blotting out the last blow in a new tidal wave of pain, a crushing monster that gobbled up every sense organ in his body.

He moaned, and now his lips moved against the dirt floor, talking to it.

He thought of a word. The word *help.*

Someone kicked his shins. A good, solid thwap with a hard boot that made Simon think of every time he ever banged his leg against something. Every time—and they all vanished compared with this intense direct hit.

He heard them laughing with great big belly laughs. Simon tried to say something but he could only mutter to the floor.

His hands covered his stomach. No matter, the next blow landed there anyway, right on his crossed hands. Another crashing wave of pain as white light filled his brain. He vomited, spewing up nothing.

One hand kept throbbing, as if awakened by some unearthly alarm clock.

Broken, he thought. Some bones are broken. He moved back to his other mental mantra. God . . . help . . . God . . . help . . .

Then the pitiful cycle, the chain of hopelessness, was interrupted. Something small—but clear and growing in brightness—dominated his mind.

Someone kicked his butt. A boot jabbed at his ass, now so flat, devoid of fleshy fat. He yelped when it hit.

The thought: *I've got to escape.*

Because if I don't escape, if I don't get away . . .

They'll kill me.

The pain came from different directions. Spaceships, envoys, beaming down, all converged on his body. He had trouble matching a pain with a body part.

It was a game. Damned difficult keeping track of so much sensation.

A few hours after the torture ended, he hacked up some blood. At least he thought it was blood. He was afraid to slip up his blindfold, afraid that someone was there, sitting in the darkness, watching him. Waiting for him to do it so they could hang *him*. He tried to sit up and found, amazingly enough, that he could.

The chain rattled behind him. He touched the wet, bloody bruises on his shins. The throbbing pain in his stomach was constant. He tried not to move—the slightest movement of his arm made his hand feel as if needles were being jabbed into the meaty parts between the broken bones.

He tried to think of how he could make it happen, how he might get away.

There had been chances before.

Once he was left alone while Big Shoes and the Smoker dealt with someone outside. They had left him unchained, and he'd felt the warm breeze from the open door.

He thought of getting away then, but he froze.

Things will change, he thought. They'll make a deal for me and I'll get out of here. Sure, that's what will happen.

The next time had come months later. His captors had left him chained to a pole while they cleaned up his basement dungeon. He flipped his blindfold and looked around. He was sure that if he yanked hard, the pole would come loose. The door was right behind him. In seconds he could be out in the streets, running away.

But again, he didn't move.

They will make a deal for me, he had thought. *Inshallah* . . . Allah willing. That's what they say.

Now my time is up. They're going to kill me, he thought. If I get another chance, no matter how small, I have to take it. I have to get out of here.

He made that vow. And then he waited.

They didn't beat him again.

In fact, the next day they gave him food—a pitifully thin soup and a dry, stale heel of bread that soaked up the cool soup nicely. And its taste was heaven, ambrosia.

It was hard for him to hobble to the bathroom. He had to limp, favoring the right leg, which also was hurt. His damned left leg couldn't stand any pain at all.

His urine was filmy red. He nearly cried at the sight, but he bit his lip and talked to himself, trying to sound like a kind, thoughtful father inside his mind.

You're Simon Farrell, he told himself. You're an American. You have a car, and a house, and a wife.

He saw her then. He *saw* Lizbeth.

The memory sneaked up on him, her auburn hair so thick, flowing down over her shoulders. The picture was so brilliant, her cheeks a pale pink, her lips red, her eyes flashing blue. This was no faded image of her that he played in his mind over and over. It was vivid, and endlessly fascinating.

He never got tired of thinking of Lizbeth.

In the early days he would think of her—

And touch himself.

When those feelings ended, when all his responsiveness disappeared as if it had never existed, her image was still enough to make him smile, and then shake with loss.

He had a little girl. He didn't know her. How old was she now? How old was she when he left? She's a person now, he thought. Probably looks like her mother.

He looked down at the hole in the ground and at his good hand holding himself, stuffing his penis back into the grimy pants.

Wouldn't she love to see me? Wouldn't that be a wonderful treat?

He knew what month it was. He was off a few days. That

couldn't be helped. He'd lost count. But he knew it was somewhere near Christmas. Maybe a little after Christmas.

Wouldn't I look wonderful under the tree? Merry Christmas,
little girl. Here's your daddy.

He slipped the blindfold down. The darkness felt good . . .
natural. He turned to the door. His broken hand brushed against it.
And he moaned, a strangled sound.

He pushed open the bathroom door, and a guard tapped his
hand, causing more pain.

"What's wrong?" he said. "Your hand. It's—"

Simon nodded. "It's broken," he said. "You—" He stopped.
No need for accusations. It was probably a mistake. Merely an
oversight. "It's broken," he said again, simply.

"I fix," the guard said.

Simon felt the guard leading him back to the radiator, to the
place where he'd be chained. The guard guided him down, pushed
him to the ground, almost gently. Was this a new guard or were
they getting into the holiday spirit?

The guard pushed him down, signaling that this was his place.
Simon heard the chain rattling. Then the guard spoke.

"I'll get bandage and—"

But the rest of the words didn't come, and the guard simply
said, "Yes," and then left.

Simon heard him go up the stairs. He waited. Then he heard
footsteps coming down. The guard was next to him, and then
Simon heard tape being unspooled and the sound of scissors.

"Give it to me," the guard said.

Simon didn't understand. He was lost, enjoying the new sounds,
a veritable feast of new sounds.

"The hand!" the guard said.

Simon nodded and nervously extended his hand. The guard took
it, and just his simple touch caused Simon terrible agony. He
chewed the inside of his cheek. This man is helping me, he
thought. I don't want to get him mad.

The guard put something cold and metallic around each finger.
More touched, more pain, and then he encased the fingers in tape.

"I don't know what is broken and what is not," the guard said.
"So I bandage everything."

Simon nodded. He tried to say thank you. But the words died on
his lips. Each finger was encased in metal splints and then
wrapped in tape. Then the back of the hand and the palm were

wrapped tight. Simon thought that maybe the guard was doing more damage than good.

Finally it was done.

Simon listened to the guard gather his things and stand up. "You'll be better," he said.

Simon nodded. The hand throbbed worse than before. How much pain can you feel before you feel no more?

I guess . . . I guess I'll find out.

Inside his head he watched the pain. He was like a shepherd watching his sheep, straying here and there. . . .

Pain everywhere.

Simon slept, and then he woke up to darkness. He slipped the blindfold up in that torturous way, the special approved Simon Farrell method. Just a bit at first, not enough to see. So if anyone was there, they would see him and he would say he was just scratching, rubbing his nose. He had an itch.

Then, after an appropriate pause, he'd slide it up a bit more until he got the first glimpse of something at the bottom of the blindfold.

Another pause. He'd count to ten, as if it were a children's game.

Then, slowly, he'd slide it all the way up until he could *see*. And no matter how horrible the sight—the dingy basement, the dirt floor dotted with his own blood, the spilled soup, the body—a decoration in the room—still it was wonderful to simply *see*.

All was quiet upstairs. He guessed it must be late at night. But there was a moon tonight; some light filtered in through the scratches on the glass.

What time is it? he wondered. 3 A.M.? 4 A.M.? I used to like the early morning. I used to like leaving my hotel and walking around a new city. I used to like watching people, watching a city come to life. . . .

He pulled away from the thoughts. They were too distracting. He couldn't be distracted. He looked at his chain, then at the padlock. He kept looking at it. The lock was always closed. Yes, it was closed. But . . .

He rattled the chain. It didn't look . . . No, it definitely didn't look as if—

Simon slid closer to the radiator, closer to the lock. He reached out. He licked his lips, but his tongue was dry and cracked. He needed some of that filmy water, he thought. No matter how bad it tasted.

With his good hand he reached out, and he—

Oh, yes, he thought. Oh . . . *yes!*

His hand touched the padlock. It was too big. The metal loop around the chain. It felt too *big.*

Because it hadn't been snapped closed. No. The guard had moved it over the hole, maybe pushed it—but not hard enough.

Not fucking hard enough!

Simon used his thumb and forefinger to move the lock, making sure that he was very quiet. His tongue lolled out of his mouth, tasting the air. He heard a creak from upstairs, a long, languorous creak, and he froze. His heart thumped. His breathing sounded loud to him, almost raucous.

Simon waited. Then, like a disabled safecracker, he worked the lock again, pushing at the metal loop with his thumb while his hand held the base of the lock still.

Maybe I'm imagining it, he thought. Yes, it's a crazy delusion. The lock is locked, pushed home tight. This is just wishful thinking—

He heard something behind him. Someone had been watching him all the time, watching. He turned and looked over his shoulder. The man—the body, the guy with no fingers—watched him with dopey interest.

Simon nodded. He imagined the body speaking.

Get me out, too, will you, pal? Take me with you, huh?

He pushed the metal loop. It didn't move, and his thumb slipped off. Simon pushed again. This time it moved just a bit—enough for him to know that the padlock wasn't locked.

I can get the chain off. I can stand up. I can walk up the stairs and—No. The door will be locked.

He shook his head. First things first. He pushed at the metal loop, grunting when it didn't move. It was a big lock, not like the little one that had kept his dirty gym stuff safe in high school. This was a heavy hunk of metal. But it moved—millimeters—but enough so that it cleared the body of the lock.

Okay, Simon thought. He stopped again and listened. He slid the lock free of one end of the chain. It rattled a bit. Then he pulled the lock free of the other end.

There was another rattle, and the lock slipped off. I'm loose, he thought. I'm loose, I'm free. He felt giddy, crazy. It was wonderful.

Now he worked the chain through the metal anklet on his feet, pulling it through the metal loop slowly, so very slowly. Each little rattle made him stop, made him suck in air and hold his breath.

I'm like that madman, he thought, in ''The Tell-Tale Heart.'' Taking an eternity for the tiniest little action, the madman inched open the door to spy the evil eye of the old man.

When Simon was finally done, he was disappointed.

He looked at the chain, a dead snake sleeping at his feet. Where was its power? He slid away from it. Then he stood up, grunting, using his good hand to get on his feet. I'm a wreck, he thought. I can barely move. How the hell can I escape? If they catch me, they'll hang me in the basement, too. They'll cut my fingers off and feed them to the next one who comes along.

He had to ask himself again, just to make sure: Did I take a bite before I tossed it away? *I didn't, did I?*

He took a step, a free step, in his dungeon. Master of his domain, a free man. He looked at the door.

It would be locked. The stairs would creak. And maybe it wasn't the moon that was making light in here, he thought, looking at the glow from the blacked-out window.

Maybe it was morning. They'd get up soon and bring him water and stale bread. They would see the chain.

He looked at the window again.

Surely there would be a guard outside the window, walking around, a rifle slung on his shoulder.

Simon took a slow, shuffling step. He dragged one foot, and the pain parade began again.

That would be better, he told himself. A man with a gun. A quick bullet. That would be better than this.

He shuffled another few steps.

I don't like this. I don't like—

This. . . .

And Simon moved to the window.

9

It was late, but Friedman flipped through the other photographs.

There were more pictures of Gail Tompkins and her son after the bodies were turned over. In some places he could see the lines that the killer had carefully cut into the boy's body.

There were photographs of the tire tracks in the dirt—sharp, stark photographs, as if the tracks were secret messages with something important to say.

The police had picked up a few fibers from the ground. Most of them belonged to Gail Tompkins or Tommy. But the investigators had also found some green acrylic fibers, perhaps from the killer's sweater. Nobody could be sure.

It had been cool that night. The Meatman probably wore a sweater, and if he did, it had to be covered with blood, like his shoes and his pants. Butchers usually wore white outfits. What did the Meatman wear? And what did he do with his clothes? Did they end up in some landfill being pecked at by a lucky sea gull?

What the hell happened to them?

Blood spatters found up to ten feet away were easily matched to both bodies. Main arteries had been sliced, and blood had sprayed the dirt.

Friedman thought of Gail Tompkins watching her little boy. God, if she had to watch . . .

Friedman picked up his beer can. It was empty, and he debated getting another. But it was late, and he had more work to do before he saw Ramirez tomorrow.

I should go to sleep, he thought.

He flipped to another page.

The time of death was easy to fix. The medical examiner put

down between 10:00 P.M. and midnight, a neat two hours. But now, unfortunately, the trail was cold. Very cold, because Gail and Tommy had died on October 20, 1986.

Over five years ago.

The Meatman had killed for three years, maybe more, depending on which cases were dropped into his growing file. And then he had disappeared.

Like the show said—an unsolved murder.

Friedman stood up and stretched, ignoring the pain. His orthopedic surgeon said it was important to get up and move around. Don't sit too long. Keep things loose, limber.

He felt about as limber as an icicle. He stretched again and, standing there, opened another folder, another murder. A change of pace.

One more nasty knife murder, this time a young coed from Riverdale. She want to Mount Saint Vincent, only minutes from the house where she lived with her parents. Her name was Tara O'Connell. Her father was a retired fire chief. And he had lost his daughter to the Meatman.

He'd killed her only minutes from her house. On Riverdale Avenue between the college and her home, she had stopped her car and gotten out. Nobody saw a thing. Nobody came forward. Her car was found . . . and so was everything else.

The killer had dragged her—there were some signs of a struggle—into a small park that bordered both Yonkers and Riverdale, a tiny dark park on a winter's night. She was found near a seesaw, sprawled in a scummy pond of her own blood.

There were dark, sprawling marks around Tara O'Connell's neck where she had been choked with a thick rope. Some of her screams probably leaked out. Anyone in the park might have heard her.

The original homicide team came up with squat.

The knife wounds to her breast didn't kill her. Death occurred because of the designs applied to her back with a thin blade roughly the same size as the one used in the other killings.

Death was due to blood loss.

The dried blood on her back spoiled some of the images, but, looking at the photo, Friedman could still make out the killer's pattern—the teardrop shapes, the familiar calligraphic scrawl, similar to that on the little boy.

Here the Meatman worked on a larger canvas. There was more detail. But there were no goddamn witnesses, no fibers, no prints.

The killer had apparently worn plastic gloves. The Meatman was smart, careful, and neat, very neat.

There were no signs of any struggle outside the park. From appearances, the victim went with the killer, maybe willingly, maybe out of fear, before being cut.

God, maybe she even knew him.

But there was one interesting clue.

Six feet away from the body, sitting on top of the cement walkway, was a tiny drop of wetness. It could have been anything—sweat, spit, bird shit . . .

It turned out to be semen. It was sent to the genetic lab, but there was so little of it—too little, the lab people said. The Meatman was nothing if not clean. When he climaxed over a victim—if all this blood and artwork made him pop his cork—he must have worn a rubber.

The Meatman practiced safe sex. But there was this drop, this dribble. A mistake. It happened.

Did he know her? Friedman wondered. Did she know him?

He pushed the folder aside. The other folders were here, the other slaughters. There were all these murders, and then they had just stopped.

Maybe the Meatman had found a new hobby. Maybe he'd died. Maybe he'd been killed by a potential victim. Maybe he fucking killed himself. Maybe he'd been nailed for something and was sitting in Attica or Sing Sing keeping his mouth shut.

But Friedman guessed that the Meatman was still alive. *Something this bad doesn't go away that easily.*

Now the TV show had everyone excited. Everyone wanted to know what had happened to the Meatman. Was he still out there waiting for a new season of madness?

Inquiring minds wanted to know.

Friedman pulled the folders closer and made a neat stack, nice and organized . . . an illusion.

He turned and walked out of his kitchen. It was so late, and now he felt exhausted, wiped out, while bloody visions danced in his head.

And, he thought, I'll have to beg for this job.

10

Later, Lizbeth would think, there were warnings, signs all around me, all at the same time. Omens . . .

She would think of Simon, of what might be happening to him, and of what she was doing. This morning, for example, she was running late, and the car, still uninspected, was almost out of gas. That always seemed to happen at the worst time, as if she blocked out the fact that the little pointer was inching closer and closer to the red, then sliding solidly into the red, finally passing the damn red mark to completely and totally empty.

Instead of hurrying to work, breezing in late—another good opportunity for people to look up at her and click their tongues—she stopped for gas. There was a small Getty station right where she got onto 9A.

She thought about the name Getty. Wasn't he the millionaire who lost a son? No. Now she remembered—his son was kidnapped, and they cut off his ear.

No. I'm crazy. That didn't happen to Getty. That happened to someone else.

The station wasn't empty this morning. There was a pickup truck, a big, burly no-nonsense truck with a spiky radio antenna reaching to the sky. The back of the black truck was filled with shovels, sledgehammers, and other tools partly covered by a gray tarp.

She couldn't see the man pumping gas. One side of the two-pump station was "self serv" and the other side was "full serv." A good ten cents a gallon separated them.

With the truck at the front pump on the "self serv" side, she'd have to pull forward and then back her car into the second ''self serv'' section.

She shut off the radio, cutting off someone cackling about the size of his penis. He said the word like a dirty-minded schoolboy. It was supposed to be a funny talk show. It was supposed to make you laugh. This morning it was only making her edgy.

Lizbeth looked at the dashboard clock of the Taurus.

It was nearly a quarter of nine, and she was going to be very late. She pulled past the pumps and stopped. The tires screeched a bit, drawing attention to her as she hit the brake.

She backed up, looking left and right. In the rearview mirror she saw someone get out of the big pickup.

She muttered, ''Don't worry, I won't''—she grunted, whipping her head back and forth—''hit you.''

She got her car in position, with the gas cap close to a short hose fitted with a ribbed rubber neck to suck up escaping fumes.

She killed the engine and got out of the car. The area stank of fumes here.

Decision time. Regular or super-lead? Two small red lights on the pump alternately flashed on and off. Cash or credit? She pushed credit and then pressed down on the handle, squeezing.

No gas came. ''Damn,'' she said.

The attendant hadn't seen her, hadn't turned on the pump.

She looked around, and noticed the driver of the pickup.

Lizbeth knew that something happened when two strangers glanced at each other. Both of them might hold the glance for the tiniest fraction of a second before one or the other looked away. It was some primal test of dominance. A game of visual chicken.

Who would look away first? She stared at the man.

He was fifty, maybe fifty-five, with a short grizzly beard. Black eyes squinted behind fleshy saddlebags drooping over the sockets. He wore the mandatory trucker's cap. It was black, bearing no cheerful emblem of a baseball team, football team, or beer manufacturer. He wore a plaid shirt-jacket in dull autumnal colors. He held the hose jammed into his truck while he looked at her.

Lizbeth felt his eyes on her. He didn't break the contact. He stood there. And for a minute she felt as if he could see straight through her, as if he knew everything about her. And not only that—*not only that*—he hated what he saw. She disgusted him. He was a man who worked hard for his few hundred dollars a week. And he was looking at her, judging her.

She looked away. The gas pump was still dead.

She felt him staring at her, not moving, not an inch. He just stared. She turned and looked straight ahead. She watched her breath create small frost clouds that dissipated quickly.

She was sure that if she turned back he'd *still* be standing there, a grim statue, watching her. Then two things happened.

The gas pump kicked into life and started making reassuring clicks and wheezes.

And a hand touched her shoulder.

"'Scuse me, miss, but I didn't see you."

She looked to her right. A small man stood there. He wore a turban and big grin. His white teeth were brilliant in the morning sun.

"Sorry," he sang.

Lizbeth nodded and turned the other way, aware that the pickup driver was still there, that he was still watching her.

But when she turned, she saw the door to the pickup truck slam shut. The truck's engine, rough and nasty, roared to life. A noxious cloud of exhaust filled her lungs.

The gas pump clicked off. Her tank was full.

She asked herself then—and again later, sitting in the office while everyone else was out for a coffee break—what had happened? What had really happened?

Nothing had.

Nothing at all.

There were signs, messages. . . .

Or maybe her mind was giving too much goddamn emotional weight to every look, every comment, every stare.

But that afternoon, when she got home from work, something really happened. Something that wasn't in her mind.

Lizbeth agreed to talk with a reporter from the *Citizen's Dispatch.* She wanted to say, "No. I'm too busy, and interviews are too upsetting for Erin."

But that was the funny thing about guilt. It could push you into some bad decisions.

The reporter said she would be brief; she only wanted to update those readers who had expressed concern for Lizbeth and her daughter. Everyone wanted to hear that she was doing just fine.

"You *are* doing fine, aren't you, Mrs. Farrell?"

The reporter had her there, but Lizbeth needed to prove something, to chase phantoms away from gas stations, to prevent the press from storming into her motel room with flashing cameras: "We have pictures of you and another man. And not only that—your inspection sticker has expired."

So she had said yes to the reporter.

And—funny thing—that was when it started.

She got home just as her daughter arrived. It was Erin's first day of school after the Christmas break. Lizbeth drove up to the house in time to see her daughter walking up the sidewalk-less street, dragging her schoolbag, looking lost.

Lizbeth beeped the horn. Erin looking up, blinded by the low winter sun, and waved. Lizbeth pulled into the driveway and down the little slope to the two garages, only one of which had room for a car.

The garage door opener had died several weeks ago, right before the bad weather came. It was a luxury she had decided to do without. Only the essentials got repaired. Now she ended up leaving the car in the driveway, parked outside in the cold.

Lizbeth went to the front door to meet Erin. "Hey, sprout, how was school today?"

She dug in her purse for her keys—so many keys, all making her sound like Santa Claus with a harness dotted with bells.

"It was okay. Mrs. Falapoop—" The door opened, and Erin giggled.

Lizbeth shook her head. "Faldoup, Erin. *Faldoup.* One of these days you'll call the poor woman that to her face."

They drifted into the foyer together, Erin dropping her schoolbag on the stone floor, Lizbeth turning on a light. The afternoons were gray, and the winter night seemed hardly able to wait until they got inside.

The Christmas tree was still standing guard in the living room. Lizbeth wanted it down, and soon. There was nothing sadder than a Christmas tree after Christmas. It was like a drunk who stayed too long at a party, wandering around wearing a lamp shade, trying to cadge a chuckle and another slug of holiday cheer.

Besides, Christmas, Thanksgiving, Easter—all of them were family times.

And we aren't a family.

"Got any homework?"

Erin scrunched up her face. "Spelling. Easy words. Simple words." She gestured dramatically, a natural ham. "Words I could teach my gerbil."

There were more giggles. Erin was bright, bored by school.

If I had the money, Lizbeth thought, I'd send her someplace

where she could soar, someplace where they'd take her as far as she could go.

But I can barely pay the bills.

Erin ran to the kitchen window and looked out at the lake. A small woods between the house and the lake nearly blocked the view of the water. "Mommy, the lake looks frozen." Erin turned to her. "Can I go skating?"

Lizbeth shook her head. "No, we need more freezing days, sprout. It's not safe. You know that. Besides, you have homework."

Erin nodded. "Can I do my homework in the kitchen?" she said. "Over milk and Oreos?"

"Two Oreos."

Erin skipped away, and Lizbeth hung up her parka in the hall closet. His coat was here, Simon's heavy camel-hair coat, looking a dark yellow, the color of sand, sleeping in the closet.

She turned and looked at the Christmas tree. That comes down, she thought. Right now.

She actually had half the ornaments off before the reporter showed up.

They sat in the kitchen with coffee for the adults and cocoa for Erin. The reporter, Mindy Zetlin, was a short, roly-poly woman with a close-cropped, short severe hairstyle. She also had a cold. She dabbed at her beet-red nose with a handkerchief that looked overwhelmed by too much goop.

The reporter set her tattered steno pad on the table. Lizbeth wished again that she had said no. Screw the story. Screw updating all the concerned people who want to know how I'm doing.

Let them guess. Let them *dream.*

But it was too late, and the reporter—all of twenty-one, maybe twenty-two—sniffed at the air, drank her coffee with two teaspoons of sugar, and asked questions.

"I'm all set," Zetlin said. "Ah, do you want your daughter to play someplace else while we talk?"

Lizbeth shook her head. "No. Erin knows everything. I *tell* her everything. She can stay"—Lizbeth looked at her daughter—"if she wants to."

Erin held the cup of cocoa between her palms and nodded.

The reporter raised her dark eyebrows. They looked bushy, especially since she had so little hair on her head. "Okay, then, Mrs. Farrell, how long has it been since your husband"—the reporter looked at Erin, who slurped her cocoa—"was taken?"

Lizbeth cleared her throat. That was an easy question. "A little over four and a half years."

What a stupid reporter. Why would she ask *that* question when she could get the answer from the morgue or whatever they call the place they keep old stories?

The reporter looked up. Lizbeth was unprepared for her next question.

"And how have you adjusted, Mrs. Farrell? What have you done to make a normal life for your daughter"—she sniffed, an unpleasant sound—"and for yourself?"

I took a lover. And my daughter is fine, except that she has nightmares about things in the house. And sometimes, when I think about him, sometimes I . . .

"We take each week, each day, as it comes. Erin has her life at school. I have a job."

Mindy Zetlin raised her pen—a baton to stop the answer, to put Lizbeth on pause. "You work at the Hudson College?"

Lizbeth nodded. "Yes. It's good for me to get—"

The reporter shook her head, disagreeing. She cocked her head and looked right at Lizbeth. "Didn't you need the money? Didn't I read somewhere that your husband— What did the State Department call him?" She flipped through her steno pad.

Tell her to get out, Lizbeth thought. Pull the plug on this crap. Tell Erin to go to her room and do the rest of her homework. And tell this dumpy little bitch to take her steno pad and—

"Yes. Here it is." Mindy Zetlin smiled catlike, satisfied. "Your husband was playing 'economic Russian roulette,' dealing with the Lebanese . . . that he was a greedy businessman who went in even after he had been warned."

"No. I don't think—"

Was she right? Lizbeth wondered. Simon had traveled a lot, sometimes to Europe, and then this one last trip to the Middle East. One more time, he had said. His business contacts were collapsing everywhere. The economy was heading for a big fall. This deal, this one oil futures deal, would have put the family ahead for a while.

That was what he said.

Lizbeth took a breath. "He was doing his job, Miss Zetlin."

The reporter opened her mouth—ready to protest the "Miss," Lizbeth wondered? Preferring "Ms."?

"Yes. I'm sure he was doing his work . . . but didn't he know the risks?"

Lizbeth stood up. "I've been over this before. Whatever sent him over there, the fact is he was taken hostage and . . . and—" She felt her lower lip quiver. She grabbed for the back of one of the wooden kitchen chairs.

She looked at her daughter. Erin had stopped sipping at her cocoa.

Mindy Zetlin pressed on. "Do you feel that your husband was treated differently by our government because he was only a businessman?"

"No. I mean, I don't know."

Yes. Of course. She knew that.

"Have you thought of flying to Syria or Lebanon to try and negotiate his release, like other hostage wives have done?"

Lizbeth let go of the chair. My eyes, she thought. They're going, goddamn it. I can feel the tears, and everything's going blurry.

"Erin honey, go upstairs. Do your homework and then play."

Erin's face was a concerned mask. The girl held her cup like a pilot steering a ship through a typhoon. She shook her head.

"Erin!" Lizbeth said.

The reporter, this foul creature, looked at Erin and smiled. And Lizbeth thought, If Ms. Zetlin reaches out and tousles Erin's hair, if she so much as touches her, I'll throw up.

Lizbeth's voice barked out, shaking, with just a hint of a tremor, "Erin. Go upstairs now."

The reporter looked back. Her pen was moving across the pad. Lizbeth could imagine the words on the page: *Distraught . . . emotionally frayed . . . fearful . . . tense . . . hostage's wife.*

I'm a hostage, too, Lizbeth thought.

Zetlin looked right at her. "Mrs. Farrell, you know that the situation is changing in Beirut. The Green Line is down, the militias have left. Do you think that this might help your husband?"

A pause. She knew the next question. She heard it rumbling like an icy breeze shooting through the door.

"Or do you think—"

"Erin!" Lizbeth's voice broke. Her daughter wasn't moving. Finally the girl stood up . . . too late.

"Do you think Simon Farrell's dead?"

Lizbeth thought she might scream.

The phone rang.

It was so unreal, so absolutely unreal Lizbeth nearly laughed. *The phone.* Imagine that! Ringing now, ringing here.

Erin was closest to the wall phone. She reached up, her small hand barely touching the phone.

The reporter paused.

"Hello?" Erin said.

Lizbeth backed away from the table. The interview was over, whether the reporter wanted it to be or not.

"Who?"

"Who is it?" Lizbeth asked. She walked over to Erin, feeling unsteady, like a bad sailor.

Erin held the phone away from her mouth. "It's a woman," she said. "And she's calling from some place."

Lizbeth took the phone.

"Someplace called the Motor Couch."

Lizbeth heard the words. It wasn't "couch." It was unreal to be in the kitchen. It was dark out, a black winter's darkness. Standing there, she could see the Christmas tree, half undressed. An old man waiting to be thrown out onto the ice.

"The Motor Couch Inn, I think she said."

Lizbeth looked straight ahead, out into the hall, to the living room, the tree. The two stockings.

Only two. She'd have no third stocking dangling there, empty or filled. She'd have none of that. She felt the reporter's eyes on her. Later she would think, I had no idea how crazy I had really become.

No idea at all.

11

Simon played with the window, which looked permanently shut. The paint on the frame formed a perfect seal over the window. He dug his black, dirt-encrusted nails into the wood and grunted. He tried to shove the window up, to make it move, even a half inch.

Come on, he thought. Just something to give me encouragement. That's all I want.

He thought he might be making too much noise. *They'll hear.* Then they'll come down and kill me.

The scratches on the glass, the pinpricks were lighter. The moon must be overhead. Or it's near dawn. He looked at the window frame, at the shadowy outline, at the dull, splintery wood.

He saw why it wouldn't open. There were two L-shaped brackets, one on either side, screwed to the window and the frame, holding it tight.

He pushed against the window. It rattled. The screws moved.

They weren't so tight. In fact, they were loose. He started digging at the brackets with his good hand grunting, resisting the urge to talk to himself. To encourage himself with words like "You can do it" and "There you go! It's coming now. Sure, it's coming."

He clawed at the wood like an animal digging for some lost buried treasure. A bone. Maybe a juicy finger. The wood splinters jabbed under his nails, causing more pain. But it didn't matter . . . no, because he saw, as he clawed at the brackets, that they were getting looser and looser.

One of the screws was wobbly. And he grabbed it between his thumb and forefinger, a prehistoric screwdriver. He unscrewed it slowly, torturously, until it came out. And he felt giddy with joy.

He put the screw into his pocket. Never can tell. Might need that later. Save everything. Waste nothing.

He tried the next screw, but it still felt snug. So it was back to the catlike scratching. Yanking at the screw, clawing the wood, loosening the bracket until the screw protruded a few millimeters, just far enough for Simon to get it out.

He heard steps upstairs. Someone was moving around. Simon heard the noisy rattle of a chair.

His breath caught in his throat. He was dizzy from the fear, the terrible fear that he had come this close—only to have them find him.

How will they kill me? What will they do to me?

The other screw came loose. Without a pause, he went to work on the remaining bracket. It already rattled loosely, ready to give up the battle. Simon felt his tongue dancing on his lips in excitement. His throat was dry.

He didn't stop.

The first screw came out easily. But the other held on until Simon thought he'd cry, until he thought he might actually have to talk to the little piece of metal, beg it.

Please. I've done all the rest. I've gotten them all out. Don't stop me now. *Please.*

The screw head tilted a bit. Simon pinched it between his thumb and finger.

It started turning sluggishly. He nodded, smiling. He felt the grateful grin on his face. He kept turning the screw, turning and grinning.

A crazy man . . .

Lizbeth listened to the voice, a light and bouncy woman's voice. Her eyes saw everything in brilliant colors—Erin, the venomous reporter, the white tiles on the kitchen floor, the shiny stainless-steel sink. Her empty coffee cup looked like a fossil from another time.

Lizbeth listened, expecting anything. She licked her lips, tasting discovery, doom, shame. A wave was about to crash over her.

A woman spoke. Lizbeth waited for her to say, "We saw you. We know who you are and what you did. And we're going to tell the whole world. Everyone will know what kind of woman you really are."

But those weren't the words that she heard.

"Hello, Mrs. Farrell. How are you today? We're calling to tell you about the Motor Coach's Weekend Romance Special. Have you heard about it?''

Lizbeth said no. It didn't occur to her to say, "Go away. Why are you calling me? I'm busy. Go away!''

"Well, for the special getaway-weekend rate of fifty-nine ninety-five you get a room for two, fresh flowers, complimentary breakfast, and a newspaper.''

"I don't think so.''

It was a joke. Someone's sick joke.

"I'd like to send you a no-obligation coupon worth ten dollars off your first night's stay. Now wouldn't that be nice? If you'll let me check your address . . .''

Lizbeth wanted to slip the handset onto the hook, quietly dismissing this person. But she had enough sense, enough awareness, to know that it would look odd to the reporter, who was watching her.

So she said, quietly, civilly: "I don't think so. I'm not interested.''

The person on the phone started to say something else. But Lizbeth said thank you and hung up.

Mindy Zetlin was staring at her.

Signs. Omens.

Zetlin said, unbelievably, "What would it be like for you and your daughter, Mrs. Farrell, if your husband came home?''

An innocuous question, a friendly question. For a moment Lizbeth pictured other wives, the Betty Crocker women, with perfect homes and small altars devoted to the memories of their lost husbands.

How *excited* they would be when their husbands came home! How they'd clean the house extra good, how they'd bake all day, how the newspaper and TV people would swarm around them, eager to catch every wonderful moment.

What would it be like?

Lizbeth smiled. A goofy, sloppy smile, an embarrassed teenage grin. She gave the only answer she could think of, the only answer in her head.

"I don't know.''

The brackets and screws rattled in the shallow pocket of Simon's pajama-style pants. He dug at the window again. This time when he pulled at it the window swung open, into his dungeon.

He felt the air, the cool delicious air. That was almost enough. But he thought, I have to keep calm. Can't get sloppy now that the window is open and freedom is right out there. A hundred things could go wrong. Thousands of things . . .

They might even be waiting for me outside. There would be a quick shout, followed by a bullet. He winced at the prospect, but he knew even that would be better than staying here.

His good hand snaked out of the window. He hoped to feel ground right there, something he could dig into. But his hand flopped around, and he felt nothing but air.

The basement window hung off the ground.

I'll just have to grab the frame and pull myself through. That's all. Nothing else I can do.

He reached up, then looked at his broken, bandaged hand. He whimpered in frustration. The hand was wrapped up with tape and metal splints.

There was no way it would help him get up. That hand was absolutely useless, absolutely fucking useless. And he certainly couldn't pull himself out with one hand. There was only one thing to do.

He made his good hand reach over, slowly creeping up on the wounded hand, surprising it. The good hand touched the bandage, feeling where the tape began.

Then, without hesitating, he started to unravel the tape, pulling at it. Even this little movement made the hand ache and throb, awakening the sleeping bones, the smashed splinters, the giant bruise that was his whole hand.

Maybe the hand won't work, he thought. Maybe the fucking thing won't even work.

There was another rattle upstairs, louder this time.

Outside, the sky was dirty blackish gray. It was morning in the Bekaa Valley. Cold air was running down the mountains. The goats stirred, waiting to be led where there might be a stand of dry grass for them to chew.

The militia were waking up, checking their guns, ready for another day of fighting the good fight for Allah or Christ or Yahweh or their homeland or their city or their dead mother or their imprisoned brothers in Jerusalem. Whatever . . .

Simon kept pulling on the tape. His eyes crossed with the pain. His vision blurred from tears. They were silent tears because he bit the inside of his cheek to fight back even the smallest whimper.

He watched his hand, a blackish-blue puffy thing, emerge from beneath layers of tape and metal. A mummy hand. He blinked to clear his vision.

It's a waste, he thought, looking at the tape, the bandage lying on the dirt floor.

Something creaked behind him. He felt the cold morning breeze rush past, through the open window.

Simon turned around. The dead man, his cell mate, spun around. So restful. At peace.

Simon looked back at his hand. Then, holding his breath, he gave it a test, clenching his fingers. They moved a tiny bit. The sensation traveled up his arm with lightning speed, demanding, screaming, Stop!

He kept holding his breath. Oh, God, it hurt too much. Beyond anything.

More, he demanded. More! The fingers, like a sluggish vise, closed around the air.

He held the hand like that.

Won't it be fun when I grab the window, when I put my weight on the hand? Won't that be something!

He turned back to the small window, to the ever-lightening sky.

It was time.

12

Captain Ramirez had meetings scheduled in the morning—another budget-crisis conference in the mayor's office. The city careened from one financial disaster to another. Then it was lunch time, and Ramirez was gone for two hours.

By the time Friedman was able to get an appointment, it was late afternoon and the city was dark again.

Friedman limped toward Ramirez's office, keeping a smile on his face, holding the folders tightly. Don't want anyone to see me in pain. Got to have everyone think, Hey, he's okay. Walks a bit funny, but Jack Friedman's *fine*. Got his kneecap blown away, but he's doing great!

With every step, Friedman kept running the bad movie, his take on what was going to happen. He could see Ramirez, jacket off, crisp white shirt glistening, leaning back.

He'll call me Jack. That will be a bad sign. He'll call me Jack and say it's time I hung it up.

Friedman reached the door to Ramirez's outer office. The captain had a good-looking secretary, a young Latina, very pretty. There were stories. The cop world lived on rumors—who was screwing whom, whose marriage just broke up, who had developed a taste for nose candy, who was on the take, who was owned by a Mafia family.

And who should pack it in because it was all over.

Friedman opened the door. Ramirez's secretary was typing—not too fast, Friedman noticed, fingers not exactly flying across the keys.

She looked up as if confused. It was dark. Time to punch out,

77

to get out of the city. "Hi. I'm Detective Friedman. I have an appointment with the captain."

She nodded and turned back to her desk. She pressed a button on the phone console and spoke quietly. Then she looked up at Friedman. "You can go in."

Friedman took a breath and walked past the secretary's desk and into the captain's office.

Ramirez smiled. "Hey, Jack, how the hell are things going?" He fiddled with papers on his desk.

Friedman could feel the captain's desire to move on, to get Friedman out of his office, to be done with it.

Ramirez looked up. "Have you given any more thought to taking your disability? You know, get some rest, travel. Hell, enjoy retirement."

Friedman nodded. He had known it was coming. If he stepped down, they could get a young guy in here for a lot less money, some young guy with a good leg.

He thought of all that time and nothing to do. I can't face it, he thought.

Ramirez looked right at him. "Is that why you wanted to see me? Did the light bulb finally go on? You ready to enjoy life a bit?"

The captain didn't mention Elaine. That would have spoiled the fantasy of leaving the department.

Friedman shook his head. He took a step closer to Ramirez, forcing himself to walk as straight as possible, and put down the folders. He cleared his throat. "You saw that show last week."

Ramirez nodded and let his face fall. Friedman fought back a smile. That was a good sign—Ramirez had caught some shit.

"These are some of the folders on the Meatman killings, right here," Friedman said.

Ramirez leaned forward, flipping through the manila folders, grimacing at all the blood in the photographs. "Sick, bad shit," he said. "Real sick."

Friedman waited, letting the pictures work their magic, and the TV show, hoping that his plan would all fall into place so neatly.

Friedman waited. Then he said, "I want these cases."

Ramirez smoothed his thinning hair back. "What do you mean, Jack? These cases are dead meat. What are they—five years old? Ancient history."

"The TV show brought them back to life, Captain."

Ramirez had told him to call him Joe. After all, the captain was younger than Friedman. But Friedman wanted to keep this very professional.

"I've heard that other shows are going to pick up the Meatman story."

Friedman had heard no such thing. It was just smoke, pure bullshit. But it sounded right, and Ramirez didn't question it.

Ramirez pursed his lips, looked at the folders again, imagining more reenactments of the killings, maybe more calls from the commissioner's office. "I don't know."

Friedman waited. "I'm not doing much good here, Captain. Moving paper around. You said it yourself. I should go blue fishing. But I looked at these folders, and I have some ideas."

Ramirez looked up. "Ideas? You mean you think this Meatman is still out there? Christ, I—"

"He was never caught," Friedman said. "I got the time. Let me take these cases."

Friedman saw Ramirez look out the window at the city and the buildings dotted with lights. He's thinking about it, Friedman thought. He's weighing the advantages, the disadvantages, the risks.

He turned back to Friedman. "Jack, why the hell do you want this? A lot of work, a lot of dead ends." Ramirez waved his hands at the folders. "A lot of cold evidence. Why the hell do you want it?"

There was one answer.

The full-scale investigation had gone on for two years. But when no new killings occurred, the special task force was cut down to a team of detectives. Then it was cut down to only one man.

Because nothing new popped up, the cases were forgotten, and filed. Until that TV show raised questions and got people all worked up.

The police still couldn't answer a very simple question: What happened to the Meatman?

Ramirez was staring at Friedman, wondering.

Friedman cleared his throat. "I want to check current homicide investigations, prison files, and the National Crime Center records. A lot of time has gone by. Maybe this guy moved. Maybe he's dead. Maybe he picked the wrong victim. Maybe he's in prison, nailed for something else, waiting until he can get out."

Ramirez made a face. He didn't like that idea.

"I'll use VICAP and the Criminalistic Lab Information Center. I'll check the state prisons."

Friedman took a breath, finishing his fast pitch, wondering if it had any credibility. "If he's still out there, maybe I can find him."

Ramirez looked down at the folders again, then scooped them up, stacked them neatly against the desk top, and handed them to Friedman. The captain wasn't smiling. "Shit, Jack. I think you're wasting your time. I think you're a fool for not getting the hell out of the department, out of the city."

Friedman saw in Ramirez's eyes that the captain knew what this was really all about. He didn't mention Elaine. But it was there, in the room with them. Friedman was grateful.

He took the folders.

"Okay. Take 'em. They're yours. Keep me posted," Ramirez said. "And don't get stupid."

Friedman smiled and left the office. He took the elevator down three flights, holding the folders close. My life's work, he thought. Old, unsolved serial murders.

The elevator door opened, and he heard the sound of electronic printers. The people here talked in hushed tones, as if respectful of the computers that sat on their desks, big TV faces watching them.

The large room was filled with the clicking of keys as people filed reports and retrieved information. There was an insectlike buzz in the air.

He walked past the sea of desks. People turned and stared at him, probably wondering why an old guy with a limp was sticking around. Friedman looked straight ahead.

They were all thinking the same thing, he guessed. Why the hell didn't he go on disability? What was wrong with him?

Each step sent pain rushing up to his head. A pain that aspirin, Tylenol, and ibuprofen did absolutely nothing to relieve.

He had some codeine—for emergencies, his neurologist told him. But every day was a goddamn emergency, every step. So he never took it.

Instead, when he went home, he opened a bottle from his closet wine cellar. He and Elaine loved white wine and had gotten to know the really good California vineyards. You didn't have to pay for pouilly-fumé or pouilly-fuissé to get a nice dry wine.

It was something they shared. Then they'd go to bed to read together. Sometimes she giggled and, like a brazen teenager, burrowed her hand under the sheets, grabbing him, playing with him. Making him suddenly, surprisingly, erect and interested.

Each step brought more pain. The chatter picked up a bit. They stopped looking at him. He felt one of the folders slipping. He adjusted it, pulled it back.

If I didn't have this work, I'd go crazy.

This big room was the main computer office of One Police Plaza. Ahead was the room he needed.

Friedman wasn't computer literate, but that was no problem, no big deal. The room ahead, with beveled glass, had three computer terminals and three operators, one of whom was assigned to help Friedman.

He opened the door. All the green screens were on, and a laser printer was pumping out sheets.

A woman looked up. There was no expression on her face.

Friedman smiled. She was a young black woman. Her hair was pulled back tight, and she wore bright red lipstick. She wasn't overly friendly. There was a nameplate sitting on her monitor. It read, Bethany Clarke.

"Hi," Friedman said, and he grabbed the back of a secretary's chair near the computer. Anything to take some of the pressure off his leg.

Clarke nodded at him and went on tapping at the keyboard.

"I'm starting to look at these." Friedman held the folders up. "I could use some help. I have an idea where I'd like to start."

Bethany Clarke was chewing gum noisily.

"I . . ." Friedman looked down at the chair, so inviting. "Do you mind?" She shook her head, and Friedman sat down, feeling uncomfortable, intrusive. The printer stopped, and another computer operator, a slim young man with a ponytail, got up and removed a stack of sheets.

"I'd like to check the New York prison population for—"

"Federal, state, or local?"

The question was unexpected. "Oh . . . state and local to start with. Only short-term convicts—four-, maybe five-year terms. I'm looking for anyone who went in for sexual assault, maybe with some knife play, or someone got into it with other prisoners, cutting them—"

Friedman wondered whether he should get more specific. Should he tell her that he was looking for someone who liked to carve designs on people?

He decided against it. Clarke wrote something down on a pad.

"Can you hook into the FBI Crime Center in Quantico?" She nodded. "Okay. So check their records for out-of-state knife murders in the past five years or so, especially ones that fall into a pattern—''

Bethany popped her gum. Her eyes were large in her coffee-with-cream-colored face. The face was pretty, aristocratic. She looked at him. ''*All* the damn knife murders? That will take—''

Friedman shook his head. ''No. Only if there's indication of'' —he looked for the right word—''a ritual.'' He had a thought. ''And if there's an element of torture in the murder.''

Another pop. Bethany Clarke wrote the information down. She looked up at Friedman, her face impassive, as if she were ordering a pepperoni pizza. ''Anything else?''

Anything else? he thought.

It would have been nice to have some fingerprints and some good fibers to work with. And enough semen to get an accurate DNA testing so that if Friedman did come up with someone, he could connect the suspect to the killings. But that was just a wish list.

''No,'' he said. ''That's it.'' He smiled. ''For now.''

Bethany Clarke nodded and began pecking at the keyboard. ''I'll bring you a printout of what I find.'' She looked up at him. ''When I get time.''

''Thanks.'' He got up, glad she didn't see the grimace that claimed his face every time he did that move.

It was late. Quitting time for most detectives. Friedman wanted to go out, to leave here, to see someone whose connection with these murders had ended years ago.

Anything to keep from going home . . .

13

"Brush your teeth, Erin," Lizbeth said. She fought the edginess, this feeling of being lost, of floating away. She sat on her daughter's bed, under the canopy. The bed spoke of a time a hundred years ago when little girls read books and played with kittens while their fathers worked in banks and their mothers sewed.

They didn't have hostages back then.

Lizbeth heard the water running and the scratchy sound of vigorous brushing. There was the sharp snap of the brush being banged against the edge of the sink, shaking off any water.

Erin came running in, squealing, "It's cold." She jumped into bed and squirmed under the covers. She pulled her stuffed bear close. It had been a present from a sympathetic neighbor during the first year of Simon's absence, when everyone was concerned about how she and Erin were doing. Before everyone tuned them out.

"Will you read some of *Samantha?*" Erin said.

It was late. Lizbeth wanted to collapse on her own bed, and leave the dinner dishes, the laundry, and everything else for tomorrow. Leave it all and watch the news.

She hoped Walt Schneider wouldn't call. She couldn't face that tonight.

"It's late, honey."

"Just a page," Erin begged.

That was an offer Lizbeth couldn't refuse. "Okay. One page."

Erin squeezed her bear in celebration.

Lizbeth took the book, smiling at the cover illustration of a Victorian-era girl with pretty ribbons in her hair. Nearby was an old-fashioned steamer trunk. Samantha was cruising to Europe with her parents. Lizbeth began to read. "The ship was a marvelous world. A world filled with shops and restaurants and fabulous people with fancy gowns and jewelry. . . ."

Lizbeth read quietly, letting the words resound gently around Erin's bed. "But by afternoon, Samantha had explored all of the top deck, from the shuffleboard courts to the rows of deck chairs facing the drab gray sea."

Lizbeth gave herself up to the image, to the warm, secure safety of the children's book, luxuriating in the illusion of safety and security.

She looked up, pages later, minutes later, and saw that Erin still squeezed the bear, but her eyes were shut tight.

Lizbeth stopped, reluctantly. She put the book down on Erin's desk and turned the light off. She stood up in the dark and then leaned down and kissed Erin's cheek.

Lizbeth straightened up, out from under the canopy. I'm not protected anymore, she thought. She turned and left the room, thinking, I'm not protected . . . and I'm all alone.

14

Both of Simon's hands grasped the frame of the window. He didn't even think about whether he could fit through the opening. I'll fit, he told himself. *I'll fit.*

He hadn't put any weight on his smashed hand, not yet.

Maybe the other hand can take most of the weight, he thought. Yeah, the other hand can do most of the work.

Right, and little elves will come out of the ground to help me.

"One," he whispered. There were sounds, the creak of a rope behind him.

Hello again . . . and then steps upstairs. It had to be breakfast time soon.

"Two." Come on. Just do it. *Come on, come on, come on.*

He didn't say three. He thought it, and then pulled. He felt fishhooks in his fingertips. He thought, My hand will be permanently mangled. Useless. He felt the bad fingers. *The bad fingers . . .*

You've been naughty, now, haven't you? We'll have to cut you off. Yes, we will. One by one.

His hands slipped, losing the little purchase they had. The temptation was too great—a temptation to stop trying, to let himself slide back into his dungeon.

But no—he grabbed the frame again, holding on to the outside wall, feeling the brittle, dry wood. He clamped his fingers around it.

"Ahhh!" He moaned, and he couldn't stop that sound. He bit his tongue, chewed at it, trying to distract his brain.

Which pain to pay attention to? There was no contest. Now he allowed his arms to actually carry some of his weight. The fishhooks turned into blades, chopping little slivers off his fingers, each slice more painful than the last.

He felt his teeth actually cut into his tongue. He tasted something, felt a wetness.

''Aw, God.'' The moan sounded pitiful even to him. But his hands held, both hands held. He let more weight land on his arms, then none, then his weight again. Up and down, ready to reach up to pull, pull—

He leaped. He grunted, his loudest sound so far. His head was just outside the window. His good hand pulled at the wood, and his shoulders reached the window.

Okay. I'm there. I'm there.

Now his shoulders were up to the window opening so that he could use his elbows to give his hand some relief. Except—

One shoulder blade was caught in the opening. It became wedged. He grunted and tried to work it loose. He felt himself slip.

''No,'' he said. It was a desperate moan, the sound a cat makes after a speeding car hurls it up in the air, a living football, spinning around, before it lands with a horrible thwap on the pavement.

His shoulder slipped free, and he was able to hold his position. He started pulling himself out. He was almost there . . . when his shirt—his dirty, filthy shirt—was caught, snagged, holding him, reluctant to let him leave.

He locked his elbows against the outside wall and kicked at the air in his dungeon. The cheap material held. It held him tight.

Suddenly it ripped. He wriggled through the opening, and fell a few inches to the cold sandy ground, his face feeling the sand and a few pebbles, not the packed dirt of the dungeon.

He flopped out, joyless. The pain still hacked at his fingers, slicing at the tips.

He waited for the shout.

The sound of a gun being readied.

And the bullet crashing into his head. . . .

He waited, and when nothing happened he crawled forward, away from the window. He dug his elbows into the sand. He counted to himself again. At three they'll start shouting at me. At ten they'll fire.

What does a bullet feel like? What is that pain like? He counted, and nothing happened. He crawled some more and counted, but still nothing happened.

I'm alive, he thought. I'm outside and I'm alive. He looked up.

And someone looked back at him.

The sky had lightened enough so that the shadows were all washed out. Sitting on the ground, leaning against the wall of a building across the sandy street, was a man. The whites of his eyes glowed, set deep in his dark face. As Simon watched, the man opened his mouth. He smiled a nearly toothless grin.

The man said nothing. Maybe he'll cry out, Simon thought. Maybe he'll yell for the guards and they'll drag me back.

I'll kill him first. I could do that. I could kill him.

One of Simon's broken fingers, unbandaged, unprotected, brushed against the sand. The pain made him blink. He gasped.

Slowly—don't want to do that again, he thought—Simon tried to stand up. Slowly, so slowly, he put his weight on one leg. It was wobbly, and the knee ached. Then he tested the other leg. The muscles were weak, but he tottered to a standing position.

The man, his head covered with a striped cloth, opened his mouth.

Simon took a step.

"Say a word," Simon whispered. "Say anything, and I'll kill you." Simon shook his head. He probably doesn't speak English, and here I'm threatening him.

The old man opened his mouth. His lips parted and Simon saw a dark hole.

The man spoke. Or tried to. "Uhl, uh-h-h-l, k-a-k-aaaa—"

He's insane, Simon thought. A crazy man. He looked at the man's mouth, at the dark pit.

The man had no tongue. He'd lost his tongue. How do you lose a tongue? Lots of ways.

Lots.

The man pointed at him. A bony finger rising, pointing at him. Marking me, Simon thought. He looked at the man's eyes, wide and terrified. What does he see?

A sudden gust of wind whipped down the street. Got to move, Simon thought, before the guards come downstairs and find me gone. Got to move. His leg ached every time he moved it.

I can't pay attention to that.

His hand swung with every step, creating agony when it banged against him or brushed against his pant leg.

I'd like to put my hand in my pocket, he thought. Just to keep it from moving. But to do that I'd have to slide it into my pocket. I'd actually have to squeeze it in.

He took another step.

I can't do that.

He kept walking. People were about, women dressed in black, their faces covered. They carried baskets as they went off to do the morning marketing. They saw him and turned away.

Simon thought of "Hogan's Heroes." Colonel Klink: *I see nothing. . . .*

He saw the sun to his left. Okay, that's east. The sun rises in the east. That's right, isn't it? Even here, that's right. So then to go north, I turn . . .

He stopped, trying to figure it out. He groaned.

Damn, to go north, I have to turn around.

He shuffled his legs, nearly screaming with every move and headed back the way he came, past men who were sitting and smoking. No alarm was being raised.

Of course not. Hostages? These men knew nothing of any hostages.

He turned down another sandy street so he wouldn't have to go past his dungeon, his prison.

The guards must have found out by now, he thought. They have to be looking for me. They'll carry sticks to beat me with. They'll hurt me really badly.

He grinned at that. Hurt me badly? Worse than this?

Can't be done. Can't . . . be . . . done.

He was moving north, up another narrow street. He came to a road stretching into the desert to the north. To Syria.

Suicide, he thought. This was absolute suicide. Still, he kept moving, kept walking, away from his dungeon, away from the village, the old man, the sand.

Despite the danger and the pain, he was free. And headed home . . .

15

It was late, Friedman realized. It was late, and dark, and cold. The city streets were dotted with black icy smears where the slush had frozen into slick patches. He drove carefully.

Eighth Avenue was clogged with cars and trucks eager to get out of the city.

I'm going to be late for my appointment, Friedman thought. But maybe that's just as well. More time to ruminate.

He looked to his right and saw a working girl. All of fifteen, maybe fourteen. Put makeup and heels on these kids, and they all look as if they were playing dress-up. Only in this version of the game they went inside a stranger's car, pulled down his fly, and sucked on his dick.

Friedman kept looking at her as he crossed Twenty-sixth Street. She saw him, with unerring human radar. She stared at him with wide eyes and an open mouth. She thought he was a potential customer. He shook his head. The girl turned away, locking her eyes on other cars creeping north toward the Lincoln Tunnel.

She was somebody's little girl. Somebody's baby. Friedman thought of birthday parties and party dresses, report cards and playing in a backyard. What went wrong to dump her here? How the hell did she get so unlucky?

The tunnel traffic veered left, clearing a lane on the right. Friedman hit the accelerator, rushing past the hopeless commuters inching their way back to Jersey.

Minutes later Friedman parked the black Celica in a lot below the West Sixty-sixth Street apartment building and hurried, as best he could, to the lobby and the elevator.

He rode up with two cadaverous young men who stood side by

side, their cheeks sunken, eyes looking straight ahead, staring, Friedman guessed, at a grim future.

The two men didn't look healthy. They got off on five. These are the plague years, Friedman thought.

He continued up five more flights, and when he got off, he smelled exotic aromas. Somebody was cooking things, peppery, spicy foods, filling the hall with a riot of smells.

He looked at the slip of paper in his hands and knocked on the door of apartment 10-A. The smells were strongest here. He heard a chain being undone. Then the door was cracked open.

A small man, about chest high to Friedman, peered out. He had full lips and rosy cheeks, and he wore a fire-engine red apron.

"Dr. Cubbage, I'm Detective Friedman. Sorry I'm late."

Dr. Lane Cubbage had been a consultant for the New York Police Department, someone who helped them when the murders got strange. His specialty had been sex-related murders. But, according to department records, not anymore.

Now he had a private practice, specializing in trauma. There were problems with Dr. Cubbage. Something had made him quit, but his file didn't get into them. Problems with what—serial killings? Catching murderers? What?

Cubbage still put some time in Riker's Island, Rahway, Sing Sing, preparing exit profiles for what he called "abused and traumatized felons." Friedman had made a note to ask him about that.

"Oh, yes. Please. Come in. I'm just finishing my Louisiana roux. It has to simmer for hours, absolute *hours*. But I have nearly everything in it."

Friedman walked into the hallway of the apartment. Faces looked at him. Long, slant-eyed faces carved in dark wood, stared down from the walls. There were at least a dozen masks in the hall.

"Oh, you've noticed my masks."

Friedman nodded.

"One of my other hobbies. The ceremonial masks of Oceania. Each one is designed to rouse a different spirit. Take that one there, for example."

Cubbage reached up and—barely—touched an oval mask that sported two curved teeth.

"This was designed to exact revenge against my enemy. The spirit invades the enemy's dreams and drives him insane."

"Very nice."

Cubbage froze. Friedman had said the wrong thing. "No. Not

very nice at all, Detective. Most of these masks do good. This one . . . well, it's not very nice at all.''

There was a sweetness about this man, Friedman thought. He was gentle. It was easy to see why he'd had trouble working with people who butchered their victims.

Cubbage sniffed the air. ''Oh, my scallions. Please, come. I'll just be a minute.''

Friedman followed the man into the kitchen. A big gray pot was filled to the brim with a brown sauce, a most revolting vision. The wonder of all the smells was spoiled by the sight of the thick liquid bubbling away.

Cubbage picked up a knife with a six-inch blade, gleaming, looking razor-sharp. He quickly sliced a bunch of scallions, dumped them into the pot, and wiped his hands on his apron. At a number of places the sauce dribbled over the side, little rivulets running down onto the already spattered stove top.

''There.'' Cubbage turned to him, beaming. ''Now we can talk. Some wine? A beer?''

Friedman was about to say no. A reflex. But he caught himself.

There wasn't anything urgent pressing. He was working on cases that were five years old. Ancient history. This wasn't the Son of Sam, with little Davie Berkowitz holding the city hostage.

''Sure. Some wine.''

Cubbage gestured at two bottles on the counter. ''Red? White?'' Friedman smiled. ''Whatever you recommend.''

''Ah. The Beaujolais Nouveau, then. Wonderfully dry. You'll love it.''

For a few surreal moments Friedman stood there while the elfin psychologist poured two glasses of wine.

Friedman had copies of Cubbage's original reports, written after the Meatman established his modus operandi, the ceremonial graphic mutilations. Cubbage's reports became clearer and more confident as the killings went on, as if he'd started to get a handle on the killer.

As a Peruvian death mask glowered at them, Friedman let Cubbage talk.

''You can see, of course, why I had to leave. It was terrible work, very upsetting. Especially since they never caught him, Lieutenant.''

''But your work might have stopped a killer, Dr. Cubbage.''

The psychologist shook his head. ''No, I couldn't have stopped him. The killings were done. Eventually, I realized that someone like this, a man who would do these things, is a victim himself. He's suffered incredible trauma, horrible abuse and pain. This is how he resolved what was done to him. I saw that my real work must be with people suffering from that sort of trauma.''

Friedman had trouble seeing the Meatman as a victim. ''The exit profiles you do, the psychological evaluations—''

''I do reports on people who have suffered severe childhood trauma. Sometimes I recommend that they see people on the outside.''

''You believe that does more than—''

''I believe in psychic determinism, Lieutenant Friedman. There are no accidents.''

''And what determined the killings you worked on, the ones by the Meatman?''

''Stupid nickname. Stupid.'' Cubbage sipped his wine. ''It wasn't at all clear at first what I was dealing with in that case.''

Friedman took a sip, too, enjoying the metallic burr the wine left on his tongue.

''I mean, here was a killer who was into pain, you know. Not unheard of, but in this case the crimes were incredibly ritualistic. That was when I began to get some uncomfortable feelings . . . while working on those cases.''

''Uncomfortable?''

''Yes. I couldn't handle it—the photographs, what he was doing. And something else bothered me about it. Serial killers usually seek strangers as victims, people they don't know. It helps them act out their fantasy, to dehumanize the people they kill. But''—Cubbage licked his full lips—''this one . . .''

Friedman waited. Then, after a long pause, said, ''Yes . . .?''

Cubbage nodded. ''It was as if this killer was into innocence. In the Tomkins killing he passed over the mother and went for the little boy. You've seen the photos?''

Friedman nodded.

''Figure twenty minutes of torture, minimum. Twenty minutes, with the mother watching, of course. That probably made it better. For the killer, I mean. It's so vile I can hardly imagine it.''

''What about the sexual aspect.''

''Yes. There was definitely a sexual component.''

''And that's unusual?''

''Not really. Most sociopaths have a completely displaced sense of sexuality. The kill is the thrill, so to speak. They are experiencing fulfillment on a level that is well removed from actual sex. But not this person.''

''Why do you say that? Because of the semen?''

''No. Even if there hadn't been that trace of fluid, I would still maintain that these killings were, at heart, *complete* acts. By that I mean they were sexually motivated. Lust murders.''

Cubbage leaned forward. Friedman saw the wine swirl in his glass. ''The killings were sexual acts, albeit on a very primitive level. I'm a Jungian, Detective Friedman. Do you know what that means?''

''No.''

''I believe we carry a lot of repressed primitivism around in our unconscious. It motivates our art; it fills our dreams. I'm talking about cannibalism, and torture and . . .'' Cubbage waved at the air, as if summoning the acts he was talking about. In the kitchen the sauce bubbled noisily, its overpowering aroma mixing headily with the wine. ''Mutilization, scarification, dismemberment, necrophilia. Dark, primitive stuff.''

Friedman took a slug of his wine.

''Here, let me show you,'' Cubbage said.

He got up from his chair and went to the shelves behind him. They were filled with books, thick, dark volumes barely visible in the soft yellow light.

''Yes, here . . .''

Cubbage selected a book and brought it back to Friedman, bending over him. Friedman saw the title: *The Search for the Modern Primitive*. The psychologist flipped through pages of photographs showing people with pierced noses, ears, nipples.

I'm too old for this shit, Friedman thought. The pictures were making him dizzy.

''Look,'' Cubbage said, pointing to a photograph of a businessman sitting at a power desk. He was a young, good-looking executive with a computer terminal facing him, a phone with half a dozen lines, a view of a city through a giant picture window behind him. Cubbage tapped the photo.

''This is a successful, highly respected businessman in the computer field.'' Cubbage looked up and grinned. ''A Republican.'' He flipped a page. ''Now look.''

The same man. Naked. Lying on a bed of nails.

A fucking bed of nails.

''Is that a trick?'' Friedman asked.

Cubbage shook his head, dismayed. ''No. It's real. You see,

there are people, Detective Friedman, who seek a certain sensation as an antidote to what they see as the numbing effect of modern society. They need something to awaken their senses, make them feel alive, excite sensual feelings.''

''Like pain?''

Cubbage nodded. ''It's not pain to them.'' He removed the book from Friedman's lap.

''They never caught the Meatman,'' Friedman said. ''So why did he stop?''

Cubbage looked thoughtful. He pursed his lips. ''I don't know . . . but let me tell you who the killer is.''

Friedman was all ears.

16

There was a sound in the house, the odd creak, the misplaced groan of a floorboard. Something very . . . small.

But it was enough of a sound to tell Lizbeth one simple, chilling fact.

I'm not alone. There's someone else here.

Then—thundering heartbeat, breath held—a possibility is checked.

Maybe it was Erin, up in the night for a drink of water or to pee. Sometimes she woke up in time to go to the bathroom, and sometimes she didn't. Sometimes she wet the bed, and she came in, sad and crying. "Mommy, I wet myself." Then she threw herself against Lizbeth, heaving. And Lizbeth didn't know a good way to tell her.

It's not your fault. Little girls aren't supposed to lose their daddies before they ever get to know them.

Lizbeth heard the noise, the creak, again. It wasn't Erin, she thought. It was different, heavier, coming from near the front door, the living room. Maybe coming up the stairs.

Why didn't I get an alarm system? How damn expensive could it be? Because now . . . now—

Another creak, louder, bolder. A real groan, a piece of wood aging into a musical instrument, a one-note virtuoso of warning. An intruder, a robber, or someone much worse . . .

We live in a world where anything can happen, anything at all.

Lizbeth sat up in bed. She watched her reflection in the bureau mirror. At least I'm alert, she thought. At least I'm awake and aware. He won't surprise me.

How do I know it's a he? Why do I assume that?

Assume that, she told herself.

A creak, another groan, the floor singing out each step. She knew there was no escape. Oh, God, another sound. Small footsteps coming into her room, and a voice, soft and plaintive.

Erin. "Mommy . . . mommee!"

She hears it, too. Erin hears the noises.

Creak. Groan. Closer together, the rhythm building. And still she didn't move.

Lizbeth watched her shadow-self in the mirror, sitting up in bed, waiting, frozen. No, Erin honey, she thought. Don't come in here. But she didn't say it. No sound came out of her mouth. There were only the light footsteps, and then—the heavy footsteps.

Coming closer together. Converging.

She grabbed the sheet, pulled it tight. Thinking, Why can't I move? Why can't I speak?

Then: "Mommy?"

Erin must have seen something. There was a hint of curiosity and concern in her sweet, sweet voice. Until—

Alarm. A scream. A warning. "Mommee!"

A useless cry. Totally useless. Because Lizbeth couldn't do anything. She couldn't do anything at all. Because this . . . this . . .

This had happened before, in her other nightmares.

She'd had this nightmare before. And it was nearly over.

The air vibrated. The black room became tinged with a color, color that streamed from the hall, where Erin's strangled cry was suddenly cut off. That was in the nightmare, Lizbeth thought. I won't hear that cry again.

Mommy.

No one will ever cry out like that to me again. Red filled the room, suffocating her. There were more screams.

Lizbeth pulled the sheets tight, tighter, and . . . Tonight there was mercy. Because tonight she woke up.

The cry summoned her. Her daughter's voice clear and real.

"Mommy?"

Lizbeth's eyes shot open. Erin stood by her bed. "I had a bad dream."

This was real, not a nightmare. Lizbeth knew that as she reached up and touched Erin's face.

Erin wanted to come into her bed. She often did that. They slept together, keeping the phantoms away.

Not a bad deal for both of them.

"Get in, honey."

I should send Erin to the bathroom, Lizbeth thought. No. I'll carry her in later, after she's asleep. Let's kill the monsters first.

Erin climbed into the bed and snuggled close, warm, fitting perfectly.

Just as she used to before.

The room was dark, the air cold, and Erin fell fast sleep.

But Lizbeth was wide awake. She turned a bit to her left, away from Erin, let her hand trail down to the floor, feeling around, her fingers searching, until—

There. She felt the baseball bat. She let her fingers play upon the smooth wood. Pretty damn primitive, she thought. A mother and her baby alone. With a club. It's prehistoric.

It would be a while before she fell asleep. But the nightmare was over . . . for tonight.

Simon tasted salt on his lips. I'm at the beach, he thought. Sure, I can hear the waves crashing. Surf's up, and the water's just fine.

The sun was burning off the thick covering of clouds as it climbed higher in the sky. Simon looked up.

Am I still going north? Yes. If the sun's still in the east, if it hasn't already slipped into the afternoon sky. In which case . . . in which case . . .

I'm going south, back to the town.

He limped, his whole body shaking with every step. He couldn't see very far ahead. The road was covered with small piles of sand, and it curved around great hummocks of sand that hid whatever was ahead.

Which might be nothing. Yes, I'm walking into nothing.

I'm thinking about water because I'm thirsty. I'm cold and thirsty. The wind is blowing tiny specks of sand into my eyes. Soon I'll be hungry. Hungry and thirsty.

And then I'll stop walking. I'll lie down and die.

Maybe I should stop and lie down now.

Conserve my energy. Marshal my resources.

He took another wobbly step, another cornucopia of pain.

If I stop, I'll never get up.

He saw something moving in the sand. Something real. A snake, mottled yellow and brown, a big snake. Was it poisonous? He didn't know. Didn't have a clue. He wasn't up on desert snakes.

It watched him as if he were simply another mouse, just another rodent that might make a good lunch.

Herds of scorpions darted from one mini-dune to the next, so full of energy, so purposeful.

So much more together than Simon.

One big scorpion stopped and—he imagined—watched him. It raised its tail to the sky and then pointed it at him.

Want a piece of me, too? he thought.

Why not? Why not, you fucking insect?

But then—step, shuffle, his jalopy of a body ready to collapse—he felt stung by that thought. He thought of a long poem he'd read in school.

An ancient mariner stopped one of three to tell the unlucky soul the story of how he didn't respect life, how he shot the albatross. And, oh, the price he paid. A cursed ship with a crew of ghosts. Life and Death played dice for the mariner's soul.

While he froze his ass off in Antarctica and wore the giant albatross around his neck.

Got to be careful. Wouldn't want something that bad to happen to me. Just because I said "fuck you" to a scorpion.

He saw something to the west—if it was the west. A dark gray patch, a dingy curtain that hung down to the ground. As he watched it, he saw bright yellow flashes.

They're in my mind, he thought.

But no, they were too brilliant, too unexpected. They were real. The curtain was rain. It was a desert thunderstorm.

He licked his lips with his dry, lizard-skin tongue. He watched the storm, imagining the water falling. Wishing he were there, amid the rain, his mouth open.

Rain on me.

He wouldn't worry about the lightning. A desert thunderstorm, over there. Why couldn't it be here?

He kept watching the light show, the rippling movement of the gray curtain as it danced around the distant dunes.

Why not here? He could have cried.

He wasn't looking where he was going. He didn't see them.

Until he heard a voice saying something in a different Arabic dialect, words that he couldn't understand. He turned away from the beautiful storm.

He saw the soldiers. They were dressed in khaki. There was a Jeep and, behind it, a green truck. A bunch of soldiers stood on the road. Militia. Yes. Druze? Shiite? *Militia* . . .

They would take him back.

"You can't leave," they would say. "You have to go back to your dungeon. Nice try."

There were more incomprehensible words. I live on a planet where everything is incomprehensible. He looked at the soldiers' uniforms.

No, Simon thought, they're not militia. They're soldiers. And they're not Lebanese.

He heard a voice and words he understood.

"Who are you?" The words were clearly enunciated, the officer taking care with his English.

Who am I? Tough question. I'll have to think. Give me a minute, Simon thought. Just don't leave. Because maybe you can help me, maybe you can . . .

The soldier, an officer wearing a blackish-green beret, came closer. "Who are you? How did you get here?"

Two questions now. Simon's tongue snaked out. The officer turned to a man behind him and said something in the other language.

Slowly it was coming to Simon. There was a small flash of light in the reluctant kindling that was his consciousness.

Another soldier ran forward and held a canteen up to Simon's lips. Water filled his mouth and streamed down his chin, wetting his clothes. The damp clothes felt cold and clammy against his skin.

He gulped the water. The soldier with the canteen said something to him. The officer took a step closer. "Not so fast. Drink slowly."

Simon shook his head. No. A stubborn child.

The officer gently pulled the canteen away. Simon licked his lips.

"I'll give you more. But who are you?"

Simon opened his mouth. "I'm Simon Farrell."

It sounded goofy, as if he was filled with a pathetic pride, a nonexistent confidence.

"I'm an American. I come from—"

He started to point back toward the town, but the turn made his leg send ice picks to his brain. He moaned.

"From Lebanon?" the officer said, finishing the thought.

Simon nodded. The dark-eyed officer stared at him for a moment, his face impassive, revealing nothing.

He'll send me back, Simon thought.

Then the officer nodded. ''You're in Syria now. We'll take you with us.''

Simon smiled. The officer said something to his men. Simon felt hands grabbing him, supporting him. One man touched his bad hand, and Simon screamed. Then the soldier was more careful, supporting Simon against his shoulder.

The men carried Simon to the truck.

The officer got into the Jeep. He said, ''You can go home.''

Simon smiled again.

It's all over, he thought.

17

Cubbage poured himself more wine, but Friedman covered his glass and shook his head. The psychologist looked up, staring into the shadowy space of his apartment, a tropical wonderland in a building where the paint still smelled fresh.

"It's not hard to know who the serial killer is, Lieutenant. His work speaks of his pain."

Cubbage smiled, a strained expression. "This man—and I'm assuming he's a man by the evidence of his sheer physical strength—this man falls into the category of a lust murderer. For these murderers, killing is a way to suppress a deep-rooted, severe traumatization from their childhood. This Meatman, as you call him, was terribly hurt as a child."

Cubbage took a breath. He seemed lost in his thoughts, perhaps wondering about that pain. He looked up at Friedman. "You're sure you won't have a drop more wine?"

"No, thanks."

"I see a lot of trauma now, in my private work and at the prison."

"Tell me about the inmates you see."

"I write exit evaluations for inmates due to be paroled from the Ossining Correctional Facility—what used to be called Sing Sing. I get to play Nostradamus, in a way. This one will end up back here; this one won't. That sort of thing. I'm not part of the parole process. I simply get a last look."

"You get to warn us what's coming back out on the streets?"

Cubbage laughed. "I wish." He leaned forward. Friedman saw the man's delicate hand wrapped around his glass. "Let me tell you a story," Cubbage said. "Do you know about Edward Beckner?"

Friedman shook his head.

"Oh, good. It's a *wonderful* story. It tells reams about our justice system. Beckner had a twisted relationship with his mother, who aroused tremendous feelings of hate and love in him. When he was fifteen, he became angry over some petty matter. In his anger—and because he was curious to know what it would feel like—he killed his grandparents."

Cubbage sipped his wine. In the roux pot a languorous bubble exploded.

"After a few years of treatment, Edward was released to his mother. The boy met with his parole officer on a regular basis, and he got counseling. He seemed to be on the path to recovery. What no one knew was that he had started picking up female hitchhikers and butchering them. In fact, his psychologist complimented Beckner on the progress he was making, while the head of one of his victims sat in the trunk of Beckner's car." Cubbage took a breath. "Bringing the head along added to the thrill, I suspect."

"Nice kid."

"He was suffering from a very severe trauma, Lieutenant. That's my point. Eventually Beckner was able to confront his demons head on, so to speak. He finally killed and decapitated his mother."

"I hope they've thrown away the key this time."

"Actually he's eligible for parole. Edward Beckner feels that he's no longer a threat to society. He really believes that." Cubbage looked thoughtful.

"You sound as if you've spoken to him."

"Oh, I have. And believe me, Beckner doesn't see himself as a danger to anyone . . . now that Mom is dead."

"So the Meatman wants to kill his mother?"

Cubbage made a face. "Perhaps. Here's what I think. . . ."

Friedman took notes, the pages building up. Old news, lots of it. But still, to him it was fascinating, riveting.

"This Meatman is totally devoted to his preoccupation. He's fastidious, sublimely careful, wonderfully neat. Which means . . ." Cubbage's eyes snapped back to Friedman, as if he were saying, *Of course you see it, too, don't you?*

Cubbage smiled impishly. "He is suffering from an over-whelmingly powerful obsessive compulsive reaction."

"Which is . . . ?"

"An OCR fixates on ritual—walking in a straight line, for example, or repeatedly washing one's hands. It could be any ritualistic behavior. But an obsession with violence is usually precipitated by a major traumatic event. The bigger the trauma, the bigger the obsession."

Cubbage drained his wineglass. "Now, some of my colleagues actually question whether an obsessive could be violent, especially *this* violent."

"Obsessives aren't usually violent?"

Cubbage raised a finger. "The captain in your homicide department brought a psychiatrist from NYU Medical Center to review my work. He completely disagreed with me." Cubbage shook his head, and Friedman wondered whether there was more to Cubbage's leaving police work than simple distress.

"But make no mistake about it, Lieutenant, the Meatman's an obsessive."

"So what does that mean?" Friedman now longed for more wine, something to make this conversation seem a bit normal. His knee throbbed, and the alcohol seemed to enhance the pain. He dug in his coat pocket for some aspirin, which he carried loose, like Tic Tacs or candy.

"The Meatman pursued—*pursues* pain, perhaps in himself and then, vicariously, through others. All the killings show evidence of a repetition complex. He commits similar acts, each time with an added wrinkle, an elaboration. He's methodical, a perfectionist."

Cubbage sipped his wine. He sniffed the air and stood up. "Let me check the roux. I don't want it to thicken too much. It's supposed to be thick"—a faint laugh—"but not so thick that it looks like sludge."

Cubbage went to the kitchen and left Friedman alone. Here in this apartment he felt close to the killer, this nut case who had murdered five people, maybe more, and then vanished.

Friedman looked at the Peruvian death mask, or maybe it was an Inca revenge mask. For a moment, sitting there, he smelled more than Cubbage's roux. He smelled the animal scent of the killer.

There was a moan from the kitchen. Startled, Friedman stood up.

Cubbage came back, still moaning. "Oh, this is *good,* Detective Friedman, I don't know if you've ever tasted a real Louisiana Roux, but this is excellent."

The psychologist extended a wooden spoon in his direction, a tiny mom offering a taste of something good to an oversized son.

"I don't—"

"I *insist,* Detective."

In the line of duty many things were asked of a detective. Getting up from the chair had made Friedman's leg hurt worse. He sniffed and then, under the watchful eyes of the psychologist, opened his mouth.

The brown liquid was hot, spicy. Friedman's lips and then his tongue burned, even though only the tiniest amount of the roux dripped in. But after the burn there was this wonderful spicy taste. "Very good." Then an even better aftertaste. Friedman wanted more. "This is wonderful," he said.

"Great. You see, a roux is a mighty thing, the heart of the sauce. Poured over duck or served with jumbo Gulf shrimp . . . well, the mind boggles." Cubbage wrinkled his nose. For a few moments the room cleared of the smoky haze of dead bodies. "I'll send some home with you."

"Thanks." Friedman sat down.

Cubbage set the spoon carefully down on the table. He looked down and noticed that Friedman still had his notebook out. "What was I saying? Oh, yes. The repetition complex here is very clear. There are other things I can guess at, too."

"Like?"

"Well, the murderer was around thirty at the time of the killings. Charming, intelligent—"

"Why do you say that?"

"He wouldn't have gotten a chance to get close to these people without some native guile, almost a talent. Most serial killers focus on strangers, but this character was different."

"Different? How?"

Cubbage looked confused. "It's in my reports. You must have seen it."

Friedman shrugged. He didn't have a clue to what Cubbage meant.

The psychologist scratched his head. "Unless they didn't put all of my report in the files. Stupid. I said that some serial murderers can turn *anyone* into a stranger."

"What do you mean?"

"Serial killers generally go after strangers. But the lust murderer is not beyond acting to *protect* his way of release. If he's intelligent, he'll act intelligently to protect his passion—and to pursue it.''

''And what about the dehumanization?''

''This Meatman selected young and innocent victims. That boy, for example, and there was a girl at Jones Beach, a college student. He was hooked on innocence, a kind of *purity*. I really don't think these people were all strangers to him. In fact, I think he *wanted* to know them before he started to hurt them.''

It felt cold in Cubbage's apartment. The psychologist kept the room at a frigid temperature.

''Go on.''

''I don't know why they would leave anything out of my report. It should be there. But I think that the Meatman knew some of his victims. And he stalked the ones that he didn't know until he *felt* as if he knew them.''

''That definitely wasn't in the report.''

''He was a classic hunter-killer. The game was probably very important to him.''

Friedman took a breath, feeling tired, overwhelmed by Cubbage and his theories. ''So who am I looking for?''

''My guess is that the Meatman is very charming and clever.'' Cubbage's face lit up. ''Charismatic! And any OCR who's into killing people would have the classic characteristics of a sociopath. To most people he'd seem like a rather nice fellow. But he'd have no remorse, no superego, no conscience, and no love. His emotional affect, under close scrutiny, would always be a tad off.''

''How did you suppose he got that way?''

As the light seemed to fade from Cubbage's eyes, Friedman wondered how much the psychologist knew about that kind of pain? What was his life like?

''Many ways, detective. Many possible ways. But I'd guess that he was physically abused. Many severely abused children die.'' A hollow laugh. ''The lucky ones die. Others become prisoners of a woman or a man working on their own pain demons. The parents, the abusers, are usually simple-minded types, but what they pass on to the kid—an outward normalcy but a life of pain and terror—is far more sinister. And far more dangerous. I—I don't like to think about what this murderer's life must have been like.''

Then Cubbage's eyes fogged over. ''One other thing is worrisome. I mean, it *should* worry you. It's bothered me ever since I read about this Meatman.''

It was late. Friedman wanted to leave. He had enough information from Cubbage . . . enough for now. Enough speculation. What the hell am I supposed to do with all this? he wondered.

"Each killing got worse," Cubbage said. "Obsessions never stay static. They grow. The feeling, the pressure . . . it mounts." He looked at Friedman. "And then overflows." Cubbage waited.

Friedman said quietly, the masks listening to his hushed words, "Then the killings stopped."

Cubbage nodded. "Yes. They stopped." He cleared his throat. "Which is impossible."

Friedman got up. He was tired. "I should go. I'd like to see you again. When I have more questions . . . when I know more."

"Yes. Certainly. I'll be at the prison tomorrow, in Ossining, and then, at the end of the week, I've been invited upstate to lecture on trauma for a month." He made a small smile.

"Where will you be?"

"Hudson College. It's not far from here, of course, but I will be staying up there. They're providing housing. A little working vacation."

Friedman nodded.

"I don't have the phone number or address yet, but the college will tell you how to contact me. If I can do anything else, please call me or come up and visit."

There wasn't any warmth in that last invitation. Friedman took a step toward the door.

"Wait," Cubbage said, smiling. "Let me give you some delicious roux to take home."

18

The morning was a blur for Lizbeth. She rushed to get Erin dressed, to get some hot cereal on the table. After breakfast there was just time to comb Erin's hair and put a ribbon in it.

There was just time for Lizbeth to be the good mother.

The TV was off. It was too distracting, the chattering of news, the weather reports that told you it was snowing in Omaha.

Erin dawdled. All little girls dawdled, Lizbeth thought, lingering over each touch, each aspect of grooming her daughter.

Lizbeth forced down her own breakfast, some oat bran cereal, tasting like soggy wood shavings by the time she got to it. The raisins had the consistency of dried boogers from a giant's nostril.

The hands of the clock moved too fast.

"Come on, Erin. It's late." Lizbeth looked at the clock. Three minutes and counting before the bus would arrive and—barely— stop at the corner. If she missed that split-second whoosh of the bus doors opening . . . those were the breaks.

If that happened, Lizbeth would have to drive Erin to school, and she'd be late for work another morning, with more people looking at her.

"Erin!" she yelled. "Erin. Please . . . come—"

The phone rang. It was an odd time for a call, Lizbeth thought. Nobody called during the takeoff hour. Everyone's personal control tower was busy dealing with getting the day launched.

There were no calls during takeoff. Well, sometimes there were play dates, last-minutes calls from friends of Erin, asking her to come over and spend a rainy afternoon with them.

The phone rang again. Erin came into the kitchen.

She wore a red plaid dress and red shoes. A red ribbon dangled from her hair. She was beautiful.

Lizbeth thought she heard the bus roaring down the block, mixing with the ringing. She snatched up the phone in the middle of its second ring. She answered it breathlessly, leaving the caller with no illusions as to what was going down in this house right now.

"Mrs. Farrell, it's Mindy Zetlin."

The bitch, the stupid, dumpy reporter bitch. Lizbeth was ready to smash the phone down, rattling the nosy bitch's ears. But she didn't want the reporter attacking her story with too much venom. *The bitch* . . .

"Mrs. Farrell, has anyone called you? Have you heard from . . . anyone?"

Thoughts raced through Lizbeth's mind. The way the reporter said those words, the tone. Only a few possibilities came to mind.

She heard the bus. No doubt about it this time. The subsonic, unmuffled bus roar traveling up through the wood floor from the very foundation of the house.

"Erin," she said, "get your coat and—"

Lizbeth turned back to the phone. "No. No one has called me this morning. Look, can I call you back?"

Erin had trouble getting one arm into the sleeve of her bulky pink and white winter coat. It was too small. She needed a new one, but there wasn't any money. Lizbeth helped her fit the arm through.

Her daughter looked up and said, "C'mon, Mommy. The bus is coming."

"Mrs. Farrell." The voice, the tone. "Your husband . . . he's free. He's out of Lebanon, Mrs. Farrell. Our wire service just picked up the story. They haven't called you yet? You haven't heard from the State Department?"

Lizbeth shook her head. The State Department . . . Why would the State Department call her?

The bus roared closer. But before it got to the house, a car pulled up to the curb. Lizbeth looked out the front window and saw the car. A black, official-looking car. There was some kind of seal on the door.

"Mommy, we've got to go."

Lizbeth hung up the phone.

It rang again. Then the doorbell rang. She held on to Erin, holding her shoulders tightly.

She took the call. This time it was someone from the State Department. The doorbell rang again.

The bus stopped, bright yellow, steaming, waiting impatiently.

"Mommy? Mom?"

"Shush," Lizbeth said.

The bus waited, then pulled away, taking away their life, the way things were.

As soon as Lizbeth hung up the phone, it rang again. And again. And again.

It would ring all day long. There would be many visitors, and plans to be made, and decisions. Erin would stay home and watch "Nickelodeon." There would be calls and visitors, visitors and calls, all day long.

The circus had begun. . . .

PART TWO

FREEDOM

Male serial killers represent the darkest, most sinister side of human existence . . . They are especially dangerous because we understand so little of their actual motivations, their lives and personalities.

—**Eric W. Hickey** *Serial Murderers and their victims*

19

Donald Pick's cell overlooked the Hudson River, covered today with giant sheets of ice, flowing down to the city. They glistened under the bright sun, looking so white and so pure. The glare was so brilliant, so bright, that it made Pick squint.

He was all ready.

His cell was as he had kept it for the past five years. It was pristine, his cot made perfectly, the sheet and blanket taut—military style, Pick liked to think.

Pick didn't permit anyone to hang things on the walls. His last roommate had wanted to put up pictures of women. The guards didn't mind that. Kept down the butt-fucking, they said. But it was against the rules, Pick said. There was supposed to be nothing on the walls, absolutely nothing.

The guards didn't care.

Pick had taken down the pictures. The cell mate, a young black man named Paris Smith, had freaked. He threatened Pick. And Pick thought, this could screw up my parole. I can't let that happen. But, on the other hand, I can't let those pictures stay on the wall. I don't like them. They make me think about what I can't do—the smiling women, the teeth glistening, the curves of the bodies.

Pick couldn't allow that. So one night he woke Paris up and grabbed him by the neck and pulled him off his upper cot. Paris had on boxer shorts. It was late, and the prison was quiet but for the sound of snores and guys waking up to beat off before going back to sleep.

The human zoo.

Pick pulled Paris to the floor. He heard Paris's knees smack against the stone. The black man started to scream at Pick. ''What the fuck you think you're doing? Get the hell off me, motherfu—''

Pick quickly covered Paris's mouth with his other hand. Paris could feel how strong Pick was. ''Yes,'' Pick whispered, looking into Paris's eyes. ''I'm a strong son of a bitch. And I'm this close to cutting off your air. Guys die here all the time. No one will give a fuck. I lose my cell, my view, my goddamn parole. But you have to understand one thing.''

Paris's dark eyes rolled around in their sockets. He was feeling wondrous pain, Pick knew. A carnival of colors exploded in the black man's skull.

''This is my cell,'' Pick told him, ''and I don't want anything on the walls, on the floor, anywhere. I want everything neat and clean so I don't get distracted, so I can wait in peace.''

Pick waited until Paris's wild eyes locked on his in the darkness, amid the snores and the wet slaps from other cells in the human zoo. He waited until Paris nodded.

''The next time,'' Pick said quietly, ''the next time I'll kill you. And no one will give a shit, no matter what you tell them.''

That was all it took. Paris became a model cell mate. He slept as much as he could, curled up in his bed. Paris snored, but Pick just smiled—there was nothing he could do about that. Otherwise, it was as if Paris wasn't there.

Now Pick turned away from the bars and the smeared window. He walked over to the cell door. He could hear morning noises— guards taking one group down to the gym, taking another group to the rec room. Pick enjoyed only one activity, lifting weights— pushing himself as far as he could, watching the veins in his arms bulge out as if they were about to burst and spray blood everywhere.

Pick liked knowing that the other men realized he could do more than they could—lift more weight, do more reps. Sometimes he could hear them holding their breath. Pick *liked* that.

He touched the bars of the cell. They felt smooth, shined to a high gloss by years of hands trailing up and down them, waiting hands, waiting. . . .

It was morning, and Donald Pick was one day away from freedom.

And all that freedom meant.

•   •   •

''Pick, the shrink's here. Come on.''

Pick walked dutifully to the open door.

''Sorry to be leaving us?''

Pick turned to the guard and smiled. He said nothing, made no wisecracks. Instead he simply nodded. The guards liked him. Sometimes they came by the cell to bullshit about sports or politics, about the wife at home or a girl on the side.

They told Pick everything because he was such a good listener, always asking the right questions, always knowing when to be quiet and listen.

Pick worked at making everyone like him. He made jokes— nothing offensive, but jokes that broke the monotony of being a keeper in the human zoo. He gave the guards money advice and advice about their families.

Pick, they said, was doing good time. He was no degenerate, no cracked-out nut case who had gone on a shooting spree. No, he just got into a bar fight and someone got cut. Punk probably deserved it.

Pick had often said he was sorry the fight happened.

And he was. Because it had ended everything.

His life ended. He lost control.

Pick thought of killing himself those first days inside his cell. He was cut off from the only thing that meant anything to him. For eight years, cut off from everything that was important to him.

But then he had decided to wait patiently, to be the best possible prisoner, to win parole the first time out.

I can do that, he thought. Cut my eight years down to four. Four years . . . That wasn't so much time, was it? Four years, a day at a time. Just like in AA. I'll do it one day at a time. Easy does it.

''How're the kids, Ernie?'' Pick said, walking beside the guard.

Pick even knew the kids' names—Mary and Tom. All-American kids. And what does your daddy do? Oh, he works in the human zoo, taking care of the animals.

''Great. They had a great Christmas. We got 'em skates, lots of toys, shit like that.''

Pick made a small laugh, as if remembering past Christmases of his own, giant trees, big turkey dinners. Actually he had no such memories. He had only the images generated by years of Holly-wood movies.

"Nothing like Christmas," Pick said. "The best time of the year."

"You can say that again."

Pick thought of one Christmas. Of driving through Canarsie to the water, past homes glowing with lights. He remembered parking outside one house, waiting for the girl to come home.

He had watched her for weeks. She had never seen him. He got to her as she was about to open her front door. He made her get into his car. She went with him. So stupid and timid.

Her skin felt wonderful. He remembered that. So smooth and tight.

"Put a big dent in the old savings," the guard said.

"Oh, I bet it did," Pick said.

The skin pulled tight, like a canvas, stretched, ready to tear, to rip, with that first cut.

Pick felt the beginning of an erection. He quickly stopped remembering.

He turned to the guard—to Ernie, who lived in Indian Point near the nuclear power plant. You could get a house cheap in Indian Point, because who the hell wanted to live next to a nuclear power plant?

Pick knew Ernie's whole pathetic story. "I'm going to miss you, Ernie."

Ernie nodded, pleased with the comment, the warmth that Pick was able to deliver.

"Yeah, me too, buddy."

They reached another gate. A different guard opened it with a cheerful "Hey, Pick."

Beyond the gate were meeting rooms where lawyers met with their clients and where the psychologist conducted his exit evaluations.

This was the final hurdle. Pick's parole had been approved, but things could still go wrong. Pick took a deep breath and turned to Ernie, who was smiling at him.

Ernie opened the door of a meeting room. He mouthed the words "good luck."

And Pick—a friend, a buddy, a regular guy—mouthed back a cheery thanks . . .

Dr. Lane Cubbage sat across the simple wooden table from Donald Pick. Cubbage made a show of looking at the folder, though he knew Pick's story well enough.

He looked up at the prisoner. Pick was an attractive man; there was no escaping that. Cubbage found himself staring at Pick's muscular chest, the few tight curls of hair. He took note of Pick's face—the deep blue eyes, the boyish smile, the sandy hair that was just a bit too long.

Cubbage cleared his throat, hoping his interest didn't show.

"This is only a formality, Donald, as you know." Cubbage picked up a pencil. He felt Pick's eyes on him, open, expressive. Cubbage looked at Pick's lips—sensitive lips, not too full, not too thin. "The parole board has spoken to you about your obligations on the outside. But I'd like to talk about your dealings with people, your reactions to the types of situations that might cause . . ."

Pick extended his hands, palms forward. He gave Cubbage a broad, warm smile. "Doctor, I think I have a good handle on the types of"—Pick looked thoughtful, as if searching for the right word—"situations and environments." He made a broader smile, and Cubbage fiddled with his pencil. "The *people* could be difficult for me, though. I have work to do. I know that. I just want you to know that I've learned a lot in here."

Cubbage nodded. He was used to these grandstand speeches by parolees. They always said they were starting anew. The past was the past—yes, sir, all buried. But more than half of them ended up coming back. And Pick's record looked ominous.

The report was thin, a quick workup completed by an over-worked prison shrink, a sketchy report written by a disinterested professional.

Pick had grown up in one of those small tract homes that sprawled north of Los Angeles. He was a foster kid. His younger sister had died when Pick was eleven and she was five. The foster mother was accused of abusing the girl, and she was found guilty of killing her after years of abuse. The woman died in prison, and Pick had entered a series of juvenile homes. He started getting into trouble.

Pick pulled back his hands. "They've given me some excellent leads for a job. I have a few shots at some computer repair work." Pick grinned. "Everyone has a PC these days."

Cubbage nodded.

Pick had been in trouble, some fights as a teenager, and there was some knife play. But he went to a technical school run by the state, and he learned how to fix computers. He had moved to San Diego and found work. There, the police records showed that Pick started roughing up prostitutes, slapping them around.

He moved east. And one night he killed a woman.

"Donald, what about relationships with women?"

Pick's face clouded over. Then he looked directly at Cubbage with those great blue eyes. It was just the two of them in this small room. Pick grinned, cutting the tension. "I'll have to build some personal relationships." The grin broadened. "I know that. Brand-new ones. But I think I can do it. I've made friends with the guards." Pick leaned close again, hands out, as if reaching for Cubbage. "I can do it on the outside."

Cubbage nodded. "I'm sure you can, Donald."

A fight in a bar. A woman was killed. Pick got eight years for manslaughter. A tough judge, a bad lawyer, or maybe both. Cubbage knew the bar where it happened. The Hammer and Nail. It was a gay bar, a rough place. Cubbage didn't go there anymore. He wondered what kind of woman would have been there. . . .

Pick tilted his head. "Doctor, is there any possibility that I might see you for some counseling on the outside?"

Cubbage looked away.

He let himself imagine Pick coming to his door a free man, his debt to society paid, looking for an end to the pain he was carrying around.

He turned back to Pick. "I—well, I don't think I can see anyone." Pick's face fell; he was disappointed. "I mean, not now. I'll be leaving tomorrow to lecture at a college."

Pick's eyes widened, interested. "Oh, really? I didn't know that."

"Yes," Cubbage said. "At Hudson College."

Pick seemed to be impressed. "What will you lecture about?"

Cubbage shifted in his seat. "Trauma and childhood pain." He watched Pick carefully, searching for a response, as if the words, dartlike, had found a mark. But Pick just smiled.

Cubbage took a breath. He dug a business card out of his pocket with his office address and phone number. No danger there. If Pick could be violent again, perhaps Cubbage could help.

He passed the card to Pick, and Pick's fingers touched his. Cubbage quickly looked down at the folder.

Donald Pick was trying to look ready to make a successful reentry into society. His social skills were good. He was smart and sensitive.

How much of it was bullshit?

The psychologist shut the folder and stood up. Pick quickly rose and stuck out a hand.

"Thank you, Doctor. For everything."

Cubbage felt Pick's strong grip holding his small hand prisoner, squeezing it. Cubbage took a breath and pulled away, ready to open the door and leave Donald Pick.

20

In the morning, Friedman didn't go to his office.

He pulled off the Henry Hudson Parkway into safe, secure Riverdale, a haven in the Bronx.

Not that secure, Friedman thought.

The Soviet diplomatic residence, a tall gray monolith, rose above the private homes, an affront to the hard-working middle class.

The ramp ended at Broadway, opposite the Hebrew Home for the Aged. A few pale yellow menorah lights shone in the windows.

He drove up 248th Street to Riverdale Avenue before turning right. At 261st Street he slowed, and to his left he saw the tall fence of Mount Saint Vincent, the sharp spires tipped in gold leaf. Corazon Aquino went to college there. She even did commercials for the school: Come here and maybe you'll get to run a country, too.

Friedman passed the entrance gate, still moving slowly, cruising by. A cab hugged his rear, impatient. The cab waited for an opening and then gunned past him on the right. Friedman saw the driver make a face at him when he passed.

Friedman came to a light. He stopped and waited, looking at the quiet avenue, nearly deserted. The light changed, and he went on to the next block, to the park.

The Louis Calhern Park. It was surrounded with thick old trees, now bare, but on a summer's night it would be a dark place, a dangerous place. Nobody nice would go there at night.

Friedman turned and looked across the street. He saw a pizza shop, Riverdale Pizza. Inside it was blindingly bright, brilliant

120

white. The pizza man smoked a cigarette, hanging over a half-eaten pie.

He turned back to the park, passing it now. In summer kids would play there, the mothers watching. Probably no one would think about what happened to Tara O'Connell inside the park. No one would notice any discoloration by the seesaw.

Friedman turned into 261st Street and counted the blocks. How many blocks from the park to her home? One, two . . . He took a breath; it wasn't far. Three. He was at Fieldstone Road.

She had been close to home, to safety, to security.

But not close enough.

Friedman turned down Fieldstone and looked for a parking space.

He found one right in front of the O'Connell house. There was a hydrant there, but Friedman put his NYPD card in the window, near the registration. He got out and pulled his coat tight. A cold wind whipped up the block, frigid and wet. He squinted against the assault.

Maybe, he thought, retiring to Florida wasn't such a bad idea.

He wasn't wearing gloves, and his fingers felt the cold. He walked quickly up the four stone steps to the house, pressed the white dot of the buzzer, and heard the dull, muffled sound inside. He waited, and the door opened.

"Mr. O'Connell, I'm Jack Friedman."

The man wore a plaid shirt. His face was wrinkled, the folds carved into his face. He nodded and opened the door.

Mrs. O'Connell went to the kitchen to make tea. Friedman said that he didn't want any, but she insisted, smiling. "It's so cold," she said.

Friedman sat on the couch, and O'Connell sat in a chair opposite him. Friedman flipped through his notebook. He knew what he wanted to ask, but he needed a minute to think. Was it fair to do this to these people after all these years?

"I want to thank you for seeing me."

O'Connell nodded. Behind the man, on the wall, Friedman saw a citation, something official-looking, perhaps from the fire department. O'Connell had done his job, and they gave him a scroll, and time to sit in his house and think.

"I have a few questions. I know that you might not remember."

"I remember everything," O'Connell said. "I've forgotten nothing about my Tara."

Friedman nodded.

"Could Tara . . . could she have had any friends, any boy-friends . . . someone you didn't know well?"

"No."

Mrs. O'Connell came into the room carrying a cup in a saucer, tiny hot plumes of steam trailing behind. She handed it to Friedman. She pulled a chair closer to her husband. Her hand reached out and encircled his.

"Tara had only a few friends, and she didn't date, Detective. She liked staying home. She always called if she stayed at school late." The woman looked at her husband. "She always called, and that's how we knew something was wrong that night."

Friedman nodded. The woman held a napkin in her left hand. It was tattered, squeezed between her fingers. Six years later, he thought, and I'm digging this up for them, bringing it back. Even in the morning, the colored lights in the window blinked on and off, on and off. . . .

"She didn't call. So we worried. Mike called the police. And then—" Her voice caught, and she looked at her husband.

O'Connell spoke. "Tara was a good girl. She was too good, too trusting. She cared for people. She'd help people. Maybe that's why this happened. Maybe she was too helpful."

"Did she ever say that she thought anyone was following her?"

"No," Mrs. O'Connell said, her eyes filmy now, her battle against the tears almost lost. "She always told us that she didn't like night classes, walking through the college parking lot. It was dark, she said. Mike offered to pick her up, but she laughed. She—she thought that was silly."

"She never said anything about someone watching her," O'Connell said.

Friedman felt trapped. The air in here was dry and hot, the radiators issuing small bangs, cooking the dry air. He took a breath. "Did your neighbors ever complain about someone walking around. Someone they didn't know? A stranger?"

The man shook his head. "Nobody saw anything," he said. Friedman saw that Mike O'Connell's eyes were wet even as he sat, stolid, his face impassive.

Friedman had no doubt what this man would do if he caught the killer and brought him here. No doubt at all.

Friedman looked directly at Tara O'Connell's mother. She was crying now, squeezing her husband's hand.

Had they seen the photographs, the sick mess of her body? Had someone told them that Tara was alive, tied up and gagged? Had the O'Connells gone to the morgue and looked at her and said, "Yes, this is our little girl"?

"She was so sweet, sweet . . . and innocent."

Friedman closed his notebook.

What did I expect here? he thought.

Maybe just to get close to one of the people he killed, to make it more real than a stupid TV show.

It was real now. Friedman felt bad about coming. He felt as if the murder had happened yesterday. For these people, the pain and the hatred would never end. Every day was one more day of living with it.

Friedman stood up. He thanked them. O'Connell nodded, and his wife got up and went for Friedman's coat.

Friedman saw them then, the pictures on the wall, of a young girl in a ballerina costume. Then a teenager with braces. Later a near-woman, ready for life.

Until someone took it away.

He took his coat and walked to the front door.

21

The circus moved quickly, the government people in their black suits, looking impressive, came first. Then, smiling, there were newspaper people, and television people with their cameras, to watch, to ask questions, to aim their cameras at Erin, to pan around Lizbeth's kitchen and living room.

It didn't occur to her that she could say no, that she could say get the hell out of here. She didn't realize that she could scream at them to take their black government cars and all these reporters, these jackals, and get the hell out.

They were in control. They were in charge. The arrangements were presented to her as a fait accompli.

She was to be driven to Stewart Field, a U.S. Air Force base up near Newburgh, that night while a very flustered Mrs. Martin watched Erin.

Simon was flying from Syria to Frankfurt and then to Stewart, where she'd meet him. They'd have a reunion, and then Simon would come home.

The plans were presented to her, and she dealt with the situation by being very quiet. She answered the few questions that were asked. And she listened thoughtfully, earnestly, when the officials told her things.

Simon would land at the airbase this afternoon. He'd be given a medical examination at a special visitors building set up by the air force.

Then Lizbeth would meet with him for their reunion. It would be a private meeting, they emphasized, smiling. "You will be alone with your husband again, Mrs. Farrell, completely alone."

She smiled and tried to look pleased.

Then they would have to decide what was to be done. The government wanted Simon to go to the Malcolm Grow Medical Center in Maryland where they had a special program and a cadre of psychiatrists to deal with the sort of mental anguish and severe trauma that her husband had endured. That was something that she and Simon would have to decide together.

She nodded, committing herself to nothing.

Mrs. Martin arrived and hugged her, telling how her glad she was. She took Erin away, and Lizbeth felt lost in her own kitchen. She made a pot of coffee. It got cold, and she dumped it and made a fresh pot.

A young man in a suit showed up with a dinner of cold cuts and soda. The reporters talked as though she wasn't there. She heard them discuss the kinds of pictures they wanted to get. They told jokes.

Lizbeth drifted. She was numb, too preoccupied to say or do anything.

My husband's coming home, she thought over and over. I had—I'll admit it—given him up for dead. And now he's coming back. My life could start again. If—if—

Other thoughts let her know it wouldn't be that easy.

Then someone tapped her shoulder and said, "It's time, Mrs. Farrell." A black car stood outside waiting for her. She grabbed a coat and let the man lead her outside.

Lizbeth got into the car and pressed her head against the back window. Her lips kissed the cold glass. Her breath made little eddies of fog.

She tried to imagine the reunion as if it were a movie.

Simon would smile to her, sweet and happy. She'd run to him and he'd enclose her in his arms.

But the image vanished. She knew it wouldn't be like that. Her dream had told her that much.

In the dream Simon didn't stand because he couldn't stand. And his hair, once black and sleek, was now a scraggly salt-and-pepper, matching the lines etched in his face.

She heard a voice on the car radio, garbled words that she didn't understand. She looked out the window. Everything was brown and gray.

In Lizbeth's dream when Simon looked up and smiled at her, Lizbeth saw that her greatest fear was well founded. This sad-eyed, disheveled man—this broken, hurt wreck—was a stranger. He reached for her. And this she saw so clearly that it made her breath catch. He reached for her and she backed away, shaking her head. No.

She looked at Simon's eyes, and he looked at hers.

And he knew, he *knew* what she had done. He could sense that she'd been seeing another man . . . and worse. He feared that she would never be able to love him again.

The man from the State Department started talking to her. His voice sounded businesslike, official. She listened, thinking, This is important. This has something to do with me.

"It's the U.S. government's position, Mrs. Farrell, that your husband was permitted to escape. His value as a hostage, as someone to trade, had become virtually nil."

"Would they have killed him?" She was surprised at how flat her voice had become, how emotionless it sounded.

"That was an option. Perhaps their actions were due to the changes in Beirut. The militias have moved out, the green line dividing the city is gone, and a rapprochement of some kind is going on. To kill your husband simply because he wasn't worth anything on the open market wouldn't have been a wise move."

She nodded.

"I imagine that his captors were pressured by the Shiites to look the other way and let him go."

She nodded. They had let him escape. How nice.

"And—excuse me for bringing this up, Mrs. Farrell—how long did you know your husband before he was taken?"

What an odd question, she thought. She looked out the window. Dirty clots of old snow were heaped on the side of the highway. It was colder here. Shiny pancakes of ice reflected the dull gray sky.

"We were married for two and a half years. Before that we had gone out for nearly a year."

No. Not true. It was more like ten months.

They had been eager to move things along, she remembered. A few of her friends suggested that she was *too* eager.

Lizbeth had made jokes about her biological clock.

The young man nodded, looking back from the front seat of the limousine, studying her. Everyone's looking at me, she thought. Observing me. This must be what it's like to be a politician's wife or to be married to a celebrity. Sometimes those wives must want to go into a bathroom, look in the mirror, and scream. I'd like that, she thought. That would feel good.

"You see, Mrs. Farrell, we've found that the returnees, the

repatriated hostages, are transformed in a number of ways. Emotionally they're on a tightrope, easily bursting into tears or laughter. They don't quite have control of their emotions.''

The man paused. Then he said the obvious, to drive his point home. ''It can be a strain.''

She nodded again.

The driver took an exit ramp off the highway. After a few minutes he passed through an open gate below a sign that read Stewart Field and past a guard station. Lizbeth looked ahead and saw squat buildings, hangars, gray sky, gray airstrips, and a large olive green plane. She wondered if that was the plane that had brought Simon home.

I'm so close now, she thought. Mere yards separate me from my old life. Her hands dug into the plush material of the seat.

''One more thing. We encourage you to persuade your husband to enter our special facility in Maryland. The doctors there will do much to heal all his wounds, physical as well as psychological.''

Still looking ahead, she said, ''I'll try.''

The man reached out and touched her shoulder. She found that odd, but still she looked at the buildings covered with snow, the overhanging gutters edged with icicles.

''Mrs. Farrell, the man you meet may seem like a stranger to you. In many ways he *will be* a stranger. But remember: he is the man you loved. Your husband, the father of your daughter.''

The car stopped in front of a low building. Someone hurried to the car. Lizbeth heard a click. The car door opened.

Lizbeth thought: I'm supposed to get out.

So she did.

They had given her a room in which to wash up, a place to wait while they got Simon ready. She looked out the window and saw the gray sky and the gray airstrips, the gray buildings, the gray roads.

What will I say? she wondered. What will my first words be?

There was a knock on the door. Lizbeth turned, and the knock was repeated.

''Yes?'' she said.

''We should go, Mrs. Farrell.'' It was the man from the car, the young man from the State Department.

''I'll be right there,'' she said. She glanced in the small mirror in the bathroom and then went to the door and opened it. The young State Department official was accompanied by an older man who didn't smile. He looked like one of those grim-faced men who guarded the president.

The State Department official saw her look at the other man. He smiled and said, ''This man is here to protect you and your husband, Mrs. Farrell. He's with the United States Marshal's Service. The president himself ordered them to watch you.''

Lizbeth smiled as if this was especially good news. She grabbed her coat and put it on.

They led her down the hallway and then out the door, out into the cold once more, to the car. They drove her a few buildings over, and Lizbeth saw several television vans waiting there.

The car stopped, and again someone opened the door, took her arm, and led her into the building. The reporters were watching her. She felt the eyes of their cameras watching.

It wasn't far. A matter of steps. She entered the open door. There was the smell of coffee and the bite of cigarette smoke, a smell more and more uncommon. Nobody smoked anymore.

She passed small office cubicles, all empty. Then she ws guided down another hall onto a plusher carpet. She looked to her left and saw a small infirmary. A doctor stood there, flanked by two nurses, watching her pass. She smiled at them as if she was in a parade.

Perhaps they had mended Simon's wounds, Lizbeth thought. He had multiple bruises, they'd told her, and broken fingers. He also had a thin but extensive fracture of the left tibia. All in all, nothing that wouldn't heal over the weeks to come.

She passed several small bedrooms with bureaus, single beds, and tiny televisions.

Lizbeth was moving toward a closed door. She took a breath and felt the man's grip on her arm tighten. She didn't know this new man, but she appreciated his firm grip. I should try to thank him, she thought. He's been nice . . . helpful.

Someone was at her other side, guiding her down the now narrow hallway. She looked at him—a man in a white jacket, wearing glasses. The doctor.

Do I look that weak? She tried to remember her image in the mirror. I looked okay, didn't I? I looked fine, didn't I?

They arrived at the door. The doctor reached out and turned the knob. He opened it.

And then—horrible moment—they let go of her.

The door glided opened slowly. The room was dark. A single

light was on near the bed. Someone was sitting in a chair. The air was warm.

The men on either side of her waited.

She turned and looked at them. A few seconds only, but in those seconds she understood. The last few feet she was to do herself.

All alone.

The reunion really would be private. She breathed in the stuffy air.

She walked into the room to see her husband.

22

Donald Pick didn't think too much about this day, the time of year, the season, the weather.

It was cold, he knew that. They had given him a cheap parka, but it did little to keep the icy breeze away. In fact, they had given him a complete wardrobe of cheap clothes.

But it didn't bother him that the day was so cold. Some of the other inmates yelled at him as he went down the yellow brick road, the stone walkway past the cells of the east wing, to the main administration building, heading for the small door that led to the outside.

To freedom.

"Hey Pick," inmates screamed. "Get some pussy for me."

Pick grinned at them. They all liked him. Everyone liked him, except some really fucked-up Nazi cons and a group that called themselves NWA—Niggers with Attitudes.

His cellmate didn't say good-bye to Pick. That didn't matter.

The warden, Martin Dickens, was in the waiting room to issue the official good-bye. The cons called him the Dickman. The Dickman was short, with wire-framed glasses. Pick asked him how his son was doing at Albany State.

"Just fine, Donald. He got three-point-oh last semester."

Pick grinned. "That's great. Tell him to keep up the hard work."

The warden smiled back and then stuck out his hand. "I hope things go well for you."

Pick pumped the Dickman's hand hard, giving it a good manly shake.

For a moment Pick let himself imagine squeezing the warden's

130

hand so tight that the man would fall to his knees and beg Pick to stop. His eyes would water, and Pick—still smiling—would *really* squeeze then.

Wouldn't that be nice?

Instead, he released the warden's hand. "Thanks for everything," Pick said.

Dickens slapped his back. "Good luck, Don."

A guard opened a small door.

Out there was freedom. Freedom and opportunity. The excitement he felt was nearly overwhelming. Each step took him a bit closer to things he had been dreaming about every night.

To wait so long—it had been cruel. They never knew what they took away from me. More than my life. They took the Work. I was a god. I had the power to create wonderful things, terrible things. I controlled sensation, feeling, *life itself.*

His legs shook with each step, he was so excited.

He tasted the cold outside air. He heard a garbage truck groaning on its rounds.

He moaned, muffling it, swallowing the sound. They shouldn't know how he felt, not now.

He felt the concrete of the outside sidewalk. He looked around. The gray sky seemed to be part of the stone wall of the prison. There were towers, one on the right and another to his left, patrolled by black figures, their guns visible and obvious.

Martin Dickens watched him. Pick smiled.

He waved, and then they shut the door.

Pick's grin widened. He turned and picked up his pace. There was so much to do, so many things to work on, all the particulars before the Work could begin again.

But now, even now, the fantasies flooded his mind, free at last to claim every part of him. . . .

23

Simon couldn't really see her, couldn't see Lizbeth. She was blocking the light from the hall, a dark shadow.

He thought, I should get up. And what? Go to her. Take her hand. Hug her close. Kiss her lips.

Lizbeth stood in the doorway. She took another step into the room. "Simon?" she said. Her voice was familiar, yes, familiar. But hearing it was like listening to an old tape or watching an old movie.

It was something from the past.

The door clicked shut noisily behind her. Now, Simon thought, it's only the two of us.

He stood up, and with the light cut off from the back, he could see Lizbeth a bit better. He could see her hair. He had dreamed of touching her hair, of feeling her hair in his hands. She wore a skirt and a cream-colored blouse. She came closer, and her eyes caught the pale yellow light from the end table lamp.

Her eyes glistened.

Simon cleared his throat, a loud rumble in the room, and it occurred to him that this—seeming so slow, taking forever—was, in actuality, happening fast.

Lizbeth kept walking toward him. A great wind roaring at him. He extended his arms, the bandaged hand encased in white. She spoke again, and it was a sound he had imagined hearing nearly every day.

"Simon," Lizbeth said. He heard her voice catch, and maybe there were tears. "Oh, God, you're really okay. You're alive and—"

She came so close, and Simon winced. When people got close

to him—when they got so close that he could smell what they had been eating, the rank smell of their clothes, and the oil from their guns—he usually got hurt.

That had been his life. But now, this time, there was a different smell. Lizbeth's perfume was exotic, as if—as if he had suddenly been whisked away to a never-never land. He sucked in the scent noisily.

There was more.

She held her arms out and encircled him, and the smell was all around him. He felt tears coming from nowhere. He was going to cry.

He croaked her name, his first word to her.

"Lizbeth . . ."

And as she hugged him close, hurting him now, not knowing that every muscle, every bone, was fragile, sensitive, he buried his face in her hair, a sea of hair, a place to bury his sobs and hide.

He felt her body. *A body close to me.*

He had hoped that he'd shed only a few tears and then emerge clear-eyed after a few minutes of sobbing. That was what he hoped.

But that was not what happened.

Lizbeth felt his hand swathed in a cast. It felt stiff at her back, pressing her hard. Still, she hugged Simon, hugged her husband.

He was a baby, crying into her hair. She found herself whispering into his ear. "Here . . . it's okay, Simon. It's fine. Yes, yes."

Still he heaved. Her words only made the sobbing worse. Lizbeth felt exposed in this small room. She heard voices in the hall.

This is like meeting in prison, she thought, a prison with a cheap rug and a single bed.

She felt her own tears, little rivers that meandered down her cheeks and flowed onto Simon's shoulder, but—she felt an icy pang—she didn't know what she was crying about. She didn't understand this great sadness.

Was she crying tears of joy? Or was that a lie? Because soon—*soon*—the lies would have to stop. But not now, not here.

She patted his back—so bony, so hard—and stood there holding him for what seemed like forever.

Erin talked Mrs. Martin into playing a game called Doogan's Playground.

The game was usually okay, sort of fun, Erin thought. But it wasn't what she *really* wanted to do.

She would much rather have been watching TV.

Erin rolled the dice and moved her piece to a yellow space, which meant a yellow question. And that, Erin knew, meant a question that didn't have any right or wrong answer.

Duh . . . pretty dumb idea, she thought. Those questions were really stupid.

She liked the blue questions, the questions about famous people, and the red ones on books and movies.

Mrs. Martin sat on the floor. She didn't look too comfortable there with her legs curled up. But she didn't complain. Erin liked Mrs. Martin, even if she wouldn't let her watch TV tonight.

Sometimes Erin closed her eyes and thought, Mrs. Martin really *is* my grandma. Erin had one grandma who was still alive, but she lived in Florida, and she didn't baby-sit or bake cookies or take her to Broadway shows. Some of the kids had grandmas who did all that neat stuff.

Erin didn't. So she sometimes pretended that Mrs. Martin, nice Mrs. Martin, was her grandma. Today when she came home from school, they had baked Toll-House cookies, big giant cookies with chocolate chips that got all gloppy and tasted wonderful with milk.

Mrs. Martin read to her, not like her mom, not *that* good, but still, she read nicely, giving all the characters a different voice.

Mrs. Martin picked up the top yellow card and read the question: "Who helps you when you're in trouble?"

Erin frowned. Another question with—yuck—no wrong answer. She could say anything—Dumbo, Peter Pan, Elvis Pretzel, or whatever his name was—and she'd still get a yellow chip. A yellow question was supposed to make you think about things.

Erin grinned. "Superman."

Mrs. Martin looked at her over her glasses. The glasses were funny. There was a line in the center of each lens. "Erin, come on. That's not a real answer."

Erin giggled. "Popeye? Super Mario?"

Mrs. Martin shook her head and then looked at her watch. "Well, it's getting near bedtime. So—"

Erin raised a hand. Not bed, she thought. Trying to sleep was hard when Mom was gone. Even with Mrs. Martin in the next room, it was hard.

"Okay . . . okay. Sorry. No more goofy answers. I promise."

The woman flipped the card over again. "All right, then—who helps you when you're in trouble?"

Erin tilted her head, so serious now. "Mommy." She nodded. "My mom."

"And?"

Erin thought that her answer had been enough.

"And you! You help me, sometimes."

"And?"

Erin was stumped. She gave the only two answers she could think of. Mrs. Martin was looking at her as if she had left out the most important answer. The one really right answer.

"And . . . ?"

"I don't know." Erin smiled. She felt the air whistle through the gap made by her two missing front teeth. She liked sucking the air in and out through the hole. It felt cool on her tongue.

"I can't think of anyone else."

Mrs. Martin smiled, a gentle smile. She didn't say, See, you goofed. You *don't* know.

"What about God, Erin? God can help you."

Erin nodded, her mouth open.

Right. She and Mom had talked about Mrs. Martin and her God. Mrs. Martin was really into God, Mom had told her. That was okay. But the only thing that Erin's mom ever said about God was that he loved all of us and we could talk to him.

Anytime. Still, Erin got the feeling that God was like the Easter Bunny and the Tooth Fairy and Santa Claus. One by one the truth about each of them had been revealed until Erin believed that God would turn out to be the same thing.

Not for Mrs. Martin, though.

"Doesn't God help you?" Mrs. Martin said. She was again peering over her glasses.

Erin thought that maybe this might be a good time to end the game. "Yeah. Sure he does. You know, Mrs. Martin, I'm kinda tired. I'll get into my pj's and—"

Mrs. Martin grabbed Erin's wrist. It didn't hurt, but still it was a powerful grip. "Erin, you know God cares about you, loves you?"

Erin nodded, snagged, trapped.

"And you can ask him for help anytime, anywhere. That's called—"

"Prayer," Erin said.

Right answer. Mrs. Martin nodded. "Do you pray?"

The big living room clock ticked noisily, the swinging thing going back and forth, click . . . click . . .

Erin didn't like this question game. Should she lie or tell the truth? "Yes," she said. It was easier to fib.

Mrs. Martin smiled. The answer made her happy. Sometimes lies could do that.

"Good." Mrs. Martin put the card down. "Remember that, Erin. You can always ask for God's help." She rubbed Erin's hair. "And my help."

Erin nodded. She'd had enough of this game.

Simon kept looking at her, as if he had to study every inch of her face, as if he was probing, searching.

Lizbeth wanted to say, I put a yellow ribbon on the tree. I made sure it didn't ever slip to the ground. And I always talked about you to Erin. I let her know she had a daddy, that her daddy was still alive, and that he would come back.

There's only one thing that I didn't do.

I didn't stay faithful.

Simon's eyes—runny, lined with red veins—studied her face. Searching, probing. He squeezed her hand too tight, not just holding it but locking on to it as if she might disappear if he let her go.

She looked at him. Do I know this man? Can I love him again? Is it possible?

And is that something that I want?

Her fingers felt mashed together. She looked down at his hand. It was covered with tiny scratches and cuts and abrasions. Some of the wounds glowed red with Mercurochrome. She looked at him, then back to his hand. "Your hand," she said, "it must hurt."

He released her, embarrassed by his wounds. A trap sprung in an instant. Simon pulled his hand back.

"It's nothing."

She patted his shoulder, remembering what the State Department official had said: "Be positive. Be reassuring. Smile as much as you can, and don't get rattled by any erratic behavior."

Simon looked as though someone had hit him in the face with a frying pan. Big pop eyes, a mouth that trembled between blubbering and a goofy smile.

I'm sweating, Lizbeth thought. It's five above zero outside, snowdrifts are piled against the building, icicles are suspended from the gutters, and I'm sweating.

But not because it's too warm.

She rubbed his shoulder. They hadn't kissed yet, not a real kiss. They had hugged close. Simon had nuzzled her hair, her neck, as if he wanted to eat her. She had kissed his cheek, leathery, marked by tiny lines that hadn't been there before.

They hadn't really kissed yet.

She tried to conjure up a vision of the Simon Farrell she had married. That Simon used to laugh a lot. He listened to her stories, laughing, while they shared a bottle of wine. He was a good lover, assured, taking his time.

But even when she married him she knew it was a leap of faith. Something told her grab him before he vanished.

She wanted children, a life, what the rest of the world had.

Not—she raised her hand to touch his cheek—*this*. Her hand seemed to calm the changes that fluttered across his face.

He looked at her. Now she knew the kiss had to happen. They had come to a bridge that had to be crossed.

She leaned closer. Her hands steadied his head. And closer still. Simon shut his eyes, and that made it easier. Lizbeth's hands went to his cheeks, holding him there. She closed her eyes.

She felt the distance between them shrink. She felt his heat. The smell of coffee on his lips.

Then she kissed him. And held it.

Fighting back tears and pain while the icy wind whistled outside the small building.

Erin tucked her feet under the down comforter. It was cold under there. The photo album slid off the bed.

Mrs. Martin picked it up. Erin fussed with her pillows, getting them right. She made sure her doll was under the blanket, just so, with only her head protruding.

The doll's name was Amy, and her eyes were closed.

"All set?" Mrs. Martin asked.

Erin nodded while Mrs. Martin flipped through the large photo album.

"That's me," Erin said, pointing to the first page. Mrs. Martin leaned closer. "That's right after I was born. Don't I look yucky?"

Mrs. Martin laughed. "All babies look like that." She flipped the page. "See? Here you are, all cleaned up. And there's your mom and your dad."

Erin stared hard at the pictures. Her mother looked tired, almost hurt. Her eyes were dark, and her hair, usually so pretty seemed to go all over the place, like a cartoon cat zapped by electricity.

She looked at the picture of her dad. Erin didn't do that often because . . . well, just because.

Who is he? She stared at the face. In the picture his head was close to hers, close to the baby's head. He was smiling. Erin saw that her tiny hand was touching, almost holding, one of his fingers.

"I was an ugly baby," Erin said.

Again Mrs. Martin laughed. "No. You were—*are* beautiful."

Erin flipped through the pages of the book, not wanting to see more baby pictures. They're boring, she thought. Babies don't do anything.

She came to a picture with cake, candles, and balloons. "My first birthday," she said.

"I can see that."

She looked at the other babies sitting on a picnic blanket in the backyard. Mom was smiling. She seemed happy in this picture. She didn't look so tired. In one picture she saw her Dad. He was standing at the barbecue grill, cooking hot dogs for the grownups.

He's smiling. He's looking at me, Erin thought. She flipped more pages.

It was Christmas. Sledding at Harley Park, sitting between Daddy's legs. Then summer, and swimming at the wading pool, wearing a little pink bikini with yellow and blue polka dots.

I remember that bathing suit, she thought. I was two. I *remember* that!

She turned the page. And . . .

He was gone. There was only a couple of more pages after that. As if all of a sudden it wasn't important to take photographs anymore.

There were none of mom. A few of Erin. The nursery school picnic. The kindergarten Thanksgiving dinner, with Erin dressed as a Pilgrim girl. On the last page there was a space where a picture was missing.

But the man, her father, was gone from the album.

Mrs. Martin patted her arm. "Nice pictures, Erin. Very nice."

Erin shut the book. It made a loud, slapping noise.

"It's bedtime, honey. I can read to you a bit." Mrs. Martin took the photo album off the bed. She put it on Erin's desk, and picked up *Matilda* by Ronald Dahl. Matilda was a crazy kid who lived with a super-mean family. So Matilda planned revenge because they were so mean.

Mrs. Martin wouldn't like the book, Erin knew. She'd think that it was a nasty book. But Erin loved it.

Mrs. Martin began reading. It took a few minutes before Erin could hear, really hear, the story . . . and not think about other things.

Lizbeth finally pulled away. Simon's lips were cracked, his mouth felt clumsy, awkward, against hers. He was a teenager again.

But she also had the memory of the life they had started, the possibility of lying in bed and not needing a baseball bat right there on the floor beside her.

"How do you feel?" she asked. It was a dumb question, a stupid question.

He laughed. A wheezy laugh, the laugh of a degenerate who had spent his life smoking cigarettes and drinking bourbon. God, what has he been through? When will he tell me? How long will it take for it all to come out? Day by day, week by week . . .

"I'm okay. My hand"—he held it up—"is a little smashed up. But . . ." A quaver there, the voice shifting keys. He didn't quite have control, not yet. . . . "The doctors here—great doctors, absolutely great. They say my hand should be in good shape in a few weeks. As for the rest of me . . . well, how do I look?" He grinned. His mouth looked dark, the teeth brown.

"Fine," she said too quickly. More lies, but this time she was sure that the truth was radiating out of her eyes. She patted his good hand. "You just need some rest and some home cooking."

His face fell as if he'd been crushed by a sudden thought. She didn't have a clue to what had made him suddenly deflate.

"Oh," she said, standing up. Keep things positive, they had told her. Say things. *Anything.*

The room was so small—a cell, a cage. He's not free yet, she realized. He's not home.

"I brought a photo," she said.

He turned and looked at her. "I know I don't look so good. I just need . . ." he muttered, not hearing her.

Lizbeth went to her purse and grabbed an envelope. She slipped out the photo. "I brought this for you."

He was shaking his head. This is too much for him, she thought. They had told her to take it easy the first time. Give him some time to absorb all that had happened. Take it slow.

She handed him the photo. He looked at it.

It was Erin, taken a few weeks ago, to show off her missing teeth. You grow up, and life makes you a clown for a year.

"It's your little girl," she said.

And it hit her. Erin *was* his little girl, his baby. God, he hadn't seen her for all those years, could only dream about her. "Your baby," she said, through her tears. She touched his shoulder.

He looked at the picture and began crying again, quiet sobs this time. He looked up at Lizbeth, then back at the picture.

"I want—" He took a breath and spoke a bit more strongly. "I need to go home."

Simon went back to staring at the picture while Lizbeth stood there and watched.

24

After leaving the O'Connells, Friedman drove up to Furnace Dock Road in Westchester, where Gail Tompkins was killed. After lunch from a hot dog van, he took the Bronx River Parkway to the Whitestone Bridge and drove to a nice neighborhood near Liberty Avenue in Queens. He then went to SoHo where a waitress-artist had met the Meatman in a parking lot.

He visited all the haunts of the Meatman.

Friedman got out of his car and walked around each spot, limping, trying to feel the place. He came away with only one thought: The Meatman could do business anywhere; he was adaptable.

By the time Friedman got back to One Police Plaza, it was late. Not that the building was deserted. It was never deserted. Crime never slept, and neither did the NYPD.

But he didn't see anybody on his floor. One office was lit, probably some hotshot working on a special project. Maybe drug stuff. Maybe gang stuff. Maybe drugs and gang stuff.

The building was cold. The department was saving money by turning the damn heat down. Friedman hobbled to his office, a modern windowless hole.

He heard something behind him and turned to say hello, ready—no, eager—for some small talk. Just doing some work, he'd say. Keeping busy with some shit-canned murders, very ugly stuff, five years old. A real cold trail.

Friedman turned around. No one was there. He heard something. There! Again. God, he heard a sound. What the—

He looked around the darkened office. The sound seemed to be moving. Over there now . . .

Was that a squeak? Okay, Friedman thought. It's a rat, only a rat. But the sound was gone. And he thought, No, there are no rats in this building. It's too new. Give them a few years. . . .

He smiled at that. Haven't seen a rat in a while.

He tried to turn away from the thought . . . the memory. Haven't seen a rat in a while. He opened his office.

Last time I saw a rat was in Sheepshead Bay two summers ago. And Elaine hugged me close. . . .

They had finished a too-large dinner at Giorgio's in Sheepshead Bay—antipasto, minestrone, pasta, and carne—some nice veal piccata, the whole nine yards. He felt no guilt ordering the veal. Screw the little calves in their pens. Some humans had it worse.

They plowed through the salad—not Giorgio's strong suit—before finally passing on dessert. Two frothy cappuccinos topped off their tanks.

Elaine said, "Let's take a walk."

It was too hot for a walk. The sun was going down, and still it was ninety degrees. The bay and the fishing boats gave off a biting aroma of old wood and salt. He said it was too hot. But Elaine smiled, looking young and lovely.

How the hell did Elaine do that? Married twenty-five years and all I can see is beauty. He knew if he ever lost her he'd be ruined.

She smiled at him, a young and infectious grin. "Come on, Jack. Maybe there'll be a nice ocean breeze."

Neither of them knew then that things could happen so fast.

One day you were happy. The next, your life was over. Riding high in April. Blown out of the water in May.

So they walked past the piers, past the men from the fishing boats spreading out their catch—the blues, the flounder—for people to buy. The crew tossed buckets of water on the fish, trying to keep them fresh. The evening was still hot.

They walked the length of Emmons Avenue, past the boats, past a few cheesy hotels, until they came to a jumble of rocks stretching down to the oil-skimmed water.

Suddenly there was breeze. Though it was hot, sticky, and he was sweating, there was a warm, sweet breeze.

So they kept walking, past houses now, leaving the fishing boats and seafood restaurants behind. The sun finally vanished, and the sky was left a dark blue.

Elaine saw some more rocks and, just at the shore, a small strip of sand. She slipped off her shoes and said she wanted to walk in the sand, to feel the wet sand under her toes.

How clean was that sand? Friedman wondered. With all the garbage, all the oil—how clean?

They climbed over the rocks and reached the strip of sand dotted with debris. Elaine didn't seem to see it. She walked, as the first stars began glowing in the east.

They passed a bum, some homeless *amigo*. Now they were called homeless. Though there were welfare benefits and shelters and Medicare, these guys *had* to sleep on the beach.

They walked around the dark shape, and Friedman saw Elaine step over something slimy and plastic, lying on the sand.

The walk lost its charm. It was time to go.

Elaine squeezed his hand. ''Maybe we should go back,'' she said.

He had nodded. The breeze vanished. It had been a tease, just to get them down here. All life was a tease. It showed you a lot of good stuff and then whipped it away.

Presto chango! See heaven? Now here's . . .

Hell.

They turned back, hurrying now, past the sleeping body. The body moved. Or rather—

Elaine squeezed Friedman's hand. Surely she felt the same tightening around her stomach that he did? The same sudden souring of the meal that he had just blown eighty dollars on?

Something moved on the bum. She squeezed his hand. ''Jack . . .'' she whispered. Then again, a bit louder this time.

The thing that moved on the bum, on the homeless man— caught enough light from the street lamps so that they could see its shape.

It was a rat.

Friedman tried to hurry his wife past, but she kept looking. ''Jack!'' she said, holding his arm tightly.

Friedman turned and saw the rat's head moving up and down. And then the sound, an unmistakable sound—unless you were heavily into denial.

Friedman thought, I've seen a lot of bodies, a lot of disgusting things. But here I am with my wife, and over there a rat's chowing down on some Ripple-ripped soul who was cashing in his chips without even the fuck knowing it.

He heard her tears and, from the bum, wet sounds and moans muffled against the sand.

Elaine screamed, "Jack! Do something! Do something!"

He ran over, yelling, pulling out his gun. Dumb idea. As if he could shoot the fucker off like some marksman.

He yelled. The shadowy rat raised its head and stood its ground. It was amazing, the rat seemed defiant. It didn't move, and Friedman froze. What do I do now? he thought.

The rat held him there. Friedman took another step. The rat looked as large as an overgrown tabby. It was a big thing, with a tail trailing down to the sand.

Friedman moved closer. He swung back his leg, ready to kick the rat into the water. He imagined it latching on to his leg and holding on. Rats didn't let go. Everyone knew that. They got you, and they wouldn't let go.

The shape—Friedman didn't know for certain whether it was a man or a woman—moaned. The Ripple was wearing off, and the chew marks were fading in.

Friedman went to kick at the rat. But it scurried away, melting into the sand, disappearing among the ice cream wrappers and the driftwood.

He walked over to the bum. He saw that it was a man. He was breathing. He had an open sore that needed attention.

Friedman rejoined Elaine. When they got back to the piers, he found a phone and called the police.

The squeak, whatever it was—maybe some computers talking to each other—was gone. The room was quiet.

Friedman licked his lips, looking around his office.

He didn't want any more of the memory, but there was nothing he could do about that.

He and Elaine had made love that night. But there was no recapturing the mood, the feelings that had been so strong during dinner. The lovemaking had been good, though. It was always good.

Another good one, he might have thought. If he had known . . .

If he'd known that they were down to one, maybe two handfuls. *We never know that.*

He felt for the switch and threw on the light in his office. And with light, the memories faded.

He expected only a sparsely furnished office and an empty desk top. Bethany Clarke had just started working on the case. It was too early for any results. It would take a while, he thought. It sure as hell wasn't a priority.

Instead, his desk was covered with computer printouts. And on top of one pile was a note.

25

Lizbeth sat beside Simon in the back of the limousine. She held his hand while he smiled and looked out the window. Sometimes he squeezed her hand hard, too hard, but she didn't let him go. She couldn't do that to him.

He said things. Once he turned to her. He had tears in his eyes.

"I—I never expected to see this again. It's like a dream."

And Lizbeth felt her own tears. She squeezed his hand back. "You're home, Simon. It's not a dream. You're *home.*"

Lizbeth fought to keep away the thoughts that made her feel like a traitor. Would he ever ask? she wondered. Would he ask her what she did while he was gone?

And what would she say?

They were on the Thruway, driving through a bitter winter landscape, when Simon turned and asked, "Does Erin do well at school?"

Lizbeth grabbed the opportunity to talk about Erin. She told him about the spelling quizzes—all A's—and how much she loved books.

Until she saw that Simon was looking out the window again at the gray road, the hills, the dark clouds.

She wanted to ask him questions, but the army psychologist had said it would be best not to. "Let it come out when he's ready," he'd said. "Talk about your life with your daughter. Talk about home. Help him start remembering his past life and thinking about his future."

Then—too soon—the limousine left the Thruway. They were nearing Harley. "Almost there," Lizbeth said lightly.

Simon turned to her. He raised his other hand, the one with the bandage. "I'm scared, Lizbeth." He looked around as if searching for a way out, as if he was trapped. "I don't know if I can do this."

She patted his good hand. "Simon, it will be fine. You'll love Erin, and she'll love you."

Simon shook his head. The limousine slowed, and the driver paid the toll. The State Department Official looked back and smiled.

Lizbeth smiled automatically and turned to Simon. Her husband had pressed his head against the window. She leaned closer to him.

He was shaking his head, muttering to himself. "I . . . I don't know."

"Shhh," she whispered. "It will be fine, Simon. It will be—"

The car started forward again, and Simon shook his head. "No. I won't know what to do or say."

Lizbeth caressed his cheek. His skin felt tight, leathery. Had it always felt that way? she wondered. Or had he changed?

She soothed him, the way a mother soothes a baby. She whispered to him.

Simon closed his eyes. His lips opened, though. He made a sound. Not a word. A sound, a pathetic sound, then louder. Lizbeth touched his shoulder, his wet cheek. "Simon. It's okay."

His mouth opened wider, a great dark cavern, an enormous yawn. "I-I—" The noise made the official from the State Department snap his head around. He looked at Simon, then at Lizbeth, as if expecting her to do something. Simon tried to speak again, shaking his head, totally overcome.

"Should I stop the car?" the driver asked.

Simon banged his head against the window. Once and then again.

"Should I—"

Lizbeth put her arm around Simon and pulled him close, away from the window, away from whatever private hell he had conjured. "No, keep going."

She pulled him closer and pressed his lips to his ear. "Simon, you're home. You don't have to be scared anymore."

He shook against her. And she whispered to him that everything was going to be all right. *He was home.* . . .

By the time Simon walked away from the car, flanked by Lizbeth and the official, he looked as if he had composed himself. That was what Lizbeth hoped.

Not another scene, please, she thought. No more weird sounds, no more sobbing. Because . . . I don't think I can handle it.

Reporters were waiting near the house. There was no way to prevent that, the officials had told her. She saw that Simon was smiling. Way to go, she thought. Good for you.

They put microphones in front of him, and his first words were "God Bless America!" Everyone clapped. There were people—strangers—crying. Reporters asked questions. NBC's Gabe Pressman squeezed close and asked the big question.

While Lizbeth held his arm tightly, smiling holding on to Simon, Gabe asked, "What will you do now, Mr. Farrell?"

Simon looked at him. Lizbeth opened her mouth. He's not going to answer, she thought. He'll just stand there. Too tough, that question's too tough.

Instead Simon nodded. The grin returned. Lizbeth knew that smile. Simon had always laughed so easily. He could be so funny. She saw that smile, and she thought: we're going to be all right. Everything's going to be all right.

Simon held Lizbeth close. He said, "I'm going to get on with my life." He gave the thumbs-up sign, and all the cameras gulped the image.

Later she'd watch it replayed on all the channels—on the six o'clock news, Eyewitness News, the "Today" show.

A path was cleared to the house. Erin was inside watching, waiting to meet her daddy. Simon took a step, the limp seemed more pronounced. She looked at him, and he still smiled. Only the way he squinted told her that he was in pain.

Lizbeth smiled. She said softly, "It won't be long."

But the walk to the door took forever.

At the steps to the house, Lizbeth hesitated. Best I stand back, she told herself. He should meet Erin on his own.

The reporters were at their backs, waiting, watching. The neighbors looked on from their doors and windows. Some of them hadn't said squat to her through the years, hiding away their own happiness, protecting it.

As if bad things were contagious.

Lizbeth stood back. The lights were on in the house. The yellow ribbon—a big strip of plastic—caught the light. She saw Simon look at it. Lizbeth chewed her lips. She carried Simon's one bag—empty really. Simon had only the clothes on his back.

The door to the house opened. Lizbeth's breath caught in her lungs. The air was so cold, unbreathable. She watched Simon walk unsteadily up to the door, his bandaged hand held rigidly beside him.

Lizbeth saw the sitter, Mrs. Martin. And standing in front of her, Erin. They were two shadowy figures, lit from the light inside.

Simon shuffled closer. She heard a sound. Simon saying something. She heard the word, croaked. His voice caught, strangled with emotion.

Oh, God, she thought. I can't handle this. I'm not handling this at all.

She was crying, then sobbing.

She heard Simon say, "Erin . . ." Then he said it louder. She thought of his crying in the car. She thought of all the things he'd been through, the way he must have dreamed about this.

"Erin . . . sweetheart."

Erin stayed close to Mrs. Martin, who was holding her hand.

Simon reached the top step, the light spilling out. She sees him now, Lizbeth thought. Erin is looking at him. And he doesn't look like the pictures in the photo album. He looks older, a lot older, and grayer. So thin.

Lizbeth worried about what Erin would do. I spoke to her. I told her how important it was to make him feel welcome, to make him feel loved.

"Erin," he said again.

Lizbeth, right behind him, heard Erin say something.

"Daddy." A quiet, gentle sound.

Simon's good arm went out to hug his daughter close. Lizbeth kept sobbing. The tears were coming as fast as she wiped them away.

Through the blur she saw Erin's arms go up to Simon, like any daughter hugging a father back from a long trip.

Then Simon, holding Erin tightly, moved into the house. Lizbeth followed. Mrs. Martin was crying. There was the smell of dinner and the warmth. The lights, dollops of warm yellow, stretched from one room to the next.

Lizbeth shut the door behind her.

They were home.

26

The feeling was on him, the electric tingle, the not-to-be denied pressure that made it difficult to breathe. He sucked in a few quick gulps of air.

Pick walked around the room, nodding, telling himself that this was okay.

"This is fine," he said. He smiled.

It was a halfway house, a place for ex-cons to mark time during their early parole period, not too far from home.

The black woman who ran the place, Mrs. Williamson, had told him that she didn't allow any trouble. No trouble, no way. She told him that she knew cons and she didn't take no shit.

Pick grinned at her.

He wouldn't be using the room much. In fact he wouldn't be using it at all. No, when he began the Work again, they'd find him if he stayed here.

That was the problem, he thought. This time if they find me and lock me away I'll never again get to see the beauty of skin covered with brilliant red swirls. I'll never hear the cries, the squealing and begging for help, the prayers to God for help, until they finally realize that *I am God. And this is my Work.*

He sat down on the bed. The springs sagged noisily.

From the window he could see one of the towers of the prison; he could see the river, hear the trains. I haven't come so far, Pick thought.

He had stopped at a sporting goods store before coming here. The kid behind the counter had looked at him funny, as if he knew. Pick asked to look at one particular knife, something good for skinning fish, and then—yes, there—something thinner, narrower.

150

He had the money he had earned in prison. He had given his savings to the scumbag lawyer. They had even sold his furniture.

He bought both knives. Then he walked into Woolworth's and bought some other things he needed. Crest toothpaste, a big tube. And Ivory soap—99 44/100 percent pure. He picked up some sugarless gum and a can of shaving cream scented with mint.

He also bought a slice of cardboard pizza. He talked to the Woolworth's counterman. Pick told him it was good pizza. "Best I had in a while," he said. "Sure is."

All the time feeling the two knives in his coat pocket.

Now he got off the sagging bed.

"I'll be in and out," Pick told Mrs. Williamson. "Traveling, going for job interviews. I want to visit some relatives."

Give her the picture.

He told the woman he'd be keeping odd hours. Here for a few days and then gone. Pick paid for two weeks. Then Mrs. Williamson left, shutting the door behind her.

Pick picked up the winter coat they had given him when he left the prison. It was a bit small. He felt the two knives in the pocket. Pick took out the thin one with the blade that folded neatly into a white plastic handle.

He opened the blade. He brought it against his thumb. He heard his breathing. Again he touched the blade to his thumb and felt his dick getting hard as he touched the blade to his thumb, a light touch, but it was enough. A thin red line magically appeared. It always *seemed* like magic.

The sting felt good.

Pick pulled the blade away. He saw the smear of red on the blade. He sucked at it, tasting salty blood.

The thin knife was nice and sharp.

Pick went to the door. He had a lot to do before he could start. It would take discipline and planning and creativity.

He started whistling. He opened the door and went down the stairs.

The Hudson River Line train to Manhattan, due at 8:05 P.M., was late. Pick stood on the platform, an icy wind from the river whipped at him, chilling him.

The train finally came, but it looked as if it was going too fast to stop. As Pick fingered his knife, the train screeched to a halt at the far end of the station, and he had to run to get into one of the three cars.

The car was hot and nearly empty. Pick saw a kid and his girl. She had spiky blond hair sticking straight up in the air. The boy's hair was short, too, but it glistened under the lights. The boy was smoking a cigarette.

Pick saw the girl look up at him. He smiled at her.

She didn't look away. She's sweet, Pick thought. He stood there a moment as the train pulled away. He imagined cutting her clothes off bit by bit. The boy could watch. That could be done. No problem. And when all her skin was exposed—she was tiny, so there wouldn't be much room—Pick imagined the design, the patterns, he'd give her.

She looked away.

Pick grinned. Maybe she read my mind. Maybe the little babette is a psychic.

Pick found a seat.

The train roared toward New York, rumbling back and forth on the tracks. And Pick thought, Life is good. Life is wonderful. I was patient, I waited, and now all those good things are going to be mine again.

He watched the two kids get off the train, and then he followed them into Grand Central. The boy draped one arm around his girl, hugging her tight. The kid looked over his shoulder as if he was going to say, "Hey, you got a problem, man? What the fuck is your problem?"

Pick kept walking behind them.

The kid looked, but he didn't do anything. Pick imagined him doing a little calculation of relative sizes, body weight, muscle. Then the kid turned away and picked up his pace.

Pick laughed to himself. That was good, but the Work would make him feel so much better. Time would stop; the whole world would shrink to insignificance. Pick had read books in prison, about meditation, Eastern religions, crap like that.

With the Work, I transcend it all, he thought.

He climbed the stairs and left Grand Central.

A car would make things much easier. But it won't be long. Just have to continue being patient.

He came out onto Forty-second Street, disoriented by the lights. Cabs were cruising in search of late-night fares; others were dropping off businessmen who were going to miss kissing their kiddies good night. Steam gushed from the sewers. They look like caldrons, Pick thought.

He turned right. I'll get a bus, he thought, and head uptown. After all I don't deserve the Work if I can't protect it. That thought made him sad. To lose it again—he couldn't bear that.

He kept walking, surrounded by people, the noise, the city.

I can protect it fine, he thought.

I'll take a bus up the West Side. Then I'll walk to West End Avenue.

To the street where Dr. Lane Cubbage has his office.

27

Erin felt her dad's hand on her forehead.

It was a rough, scratchy hand, not like Mommy's at all. It wasn't soft. In the dark room she couldn't really see him anymore.

My dad, she thought. He's my daddy.

Kids used to tease her. Where's your dad? Don't you even have a daddy?

"*I do!*" she'd yelled at them. Once, in first grade, she'd kicked Timmy Cirullo. A real good one, in the shin. "I *do* have a daddy," she'd yelled.

"Oh, yeah? Then where is he?"

Erin made a good ugly face, all scrunched up. Mommy called it her mean old man face. And she had said, "He's a hostage."

She didn't really understand how someone got to be a hostage and why it had to be her daddy. She just knew that that was what he was. And it made Timmy Cirullo shut up.

Now he was here, her daddy was here, and she didn't know him at all.

His hand trailed down her cheek. The other hand was all bandaged up, and the arm was in a sling. And he didn't walk too well. It must hurt him to walk, Erin thought. His hair was short, as if someone had cut it with a lawn mower—and it had big patches of gray.

He looked old, but Mommy looked young and pretty. He spoke. "Good night, Erin."

She nodded. Then she made a small smile. "Good night, Daddy." She thought she heard something else. Was he crying? She heard him sniff. Did he have a cold or was he crying? Why would he cry?

She couldn't see him. Then Mom came to the doorway. She walked in. "Good night, sweetheart," she said. She leaned over the bed and kissed her.

Then he did it, too. Her dad kissed her. And Erin thought, I don't know him. He's like a stranger. But I have a daddy now, someone to watch over me, to protect me . . . me and Mommy.

He stood up, pushing on the bed with his good arm.

When they both left, when the door was shut and there was only the glow of the Mickey Mouse nite-light, Erin hugged her Cabbage Patch Preemie real close.

Simon walked around the house, moving from room to room. There are no chains here, he thought. No guards to come and kick me if I move too much. No dog bowls of bad food on the floor.

No bodies hanging from the ceiling, swinging with every breeze that snakes through the room.

Sometimes Simon had to feel his forehead to make sure that he didn't have a blindfold there, that it wasn't pushed up onto his forehead.

If this was a dream, it was very real. It was so lifelike. The lights were so bright; the couch looked so soft. There was a TV. And brilliant white light in the kitchen. He stood still for a moment and heard the hum of the refrigerator.

He knew that Lizbeth was watching him. He moved into the kitchen. He saw Erin's spelling quizzes held to the refrigerator by magnets. He turned around and saw a coffeemaker. A digital clock hung on the wall.

He left the kitchen and walked up a few steps to the living room.

"Simon, are you okay? Maybe you should rest."

He nodded at Lizbeth as he went up the steps. The Christmas tree was still there, the lights off, no gifts under the tree, just hundreds of green needles on the floor.

"Come. Sit down. I'll get you a beer."

Yes, I used to like beer. Beer and a baseball game. I loved that. And the opera broadcasts on Saturdays.

He saw some photos on the wall beside the fireplace. He went to them. "They're all new," he said. "These are all things that I missed."

He heard Lizbeth come up beside him. She touched his good arm. "I'll tell you everything that happened"—she reached out and touched a photo of three-year-old Erin on a merry-go-round— "all the things we did while you were gone."

"I missed so much," he said flatly. "They took it away from me."

He felt Lizbeth's grip tighten on his arm. "Don't think about that. We're together now. We have our lives back."

Simon turned to her. "Those years are gone, Liz. Everything is different now. But I'll make it up to you and to Erin." He smiled. "And to myself."

He thought then of Erin, a little girl who needed a dad, someone big and strong to protect her. But I couldn't even protect myself. I was a chained animal. I sat in my own filth. I can't be a dad to her.

Lizbeth hugged him. She kissed his cheek, and he felt her lips pressing against him, warm and soft.

The tears didn't claim him this time.

No, he thought, there's something here I haven't known, something I thought was gone.

God, please, let there be a *future* here.

He prayed while Lizbeth held him.

Lizbeth gave Simon a hug. She held him tight, trying to keep her thoughts, her fears, away.

She had watched him walk through the house noticing every change, every added knickknack. When he saw the photos, he'd looked so pathetic.

It was late. It had been a long day, a crazy day, and Lizbeth was exhausted. But she kept asking herself, What must he be feeling? What's going on inside his head?

Now he took her hand, and they walked upstairs to their bedroom. The steps were hard for him. He took them slowly.

He stopped and looked at the king-size bed, grinning. "I'm used to sleeping on the ground," he said. It was a joke. He went to his bureau and started opening drawers. He pulled out socks and underwear. Years old, but perfectly preserved.

"It's like I've never been gone," he said.

While Lizbeth walked around with him, she wondered why this was so hard for her. I feel as if he's inspecting the house, feeling around for any changes, any deep changes. As if he might sense that I cheated. That I wasn't one of the good wives.

And I'm following him, hoping to catch any little clue, like "Whose shoes are these? I've never had Reeboks." Or "I don't smoke cigarillos. Whose stogies are these?"

Moments from a lost "Lucy" episode.

The odd part was that she had nothing to fear. Walt Schneider—she let herself think his name, picture him for the first time today—had never even been here.

She had nothing to fear.

Simon shut the drawers and turned to her. "I can't get enough of this," he said. "There were months when I thought I'd never see any of it again." He looked around.

"I can't believe it, either," she said. "You were gone so long. I tried not to give up hope."

He looked at her. For the first time she felt as if he really saw her.

And she really saw him.

"I can't explain to you what thinking about this house and Erin and you—what it meant to me. I went mad thinking about it. Everything was so important—the holidays, family dinners, movies together, and . . . and—"

He started to lose control again. He slipped another few notches. Lizbeth felt something stir inside her. For a moment Simon wasn't some strange creature out of a time warp.

He was someone she knew, someone she loved. The image was there, and the hint of feeling. Call it hope, she thought. Call that feeling hope.

"I'm going to try to make everything good again," he said. "The way it was."

She was crying. Got to stop crying, she thought. Somehow I've got to stop all this crying.

Lizbeth put a finger to his lips. "You don't have to do anything, Simon. Just get better, and everything will be fine."

She said the words, and she hoped that they were true.

When he came to their bed, Lizbeth looked at the bruises, the cuts, the discolored patches on his body.

Then she got into bed beside him. She wore perfume.

Simon's pajamas ballooned around him. He made a joke about how gaunt he looked in them. She turned the light off.

He touched her, slowly, tentatively.

"Lizbeth," he whispered. "God, I . . ."

This would be difficult. For many reasons.

But she knew it had to happen. Lizbeth wanted it to happen. I want my life back, too, she thought. I want my family.

She touched him gently, afraid of hurting him, but also afraid that nothing would happen. She moved beside him, touching him, replacing his pain with pleasure. He said her name. Then he said, ''I love you.''

She took away the pain and whispered back to him, ''And I love you.''

Later Simon fell fast asleep, his head cradled in her arms.
It was near dawn.
Lizbeth was still awake.

28

Friedman picked up the note, a sheet of purple paper marked with a handwritten scrawl, sitting on the stack of printouts: "Here's what I've come up with so far. More on the way. Bethany."

He'd expected nothing, and here was enough information to keep him busy for days. He wanted to get some dinner. Maybe catch a movie . . . fill the hours. Now he had all this. He sat down in the chair.

The first pile was labeled "Sexual Assault Cases Corresponding to the Target Period." He was dealing with speculation here, he knew. Just guess work.

The last acknowledged Meatman killing was in December of 1987. So he figured that only people incarcerated after that could be of interest. There were pages of them, listed by prison—Attica, Ossining, Elmira. There were also some light houses, the easy joints—a work farm, a country club. Only a few names there, probably mob goodfellows with pull.

There was a list from the state correctional medical facility. Friedman had been there once. It was supposed to handle only Level II and Level III felons—psychotics, schizophrenics. They had group therapy and a nice arts program for the inmates. They made baskets and key chain holders. They talked out their antisocial problems.

But budget problems and the general popularity of crime had put the crunch on all the state's institutions. And the medical facility started to get a few very violent sociopaths.

They gave them a set of oils and a canvas, these people who admired John Wayne Gacy, who liked to draw clowns. Gacy dressed like a clown to attract little children. And then he killed them. Very slowly.

I never liked clowns, thought Friedman.

There were twenty pages of names and case histories of violent sexual assault. Lots of nasty stuff. No surprise there, he thought.

The next two pages pertained to a more select crowd—cases involving knives and sexual assault. Most of the convicts had been seen by a psychologist as part of their rehabilitation.

Then, on the bottom sheet, he saw a note from Clarke: "Pulled these out. Two recent parolees from Sing Sing. Might be a good place to start."

Might be, but Friedman was suddenly interested in something else. He saw a name he knew. Dr. Lane Cubbage, in addition to his private practice in New York and his consulting work for the department, had a good-paying sideline with the State Correctional System.

Now, that's interesting, Friedman thought. Cubbage saw, at least, two mental cases with violent tendencies.

He looked at the names of the two men who saw Cubbage. Both candidates made the cut-off period. And both of them were now on parole.

I don't like that, he thought. Everyone else on the lists is under lock and key. If one of them is the Meatman, he ain't going anywhere. But these two guys are out on the streets.

He checked their release dates. One had been out for eight weeks, another since last June. He thought of what Cubbage told him about the pressure. The obsession would build, he'd said.

It would mount. It would overflow. If Cubbage worked with these men, he should damn well know if one of them could be the Meatman.

And if the Meatman was out, how long would it be before he picked up his old pastime?

He wrote down the two names: Ed Hogue and Mohamed Greene. It was good news that both of them had been out for a while. Nothing had happened, not yet. Greene was living with a wife in Yonkers. Hogue was staying at a Y right here in the city.

Friedman could check on these suckers right away.

His stomach growled, insisting on food.

But he wanted to leave a note thanking Clarke and her wonderful computer and asking her to check one more thing that might help.

He wrote the note and ripped it out of his notebook. He'd drop it on her desk on the way out. It was late. There was enough for him to do tomorrow, plenty to keep him busy. That was the important thing.

Because, he thought, I don't really expect to nail this guy, do I? I don't think so. . . .

He got up. The knee sent him a quick jolt of pain, a little pick-me-up. Friedman limped out of the deserted office.

29

Pussy has amazing powers, magical powers, Ink thought. Damn, it has to . . .

He looked at the girl sitting on his desk, thighs open to view, luscious, yummy.

To die for, right?

He looked back at the kid. The kid was what—eight-fucking-teen? Good-looking kid.

Ink turned on the compressor, and his tattoo needle vibrated in his hand. It would hurt a lot less than it used to. In the old days, before the industrial revolution came to tattooing.

Still, the kid went bug-eyed. And—as if sensing that the boy was having second, third, a whole six-pack of thoughts—the girl slid off the desk.

She wasn't that young. Pushing thirty. But damn, she was a sexy-looking babe. Wearing a goddamn miniskirt, blond hair. What did she think it was, the sixties? She came close to the boy's body and patted his head.

The compressor whirred. The tattoo was going to be all black, something interesting. That was good. Ink was sick of the stuff the drunken townies usually asked for, their tires screeching when they came up to his beat-up farmhouse, digging up his gravel driveway.

Ink always heard their tires kicking up the gravel as they arrived from Telluride, and even when the rich snots came from Aspen.

They'd ask for anchors, hearts with girls' names, or just "Mom"—more power to the pussy. More incantations of the flesh. Ink usually had to remind himself, sitting there as their beery vapors filled his studio, I'm a damn artist. All this does is pay the rent.

The girl looked at Ink, smiled, then turned back to the boy.

"It's going to look great, Bobby."

Ink waited.

At least this was going to be one hell of an interesting tattoo. If the kid could stay still. If he didn't jump the hell out of his skin and go running bare-assed down the icy road and out of the mountains.

Maybe the kid was from Denver. He wasn't from the college, though, that was for sure. They didn't take them that slack-jawed at Colorado State. Not yet, anyway.

She knelt down. The girl fucking knelt down.

The studio was cold despite the big kerosene heater pumping out a steady stream of smelly hot air. There were too many cracks around the window frame, too many gaps between the planks of the walls.

It was so cold, and the kid was sweating as if he were in the rain forest.

She knelt down between his open legs, close to the boy's naked thighs.

"It's going to look so good, Bobby. Really good."

She reached out and touched the point where the tattoo of a serpent—a design from Java—was to begin. Right above the kneecap.

Drops of the kid's sweat hit the floor like heavy plops of rain.

If I didn't need the bread, Ink thought, I'd kick them out. I shouldn't be doing this shit to a kid who's so damned scared. He'll wake up tomorrow with that snake and, at the tip, right near his wang, her name.

I shouldn't do it.

But times are fucking tough.

The girl's hand trailed up near the boy's thing. "I'm just gonna love it, Bobby." Then, kneeling, she looked right up into the boy's eyes, leaving absolutely no question as to what she was talking about.

Ink felt himself sprouting a boner. He shook his head and pushed his beard back. He didn't want to jab the poor sucker with his gray bristles.

What the hell would the kid think if he knew that this little fox, this little beauty, had been here before? If he knew there were other wide-eyed guys walking around with serpents inside their thighs, stretching up to nibble at the family jewels.

And at the head of the snake—her name.

Syn.

For Synthia or some shit. Good name.

"You ready, son?" Ink said.

It was getting late. He wanted to shut down and turn the lights off so no drunken kids would show up looking for their manhood at three fucking A.M.

The boy turned, but Syn's hand stayed where it was, feathery and sweet. That wasn't how the needle would feel. It wasn't too bad, now that the needles were so damned good. There was pain, but, shit, it wasn't terminal.

Still, *that* was one damned sensitive area.

The boy looked at Ink—sad puppy—and then nodded. Ink looked at the girl. "Miss, I gotta get in there."

She smiled and then backed away and went back to her arena seat, ready to watch the show.

The tattoo would be all black. The girl knew her stuff. Color only made a tattoo look garish. The design was stylized, great swirls of black ink, twisting on one another so that there were actually two serpents, one made by the ink and another by the white skin of the boy's inner thigh.

M. C. fucking Escher. The girl knew her tattoos. She had a few herself, one of which Ink had done. She'd paid for it.

Ink had wished he could take it out in trade. But a fat middle-aged guy with a beard wasn't her type, he guessed. Judging from his social life, he was nobody's type.

Of course, who was there to date in the goddamn mountains?

"Hold the arms of the chair, son," Ink said. The boy did so. "And just roll with the sensation. It will hurt. I'm not shitting you there. But no worse than that first . . . bite. Don't tense up. Makes it harder to work. Try breathing."

Ink looked up at the girl.

"Tell him to take slow, deep breaths. Nice and calm. Think about other things." Ink leaned close, to where the girl had been, in the valley made by the boy's legs.

He checked his works, making sure he had enough hose. Nice and smooth. He wanted to get the sweep of the thing.

Ink wanted the tattoo to look good even though this wasn't the type of job he liked. He might have turned this one away in better days.

But still he told himself, *I'm a fucking artist.*

There was a sign in the studio, surrounded by pictures of people with full suits, their entire bodies covered by tattoos.

The sign said, Skin Is My Canvas. He'd tell people, "My work will live as long as you do."

He moved the tip of the needle closer, to just behind the knee. Right there . . .

The needle hovered a second. Get this close, and it looked big. "Ready, son?"

The girl, the prize, jiggled around on his desk. The boy spoke, a voice from Mars: from the planet "Get me outta here."

Ink looked at the leg. He imagined the serpent. It was *there.* All he'd have to do was make it appear by his own magic.

And he brought the needle down to the boy's skin.

30

Getting here had been easy for Pick. Getting *in* was going to be harder.

He walked past the building. He saw the doorman sitting at a big desk behind two sets of glass doors. Then he came to the building's private underground garage with a corrugated metal door.

No, it wouldn't be as easy as finding Cubbage's home address. He had been counting on Cubbage's apartment being near his office, and he had figured Cubbage for someone who liked his alcohol. He tried three liquor stores in the area until he found one where they knew Dr. Cubbage, smiled at his name. Pick smiled, too, said he wanted to send a bottle of wine to the good doctor, "But damn it, jeez, I forgot which building he's in."

No problem, the guy behind the counter had said. He was a burly guy, sleeves rolled up, showing off good-sized biceps. Nearly as big as mine, Pick thought.

The guy opened some kind of account book. Pick asked about some California white wines. Yeah, a nice white wine would be good to send.

The guy had moved away from the book. Pick looked over: an apartment on West Seventy-sixth Street, Apartment 10A. It was easy.

Pick had decided to send the bottle anyhow. Why the hell not?

Now he looked at the glass doors and the doorman. He walked past them, heading toward the garage.

He stood by the door.

He saw some kids over on West End Avenue, standing around, trying to look dangerous.

A car came up to the building. It slowed and then turned into the garage. The driver stopped and rolled down his window.

Pick watched the driver stick a card into a machine in the wall. There was a click and an electronic buzz. The door started sliding up.

It rose quickly and then slid down, triggered by the movement of the car into the garage.

It won't be easy, thought Pick. No fucking way. He weighed the other possibilities.

Then he felt someone staring at him.

Pick turned around and saw the doorman, out on the sidewalk now, looking at him. Shit! Pick started walking casually. The cold breeze off the Hudson slammed into him. He saw Jersey twinkling in the distance. His hand was in his pocket, fingering the thin knife.

You have to protect what you love. He knew that; he accepted that. If you protected it, you could keep it.

He fingered the sleek plastic sheath and imagined the blade inside it.

He walked toward the black river.

Moments later his fingers locked on a mesh fence. The Henry Hudson Highway was below him, the traffic moving smoothly, cars streaming out of the city and just as many streaming in.

Pick felt his nose. It was cold, and so were his feet. His toes felt frozen. He waited another few minutes and then turned back.

He walked back across Seventy-sixth Street toward the apartment building. He didn't see the doorman outside. It was too cold. He was inside, nice and warm.

Pick walked up the block until he was next to the garage. He pressed himself against the building, trying to disappear. He stood there and waited.

The traffic light on the corner clicked from green to yellow to red, then green again. Cars drove by, leaving a trail of exhaust that danced in the air. Pick wished he smoked. It wouldn't be so bad, standing here, with a cigarette. He could look as if he was waiting for someone.

He waited.

The he heard the click of some mechanism inside the garage door, and the clank of the metal door sliding up. Pick took a deep breath of the ice cold air.

A black Lincoln pulled out, with a man and a woman inside. He got a look at the woman's legs catching the light from a street lamp.

It was hard to wait.

He heard a click. The car had barely reached the curb when the garage door started coming down. Pick moved fast, slipping closer to the garage.

If the driver looks in the rearview mirror, he'll see me, Pick thought. And then what will the fucker do? Use his cellular phone to call 911? Get out and stop him? What the hell would he do?

The door was closing quickly. Obviously it was for cars only.

When the door was within three feet of the concrete, Pick rolled inside the garage, smelling the oil and the other car odors.

He heard the loud clank as the metal door shut behind him.

And he was inside the building.

The elevator also required some damn plastic card. Pick looked at the slit in the wall. "Insert resident's pass here," it said.

The door to the stairwell was locked.

Pick heard a voice. Someone was down here, walking around. A guard, he thought. They must have a fucking security guard for the garage.

He heard the steps come closer, but he couldn't see anyone.

Of course, Pick thought, I could kill him. But that would be stupid. If I kill him, the police will know I've been here.

And that's not my plan. He smiled when he thought of his plan. It was brilliant, creative.

He crouched behind a car while the footsteps came closer. They seemed to slow down. Pick took a breath.

I don't want to kill him, he thought.

He put his hand on the knife and held it, pressing it tightly into his palm.

The steps slowed and then stopped.

Pick tried to breathe very quietly. He heard a click, and he smelled smoke. The guy was lighting a butt, that was all. The steps started again; the smell of the cigarette grew faint. Pick still crouched and waited.

When he stood up, he heard the elevator running. Pick stood to one side of the doors. He listened, wondering if someone was getting off at the lobby or coming down to get a car?

He waited. The sound grew louder. The elevator stopped, and the door slid open.

A man walked out. He was dressed in a suit. He wore glasses and had a small mustache.

Pick put a smile on his face and caught the closing elevator door.

The man turned and looked.

"Whoa," Pick said, grinning. "Almost missed it."

The man looked concerned. Pick kept his smile on as he got into the elevator. Then he released the door and said, "Have a good night."

The man in the suit nodded and kept walking.

The elevator door shut. Pick pressed 8, hoping that no one was waiting in the lobby to go up. If the doors opened, the goddamn doorman might see him.

And if the doorman saw him, he might remember. He might call the police.

Pick shook his head. That couldn't happen. There could be no more bad luck. Nothing to interfere with the Work.

The elevator went up. He looked at the small circles of light indicating the floors. He saw the lobby light come on. He thought he felt the elevator slow, but no, it went on moving, past the lobby, past one, all the way to the tenth floor.

31

Ink shut the lights off, and his driveway went black. There was a faint glow of snow on the mountains. Snow-topped mountains mixing with clouds. . . .

He stood at the window for a moment, staring into the dark, and he saw white patches of snow near the house—old, crusty snow. The night was so fucking cold. The glass panes in the door were decorated with crystal patterns that would have been pretty except that he could scrape them with his fingernail and scratch off an icy peel.

Old man winter wanted in. . . .

His studio was in an attached garage. Ink shut the lights off there and moved through the walkway into his house.

He thought of the girl. He had trouble getting something like that off his mind. Sure, he thought. Anyone would.

He thought of the girl, and the kid with his tattoo, the boy's thigh still aching, the skin tender. Maybe the kid would get his reward. Maybe the girl would nibble her way right up to where the serpent was slithering. . . .

Ink stopped in his kitchen, in front of a refrigerator with a cylindrical compressor on top. A real dinosaur. He opened it and took out a Coors, popped it open, took a slug, and then continued upstairs to his bedroom.

I'm a bit jittery tonight, he thought. Usually don't mind being out here all alone. That's why I came to the mountains. To get away from the whole scene.

But tonight . . .

Could be the snow, the cold. I'm starting to get cabin fever. Should get out more. Hit a movie.

He trudged upstairs.

Gets colder out here than in the valley. Up here in the goddamn foothills, gets so fucking cold.

His bed was a mess, the quilt all twisted madly around the pillows. Books, empty beer cans, a real shit hole. I'll clean it up tomorrow, he thought.

He took another slug of beer and thought of the way it used to be, in his old digs by the ocean, his workshop in San Diego. There were lots of studios there, lots of people doing real good tattoo work. And lots of babes. Life was good, except . . .

He heard a voice inside his head reminding him, clearly, sternly . . .

Reminding him exactly why he had left San Diego, why he had come to the mountains. This place wasn't just for the rich ski pricks.

He couldn't lie to himself.

I had a studio, and it was real nice. People came to see my work. People like Travis Tyler, a real tattoo artist. And old Daniel Hardy, whose full-skin suits were mind-blowing. And Carol Slover, a woman tattooist for women only. Decorations for Dykes.

Once, these guys from Japan had come, little runty guys dressed in gray and black business suits. Shit, they had money to spend. They showed him pictures of their museum, their goddamn tattoo museum, where whole skins were displayed, as objets d'art. They talked about Polynesian designs, Indo-Chinese patterns, the body as canvas. Tattooing as a real living art.

The one thing the fucking IRS can't take away from you. Your fucking skin.

San Diego had been a great scene. He took another slug of beer.

Then why did you leave, Ink? What the hell made you leave? Was it just to clear out the old head in the mountains? To do tattoos of butterflies on the ski bunnies' white butts?

The reason wasn't really hard to remember after all these years. It was still *there*. He thought, From the first, I knew that the sicko who cut Mary Nova was one of us.

There wasn't a lot in the papers. But there were rumors. People spoke to the police. Everyone knew. They buzzed about it.

"Look what he did."

"*He was one of us.*"

Mary was killed by someone we knew. *Had to be*. Then everyone had started to wonder who the hell might have killed her.

Until someone suggested that maybe, just maybe, wondering might not be healthy.

Mary Nova had been at Ink's big New Year's bash. Everyone knew she was heavy into the S/M scene. In too deep. She was over the top, way over.

Ink had limits. But not everyone did.

Mary Nova had a diamond pin right through her nose. And through her blouse—sheer, black—you could see the goddamn nipple clips—big, nasty chunks of metal. Ink knew she had other stuff, too. Mary wore rings in her cunt lips.

There were limits.

Mary didn't think it was any big deal. She talked about her piercings as if they were just another form of art. She thought that scarification, cutting designs into her body, was interesting. Now, that was the outer edge, the real outer edge.

Human canvases. Human pincushions. *Far out.*

Ink had laughed with her, hoping he'd get lucky. Mary was gorgeous. But even then he'd been way too fat. Everybody loved him, loved his work. But no one particularly wanted to fuck him.

Then he'd thrown a party at his studio.

Ink had looked around at his guests, the slaves and masters, the S/M crowd—the dog and pony show. Girls in latex boots and leather bras were leading bare-assed guys around on leashes. Or maybe they were really guys dressed in latex boots and leather bras.

Who the hell knew?

The slaves licked their masters' boot heels. They were folks with real healthy self-images. There were beautifully tattooed people there, too, chicks wearing full-body suits. Gorgeous parrots perched between their shoulder blades. And fish—stylized black fish—leaping from one titty to the other.

Ink remembered how he'd felt at the party. He remembered looking around, staring at the circus, the freak show. He remembered thinking, It's getting too strange, man.

Suddenly Ink had wanted the party to end; he'd wanted everyone to leave.

He'd seen Mary Nova talking with someone—a man who looked too straight, who didn't belong. Ink had asked about him. They said he was Mary's toy. They played together. Ink could guess what games Mary Nova was playing. But the guy looked all wrong. Too fucking straight, too good-looking, too damn muscular.

He had big arms and a full head of sandy hair. He looked as if he belonged in a gym.

As Ink watched, he saw the guy looking at the designs on the walls. Mary stayed next to him, getting close to him. Ink remembered thinking: Moth to the flame. She goes for the mean ones.

Ink had never seen the guy before that night.

A week later, Mary was dead. There wasn't too much in the papers, but Louise Welles, Mary's boss at the S/M joint, had to identify Mary Nova's corpse, and she described exactly how Mary's tiny body had been butchered.

Ink had nodded, listening, thinking, as Welles described the patterns neatly carved into Mary's body.

Welles was a sick puppy, too. She should have been crying, screaming. But she wasn't. She had calmly pointed to something on Ink's wall.

It was one of the sketches Ink used as a model. Welles had said, "That's what the cuts on Mary looked like, Ink. Shit, just like that."

Then Ink had known who did it. Not his name or where he lived. He'd found that out later, after the guy was gone. But Ink knew what the killer looked like. A straight arrow, a muscular guy with a big smile.

Ink remembered feeling as if he was going to throw up.

He had thought, back then, of going to the police. But they knew who Mary Nova was. Just a dead sicko, though they spoke to her clients, the ones they could find. I should have talked to them, Ink thought. That's what I should have done. But . . .

I'm a coward.

And what if they couldn't pull the guy in right away? What evidence, what fucking proof, do I really have?

He had nothing. Absolutely nothing.

So the guy might be left out on the streets. And then maybe he'd come for Ink. What would another body be? What would be the fucking big deal?

No fucking way, Ink had thought. Hell, they might even think I fucking did it.

There was only one thing for a coward to do. Ink left. The scene was getting too *out there*.

He left as soon as he could. He packed up all his shit and went on a long vacation. He moved to Colorado, found this old house in the hills.

Later he saw stories of other killings in New York. But he tried not to think about them. A girl in Queens, and that boy and his mother. The stories had been on TV. People had started calling the killer the Meatman. Maybe there was no connection.

Ink tried not to think about the murders.

What do I know? he thought. I don't know shit. I moved to the woods, so what the fuck do I know?

Maybe that was why he was so fucking cold tonight. . . .

Ink woke up suddenly and looked at the clock. He saw blurry green letters. He blinked. It was 3:20 A.M.

He felt as if he'd been asleep for hours. He looked at the clock again. Oh. He'd been asleep for only ten, maybe twenty minutes when—

Something woke him up.

He was aware of a *sound.* Maybe some fucker looking for a tattoo after closing hours. Lights off, house dark, and—goddamn—someone was down there.

He heard the sound again. Some kid knocking on the door? Some drunken shit? He heard another bang.

It sounded as if it had come from inside the house.

The house was frigid now, the heat topping off at 50 degrees, maybe sinking lower. Ink blinked again. His nose was cold.

Another bang. Shit. I got to get up. *I've got to get the fuck up.* But first he reached over to his table and scooped up a knife in a sheath. Wouldn't mind having a gun, he thought. But guns scared him. Things happened to people who kept guns in their homes.

He sat up, feet on the floor. He pulled the knife out of its sheath. He went to the window, slowly, tiptoeing, not wanting to let the intruder know he was there.

Or maybe I should make a lot of noise. Maybe they think the house is empty. Or—shit—maybe that would be bad? Maybe they'll decide to rob me, and they'll come in. And if they come in, if they see me—if I see them—they'll have to kill me. . . .

There was another bang from outside. The big bang of someone knocking on the wall, louder.

Ink was breathing fast, in and out, trying to find an explanation—a nice safe explanation.

"Okay," he said. He moved to the window.

The driveway was empty. There was no car, only the dusty patch of snow.

Another bang, still from outside. He moved past his open

bedroom door slowly, quietly, holding the pig-sticker out in front of him, then started down the stairs.

Bang. The sound was closer now. Shit, it was close.

He said, ''You better the fuck leave. You just better get the hell—''

There was a series of thumps in answer. The knife led him down to the foot of the stairs. Ink stopped at the bottom. He waited. There was another bang. Oh, shit, he thought, it's coming from the kitchen door.

I don't like this.

His feet were icy.

My toes are gonna break the hell off. It's so cold. Jeez, did I remember to bolt the door? Is the fucking door locked?

He turned. He took a step. A splinter dug into his foot. He winced, but he didn't stop.

The phone was in the kitchen. The good old phone. Good old 911. If he was going to call for help, he'd have to get to the phone.

Even though—too bad—that was where the sound was coming from.

He took a few more steps. The sound stopped. He walked into the kitchen. Everything was quiet; the phone was steps away.

I'll pick it up, he thought. I'll very quietly dial 911 and say, very quietly, that I'm at—

Another bang sounded so loud in the room that it made Ink jump. He groaned and he moved away. It was right *there,* outside the back door.

Ink couldn't move.

Then something drifted in front of the window right over the sink, the one that looked out on his backyard with its tall frozen clumps of weedy grass.

It was a shaggy dark head with curled horns. Big rheumy eyes looked in. The horns banged against the side of the house.

Ink started laughing at the bighorn sheep, hungry, the winter driving it down. Hungry bastard, it watched him. Another bang, and then the bighorn moved away, hungry, cold, and fed up with winter.

Ink kept laughing out loud, hooting, howling, leaning against the wall.

Laughing . . .

32

Pick rang the buzzer of apartment 10A. He didn't hear any-thing—no steps, no one coming to answer.

Now that was a bad possibility. What if Dr. Cubbage was not in? What would Pick do then? Where would he go? Where would he wait?

He pressed the buzzer again.

This time he heard steps; he heard Cubbage hurrying to the door.

Pick smiled.

"Hello? Who is it?"

Pick knew that the psychologist was scrutinizing him through the door's fish-eye lens. He smiled at the lens.

"Dr. Cubbage. Good! You're here. Jeez, I was just released yesterday, and I wanted to see you before you left for your lectures."

Cubbage's voice was muffled behind the door. "How did you find out where I live? How did you get up here?"

Pick ran a hand through his hair. He had his coat open, the shirt unbuttoned. He shook his head, trying to look confused, trying to look like someone who needed help. That was what Cubbage did, wasn't it? He helped people.

But Cubbage wasn't stupid.

At least Pick didn't think so.

"God, I don't know, Dr. Cubbage. There was no one down-stairs. I asked someone where you lived."

Pick looked right at the lens. "Dr. Cubbage, I need to talk about things. I'm nervous, being out." He nodded, trying to play on Cubbage's sympathy.

"Er, I understand. But I'm packing. I leave in the morning."

Pick heard the man clearly, but he scrunched up his face and said, "What? I can't hear you. What did you say?"

Cubbage repeated himself, but Pick kept the frown on his face. The door opened. The chain was still on, but Pick saw Cubbage's face through the crack.

"I'm *leaving* in the morning, Mr. Pick."

Pick made a surprised O with his mouth. "Right. Yes, of course, you're going away. Well, if I could just talk to you for a minute."

Cubbage shook his head. "No. That won't be possible."

Pick nodded. He looked down the hallway. He thought he'd heard someone rattling with a door lock, getting nosy . . . or scared.

Pick's hand closed over the knife in his jacket pocket.

Cubbage said, "Now, please, I—"

Pick looked up and—so fast—threw his weight against the door. Cubbage backed away, startled. Pick heard him yelp. It was a good sound.

But the door held. Pick pulled back and, grunting, he went at the door again. This time the chain snapped as the door flew open, smacking Cubbage in the head.

Pick, now inside, quickly shut and bolted the door.

Cubbage had a red mark where the door had hit him. He looked up. Pick saw that he was wearing a robe, something shiny, Oriental. Perhaps he wore nothing underneath it.

Pick sniffed the air, his excitement growing.

"Mr. Pick . . . Donald," Cubbage said quietly, backing up. "This is very bad for your parole, your future. You shouldn't be doing this. I said we could talk, if only you—"

Pick took another deep breath. He smelled whatever food Cubbage had been cooking and something like perfume, and fear. Fear had a smell, a wonderful smell.

Cubbage backed up against the wall next to his small kitchen. "You have pain. I know that. That's what all this is about, Donald."

Pick pulled out the knife.

Cubbage moaned, another pathetic sound. A moan, and the little psychologist was all eyes for the knife. It was an amazing thing about knives, the way they caught the light, the way they caught people's eyes, silvery, shining.

Pick raised the knife.

Cubbage would scream soon.

He stuttered. The sound appeared full blown. The stuttering.

"I-I know wha-what did this t-t-t-to you."

Cubbage opened his mouth and raised his small white hands in front of him in a primal, primitive gesture obeying a message from deep inside the brain, overriding everything else. Then the psychologist's hands fluttered in front of him, ready to ward off the blow.

Pick stepped forward. Cubbage watched the knife, but he didn't see Pick's other hand cover his mouth.

Pick felt the psychologist's fleshy lips beneath his palm, rubber lips, dry, so dry. All the moisture gone.

Pick pressed the knife against the man's stomach. He leaned close and whispered in his ear. "Who knows you at the college? Who fucking knows you?"

Cubbage didn't say anything.

Pick dug the knife into the robe, cutting, tasting skin. "Who the fuck knows you?"

Cubbage shook his head. He was crying. Pick felt the tears dripping onto his hand. He moved his hand the merest fraction of an inch away from the man's mouth. He felt the featherlike movement of Cubbage's lips.

"No one. No one knows me there. Please—"

Clamp. The hand went down again, tight this time, squeezing those lips hard against the teeth. More tears, and Cubbage started squirming while Pick made the knife play with his stomach.

He used his grip to move Cubbage into the living room, and there, for the first time, Pick saw the wooden faces of the masks looking down at him, leering, approving.

It was better with an audience.

He pushed Cubbage into a leather easy chair, still keeping one hand over his mouth. Pick knelt before Cubbage, grinning.

He pulled the knife away. Cubbage's eyes went wide, so hopeful now. Pick pushed the silken robe aside, then placed his hand on Cubbage's leg and moved it up, higher.

Bad skin, Pick thought. Not tight. All speckled with little fatty growths. Garbage skin. Of no interest.

His hand trailed up a bit farther. "You have no friends there?" Pick said.

Cubbage shook his head. Then he stammered, "Wait. I forgot . . . the department head."

Up to the meaty white skin of Cubbage's inner thigh. Pick knew he was lying.

Pick pinched the flabby flesh of Cubbage's thigh. He kept squeezing until Cubbage struggled to make little dog yelps.

Then Pick reached in with his other hand and grabbed Cubbage's scrotum. He squeezed as if working with the exercise springs in the prison gym. He quickly mashed the testes in his hands until they collapsed into a hemorrhaging paste.

Too bad that Cubbage's scream, bloodcurdling and wonderful, had to be muffled by Pick's hand.

The fat man kept screaming and writhing, kicking like a living frog about to be cut from head to flippered foot.

Which was exactly what Pick did.

Letting go of Cubbage's crushed balls, he picked up the knife. Cubbage's eyes were closed. He was lost in some never-never land of pain. He feebly pushed against Pick's muffling hand.

The psychologist never saw the blade coming at him.

This wasn't the Work. The Work was about mixing innocence and pain, creating art from human sensation.

This was business. Pick was merely protecting his life.

Still, he couldn't deny that there was a small, warm pleasure in touching the blade to Cubbage's fleshy neck and then, hurrying to end the struggle, digging in and watching blood spurt out. God, it shot all over the apartment like liquid confetti.

And over Pick, who laughed.

Cubbage's struggles increased. Pick was surprised and impressed. He brought the blade down, not in the most effective way to kill Cubbage, for now this was too good to hurry. So he brought the knife straight down, still thinking of a lab frog as he watched Cubbage's chest split, his belly come apart, his abdomen open like a balloon too full of air.

The blood shot over Pick from half a dozen geysers.

Cubbage's struggles lessened.

It was a beautiful moment. Pick was aware that death was *here*, that the struggle was pointless, and only Pick and Cubbage existed. Next would come the surprise of what lay beneath his skin.

Pick giggled. He talked to Cubbage. He always talked to them. It was something he did.

He cooed to the body. He called it names.

"Sweet baby, sweet boy."

The words made Pick feel even better. They made the warmth, the glow, all that much more delicious.

This was business. This was protection. But still he could enjoy it.

Finally there was no movement, no breathing from Cubbage. Pick rested his blood-soaked head against Cubbage's knee.

It was over.

Pick rested. He sat there for several minutes, or maybe for an hour. He listened to the blood dripping onto the carpet.

He listened until there were no more dripping sounds.

And then, taking a deep breath, a relieved breath, he stood up. It was late, and he still had so much cleaning to do, before he'd be ready to leave.

He would have to clean the floor as best he could. Not to perfection, but enough to cut down the rank, coppery smell. He didn't want to upset the neighbors.

He knew what he was going to do with the body. He'd cut it up—work best done in the bathroom—and then seal the parts in plastic bags and store them in the refrigerator and freezer.

Any food Cubbage had could be tossed into the incinerator.

Pick also needed to look for the things he'd need—Cubbage's credit cards, car keys, registration, maybe some cash.

He'd find the address of the college and the name of the person Cubbage was supposed to contact. Cubbage obviously was very organized about such things.

This was going to be a long night. But when it was over Pick would be ready. He didn't feel that he was rushing—after five years that would be the temptation. He was proud of his plan. It showed that he could be disciplined and careful.

It shows that I respect the Work, he thought.

And it means that now I can begin.

PART THREE

THE WORK

Psychosis is a major mental disorder involving misinterpretation of reality and an obvious departure from normal patterns of thinking, feeling and acting.

—Ian Gregory and Ephraim Rosen, *Abnormal Psychology*

33

Lizbeth didn't work that first week. During Simon's second week home, she went back, relieved to be out of the house, to be among people who now—if possible—treated her with even more diffidence and regarded her as even more of a curiosity.

A man from the State Department called every day that first week. His name was Ted Rice, and she spoke to him every morning as she stared at Erin's bowl of cereal, the uneaten Rice Krispies stuck around the rim.

Isn't that funny? she thought. His name is Ted Rice . . . while she looked at the Rice Krispies that hadn't made it to Erin's mouth.

He asked how things were going. He spoke to Simon. Simon's face went solemn, grim, determined.

Then he spoke to Lizbeth again. He talked about the Stockholm syndrome, about how hostages sometimes began to accept the rationale of their captors. He said other things that had little impact on her.

He told her about posttraumatic stress syndrome. The second wound, it was called, the wound you felt after the trauma was over.

She wanted to tell Tim Rice that Simon didn't want to talk about what had happened, how he grew quiet and looked way from her. And then, other times, how he watched TV, laughing too loud at the stupid sitcoms, how he shook his head at the game shows and called people fools who made dumb decisions.

She wanted to tell Rice that she had tried to get Simon to maybe think about getting help and that her suggestions made him mad.

"The government wants me to be quiet, that's all," Simon said. "They just want me to shut up."

If there was something wrong with him, he said, he was going to get better all by himself—the way he'd gotten free.

She wanted to tell Ted Rice other things, too.

But Simon was sitting right there, TV blaring. If Rice had called her at work she could have told him how Simon woke up two or three times every night, yelling and screaming loud enough to awaken Erin.

In a way, Simon was still a prisoner.

And so was Lizbeth.

There was one last thing she might have told Rice. Simon took long walks. Getting fresh air, learning how to be free—that was how he put it. "I need to be out," he said. Then he disappeared for hours.

Lizbeth didn't mind because, when he came back, he seemed better, as if every step brought him closer to being normal, closer to really being home. He smiled. Sometimes he'd give Lizbeth a hug and ask her to be patient.

Tim Rice told her to keep talking to Simon, to keep trying to get him to go to that hospital in Maryland. "He'll need help," Rice said.

"I know," she answered.

Rice gave her his number. He told her to call. "If you need help," he said, "if it all gets to be too much, call me." She copied the number down. She put it in her purse.

She kept it close to her. . . .

During the second week Lizbeth went back to work. And Simon's bandages came off. His walking started improving—he was practicing so much.

He said he was ready to start driving.

Lizbeth felt good. Every day was another step for Simon. He was getting better every day.

Then one day, when she was eating lunch in her office, all alone, Walt Schneider came to see her. She looked up from a ham sandwich, and Walt was there, standing by her cubicle, looking at her.

"What are you—"

He put a hand up. "I tried calling. You wouldn't speak to me. How many times did I call?" Lizbeth looked around. The registrar's office was still deserted. It wasn't good to be talking to Walt here, where anyone could see them.

"I can't talk to you. Not now."

He shook his head and looked annoyed. "Tell me *when* I can talk to you."

He won't go away, she thought. He won't just disappear. I can't have him here. I can't have him in my life.

She had wondered if she could tell Simon, confess to him what she had done. He'd understand, wouldn't he?

"I don't know. I can't talk now." Lizbeth took another look around the office. Her supervisor strolled in with two of her friends. They looked like the bookkeepers that they were, with silver-gray hair, bifocals, purses filled with the wonders of Aladdin.

Walt shook his head. "Then when can I see you?"

"I don't know."

Her boss looked over. When she saw Lizbeth and Walt, the woman smiled. Then a quizzical look crossed her face.

Lizbeth saw her end her conversation and start toward her.

"Okay then, we'll talk now," Walt said.

She shook her head, thinking, thinking, until: "All right. Erin has ballet on Thursday . . . tomorrow. I usually do chores while I'm waiting for her. I can meet you."

Walt Schneider smiled. "Good. Where?"

Lizbeth thought. It would have to be someplace deserted, someplace where no one would see them. She didn't want to hurt Simon.

He didn't deserve a wife with a little affair to clean up. The good wife, the patient wife, waiting for her husband to come back.

But not waiting too well.

"Riverfront Park," she said. No one would be there, she thought. It was a summer place. The ground would be covered with ice; the wind would blow off the river, cold, freezing cold. "About four."

Walt stood up. His fingers gently touched her hand, and then he left.

The supervisor appeared. Lizbeth grabbed a piece of paper, any paper, as if she was checking something. The woman asked, "Are you okay, dear? Are you all right?"

Lizbeth looked up and smiled, knowing she looked a mess. The situation is out of control, she thought. And I'm not too sure I can do anything about it.

''I'm fine, thank you. Fine.'' She kept the smile.

The woman nodded, then pursed her lips and said, ''If there's anything I can do for you—*anything*—just let me know.'' They were empty, silly promises. Then the woman left her.

And Lizbeth was allowed to be alone, and to think. . . .

34

Friedman felt like a ghoul.

He sat in the squeaky chair and looked at the walls of his temporary office, now decorated with photocopied pages from prison records, photographs, and notes. The papers rustled every time he walked in or out of the small room.

On a map he had marked all the murders, but he could see no pattern there—no mystic pentagram, no astrological sign. But after a lot of reading and looking at dozens of arrest histories, most of them sketchy, he had come to a few conclusions.

What might have become of the Meatman?

He could be dead—a lucky break for whoever was next on his shopping list. Maybe a heart attack from eating too many burgers and fries soaked in ketchup.

Maybe he was hit by a car.

Or maybe the Meatman was killed by someone a bit faster, someone with a knife of his own.

They were all good possibilities. But Friedman did not believe in them.

The Meatman was young and strong. He had to be, to kill the way he did. He had to be fit, intelligent, and careful. He hadn't screwed up in five times. So there had been no heart attack, no car crash, nobody faster with a knife. The guy couldn't be beaten that easy.

On to another possibility. Call it the front-runner, Friedman thought. Call it the possibility that smelled the best.

The Meatman had gotten nailed for a lesser felony, something that took him off the streets. It wasn't a speeding ticket; it had to be something that would give him some real time to do.

Probably not premeditated murder. That might have led the police to the other murders.

Friedman nodded.

We're looking at four, five years here. The Meatman's been out of circulation for that length of time. So what could it be? Friedman wondered. A criminal assault charge? An involuntary manslaughter? Probably a crime involving a knife, somebody getting cut.

And that was the problem.

He had literally hundreds of records of stabbings taped to the walls, hundreds of guys, every one of them a real great guy. All of them had stuck somebody with a blade.

Too fucking big a net, he thought.

A net with too many holes.

He was feeling lost, hopeless. And then Bethany Clarke found something interesting. She walked into his office carrying several sheets of paper.

Friedman had been daydreaming, staring idly at the gory crime-scene photos on the walls.

"I got something," she said.

He looked up, not knowing what she was talking about.

"Your idea about moving backwards—you know, back from the first Meatman case." She popped her gum. "I came up with something."

Clarke handed him the papers. Friedman saw a name: "Maria Torelli, a.k.a. Mary Nova. Unsolved homicide, Oct. 6, 1985." Killed in San Diego, California.

"She was . . . what do you call it? A mistress or some shit. Mind if I . . ." Clarke pointed to the chair facing Friedman's desk. He flipped the page and saw a photograph. It had been faxed, and the contrast was way too high. He saw a whitish outline and black smears running from it, more smears on the ground, and dark bruiselike spots. Friedman leaned closer—and he saw pictures. Maria—Mary Nova—had barely visible pictures on her skin.

"She worked at this place down by the bay, there in San Diego, in a warehouse. It wasn't hooking, the report says. It was stuff with whips and leather and sick guys."

I need a better photograph, Friedman thought. I got to see this more clearly.

"Why did you pull it?"

Clarke popped her gum again. "I didn't. I put the particulars in and then changed the time frame before sending the data to VICAP. It came out labeled 'close match.'"

Friedman shook his head. It looked like a simple stabbing. One of Nova's clients got out of control, chased her down to a—he flipped back to the first page—down to the beach. And he took his sweet time cutting her up. The San Diego medical examiner said it took nearly an hour for Mary Nova to die.

What was the connection?

"It fit the pattern," Clarke said. "She had all these tattoos, and some of them had been cut right off her. But there was this whole pattern carved on her back. The killer did that. There's a sketch."

Friedman went to the third page. On a sheet of off-white paper was a simple line drawing of a woman's back. There was an intricate pattern carved into her back. Great swirls and teardrop shapes.

"The blood made it hard for the M.E. to see." Clarke stood up. "But when they cleaned her off, there it was." She moved to the door. "And that's why VICAP picked it up."

San Diego, 1985. Far away and long ago.

Too damn unlikely, too goddamn unlikely. He looked up at Clarke.

"Thanks. Thanks a lot."

She grinned, popped her gum, and left the room.

Friedman read the report and then reread it slowly until he was convinced that what he wanted to do made sense. The trail was so fucking cold. But there was one thing that he kept thinking about as he watched TV at home while eating Healthy Choice dinners, pasty near-food.

Where does a Meatman come from? Does he just spring onto the scene full-blown? Is that what happens?

Where do they learn what they do?

Friedman nodded to himself. He could get some information directly from San Diego—crime-scene evidence, spatters, fibers, whatever they had, if anything.

But some things he had to do in person.

He got up and left his office.

Captain Ramirez asked Friedman to wait outside his office while he made some phone calls.

Ramirez's secretary answered the phone in a hushed voice. Occasionally she looked up at Friedman and smiled.

Finally the intercom buzzed, and the secretary looked up, smiling, and said, "You may go in, Lieutenant."

Ramirez met him at the door.

"Jack, come in. Want some coffee? Susan can—"

Friedman held up a hand. "No, thanks. Already had my quota for the day. I get rattled when the caffeine kicks in."

Ramirez laughed, even though what Friedman had said wasn't that funny. Wasn't funny at all.

Ramirez shut the door. It closed with a healthy click. The captain had his shirtsleeves rolled up. He gestured at a comfy-looking chair. Friedman sat down while Ramirez perched on his desk.

"Captain, about the Meatman case. Something's come up."

"Hell. Jack. Do you know that Channel 6 News wanted to interview me? They wanted to ask me what the hell we're doing about all those unsolved murders? Stupid goddamn show. Hey, Jack, if you're sick of it—I mean, it's all shit-canned stuff, ancient history—just say the word. I'll put you on something else."

Another desk job. Of course, that's how they see it. Keep me busy. Out of trouble. I'm surprised that Ramirez hasn't asked me how I'm doing. Trying to look deep. Wanting to really know.

How are you doing now that your life is over, now that you sleep in an empty bed, now that your kids have moved away and there's no good reason to live?

How are you doing?

"Say the word. That damn TV show got everybody stirred up, and it's ancient history."

Friedman laughed, a shallow, breathy flutter. Because Ramirez had it all wrong. Friedman looked up, and the Captain was looking at him.

"No, Captain, that's not why I'm here."

"Then why? You didn't get a break, did you? Crack the case?" Ramirez laughed.

Wiseass.

"No. Not exactly. But . . ."

He opened a folder and handed the photograph of Mary Nova to Ramirez. "The Meatman came from somewhere. He didn't just happen. Maybe this is where."

Ramirez moved around to his desk.

"If he vanished because he's in the slammer, the killings could start again when he gets out," Friedman said.

Ramirez took a breath. "But they haven't started."

"Yet. I think this killing might be connected."

Ramirez looked up. "San Diego? You've got to be kidding me?"

"I want to go there, speak to the people the woman worked with, see the people who knew her, her friends. Maybe we already have this guy right here."

Ramirez wrote something down on a small Post-it in front of him.

Then he looked up at Friedman. Very serious now, his dark eyes locked on Friedman. "Go on. You've got my attention."

Friedman took a breath.

"I want mostly to talk to the person she worked for, find out if Mary Nova helped get herself killed."

"When?"

"I've booked a cheap flight. And I can be back tomorrow." Friedman smiled. "No overnight stay. If the NYPD will just pay my freight."

Ramirez looked away.

Probably figuring, Friedman guessed. Evaluating. Wondering if there was any way this could boomerang and hurt him. Staring out the window. The day was turning sunny. Maybe the cold would go away.

Ramirez looked back. "Okay. Permission granted, Jack. Need anything else?"

"Petty cash for a car, gas, a meal. That's all."

Ramirez said, "Great. No problem." Friedman moved to the door. "Jack, if you find anything we should know, call it in, will you? Maybe I can put some more detectives on the case." Ramirez smiled. A nervous smile. "Who knows? Maybe you got something here."

Friedman nodded.

Maybe.

Maybe not.

35

The plane ride was bumpy. Friedman passed on the meat roll soaked in a blood-red gravy with stringy bits of onion draped over it.

The movie was a comedy with two of his favorite actors. Friedman didn't get headphones but he heard people laughing. He watched as one actor slipped and knocked someone into a wedding cake. Friedman grinned at that.

There was a phone on the back of the seat in front of him. He was tempted to call Clarke. He had some other things he wanted her to do.

He reached for the phone, stuck in his credit card, and the phone popped out. But then he shook his head.

It can wait, he thought.

A woman sat next to him, middle-aged, plump. He already felt her looking at him, eager to start talking.

"Visiting someone?" she asked.

He turned to her and smiled. "No. Business trip."

She smiled. "I'm visiting my children."

Friedman smiled and turned away, but the woman asked, "Do you have children?"

With a minimum of encouragement, the woman talked to him, carrying on a conversation, sharing bits of her life, while Friedman thought, You don't want to hear about mine.

I walk around with photographs of cut-up girls in my coat.

You don't want to hear about my life.

When the chance arose, he pretended to be asleep. And soon he really was asleep. He awakened—seemingly minutes later—as the plane touched down.

Friedman passed crowds fighting to remove their carry-on luggage from the compartments. He moved—so slowly—to the terminal, feeling the light and the airiness of the building. He saw smiling faces. Friedman pushed past them.

"Detective Friedman?"

Friedman turned to his left. He saw a young man in sports clothes standing to one side holding a brown document envelope.

"Yes?"

"They gave us a good description." The man smiled.

Someone had called and arranged for the San Diego Homicide to meet him.

"I'm Detective Tom Broley. My parents were native New Yorkers."

Friedman nodded. He looked like a kid, all of twenty. Friedman stuck out his hand and told Broley to call him Jack.

"I've got a car, and I'm at your disposal. The detectives who worked on the Nova case have retired, but we've copied everything. It's all in here."

Friedman took the folder. Everything, he thought, but the killer.

"Can you drive me to the places where Mary Nova worked, where she was killed, where she hung out?"

"Yes, I've got maps. We've called ahead."

The crowd exiting from the plane thinned out, and the waiting area lost its festive glow.

"Then let's go," Friedman said. He followed Broley to his car.

Palm trees and a golden afternoon sun. They hit traffic, and Broley apologized. There was nothing he could do. The air conditioner was on full force, and Friedman caught glimpses of the Pacific, a mythic sea, glistening a burnished yellow.

Fucking palm trees, he thought. His winter coat lay across the seat, looking ridiculous.

Broley got on the San Diego Freeway. The S/M parlor where Mary Nova worked was near the beach on the way toward Coronado, Broley said.

As they left the freeway, Friedman saw a girl in a bikini top and cutoffs Rollerblading beside the car. The stores looked new and clean. The bars looked safe.

He saw a tattoo parlor. Wild Man Ed's. There were designs in the window. A block down, next to Taco Bell, was another tattoo place, Living Art.

Mary Nova had tattoos. Maybe she had come here to get them.

Broley took a right, toward the water.

"There's a lot of tattoo places," Friedman said.

"Yeah. Kind of a San Diego specialty. That and heat and sun and—" A dark-skinned girl skated by them. Broley grinned. "And good Mexican food."

He went down a hill. Friedman looked at the sign: Coronado Drive. Broley turned left and pulled over to the curb. He killed the engine. "We're here." Broley popped open his door.

"Where?" Friedman touched the young detective's arm.

Broley pointed to a black door. "Right there, and up the stairs."

Friedman patted his arm. "Wait here, please. I don't want to overwhelm the woman with firepower. Maybe . . . maybe I'll get more if I go up myself."

"Fine." Broley sounded annoyed, but Friedman couldn't be concerned.

As Friedman got out of the car and walked, in the hot sun, to the black door, a woman passed him. There was something odd about her. She wore too much makeup, and her heels strained to hold up her egg-shaped body.

The woman turned and looked back, as if she knew he was watching her.

Friedman saw something, a bulge, right in the throat. She smiled, a big, toothy grin framed by stoplight-colored lips.

Friedman looked away. It was a guy. A fucking guy.

He got to the door and pulled on it. It opened. No security guard here, no surveillance cameras. Everything was very laid back.

He walked up the stairs, five flights; the walls were painted black. How cheery, Friedman thought. At the top he saw a black metal door to his left with a business card taped to the door: Icarus Productions, Film and Video Production.

They made S/M movies, Friedman knew. That was in the report. Nothing too heavy, no snuff flicks, just movies about sexy ladies dressed in boots hitting chubby guys with whips.

Different strokes for different folks.

He passed another door with big painted letters that screamed, *Private!* Probably an office.

The last door had a brass knocker shaped like a lion's head. No normal buzzer was used to enter the dungeon. Friedman felt nervous, as if he had entered the Twilight Zone, as if he was going to learn more here than he wanted to know.

He lifted the lion's head knocker and let it smash down. The sound echoed in the hall. He heard nothing. He did it again.

He heard the sound of heels clicking against a wood floor.

Friedman took a breath as the door was opened.

A young woman swathed in black leather led him to a waiting room.

''Sit here,'' she said, sounding like a Nazi commandant, junior grade. She left.

He sat on a cheap couch, a blur of red and orange, autumn gone amok. There were two matching chairs, equally ugly, and a teardrop coffee table—an antique from the fifties.

There were some newspapers and magazines on the table, periodicals that you didn't see in the average waiting room: the *Whip,* the *He/She Newsletter,* the *Bondage Connection,* and an old favorite, a tabloid called *Water Sports.* And *PFQ—Piercing Fan's Quarterly.* Lots of good reading here.

He shook his head. Where was *Newsweek? Working Mother?*

He heard footsteps in the hallway. Again the clear staccato click of heels on linoleum. He heard hushed voices.

The sound faded again. Friedman leaned forward and flipped open the latest copy of good old *PFQ.* And though Friedman had seen a lot in his twenty-two years on the force—you name it—he wasn't quite prepared for this.

It was indeed a magazine for those who liked to get pierced.

He turned the unbelievable pages. There were rings through nipples, holes through the nose, multiple piercings of the ear. And then—for the real fans, for the die-hard aficionados of self-mutilation—there were rings that dangled from the fleshy lips of vaginas, brass rings from a carousel ride in hell.

He kept turning the pages and winced when he saw a dick covered with metal studs. It was a real close shot, and the head looked like a pomander.

''Shit,'' he said, and he flipped the page. There was a color photograph of rings that ran right through the shaft of the penis.

God, Friedman thought, I'm sweating. He turned the page, and the horror show continued.

There was a guy suspended from a tree by dozens of hooks in his chest and neck. The next page showed a picture of the same man, off the tree—the ''after'' shot. He looked none the worse for wear except for some puffy protrusions where the flesh hadn't quite returned to its natural state.

''Into piercing?''

Friedman hadn't heard anyone come into the small waiting room. The voice startled him. He looked up from the magazine.

The woman was about forty-five, maybe a bit older. She had very short black hair and wore silver eye shadow. She was encased in leather—no surprise there. A leather jacket, leather gloves that nearly reached her shoulders, leather pants, leather boots.

Wanda the Whip here was just about wearing a whole cow.

And for that added effect she carried a black riding crop.

"What?" Friedman said, still taking it all in. Someone else appeared from the dark recesses of the dungeons, a willowy redhead dressed more conservatively in a black lace *bustier* and a leather skirt. There was a good inch or two of creamy flesh between the tops of her stockings and the skirt.

It was nice to see skin after so much black cowhide.

Friedman thought, We're not in Kansas anymore, Toto.

The older woman took a step toward him. She struck the magazine with her riding crop, making a noise. "I *said,* dickhead, are you into piercing? Is that what you like?"

Friedman shook his head. No. Not really.

"Because"—she sighed, exasperated, eager to get at Friedman with her whip—"we don't do that here. We can refer you to some very good people, people who know what they're doing. You have to be careful, you know."

She took some steps to his left so that Friedman was flanked by the two women.

Friedman said, "That's not why I'm here."

"Good. Let me explain what we offer, our fee structure, and—"

That might be interesting to hear, Friedman thought. But he didn't want to waste any more time. "No." He dug into his coat pocket.

The women reacted, backing up a bit. They probably worried about the true nut cases. Friedman guessed there was a gorilla on duty, lurking in some back room, ready to eject out-of-control patrons from the fifth floor.

Friedman flashed his badge. "I believe the San Diego police called—"

"Shit. Right." The woman stormed to the right, then spun back, glaring at him. "One thing you gotta know." She used her riding crop to gesture. "I don't do anything illegal. I never did, even back when Mary Nova worked here. We deal in fantasies, that's all."

Friedman held up his hand. The other girl slid away into the back alcoves, leaving the owner alone.

"Easy. Take it easy. I'm not here to bust you, Ms. Welles." Her name was Louise Welles, at least that was the name on the police records from seven years ago. She stood there, waiting for him.

"Please, sit. I just want to talk with you."

She sat down on one of the ugly orange chairs. She looked silly in her leather now, as if she'd shown up for a costume party only to find everyone else dressed normally.

Oops.

"I want to talk to you about Mary Nova."

Welles shook her head. "I don't know anything new. That was years ago . . . years. I told the cops everything I could. I don't—"

Friedman held up a hand again. "I know. You were very cooperative. It says so in the files. But humor me, okay? I'm just going over some stuff. It's all new to me."

Friedman thought of the photograph of Mary Nova. She was a thin blonde with fine long hair. Her face had a sweet kind of beauty to it, round, soft, and vulnerable.

In the photo she'd looked real vulnerable. She had been—what was the word the medical examiner used?

Eviscerated. While she was still alive. The rock she was cut on looked like a slaughterhouse. There were bits of Mary's insides all over the sand.

An image had come to Friedman's mind when he saw the photo of Mary Nova. He remembered the frog he'd dissected in high school.

Mary Nova looked exactly like that.

Friedman took out his small spiral notebook and wrote down what Welles had to say.

Welles stood up and marched around as she talked and smoked.

"Mary was, y'know, into the scene heavy, more than most girls who work for me. She liked videos, bloody stuff, faces of death . . . things like that."

The woman's long red fingernails played with her leather, pressing into it. She looked up.

"I worried about her. She had tattoos—that was no big deal. But then she started with the other stuff."

"The other stuff?"

"Body modifications. Piercings, scarification . . ."

Friedman opened his mouth, mouthing "Oh."

"She started getting into decorative scars. Mary thought they were beautiful, but that stuff freaked the clients out. She had nipple rings that she could pop in whenever she wanted, and a chunk of metal that went right through her nose. She also had thin scars on her butt, like some sort of aboriginal. I told her to ease up. But she kept wanting more stuff done to her.''

''Didn't it hurt?''

Welles laughed. ''Hell, sure it did. But Mary always walked both sides of the S/M scene. She could be a dominatrix—''

Was that like an aviatrix? An image of Amelia Earhart in jackboots.

''Or—her preference—submissive.'' Welles took a breath. ''I think she got into the pain.''

''Got into the pain?''

''Like our clients. She got off on pain, pushing her limits, getting into the feeling. One day one of the girls told me that Mary had a bunch of rings in her cunt. I didn't ask to see them.''

''Too squeamish?''

The woman smiled, momentarily exposed. ''I'm into the theatrics of this, Lieutenant. For me it's fantasy play. For Mary Nova it became real. I didn't know what kind of trip she was on.''

Nova was no innocent, that was obvious. No innocent. So far from the Meatman pattern, Friedman thought.

But there was something here.

''What did her customers . . . her clients say.''

Welles looked discomfited by the question. Friedman noted that on his pad.

''Some of them said that Mary was too sick for them. She was good-looking, though. A real fantasy doll. But she was into the stuff for real. It was like she worked on her clients, getting them more into it too, pushing them into a real taste for pain.''

''Getting pain or giving it?''

''Both.''

Friedman nodded. ''I'm sure you were asked this question years ago. A lot of time has passed, but it's important.''

Welles shifted in her seat. There were voices out in the hall, someone stopping a customer, warning him away. Business was on hold until this interview was over.

''After Nova's death you were asked if you thought any of your customers might have done this.''

''Right, I remember. And I said no. The people who come to us are . . . well, most of them are businessmen looking for some kinky thrills. Otherwise they're normal middle-class guys. Shit, a lot of them are married, with kids. You wouldn't believe it.''

Friedman nodded.

Honey, I'm home. And, hey! Want to see my nipple clamps?

Friedman raised his hand. "But what about this. Couldn't someone come here looking for someone exactly like Mary, someone who was into receiving more than giving?"

The woman hesitated. "No. Not to the extent of what was done to Mary. No, if anything—"

Friedman interrupted, shook his head. "No, right, not at first. But if this person, say, came upon Mary, it would be like hitting the mother lode. Here was someone willing to explore the outer limits, right? Someone who was into inflicting pain on herself."

Welles said nothing.

"You might not even know. It could have been between Mary and her customer—er, client. Right?"

Welles shrugged. "Maybe. But, if anything, I think it would be Mary Nova who was looking for someone who had a switch to throw."

Friedman knew the answer to his next question. "What kind of records do you keep on your clients?"

She shook her head. "I'm sorry. Nothing. Nothing at all."

He took a breath. "Do you remember anyone who saw Mary regularly, someone who was unusually interested in her, who only wanted her?"

"I was asked that. No, I think— I think . . ."

"Yes?"

"If she met someone here, she might have seen him outside. She left here just before she was killed. I had to let her go. She'd gotten *too* weird." She stopped walking around. "Some of the girls, the stupid ones, start seeing people outside. It's a bad idea. I tell them that."

How thoughtful.

"Look, Ms. Welles. This man, the person who did this, was never found."

"I know."

"Is there anything you can tell me, anything at all, that we might have missed?"

Welles hesitated. Then she spoke. "Only this. My guess is that whatever's wrong with that fucker, it wouldn't just go away. If anything, it would get worse. They tend to get deeper into this shit." She paused. "If the killer is alive, he's *still* into it."

Friedman closed his notebook.

"Unless something stopped him," she said.

Friedman stood up. "Right."

He stood up. The sharp pain in his knee seemed appropriate in this place. He looked at the magazines on the table. He reached down and picked up *Piercing Fans Quarterly*. "Mind if I keep this?"

Welles shook her head. "No. Go ahead." She smiled. "I have lots of issues."

What a way to make a buck, Friedman thought. He started for the door. "Thanks for your help. I may call. I may need more." He smiled. "But I doubt if I'll be dropping in on you."

Welles nodded.

Friedman walked out into the hallway.

Everything the San Diego homicide cops had on the murder was in the folder. It wasn't much, and it was old. Friedman took a look at where Mary Nova lived. No one there knew of her. It was a long time ago.

But before he had Broley take him back to the airport, Friedman wanted to see where she was killed.

Why ruin my record? Friedman thought. I've seen all the other murder locations.

Broley drove north to a town called Ocean Beach. There was a cliff with a rough trail leading down to where the sun was dipping into the Pacific.

"It's a bitch of a walk down there," Broley said.

Friedman nodded and told him to lead on.

Once, on a sandy hummock, Friedman slipped. His knee bent in a funny way, and he grabbed at the sand and some reedy grass while he slid half a dozen feet.

Broley helped him up, and Friedman proceeded more carefully.

"There's a jump at the bottom," Broley said. "It looks like a fault line."

He thinks I'm too old for this shit. And he's probably right.

Broley made the jump first, a four-foot drop into the sand. Friedman jumped and landed in a clumsy roll. He got up and felt the salty spray on his face. The waves were that close.

"Down here," Broley said, moving to the left. The sun was hidden by the sea now, and the sky had lost its bright blue color. Broley moved around a curve of the cliff. Friedman hurried to follow, and he came to where Broley stood, pointing at a small indentation, almost a cave.

"Kids come down here. Build a fire, drink beer. Screw."

Broley pointed at a flat gray rock as big as a sofa, with a line of rose quartz.

"That's where he did it. She must have come with him willingly. She must have wanted to . . ."

Friedman went close to the rock. He knelt down and touched it, the crashing of the waves behind him. "It's still stained," he said. "Some of her blood ran into the cracks." He ran his fingers along the veins of reddish quartz, up one vein and down the other, thinking, believing, knowing . . .

It had started here. That was why they'd never caught him. One killing and then he was gone, off to perfect his technique.

This was where it had started.

Friedman stood up.

And, God . . . I don't think it's over.

36

The residence for visiting professors looked like a ranch house, a suburban Ponderosa made of dark wood planks resting on great chunks of fieldstone.

Pick smelled something when he walked into the house. He wasn't sure what the smell was, but he didn't like it. It wasn't like prison; it didn't smell of sweat and semen and the food odors that mixed and lingered. And it didn't smell like death. That was a rich, sweet smell from all the blood and from the steamy pockets of gas that burped from inside the secret parts of the bodies.

This house smelled stale and dry, and Pick didn't like it.

Pick had met a woman at the college, a middle-aged assistant dean. Her body was thin, still shapely. Pick had felt her warm response to him. He always felt that. He enjoyed the way women reacted to him.

She had smiled and offered to help him in any way she could. Pick nodded and smiled, leaving all doors open. She told him to ask the security guard at the college gate for directions to this house for guests of the college.

"I'm so bad at directions," she'd said, laughing.

Pick didn't like the house. He walked through the downstairs, past a small living room filled with books, then upstairs to a pair of dark bedrooms. He stopped there, looking at the big beds, and grinned.

I've disappeared, he thought. I've become someone else.

I'm safe.

He left and went shopping at the Pleasantville hardware store, using Cubbage's charge card, buying all the things that he'd need. Then he started planning what he was going to do.

• • •

Pick actually lectured that first week. It was surprisingly easy. He had found Cubbage's extensive notes on what he was going to say. Pick had no trouble expanding on those notes, telling stories. One lecture was on trauma, and Pick enjoyed telling horrible stories that he made up.

He spoke of a family he treated. The father fell off the family boat while the engine was running. Everyone looked over the side to see him, two little children, a boy and a girl, and Mom. They all saw Dad's head float by, severed by the boat's propeller. The graduate students gasped. It was a good moment.

Pick talked about the primacy of pain in human life. He said that trauma was the refusal to deal with that pain. That was something he added to Cubbage's notes.

He even took questions, telling jokes, smiling at the grad students, noticing some of the young women crossing their legs, watching him.

I've disappeared, he thought.

This was a good plan. A good way to protect the Work so that he could begin again.

He had Cubbage's money, his credit cards, his car. And one night Pick went out. . . .

Simon flipped through the cable channels, a blur of images. A word or two, then he moved on to the next channel.

He sat alone in the living room watching TV.

There had been another interview this morning, a show called "Good Morning America." He'd never seen it. But the reporter had come to the house with three cameras.

Erin had been getting ready for school, and Lizbeth was combing her hair. They wanted to film the family in its natural state. Lizbeth didn't want to do the interview.

"Not here," she had told him. "Let's try to get back to normal. Enough interviews, " she'd said.

Simon had said something stupid. He knew that what he said was stupid, hurtful. Simon said to her, "You want me to forget. You want me to pretend it never happened."

He looked at her and then regretted what he had said. He thought, Who is she? Who is this person? My wife? *I don't know her.*

I want to tell people that I'm okay now, that I'm not crazy. I came out *okay.* Just fine . . .

He wanted to believe that as he swooped through the channels, the electronic flutter making a static rhythm. He came to a Chicago TV station. Chicagoland's Number One station. A movie was beginning in Chicago, sent here by satellite.

The movie was *Midnight Express*. Simon started watching it. . . .

J.C. met the man outside DiOro's.

It was near dark, and most of the other high school kids had gone home. It was fuckin' *cold.* The wind whipped down Route 9, so cold, biting. His name was Jerome Conneley, but he called himself J.C. He joked about it. "You know, J.C., like the Messiah." He liked the sound of it much better than Jerome or Jerry or Jer. *Mucho* better. He stood outside DiOro's—always doing a big business in lottery tickets, six-packs, and shitty crullers.

He'd done this before, and it had worked. You stand there and some guy comes along. He looks at you, you look back. Some guy looks at you like he hasn't had a meal in a month. He gives you *hungry* looks.

It wasn't a bad way to make money. J.C. liked having money. That's what it's all about, he told himself. Isn't that what it's all about?

He had to watch for the Fresh Spring Police. There were two patrol cars, and they always slowed down when they saw him, as if they knew what he was doing. But so far tonight there had been no police cars.

A guy came along while the sky was still a light blue, and the stars—shit, they looked like jewels, like diamonds.

This dude stopped, a big guy, good-looking, not like the usual. He said something, and J.C. laughed at his joke.

He asked J.C. if he was cold. He asked if J.C. wanted to hang out, maybe go for a ride. J.C. stood his ground. He knew enough to wait until he saw some money.

The guy pulled out some tens. "Got some spending money," the man said. His arms were big, like he worked out. He had a nice smile. "We could party," the guy said.

J.C. nodded, and then, looking around, he took the money. There were five bills at least, maybe more. *Maybe more* . . .

The man said his name was Donald. He laughed when he told J.C. his name.

J.C. followed Donald to his car.

• • •

Erin felt her mom put a hand on each shoulder—a sign that she was about to say something important, something serious. Erin looked up.

She put on her best listening face. She guessed what Mom was going to ask.

"Erin." Her mom's voice was low, a whisper. Erin heard the sound of the TV in the living room, as if someone had fallen asleep sitting on the remote control, going up the channels and then down, up and down.

"Erin, is your homework done?"

Erin nodded, thinking, I should have stayed in my room. I should have done extra spelling and some more work in my *Mathematic's Around Us* book. It was a dumb book, pages and pages of dumb problems.

I should have stayed in my room.

"I want you to go into the living room." Her mom lowered her voice even more. "Stay with your father. Just play in there."

Erin started shaking her head. Erin knew he was her daddy, but it didn't feel right. The way he talked, the way he acted—it wasn't right.

I should have stayed in my room.

He didn't feel like her daddy. He sat in that room and watched TV. He was like a stranger. And he was drinking. That clear stuff in his glass was alcohol. Erin knew that drinking wasn't good for people. It made them act funny. Sometimes they laughed; they got goofy.

But her daddy's laughing scared her.

Erin knew what her mother wanted, but she didn't like to stay with her Dad alone. If Mom was there, okay, If not . . .

Erin coughed.

Her mother's hand slipped from her shoulder and took her chin, holding it, examining her face. "Hey, what's that cough? Are you okay?"

Erin felt something at the back of her throat. The beginnings of something. She was getting a sore throat. She felt that tickling. But she wasn't going to tell her mom, because then, well, then she'd have to stay home from school while her mom went to work.

Erin said quickly, "I'm fine."

Lizbeth nodded. "Then go to the living room, honey. Play with your Barbies, or watch TV." Her mom smiled. A pretty smile, so warm and safe. "I'll join you in a few minutes, soon as I'm done with the dishes. Okay?"

Erin still heard the sound of the TV jumping from station to station. She chewed her lower lip. "Okay."

Erin went into the living room.

The man, Donald, wanted to go to the gorge.

He must have known about it. Maybe he watched kids go down there. The guy wanted to go even though it was so fucking cold. But that was okay. J.C. had been there before.

Donald held a big brown paper bag. He said he had something really special to drink, something really good . . . something to take the chill off.

Already J.C. was wondering what this guy wanted. What was his thing? Maybe he only wanted to touch him. A lot of guys wanted that. Maybe he wanted to do things to him. That wasn't so bad. J.C. could close his eyes and think about other stuff. Shit, he could even pretend it was a girl. He'd done that before.

The guy led the way, smiling back at J.C.

J.C. knew that he wouldn't *do* anything to the guy. No, sir. No way. He didn't do that. Not without more money.

The gorge was secluded from the highway and protected from the cold wind from the river. The gorge kept the wind out. The kids from Horatio Alger were always down there boozing and screwing. There were fucking used rubbers everywhere. But not when it was this cold.

There'd be no one down there now.

In the movie this kid—nineteen, maybe twenty—was caught sneaking drugs out of Turkey. He was arrested right at the airport.

Simon took a breath and shifted in his seat. His glass was empty; there was only the water from the melting ice cubes now. He sucked at the cubes. When he was a prisoner he had dreamed about the slippery feel of an ice cube against his lips, so cold and wet.

He kept staring at the TV. Simon looked at the Turkish guards, at their dark faces, as they snarled and grabbed the American kid roughly, shaking him around, dragging him someplace.

They got him, Simon thought. Yes, they've got him. Simon took another big breath. This movie is getting to me, he thought. I shouldn't let it get to me . . .

He looked to his right and saw Erin sitting on the floor. She had slipped into the room, and he hadn't noticed. She played with a long-legged doll, pulling off the doll's clothes, stripping her down.

They were taking the clothes off the boy in the movie. The boy was trying to explain. It was all a misunderstanding. He tried to explain . . .

Erin's little plastic doll wore a big smile. She didn't mind her clothes being pulled off.

The American was thrown into a cell, a small dirty cell. A giant cockroach skittered across the floor. It was his domain. There was a hole in the ground.

I know what that is, Simon thought. Sure, it's a place to piss, a place to shit. You need that. If you're going to hold people captive, you got to have someplace like that.

Simon felt himself breathing harder, faster. Gulping the air in. He looked back at his little girl.

The doll was naked. She leaned against a chair on her pointy toes even though she wore no shoes. Erin started tugging at something in the doll's hair. She pulled roughly at a pink headband stuck in the blond tangle. She yanked at the band, at the doll's hair, tugging at its head.

She's going to pull it off, Simon thought. She's going to pull that poor doll's head *right off.*

"Erin," he said, but much too quietly, he realized. I'll have to speak much louder than that if I want her to hear me.

"Erin!" Still she yanked. She's not being careful, he thought. She's getting frustrated.

I should help her. Why don't I just help her? But he didn't move. So what if the doll's head came off? So what? That wasn't the worst thing that could happen.

The sound of the TV changed, and a commercial came on.

There were worse things. He thought about this morning, about the TV show and the question the reporter had asked. . . .

The reporter had asked one last question after Simon thought the interview was over and he'd done a pretty good job, smiling, saying he was okay, that he prayed for the other hostages still over there.

The reporter had asked one last question this morning, in this same room: "What was the worst thing you saw, Mr. Farrell?"

Simon had felt Lizbeth watching him from the kitchen entrance. Erin was eating breakfast away from the cameras, away from the TV reporter.

Simon had licked his lips and looked at Lizbeth. He saw her move Erin away, where she couldn't hear his answer.

The worst thing, they wanted to know. That was easy to answer because it was so fresh in his mind. Simon smiled, which must have looked weird on the television.

The show was live. His breathing went funny, as if he'd forgotten the natural rhythm. Simon licked his lips again. The reporter asked the question. Simon knew he should answer it. When he spoke, his voice was quieter than before.

"They hanged a man," Simon said.

He felt the smile on his face, a frozen grin of rictus, but he couldn't shake it. I gave you the answer. That's what you wanted, right? The answer, and now you'll let me go, right? Now I can leave?

"They hanged this man. They cut off his hands."

The reporter's face fell. Was it because Simon's answer wasn't good? Or maybe it was *too* good? Or maybe it was the wrong kind of answer?

Maybe, he thought, the reporter needed the *whole* story. She had asked for the worst thing. The bright lights made all the crew members standing around look like shadow people. They weren't real. Simon felt as if he had died, as if he was in heaven, a dead man being interviewed.

"Then . . . then . . ."

He was there, chained to the radiator in the basement, with the body . . . *He was there.*

"They fed the fingers to me. I was blindfolded. And in my food bowl . . ."

The TV reporter was a pretty woman. No, she was more than that. She was beautiful, with her red lips, her blond hair. She pulled away. Simon saw her pull back from him.

She said some words. Simon didn't hear anything. The lights went out, so fast. The reporter looked at him and said, "Thank you." But it didn't sound as if she meant it.

And Simon was alone with his memories.

I'm not home, he thought then.

Now he looked from Erin and her doll to the TV. He shook his head.

I'm still not home. . . .

The man, this Donald, is a head case, J.C. thought. Big time, no fucking doubt about it. The man talked to J.C. mumbling shit like he was talking to a girl.

"Nice ass," he said. He had J.C. turn around. Though there was no wind down here, none at all, it was bitchin' cold. There was also no light. J.C. stood on a flat piece of ground near the rocky ledge of the gorge.

The man's hands, strong hands, moved on him. "Turn around," the man said.

He's just into watching, feeling. That's all, J.C. thought. That's okay.

"Bring your arms back," Donald said. J.C. nodded and looked at this Donald. His blue eyes sparkled while the rest of him was all shadow.

This was okay. J.C. looked into the darkness. This wasn't so bad.

He looked at the small stream that ran through the gorge, frozen now. Maybe water moved underneath the ice. Maybe there were salamanders under the ice, maybe crayfish.

I used to come here and capture crayfish when I was a kid, he thought. I didn't know what the gorge was really for. I'd watch the crayfish scuttle under a rock. Then they'd stop moving, just hiding there.

J.C. heard something rattle. He turned around. Then—so fast—he felt metal, ice-cold metal against one wrist. "Hey," he said. "What the—"

He heard a latch close. J.C. knew what was going on. Donald had handcuffs. Pretty fucking kinky, the guy traveled with handcuffs. J.C. had to fight to get a breath. This was getting weird.

He tried to whip his other arm away, but the man quickly grabbed it. He was so damn strong. He snapped the hand into the other cuff. J.C. heard the clasp close.

"Get the fuck off!" J.C. yelled, not caring how much noise he made. I don't give a damn, he thought. "Get the fuck off me!"

J.C.'s arms were pinned behind him. He turned around fast and kicked, but the man backed away, laughing. And now J.C. saw something flash behind Donald's eyes. He saw the man smiling, his teeth glowing, catching whatever light there was here. He heard the man breathing heavily.

He saw something silver in the man's hand.

"Oh, Christ, no. Oh, shit!" J.C. legs turned to rubber. He had crossed over into a strange land, a land where his life could disappear.

He had wished *he* could disappear. Now this man was standing there, ready to make it happen. And J.C. didn't want it.

He backed up, trying to think.

How can I get out of here? What's the best fucking way out of this?

"Get the fuck away from me!" he bellowed. Maybe somebody could hear, up there on Route 9. But he knew there wasn't a chance, not a fucking chance.

J.C. stepped on something, something long and dark, lying on the ground. He yelped. He thought it was a snake.

But it wasn't. It didn't *give* the way the body of a snake would. It was harder, more compact.

What is it? he wondered. What the hell is it?

The man started moving toward him.

37

J.C. turned and ran deeper into the gorge.

I know this place, he thought. I can get the hell away.

But his steps were wobbly. He tripped on an icy rock and fell onto wet clumps of moss and dead leaves. He craned his neck as he was falling and let his chest take the blow. I need to see him, J.C. thought, to see whether he's coming after me. Or maybe—oh, God, please—maybe he got scared and ran away.

J.C. didn't see the man. Donald wasn't after him. It was only a scare—that was all. Maybe just a game.

He quickly got to his knees and started scrambling to his feet.

It's not so easy with no hands, he thought. Not so fucking easy.

He was screaming too. Maybe someone would hear him. He kept yelling. He hollered, "Help!" and "Get the fuck out of here!"

But no one heard him. The gorge was a quiet, deserted place, a place to drink . . . a place to fuck.

He saw a steep path leading up, to his right. It wasn't the best path, so damn steep. It was used by the runty kids who sneaked down here to smoke cigarettes and light cherry bombs.

I've done that, J.C. thought. I used to do that. He started up the path.

The ground and the leaves gave way. With his hands cuffed behind him there was no way he could grab anything. He slid down.

"Oh, shit," he said. He tried to scramble to his feet again.

Then the man was there. Donald was there.

The man had him. J.C. kicked against him.

''Get the fuck . . . away!''
But the man was strong. . . .

The commercial ended, and someone screamed. Erin looked up
at the TV screen, at the movie her dad was watching.

A big man was kicking someone in a jail cell. A fat guy kicked
a man . . . No, he was kicking a *boy* lying on the ground. The fat
man kicked him once, and then again.

At first Erin didn't look at her father. Instead, she tried to pull
the pink jumpsuit onto Barbie's body. The stupid jumpsuit never
went on easily. It always caught at the elbows and on her head, on
all that hair. And Barbie's boobies were *way* too big.

Then she did look. She was something wet on her father's
cheek. Erin saw a drop fall from his chin. She looked out at her
mother, who was finishing up the dishes. Erin heard her father
sniff.

She coughed again. Her scratchy throat hurt now, and she knew
she was getting sick. Erin stood up. Maybe she should get her
mom. But she kept looking at her father, this strange man she
really didn't know, watching the TV.

The screen was filled with the boy's face, all bloody, one eye
shut, and the boy's mouth was black and bloody.

Erin heard noises coming from the big chair where her father
sat. Daddy was making a sound. He was crying, Erin realized. The
movie made him sad, and he was crying. Again she looked out to
the kitchen. She heard the clatter of dishes.

Daddy's crying.

She took a step toward her father, bringing Barbie with her.

''Daddy . . .''

She didn't want to do this. But he sounded so sad. He needs me,
Erin thought. *My daddy needs me.*

She took another step, and she was close enough to touch his
shoulder. It was shaking, something was making him shake.

''Daddy . . . ?''

He looked up, and Erin saw his tears, and she felt sad. She felt
her own tears coming. ''Daddy,'' she said, rubbing his shoulder
and touching his cheek. ''Daddy, don't cry.''

She had waited so long for him to come home, to make them a
family again. She'd waited so long.

''Daddy, don't cry. Mommy and I are here. Daddy, we love
you.''

Erin touched her dad's wet cheek; her fingertips felt the

streams. Her fingers stopped the streams, as if she could make the tears go back.

His eyes seemed to open wider, and he took a breath. He smiled. It was a real smile.

"And I love you," he said.

He reached for her with both his good arm and his bad arm. He reached for her and pulled Erin close.

He said the words again, the wonderful words, his face pressing into her shoulder.

"I love you."

Pick held the knife to J.C.'s throat. I've disappeared, Pick thought. I've vanished. So who could be doing this wonderful thing? Nobody . . .

The boy didn't move now. Pick knew what was going through his head. He was trying to convince himself that it was a game, just a sex game that a freak was playing.

That annoyed Pick. That wasn't true at all. This was the Work. Secrets were being uncovered here. There were experiences ahead, experiences that would take them both beyond the dullness of normal life.

Pick kept the knife at the boy's throat and then, with his other hand, slid the noose over his neck. J.C. moaned.

Pick heard a sound. Christ, he heard a sound coming from the road. Shit, was someone else coming down here? Why the hell would anyone else come down here?

To rush would spoil everything. Pick had learned some things about the Work. He had spent years thinking about it in prison, trying to understand it.

Time was important. Maybe it was all about time, about making each sensation as prolonged as possible. The first ones, so many years ago, had been fast, much too fast, and that had been all wrong.

Pick knew that it was important to be watched, to be able to look in the person's eyes, to have that bond, that understanding.

He also knew it was better with someone young. They *felt* so much more. They were ready for life to begin, not end. That made it all the more powerful.

"Please," J.C. said. "C'mon, man. Please let me go. I've had enough. C'mon."

Pick didn't say anything. He listened for the sound from the highway. The boy obviously didn't hear it; otherwise he would have tried screaming again, even with the knife at his throat. There were voices there, above them. The kid was too scared, probably nothing was getting through except the thumping of blood in his ears.

He was young. But not young enough.

The voices faded, people hurrying home from the cold.

Pick made the knife's edge twitch on J.C.'s skin. The skin, the canvas, was good, nice and tight. It looked grayish white in the gloom.

He pulled the noose tight.

J.C. shook his head. "Oh, God. Oh, Jesus. C'mon, man, let me the fuck go? Please!" The boy was yelling now, but there was no one to hear.

"Turn around," Pick said. The words were spoken quietly, reasonably, like a doctor doing an examination. Flip over. Cough. Drop trow.

"Hey, man—"

Pick pushed the knife blade in the tiniest bit. And the boy felt it. It probably felt like the sting of a shaving cut, that kind of sting. The boy started crying. Pick saw a thin line of red at his neck, just above the noose.

"Turn around."

J.C. turned around. Pick felt his erection, the metal bar pressing against the head of his penis. *There are secrets here. We're on a journey together.*

Pick kicked at the back of J.C.'s knees, and the boy fell. His head swung forward, smacking into the ground, making a cracking noise. He put a foot on J.C.'s back.

The boy tried to push against the foot. He kept yelling and bucking up against Pick's foot. But without his arms, the boy couldn't get up.

Pick grabbed one end of the rope.

The boy heard the rope being thrown in the air. He started screaming. Please let someone hear. Please.

There was the whistle of the rope flying through the air, then a whoosh and a thump. The rope fell to the ground. The man's foot pinned J.C. to the ground.

"Let me go!" J.C. screamed. He bucked some more. The man kicked his back, jamming the heel of his shoe down hard. "Let me go!"

J.C. heard the rope being thrown again. This time it didn't fall back. It caught on something. J.C. heard it being pulled tight.

Then there was a tug on his neck. The noose tightened more.

"Oh, no, please." J.C. tried to clean his lips, using his tongue to push off the needles, the dirt.

The man took his foot off J.C.'s back. The rope tugged at his neck.

J.C. cried and begged and thought about his sixteen years on the planet.

All at once . . .

38

Jimmy McGovern, "the Jimbo," ace linebacker for the Fresh Spring Trojans, hated the name of the team. The *whole team* hated it, wanted it changed.

We are the Trojans! Fight, fight, fight!

Put us on your wieners! Tight, tight, tight!

It was a sucky name. But then, Fresh Spring was a sucky town. Jimbo wasn't even looking forward to college next fall. SUNY Binghamton was going to be even more of a pit stop than this burg.

If I had been a better football player, he thought, it would have made a difference. But I was just okay, just your average dumb-ass linebacker.

The season, his last, was over, though. And he had his number one girl, Samantha, sitting next to him. There would be no more training, no more shit from the lard-ass coach.

"I got us some Ole Grand-Dad," he told Samantha. Sam liked to drink. It made her laugh a lot, got her nice and loose. But the old Mayberry R.D. police were a problem. They didn't like parked cars with drinking teenagers, no sir, didn't like to see them drinking while steaming the car up. Underage drinking was against the law. Underage screwing wasn't. . . .

"We'll head down to the gorge," he told Samantha.

Yeah, thought McGovern, we'll drink the bourbon down there, get the chill off, and then come back to the car. They can't arrest us for screwing.

Samantha looked unsure. She looked left and right. "I don't know, Jim. It's real cold."

McGovern turned the music louder in the Toyota. He reached over and gave her leg a squeeze. "I'll get you warmed up."

She didn't say anything else after that.

Lizbeth tucked Erin in tight, pulling the quilt snug. Erin's doll was already fast asleep, her eyes closed tight.

She put the book, *The Little Witch,* on Erin's desk.

"We'll finish this tomorrow," Lizbeth said.

Erin nodded. "Mommy . . . is Daddy going to get better?"

Lizbeth brushed a stray lock of Erin's hair off her forehead. She leaned forward and kissed Erin. "Yes, sweet pea. He'll get better. Daddy just needs time." *If time works.* If that's all we need here. Is time all that we need?

Erin nodded again, a little girl at sea in a big girl's world. Lizbeth shut off the light. She started singing. She always had to end the evening with a song. "Lullaby . . . and good night. Guardian angels . . ."

Erin scrunched under the blankets. Lizbeth heard a sound. The front door slammed shut. Simon was leaving, going out.

". . . are watching . . ."

The car started. He wasn't walking tonight.

"They watch, they keep . . ."

The car pulled away. He was driving.

"While God's children go to sleep. . . ."

Erin was asleep. But Lizbeth sat there thinking, He's not home yet. He's not really home. . . .

McGovern held Samantha's hand while climbing down the gorge, but she slipped anyway.

"Shit," she said.

"Watch your language, young lady." He laughed and helped her up. When they got to the bottom, they found that the gorge was deserted.

Naturally. Who else would come down here? Except maybe the rest of the football team, with their dates. They held regular tailgate parties in the woods. But it was early.

Samantha wrapped her arms around herself. She hugged herself tightly.

"I don't like it here, Jimmy. It's so *cold.*"

"Easy, babe. Antifreeze is on its way."

McGovern whipped the bottle of bourbon out of a bag. He unscrewed the cap, breaking the seal.

"I'd best taste it first," he said, passing the bottle under his nose. He took a big swig. And, damn, did that taste warm and wonderful. It started by burning his tongue and then sent a fireball down into his belly.

"It's *perfect.*" He handed the bottle to Samantha, who took it without enthusiasm.

She looked around, and then she took a small sip. She coughed. "Ow. That burns."

"No pain, no gain, babe. Fire up another."

She took another sip, but this time she kept the bottle to her lips a bit longer.

"Yo, leave some for the Man," he said, snatching the bottle away. McGovern took another chug. The warmth sat in his belly now. Samantha stood close, and he smelled the bourbon on her lips mixing with her perfume.

He saw her lips, the lipstick glistening from the wetness. He leaned down and kissed her. He made his tongue scour her mouth. She liked that, he knew. Yeah, tongue action drove her crazy. He wasn't surprised when she flicked her tongue back at him.

The warmth went lower. It was almost time to go back to the car and have some real fun. He broke the huddle. "Have another," he said, giving her the bottle.

He handed it to her. A sudden wind blew through the gorge.

She turned around, holding the bottle.

"Jim? Jimmy . . ." Samantha was still turned around, still looking into the gorge.

"What, babe? What's up."

"Jim. God, I think I see something . . . somebody."

McGovern froze. It was usually all fun and games down here. Samantha liked getting laid more than any girl he'd ever had, bar none—and the booze helped. Fun and games, but now—what she'd said—he felt the darkness.

The car seemed far away. "What? What the hell are you talking about? There's nobody down here, Sam, nobody but a frozen beaver." He took the bottle from her, swallowed a slug, and pulled her close. Yeah, it was time to go back. Time to start the play action. . . .

Samantha kept her head turned, looking into the narrow path of the gorge.

"No. There's someone there. Right there. I see—"

McGovern looked into the darkness. He saw the icy frosting on the rocks, catching the light. He saw the outline of a big pine tree. And then he saw something else.

It might be somebody watching them, he thought. Some peeping asshole.

If there was someone there . . .

"Hey," McGovern yelled. "Hey, you. Yo, Darkman! What the hell?" He turned to Samantha. "It's no one, just . . ."

He looked back. Well, he thought, *what was it?* He started walking toward the tree.

"No, Jim. Please."

He stepped on the frozen rocks. He heard the icy covering of the stream crack. He got closer, right under the pine tree. He heard Samantha behind him, following him. He held the bottle of Old Grand-Dad like a weapon. He wanted another swig. All the warmth was gone now; all the heat had vanished. There was no warmth now, nothing, except . . .

He took another step closer, until he saw—

"Oh, shit. Oh—"

"What, Jimmy? Tell me. What is it?"

He tried to try to block her. That's what you do, he thought. You don't let women see things like this. But he was too late.

She was beside him. "What is it? Is it somebody? Is it—" She was in the gloom beside him. He knew she could see the body.

The naked body swinging from the tree. McGovern knew the kid. *He knew the kid.* He'd seen him in the halls at school. He was a weird kid, a real weird dude. Called himself J.C.

Now he was here. His eyes were open, bulging out of his head.

A thought came to McGovern: *We should move.* We should get the hell out of here. That's what we should do.

He stepped back, and his foot slipped on an icy rock. He had to grab Samantha to get his balance. "Shit, we've gotta get out of here, Sam. We gotta."

That breeze came again, and Jim McGovern looked up to see the body spin in the breeze. And something moved on the kid's body.

A flap of skin on his stomach moved. While McGovern watched, the skin kind of fell. It just *peeled away* . . . like a chrysalis opening, like in Junior Biology, when the monarch butterfly squirmed out of its case.

Then another piece—a thin, narrow piece of milky white skin—fell from the kid's arm.

McGovern thought of fishing with his father . . . before he'd had a heart attack. He remembered how they had neatly cut the scaly skin before filleting the fish.

That's what had happened to J.C.

Samantha screamed and cried, hitting McGovern with her fists. "Jimmy, please. Take me out of here." He kept staring at the body. "Please, Jimmy."

He moved backwards, walking backwards, his hand locked on Samantha's arm. But he kept his eyes on the body, on the flaps of dangling skin. He kept looking at the bug eyes, the open mouth.

The open mouth, silently screaming.

Jimbo let the bottle of Old Grand-Dad fall to the frozen stream.

It was the same procedure he'd used years before, the methodical way Pick cleaned up. It was important to take time to do it right, Pick knew.

As soon as he was back in the car, he had stripped off the blood-spattered pants and sweater and changed into clean clothes. Eventually he'd look for an appropriate place to toss the bloody garments.

Then he peeled off his gloves and put them into the paper bag with the bloody clothes. For the moment he simply brushed the knife blade against some paper towels.

When he got back to the small college house, a newspaper lay on the wood porch and the outside lights were on, just as he'd left them.

He hurried inside to the small kitchen.

He used detergent to scrub his knife thoroughly, holding the blade up to the light, looking over every millimeter for any sign of red. He then put it in the hall closet.

He took a bath, filling the tub with blistering hot water and soapy bubbles. He soaked and let himself think about how he felt.

It had been good. That was true. After all those years of waiting, it had been *very good*. He felt as if he should be able to relax. But even as he thought that, he knew it wasn't as good as it could have been.

He still had this pit inside his gut. The fantasies, the pictures, were still there.

No, he admitted, something had been wrong. And he knew what it was.

He lowered himself until only his head stuck out of the water. The water was so hot it made his skin tingle. He was sweating into the tub.

The boy should have been younger . . . much younger. Already—at fifteen, sixteen—the punk was jaded. He didn't have that fresh look in his eyes, that sweet spark of life, of expectation. That was what Pick wanted to see.

Because then he knew that he was doing the Work.

He lowered his chin until the scalding bathwater touched his lower lip.

Yes, he thought. When I see that look, I know I'm teaching them that I'm not the only one taking pleasure from the groans, the flailing, the eye-popping screams.

No, he thought. I need that look that says, This is *new*. I never expected this. And this feeling has no end, no bottom. It just goes on and on and on.

Like the universe . . .

He lowered his mouth into the water, then his eyes. He shut them, and he felt the heat on his eyeballs. The water could even be hotter, he thought, a bit . . . hotter.

He went all the way under, cooking, completely enveloped by the water. He stayed under while his lungs began a slow burn, demanding air. He waited past the first alarm, the first scream for oxygen. Then there were two burning sensations, the hot water on his skin and the heat inside, his lungs, on fire, burning madly.

He waited until he knew he'd have to gulp down the hot water.

Then he popped up, gulping at the air, and again gulping, sucking it in.

Almost expecting to see *her* there, waiting for him, screaming at him, with clothespins in her hands. Clothespins, God—or maybe a plate of his own shit.

He could almost see her, his mother, standing there. The room was empty, but the memories were here now, walking around, filling this house, always with him. . . .

It was a normal night, just another night. The man he and his sister called Uncle Pete had gone. Another uncle was gone, and this time there would be no more uncles after him. No more . . . and Mom was mad.

She always got mad when the uncles left. It always got worse when they left. . . .

She had punished him, screaming at him, calling him Dirty Donny.

He didn't know what he'd done, but still she got out the big strap and started swinging the buckle end. Some of the blows bounced off his head. He heard the thwack echo inside his head. *Thwack* . . . It was a cartoon sound.

After a while it sounded as if it was happening to someone else.

Eventually she got tired of hitting him. Donny didn't do anything, and that always made her stop. He didn't scream; he didn't cry much. So she turned to his little sister, Patricia . . . Patty. But little Patty wasn't his real sister. They were both adopted.

Later he found out that they hadn't even been really adopted. Mom was only a foster parent.

She started in on Patty. Patty was little—five, maybe four maybe even younger. And she cried so much.

He heard her hollering at Patty, slapping her. There was nothing new there. But then he heard Patty scream, and it was a worse sound. This was going to be a bad night.

Patty had been bad. She had done something. So now Mom was doing something to her.

Sometimes Patty made a mess in her pants. She got scared and peed. And Mom punished her. She used certain things—wire brushes and fluids—*right down there.*

Pick remember watching the way she held the little girl's legs apart.

Patty's shrieks and his own riotous screams filled the house. He used to wonder, doesn't anyone hear? What's wrong with everyone?

Later he knew, of course, that they did. *They heard.* But it wasn't their business. Mothers had the right to discipline their kids. It was a parent's right. And the little girl, his sister, screamed.

But this night it was worse than ever before.

Pick remembered how cold his skin had felt as he sat and listened.

The screaming, *screaming*—until there was no more. It stopped. Pick thought it was over for that night. But he was wrong.

That night was to be different. That night the beating was only the beginning. . . .

Pick walked out of the bathroom, as if he could escape the memory. But it followed him, ever faithful.

The guesthouse was transformed.

Now it was the house where he'd lived as a boy. The screams, the cries, were everywhere. He *heard* them. His mother yelling, rummaging through kitchen drawers, looking for her tools—her "things," she called them.

"I have something for you," she said.

Pick looked down at the newspaper on the bed. It's no good, he thought. I haven't done anything to make it go away. Christ, they're still here with me. They haven't gone away.

The boy in the gorge was no good.

Pick thought of the knife, like a lover, lying in the hall closet, waiting seductively. He clenched and unclenched his fists.

No fucking good, he thought.

He looked down at the newspaper. There was a photo of a man, a woman . . . and a girl. Above the picture—they were all smiling—were the words "Home at last."

The guesthouse was filled with ancient screams while Donald Pick grabbed the newspaper off the bed and read the story.

"Home at last," he read. And the fire was there, with him, filling him completely.

39

Friedman's plane sat on the runway for over an hour, until the one o'clock flight turned into a 3:00 A.M. jaunt.

He asked for a pillow and a blanket to help sleep.

But even after the plane took off, Friedman was wide awake, looking down at a black earth, imagining the deserts below, the canyons, so much vast empty space. He tried closing his eyes, pushing his seat back, ignoring yet another movie. He didn't hear anyone laugh at this movie. Too damn early for laughs.

The sky lightened. They were traveling toward the sun, racing to meet dawn in a dozen different cities. Once Friedman looked down and saw mountains and snow, pure and clean. He glanced to his right. The man next to him was snoring. He looked like a businessman—a nice suit, a stylish tie. Friedman felt old and rumpled sitting next to him.

But now he could open his folder without upsetting the man.

He reached under the seat in front of him and pulled the brown folder out of his bag. He wished he could stand up. His doctor had said, "Don't sit too long. Keep things loose, limber."

He felt about as limber as an icicle. He stretched again and, sitting there, opened the folder.

There was a photograph of Mary Nova, a before picture, probably from Madam Welles's files. Mary Nova was young, very pretty, into punk stuff, with purple streaks in her blond hair and tattoos. She had one especially large tattoo, a brilliant magenta bird of paradise drilled right onto her butt.

He could see that tattoo clearly in the photo. The Meatman hadn't touched the bird. Friedman looked at the other photos, nice and clear now. He saw where the killer had worked, the design he'd carved on her back and the two-inch nails—big mother nails, the type used to hold two-by-fours together—he'd put through her breasts.

There were dark, sprawling ligature marks around Mary Nova's neck where she had been choked. Some of her screams had probably leaked out. Anyone who was on that deserted beach might have heard her.

The original homicide team had come up with squat. There was one interesting item, though. "The victim's anterior labial lips were pierced with a small silver ring," the M.E. had written. She was into piercings, Welles had said. Mary Nova was "out there."

The girl had a ring in her cunt. For decorative purposes, for fun, for her clients. She had done that to herself—that and the tattoo—before her killer ever added to her cosmetic changes.

But the wounds in her breasts hadn't killed her. Death had occurred because of the psychedelic designs applied to her back, not with a tattoo needle but with a thin knife, with a blade roughly the same size as the one used in the Meatman killings.

Death was due to blood loss.

The dried blood on her back spoiled some of the imagery, but Friedman could still make out the killer's pattern—the teardrop shapes, the familiar calligraphic sprawl, so similiar to that seen on the little boy, on the coed from Riverdale, and on the quiet girl from Canarsie.

There were no goddamn witnesses, no fibers, no prints. Plastic gloves had been the order of the day. The killer had been smart, careful, and neat, very neat.

Surfers had found the body in the morning.

There was no signs of a struggle leading down to the beach, no dripping blood. From appearances, the victim had gone with the killer willingly before being cut.

She might have known him.

Friedman pushed the folder aside. The other folders contained lab reports, statements from Welles, friends, neighbors who lived in the large house where Mary Nova rented a room. He found nothing but dead ends.

And there were no other murders.

Not in San Diego.

Still, something this bad didn't go away that easily.

Friedman pulled the folders close, making a neat stack, nice and organized . . . an illusion.

He looked out the window. The sun broke the horizon. It was

daytime, already midmorning in New York, and he still had hours of flying left.

The cold was an assault waiting for Friedman as he left the terminal at Kennedy and walked to his car.

San Diego—the warmth, the palm trees, the golden Pacific— would have seemed like a dream if he hadn't had the folder tucked in his bag.

He wanted to go home to Bay Ridge and sleep in a real bed. Everything ached.

That is what I want to do.

Instead, he got into his car and crawled to Manhattan, fighting construction and one-lane traffic all the way back to his office.

He went straight to Clarke's station, but she was at lunch. Friedman waited, standing by the computer, an alien machine. I should learn how to use one, he thought.

Can't teach an old dog new tricks. . . .

He pulled out a piece of computer paper and wrote Clarke a note.

He had hundreds of names, he told her, of guys connected with knives, sexual assault, manslaughter—a real nice crowd. If one of them came from California, he could have buried that fact and used an alias. That wouldn't be hard.

But if he'd danced with Mary Nova, if that was where he got his taste for pain—if she was the trigger—then maybe he'd brought something east with him.

"Can we get physical descriptions of these men?" Friedman wrote. "Look for elaborate tattoos, piercings, any unusual body modification."

If the killings had started with Mary Nova, then maybe the Meatman had brought the technique back here, something from the wonderful kinky world of S/M.

He walked to his office, needing a good cup of coffee.

Clarke had an answer for him a few hours later. Her terminal worked fast, he thought.

"You look like—excuse me, Friedman—you look like shit."

Friedman nodded. "Which is exactly how I feel. Did you come up with anything?" Clarke was wearing a metallic orange skirt and matching blouse. She could have stopped a firetruck.

"Yes . . . and no. Some arrest records mention the presence of tattoos. But half the damn prison population has got tattoos.

And some reports don't mention them one way or the other. So who knows?"

Friedman smelled a strikeout.

"The big prisons, though, note any distinguishing marks," Clarke said. "In the county prisons it depends on where the tattoo is. If a guy has a skull and crossbones on his butt, I don't think anyone would care. If it's visible . . ."

Welcome to the almost-twenty-first century, Friedman thought. You'd think there'd be a uniform system of identification, noting every mole, to keep track of these sweethearts.

Clarke handed him some pages. "Here's what the computer gave me."

Friedman looked at the pages. At least it cut his list of names down.

"Neither of the recent parolees has tattoos, Friedman."

He wasn't interested in them. Both Ed Hogue and Mohamed Greene were exactly where they were supposed to be, checking in with their parole officer, working at their jobs.

He looked at the other names, most drawn from the big state prisons like Attica and Sing Sing. Here were guys still in cold storage, with tattoos—big hearts with "Mom," naked ladies, dragons, skulls, and swastikas—nothing too far out.

But one guy had something that Friedman had never heard of. Not a tattoo—something called an ampallang.

"What the hell is an ampallang?"

Clarke shook her head. "Damned if I know. It came out on the list. Must be something like a tattoo."

Like a tattoo? What the hell was *like* a tattoo?

Friedman circled the guy's name—Donald Pick. He put a question mark next to it.

"Could you look into it? And could you get this guy's record? Not just his arrest and conviction summary, but the full report."

"There's just so many hours in the day, Friedman. You're not the only one wanting on-line time."

He looked up at Clarke and smiled. "Bethany, I'm tired. I'd like to go home. I'd really appreciate it if you'd get this for me. Please?"

She took the sheet of paper with the man's name. She shook her head as she walked out. "Donald Pick," she said. She wrinkled her nose at Friedman. "That's a nasty name . . . Donald Pick."

She walked away.

• • •

Twenty-five minutes later Clarke knocked at his open door.
"Yes?"

She came in carrying pages, smiling as if she was going to a
surprise party. "I got what you wanted." she held the papers tight.

She's teasing me, he thought. He sat there, looking at his lists,
his columns with dates. Clarke was grinning. She sat down and
crossed her long, dark legs. She smiled at him.

She waited for Friedman to ask her, her smile catlike.

"Okay, so what the hell is an ampallang?"

Clarke grinned, showing white teeth framed by red lips. "Are
you ready for *this?*"

Friedman nodded.

"An ampallang is a piercing of the head of the penis."

She emphasized the last word so that the full weight of the two
syllables sounded in the room. It took a second for her explanation
to register.

"What?"

Clarke hooted. "It's a piercing, Friedman. The head of this
guy's dick is pierced by a metal bar."

Friedman winced, but at the same time he sat up in his chair.

"Pick has a metal bar, what's called a lateral apadura, right
through the head of his dick."

Friedman took a breath. It was an image to give one pause.

"Can you believe it?" she said. "Why the hell would anyone
do that?" Clarke grinned.

Friedman noticed something besides her legs, her lips, her
sensual body. He saw something glistening on her nose. A tiny
mite-sized diamond.

In her nose.

"Maybe it's a decoration," she said, laughing. "Shit, maybe"—
she laughed louder—"maybe it *feels* good."

Friedman shook his head. "God. What about the pain?"

Clarke shrugged. "Different strokes . . ."

Different strokes . . .

Friedman thought about this guy, Donald Pick, doing his time,
looking normal. Friedman glanced at his picture. Pick was a big
guy, good-looking. With just this one little odd thing.

He's got a chunk of metal through his dick.

Now what the hell did that say about Pick? He thought of a
word connected with the Meatman killings—the "ritual." The
decoration.

Pain. The Meatman was into pain. Because, you see, once the victims were mutilated, once they could see what he'd done to them, they knew they were going to die.

You'd know that, after you had your skin cut, then—Christ—peeled away, the flaps neatly arranged, long lines streaming down your side.

You'd know you weren't going to live.

Then this guy, this maniac. A *real* maniac. He'd sit there or stand there—whatever—his pants down around his ankles, plastic gloves on, getting off on the whole thing.

"Friedman . . . Friedman? You listening?"

He came back.

I got pulled away a bit there, he thought. I got caught daydreaming.

"Yeah. I was just thinking."

Bethany Clarke stood up. "The report's there. Pick killed a dyke in a bar. Manslaughter. They were fighting over some underage girl. Too fucking weird. He's from California. Guess they're into that stuff there."

Friedman sat up. "He's from California? Where?"

Clarke shrugged. "It's there, in the report."

She went to the door, and Friedman—so tired—wished she wouldn't. He wished she'd sit back down, and maybe he could ask her out to dinner. She could tell him what her life was like.

And he could try to talk to her.

"Oh, there's something else," she said. "We didn't catch it. It came in after your first check."

Friedman wasn't listening, not really. He was thinking about Clarke, and about Pick. Of course Pick used to live in San Diego. Friedman had known that before he even looked down.

He had the magazine in his desk. *PFQ* . . .

It showed guys with clips in their nipples and hooks in their skin and wires and chains cutting into their penises.

"Donald Pick"—Clarke was smirking—"your Mr. Iron Dick there, isn't in jail anymore." Friedman opened his mouth. "He got out on parole right after we did the sweep with the computer. There's a parole address there—a halfway house.

Pick was out.

If he was out, Friedman had to talk to him. He looked at his watch. I have to ask him questions, he thought, but I can't do it now. I can't do anything now. . . .

Clarke walked to the door. Her fingers with brilliant purple fingernails, she grabbed the doorknob, ready to shut it behind her.

Friedman nodded. "Thanks." He tried to smile. "Thanks a lot." She started out.

She shut the office door, and Friedman picked up the paper. There was no phone number, only the address of the halfway house, blocks from the prison.

He was still close. That's was good.

Couldn't bring himself to leave home. Some cons did that. Like they were graduating from college, they couldn't leave the old alma mater.

Friedman sat back in his chair. It creaked, and he looked at the folders, his notes, and always the photos, wondering: Is it going to happen again?

And can I stop it?

40

Erin coughed as she got out of the car. Lizbeth watched her hack when she felt the cold air. Mona's driveway was filled with cars—other moms dropping their kids off for ballet. Most of them stayed to watch the class, to watch and dream about their little girls.

"Honey, are you okay?" Lizbeth felt a sharp pang of worry. Erin didn't look good. She could be so feisty, so independent. But when she got sick it was like the air escaping from a balloon, the life wheezing away.

When Erin got sick it terrified Lizbeth. Three years ago Erin had gone into the hospital with pneumonia. It was around her birthday, and Erin had said, "This isn't fair. I shouldn't get sick on my birthday." She went in with pneumonia, and she didn't get better.

They had put her on an I.V., and the plastic bottle dangling over her seemed to be a warning: *Something very bad is happening here.*

Lizbeth had stayed at the hospital, not really sleeping, but listening to all the sounds—the nurses laughing, the children waking up in pain, and then in the darkest hour of the night, Erin calling out, a breathy word, barely audible.

The whispered word had cut through everything—the heavy sleep, the noisy nurses. It was a faint, ragged whisper of immense power.

"Mommy . . ." One word, and Lizbeth was there beside her on the bed, holding her hand. That was all she could do, and it felt like so little.

Lizbeth thought of that moment as Erin got out of the car. She

231

stopped, and though she had dark rings under her eyes, she turned and smiled.

"I'm fine, Mom. Don't worry." Her voice sounded raspy.

I shouldn't let her go to ballet, Lizbeth thought. No, I should take her home. But she had told Walt Schneider she would meet him. Otherwise he'd keep calling. Simon would pick up the phone and . . .

He wasn't stupid. The thought of her having a lover must have occurred to him. At times she thought Simon could sense it. If he could, she hoped he could also sense that it was over. . . .

Lizbeth reached out and touched Erin's hand. "Have a good class, sweetheart. See you after ballet." Erin smiled, then turned and ran across the frozen lawn, stepping on isolated patches of snow.

Lizbeth waited, breathing fast. Then she backed out of the driveway.

Simon knew Lizbeth wasn't coming back while Erin was at class. And he thought he knew why.

The phone rang once while she was out of the house. Simon picked it up and said hello. There was a rude click as the caller hung up.

Suddenly the thought was there, so clear, so obvious, he wondered why he hadn't considered it before.

He walked around the house, thinking about it, trying to figure out what it meant.

Of course, she had someone, Simon thought. Why, it was crazy to expect anything else. He'd had no right to assume that he could come back after so much time and reclaim his place.

He walked through the house. He looked at his little girl's room. He walked into Lizbeth's bedroom. Simon shook his head. I want this, he thought. So much. I want this, and . . . maybe I can't have it. He turned and went downstairs. He took his coat out of the closet. He opened the door and went outside.

His car was there. Walt Schneider's beat-up Escort was already in the otherwise deserted parking lot at the river's edge. The Andrew H. Looman Memorial Park was empty, a children's ghost town. The wooden climbing apparatus—the piles of tires, the slides—was deserted, coated with an icy frosting of white.

Lizbeth pulled close to Walt's car, five spaces away, not next to it. That would have been too obvious. Anyone could look, it would be so obvious. She parked well away, her car pointing right out at the river.

She let the car engine run, pumping heat out. The river was so close, only yards away, lapping at the jumble of rocks, a deeper gray than the sky.

The river was dotted with whitecaps. The water—some days as still as a lake—was churning, active, alive.

The side door of her car opened. There was a gust of cold air. Lizbeth stiffened but didn't turn. Walt Schneider got in.

He leaned close to kiss her. Lizbeth pulled away, but not enough to escape the touch of his lips. It was a reminder of the world she had created.

"What's wrong, Lizbeth? You could hurt my feelings." It was a joke, something light. But she didn't smile. She looked up at the rearview mirror. She saw the train station behind them, the crossover, the empty tracks.

"Walt . . ." She turned and looked into his eyes. She hoped she was masking her feelings, her fear. "I said I'd *meet* with you, to let you talk. But this is it. One time only. I can't do this anymore."

He patted her leg. Another touch. It sent alarms through her. Warnings. "I know. I understand that. It's just that you seem sad, very upset. I was wondering if I could do anything."

She smiled at that. Upset, yes, you could say that. I guess you could say I'm in over my head, dealing with something beyond me. "No. I'm fine. It's hard now, but it will get better. Simon will get better."

"Bullshit. Not without help."

She turned to him. "What gives you the right—"

"I wasn't someone who drifted into your life, someone to screw you. I care about you."

Lizbeth turned away, looking at the river. "I can't."

"What? Can't have a lover anymore? Fine. I understand that. That's okay."

He touched her shoulder, his hand rested there, and she thought, I shouldn't be here, shouldn't be talking to him.

His hand trailed up to her cheek, and she brushed it lightly with just one finger. "But I can still be your friend."

She turned back to Walt. She didn't know that she had been crying. She nodded. "I'm sorry. Yes. We can be friends. But I don't want Simon hurt anymore. I couldn't bear that."

"I know. I have an idea. There's someone at the college

lecturing for a few weeks. He specializes in trauma. I spoke to him, and he'll see Simon. It might help.''

Lizbeth shook her head. ''I don't know. . . . Simon said he didn't want to see anyone—not yet.''

''Look, let me set up a meeting for tomorrow. You talk to Simon. Present it to him as a fait accompli. At least give him the chance to get help.''

Lizbeth looked at Walt. He was being sweet. Some men would be pushing her to keep the affair going. She squeezed his hand. ''Okay. I'll try it.''

Walt smiled. ''Remember, I'm your friend, Lizbeth. I don't want you telling me that I'm not.''

She grinned, even though she still felt her fresh tears. ''Okay,'' she said. ''I promise.'' She took a breath and let go of Walt's hand. ''What is the psychologist's name?''

''Cubbage,'' Walt said. ''Dr. Lane Cubbage.''

Lizbeth nodded. It was dark now by the river, and even the frothy whitecaps had disappeared. . . .

Ink took his Hearty Man pot pie out of the oven. He sat down with a Coors and turned on the TV. Donahue was dishing up three happily married cross dressers.

The show was just ending, and Ink took a slug of his beer.

Real family entertainment, thought Ink. Donahue presenting modern-day freaks, giving his viewers an opportunity to click their tongues and feel superior.

A-holes.

He clicked around the dial, and caught a headline on CNN. ''And in New York, a brutal murder horrifies authorities. Coming up next.'' His hand froze as he raised the beer can to his lips.

There was video footage of a body. Grisly stuff, the cuts were visible. There was a rope hanging from a tree, and—

Ink had the thought, *Look at that.* Look the fuck at that. Why, doesn't that seem like the same shit the same *goddamn* shit from years ago?

Ink waited through a few commercials and the stupid news jingle.

He listened to the story. He watched the videotape. He saw the cuts in the body—so fast. He wished he had it on tape so that he could slow it down, look, at the cuts, at the design, at the *fucking pattern.*

Ink licked his lips. The victim was a teenager. Some poor fuck, cut up, his skin sliced away. He waited for the story of the killing.

"The Putnam County Medical Examiner gave the time of death as between four and eight P.M. yesterday. State police say that they have no suspects in the horrible case."

The next story was about a teachers' strike in Denver. Ink sat there licking his lips, feeling frozen in his cold house.

Can't be, he thought. Some other freak, that's all. Can't be anything else.

I thought he died. Or got nailed for something. He disappeared. Mary Nova pushed him too far, playing her games. She pushed the freak too far, that's all. She got burned. That's all it was. . . .

I don't have to worry about shit.

Can't be him.

But he couldn't force the images away, the quick video snippets of the body, cut down from the tree, the gashes swirling up and down the boy's torso.

He took his time, the killer, the fucker. He took his time.

Can't be, Ink thought. Can't be him. Not after all this time. Something happened to him. He went away. Like I moved away, to the mountains. The guy gave it all up.

Ink walked around. No, he told himself. No, you can't bullshit yourself. This is the same deal, the same crap. But they'll never figure that out—the cops will never *get* it.

They won't know who he is.

Ink walked to the window and looked out at the dark woods, at the thin covering of ice and snow on the ground.

They won't know who did it. They never knew.

He touched the windowpane with his fingers. So dark out there. Anyone could come creeping up. *Anyone* . . .

One sick puppy . . . and if he'd started again, who would he go after?

Ink shook his head. He said, "Shit. I should call and tell them. I should do that."

The phone was in the kitchen.

But Ink didn't call anyone.

There was a knock on Friedman's office door.

Bethany Clarke walked in. She wasn't smiling.

"Did you get Cubbage's number?" Friedman said.

She nodded. "Yes." She put a slip of paper down on his desk. "But there's something else, Friedman."

"Yeah?"

"You haven't seen the news. I mean, you don't know what happened."

Then Friedman saw that she had papers, curled papers, fresh off the fax machine. "No, I haven't seen the news. Maybe you have something that you'd like to share with me." Friedman was getting impatient.

She put one sheet down. It was a faxed photo, lousy quality, but clear enough for Friedman to see. It was a Meatman photo. Must have slipped out of the folder. Sure, it belonged in his folder with all the other photos of mutilated bodies . . . his collection.

But Friedman hadn't seen this one before.

"This boy was cut last night," Clarke said. "We just got it on our network this morning. I've got a permanent search flag on for relevant homicides."

Friedman smoothed the sheet out with his hand. It was blurry, and the contrast too high, but it was clear enough for him to see that the boy had been tortured, each cut adding to the pain, doing nothing to hurry the kid's death along.

"There's another sick fuck out there," Friedman said.

That's what he hoped. This investigation was only an exercise, after all, something to keep him busy. An object of curiosity, a game. What ever happened to . . . ?

"You think so? Jesus, look at that," Clarke said. "You really think so?"

Friedman looked up. Deliberately, without a sense of joy, he shook his head.

No. He felt something that he hadn't felt since he was shot, a strange mixture of fear and excitement. It was a cop feeling, a feeling that there was someone bad out there, *close now,* and it was Friedman's job to hunt him down, to corner him, to capture him if he could . . . or kill him if he couldn't.

The feeling, gone for such a long time, hit him like a gale-force wind, stronger than it had ever been before.

Cops believed in fate. They had to, when their number could be up any moment, any day. One day you have a wife and two kids, a backyard with a gas-jet barbecue. Friends and a cooler full of Coors Light.

The next day you walk into an abandoned building and your head gets blown off.

Fate.

Fate's in charge now, Friedman thought. Here, now, wherever

the hell this is going. It was a whim, this case, just something I got interested in. It was supposed to happen. I was supposed to get involved in this.

There's something I'm supposed to do.

He felt the anxiety, the gooseflesh on his arms.

"No," he finally said to Clarke. "I *don't* think it's someone else."

41

Lizbeth hurried back to Mona's house before the ballet class was to end.

She found Erin inside, sitting on the steps leading down to what would have been the family room, now outfitted with a barre and mirrored walls.

The class was still working, dancing to something light and bouncy from Tchaikovsky. The mothers stood to the side, their winter coats unbuttoned, watching their awkward little ballerinas. Erin looked abandoned.

Mona talked loud. "Girls . . . now, girls, ready on three!"

"Erin?" Lizbeth said.

Her little girl looked up. She smiled, then coughed. Her eyes were underlined with thick dark smudges. She looked terrible.

"Back to second position and—"

Lizbeth crouched low beside Erin. "Honey? What happened?"

"I feel sick."

Lizbeth saw Mona shoot her a stern look of disapproval, a look that said, How could you bring the poor girl today? Why on *earth* would you bring such a sick child to ballet? What kind of mother are you?

Lizbeth took Erin's hand. You see, she thought . . . you see, I had to talk with my lover. I had to talk about my husband. He's not well. I watched the river, so gray, so cold and empty.

She squeezed Erin's hand. The other mothers, the full-time soldiers, stared at her. Tongues clucking.

She caught another glance from Mona while Erin hacked out more coughs, really horrible. The little girl let her full weight hang on her, dragging. . . .

Lizbeth guided her out to the strains of fairy music.

∙ ∙ ∙

The house was empty, and Simon went for a walk.

It was still strange to simply walk out the door anytime he wanted. He could walk around the block and keep walking, and no one would stop him.

Maybe that's exactly what I should do, he thought. Because— because I thought I was coming back to my life here.

But too much time has passed.

Yes, I can feel that. Maybe I should just leave.

I have a little girl, and she needs a father. She needs a dad she can depend on. Someone to watch her, to protect her.

And I can't do it.

The wind was cold, and he pulled his old coat tighter. His eyes stung from the bite of the wind. He kept walking, avoiding icy patches on the sidewalk.

I should just keep walking . . . right out of their lives.

Lizbeth hurried Erin into the house.

"Go upstairs to bed. I'll call the doctor, honey, and bring you some Tylenol and something to drink."

Erin stood there. "Where's Daddy?"

"Erin, just go. Now." Erin turned to the stairs.

The front door opened. Lizbeth turned and looked at Simon. She had to talk to him, tell him about the doctor, get him to see the psychologist.

"What's wrong?" he said.

"Erin's sick. She has a fever. She gets these fevers, and they scare me."

Simon nodded. "Can I do anything to help?"

"I—"

The phone rang, and Simon picked it up.

"Hello."

Lizbeth looked at him, wondering who it could be. Then she knew. Simon held out the handset to her. "It's for you."

Lizbeth walked over to the phone, and Walt was there, telling her that it was all set. Simon could meet the psychologist, Cubbage, tomorrow.

She felt Simon's eyes on her.

"Yes. Oh, good. Right, yes. What time? Thank you." Simon watched her as she hung up.

He looked away. "Lizbeth, I've been thinking. I was walking around before, and I was thinking . . ."

"Simon, that was—"

He turned his back to her, and she saw the terrible sadness in his eyes. Oh, God, she thought, there's more pain, more hurt there. . . .

"I know you have somebody, Lizbeth. I mean, it's only natural. I can't come back here and expect—"

Lizbeth shook her head. This wasn't supposed to happen. "No, Simon, you don't—"

"I'm going to leave. There are some places I can stay. I think—"

Lizbeth took his hand. "Simon, please. Please, don't say this."

Simon nodded. "You have someone else. I know it. And it's—it's okay. I was gone"—he smiled sadly—"for too long."

But Lizbeth shook her head. "No. "We—we need you. We need you to get better."

He looked away and said, "When I was a prisoner, there was one thought that never left me." His hands rose, sculpting the scene, shaping it in front of his eyes. "I thought about *home,* all the time. Every detail I could remember." He turned to Lizbeth, hands still suspended in midair. *"Everything.* I thought about the way the house looked, about the furniture, where every picture was hung. I pictured you here, and Erin, growing up strong and beautiful. I saw it all—and now I can't touch it."

His hands fell slowly. . . .

"Simon . . ."

"I'm here. I'm safe now. But I can't touch what's here. I can't be part of this dream I had, this thing that kept me alive."

His eyes lost their steely glow, turning filmy. His breath caught.

Lizbeth touched his arm, feeling his pain, his terrible sadness. "We want you back. *I* want you back."

Simon clung to the precipice, barely holding on. "I don't know. I don't want to—"

"There's someone at the college. He's a doctor, a psychologist. He deals with people who've been through . . . extraordinary things. He's a specialist in trauma. He'll only be here for about a month. But he can see you."

"I don't—"

"Simon, he can help the family."

Simon looked away, lost, shaking his head, and Lizbeth raised her hand to his cheek. Her smooth fingers felt the valleys, the furrows. All new . . .

"He can help us."

Simon looked at her, shaking his head. "I don't know."

"Please," she said.

He stopped shaking his head.

"Please . . ." Then Lizbeth turned and saw Erin standing there.

"I don't want Daddy to go," she said. "I don't want to lose Daddy. I don't want to lose him again."

"Please," Lizbeth whispered against him, thinking, Let me have another chance at this. "Please. See the doctor. Don't leave us."

Simon cleared his throat. "Erin, you should be in bed, honey. Go to bed, baby."

"But, Daddy, I don't want you to leave."

"Okay. I'll see the doctor. I won't go anywhere," he said.

Lizbeth didn't know whether to believe him or not.

42

Somehow Friedman had sleepily flailed at his alarm, hitting it and shutting it off. So he slept late.

When he finally woke up, aching all over, he microwaved a cup of instant coffee and hurried to the office.

Today, he'd go see Pick. Donald Pick from California. Donald Pick with the ampallang.

When he got to his desk, he looked over Pick's papers. Friedman was so tired he almost didn't see it.

There was an exit profile, a routine document, on Pick. And it was signed by Dr. Lane Cubbage.

Friedman picked up the phone, recalling the name of the college where Cubbage was lecturing: Hudson College. He called, working his way through the electronic switchboard, fighting to speak to a real operator. He asked for the psychology department, and an assistant dean answered.

Yes, she said, Dr. Cubbage was a guest lecturer at the school. He was staying at a guesthouse.

Friedman asked for the number, then hung up and hit the buttons.

Friedman let the phone ring eight times. Then, thinking that he might have made a mistake, he hung up and called again.

The phone rang, but Pick didn't touch it. He was too busy thinking.

Now, this is truly a remarkable occurrence, he thought, an amazing gift. That man came to me, asking *me* to see the freed hostage.

Pick fingered the photo from the newspaper, pushed it around. They were all smiling in the photo. Pick saw that, but . . .

I very much doubt that they are happy. Happiness seem to have eluded this family . . . the Farrells.

The father, the hostage, must have wonderful stories to tell, Pick thought. And I'll get to hear those stories.

The phone rang again. Pick let it ring five, six times, each ring making his nerves jangle.

This won't work, he thought.

It was an interesting idea, taking Cubbage's place, trying to disappear. He'd heard about that TV show, "Unsolved Murders." He figured people would be looking for the Meatman again. Looking for *him*. But Donald Pick would be gone.

It had seemed like a good idea—until that incident in the lecture hall.

I used Cubbage's notes. It was easy to talk, it was fun. Everyone listened. They believed me. But then that girl asked me a stupid question.

Pick opened the desk drawer and pulled out a pair of scissors.

It was a question about something called a reaction formation . . . a fucking *reaction formation.*

I made a joke. They didn't laugh. The girl wanted an answer. Reaction formation, I thought. Christ, what the hell is a reaction formation?

Then it was over. I had to get off that goddamn stage. The students were talking, buzzing like insects.

Pick took the scissors and started cutting the photo.

First he cut away the man, Simon Farrell. The woman's hand, dismembered, still rested on his shoulder.

Then he separated the woman and the girl.

"Fucking bitch," he said, thinking about the girl who had asked the question. "Goddamn stupid fucking bitch."

He told them he was ill. He told the assistant dean bitch that he was under the weather. Fucking-A, under the weather, and put a hold on any more lectures.

I've got to disappear again.

But then this gift, this wonderful gift, fell into my lap.

Pick picked up the three people and stacked the sliced photos together. He cut them in half and then cut them again.

The hard part now was waiting. . . .

Just before dawn Ink heard a car slowing down on the road. He pushed aside his gray curtain and checked the road.

Keep moving, asshole, Ink thought. Can't you see that the place is closed? Can't you see that I'm not open for business?

Ink turned around. The picture from the newspaper was sitting on his kitchen table.

I could ignore it, he thought. I don't have to do anything about it. Nothing at all. I don't have to do shit.

Maybe there's no connection. What's it been, six years? Seven years?

I moved away from California because the police couldn't get him, and I thought maybe he'd come after me. And I didn't want him to do that.

Ink looked at the grainy newspaper photo. The swirling lines cut into the boy's skin were ridged with dry blood. The story in the paper said that the kid was awake through the whole thing. Sure, that was how he liked it, how he wanted it.

He wanted them awake.

Ink looked at the phone.

All I gotta do is call, he thought, give them a name. What could happen? What could fucking happen to me?

Still Ink didn't do anything.

Friedman hung up the phone. Clarke was waiting for him. Magenta was the color of the day—her lips, eye shadow, shirt, and pants.

"And I got you this." she said.

She handed him a photo. For a second he didn't know what it could be. A cannon? An animal with a bone through its head? A chubby worm with a spike right through one end?

It looked like a snake with a mouth at the top. He looked, and suddenly he knew what the larger-than-life picture showed.

"That," Clarke said, "is an ampallang. Can you believe it?"

The enormous penis, a chunk of metal through its head, looked back.

"Ouch."

"Ouch is right. I also found some information in the on-line encyclopedia."

Clarke read from a piece of paper. "'The ampallang was believed by primitive societies to keep demons from entering either party during a sexual union.'" She looked at Friedman. "Keep the demons away," she said. "It would keep *me* away."

She laughed. Friedman only smiled. He was preoccupied.

Clarke studied the photo. "You know, you have to wonder what it would feel like." She looked at Friedman.

Clarke turned to leave.

"I'm going to go talk to Pick this afternoon," Friedman said, "and to Lane Cubbage. I'll check in to see if you learn anything else about this Conneley murder."

She looked at him. "You be careful. I don't like the sound of that guy, Donald Pick."

Friedman smiled. "I'll be very careful."

Clarke left. Friedman pinned the photo of the ampallang, the monster wiener from hell, on the wall, along with the other pictures.

The others . . . The dissected bodies, the faces, the wide-open mouths frozen into screams of horror. The old pictures, asking— even after all these years—for help.

And the brand-new one of Jerome Conneley.

The demons got out, Friedman thought. The demons are hungry. They can only want more. . . .

Maybe I'm the only one who can stop them.

He scooped up file folders, the photo of Pick, his record. He picked up the phone and called the number for Cubbage again, and listened to the phone ring and ring. . . .

PART FOUR

HOME

The obsessive-compulsive is rarely violent. But when a sociopath has an obsessive-compulsive disorder, the violence will be ritualistic and immense. He will strive for *perfection* in his killing.

—**Martin Hayes,** *The Violent Mind*

43

Friday morning Lizbeth called her office and told them she wouldn't be coming in. "My baby's sick," she said.

The secretary didn't sound as if she understood or cared. "All right," she said. "I'll let them know."

Lizbeth made some toast for Erin and cut it into fingers. She realized she hadn't seen Simon for a while. Where is he? She wondered. What happened to him?

She went upstairs, calling his name, quietly, gently, "Simon? Simon . . . are you up?"

Lizbeth heard voices coming from Erin's room. She walked to the door quietly, and stopped.

Simon touched his daughter's brow. She felt hot, and the doctor had her on antibiotics. A soft white bear was nestled next to her cheek. Simon rested his broken hand in his lap.

What can I do for her? he thought.

"The children in school," Erin said, "they used to tease me."

"Oh, really? How?"

"They said you weren't real, that I didn't have a daddy."

Simon nodded. "Did that make you sad?"

"Sometimes I cried." Erin took a breath and looked at Simon.

She so much wants this to work, he thought. She's just a little girl who wants a family, who wants to feel safe and loved. . . .

"You won't ever leave, will you?"

Simon smiled. He heard a noise behind him, and he turned to see Lizbeth waiting at the door.

Simon turned back to Erin. "No, honey. I'll stay with you."

"Daddy has to go now," Lizbeth said. "He has to see someone."

Simon nodded. He got up, and Erin reached out and grabbed his hand. "Come back to see me when you get home."

Simon smiled, his heart breaking, the sweet pain more than he could stand. "I'll come right upstairs," he said. "Just as soon as I come back."

He walked to Lizbeth and together they went downstairs.

Later Lizbeth turned on the TV in the kitchen.

She thought of Simon driving to see the psychologist, wondering if it might help him.

The midday news began. The third story, right after the report about New York City's budget crisis and the mayor's fraud trial, was about the murder of the boy up in Putnam.

He was killed in a gorge, just outside town. The camera panned down to where the stones were stained by the boy's blood, then up to the tree where he had been hanged. Butchered. That was the word used.

"The boy died slowly," the reporter said.

Designs, decorations, had been cut into the boy's body while he watched.

"It must have taken him an hour to die," a state police detective said. "Maybe more," he told the reporter.

"It's a grisly murder," the reporter observed redundantly.

It was horrible, so sick. Lizbeth shut the TV off.

Simon parked the car in front of the house, this dark wood house with great stained timbers and curved beams and a foundation of fieldstone. It was so dark, the wood stained a deep earth brown. The windows all had curtains, and all the curtains were drawn.

Simon got out. The house belonged to Hudson College, Lizbeth had told him, a residence to be used by visiting professors. It was such a gloomy place from the outside, he imagined that it could only be worse inside.

He didn't want to go in.

He stood there on the stone walkway.

I don't want to go in there.

He thought of other houses, places he was dragged into, his legs smashing against wood. The men, the smell of the men, their curses in his ear.

He walked along the path and up the steps—wood planks resting on more stone—to the porch, stained the same dirt brown that made the whole house so dark.

Simon pressed the doorbell and waited. He didn't hear anything. He pressed again, waited, and then knocked.

He looked around and then checked the piece of paper in his coat. Maybe he had the wrong address. This house looked abandoned.

No one home. Just as well, he was thinking. I don't think I'm in any shape to talk.

He heard a sound coming from the back. Maybe it was a neighbor putting out some garbage, Simon thought. Except the nearest house was a couple hundred yards away, shielded by a stand of pine trees. No neighbors out here.

Simon walked to the edge of the porch and leaned out. He heard another sound from the back.

Someone's here, he thought. Inside this house. Someone *is* home.

He turned back to the front door. One more knock, he thought. I'll give it just one more knock.

Simon raised his hand, and the door opened.

44

Friedman filed a preliminary investigation report, writing up his trip to San Diego, marking down his expenses.

Then it was time to go. His stomach rumbled. He was hungry.

He left the office and took the elevator to the lobby. On his way out of the building, he bought a hot dog from the dwarflike man who parked his cart on the corner outside One Police Plaza. Throwing caution to the wind, Friedman got a dog with the works, including chile and fried onions.

He ate the hot dog while he walked to his car.

Friday was a busy day for Karin Ostrom. All of her clients wanted their apartments cleaned on Friday. She was only doing this work until she could get a better job. Her parents in Amsterdam thought she was a secretary. She sent money to them, and they were proud.

She wondered how they would feel if they knew she had to get down on her hands and knees and clean toilets.

Friday was too busy. There was the Curtises' apartment—neat people, but a big place. And they wanted things just so. Then Mr. Mandelbaum, a lawyer. His place had lots of knickknacks, lots of dusting. Finally, when she was dead on her feet, she had to clean Dr. Cubbage's place. It spooked her, that apartment, with its weird masks.

Yes, she'd be dead by the time she got to Dr. Cubbage's place. . . .

The door to the dark brown house opened as Simon was about to knock. A man stood there, wiping his face with a towel.

Simon's first thought was that he had gotten Cubbage out of the shower. His hair was wet, and there were foamy white puffs near his ears.

Dr. Cubbage was a big man with sandy hair and big powerful arms. He wasn't what Simon expected.

"Mr. Farrell? Simon Farrell? I'm sorry. You must have been knocking." The man smiled, a warm smile; his blue eyes were bright, piercing.

"I was shaving. Running the water." He wiped his hand and extended it toward Simon. "Lane Cubbage," he said. Simon took his hand. "Come in. Come. It's a nasty morning out there."

Simon followed Cubbage into the house, as dark as Simon suspected. The psychologist pointed to the left. "Why don't we talk in here? There's an office we can use. Here—give me your coat."

"Thank you."

The psychologist took Simon's coat. Simon imagined him saying, Now, where is your chain? We have to chain you up. We have to kick you. If you'll wait just a minute . . .

There was no light in the house. Simon didn't see any moose heads hanging from the wall, but he wouldn't have been surprised.

The grim hallway ended in a broad staircase leading up to the second floor. To the musty guest rooms, Simon guessed.

The office, to the left, was only slightly more cheery. It faced the porch and the midday glare of an overcast day.

The psychologist hung up Simon's coat and turned back to him. Simon felt this pressure to say something.

"Thank you for seeing me, Doctor."

"Don't mention it. I'll be glad to do whatever I can to help you."

The psychologist pointed to a seat facing a giant desk. A pale light filtered through the curtains.

Simon sat down. "I've been home for two weeks. And I . . ."

The man nodded his head, smiling, his eyes still bright and warm.

I've started wrong, Simon thought. I said something, and it was wrong.

"Simon . . ." The familiarity of the name seemed natural, soothing. Cubbage was obviously experienced at gaining people's trust quickly. Simon let himself submit to it. "Let's start with *before*—when you were a prisoner. Let's start by talking about that."

Simon chewed his lip and looked away to the windows. Then he turned back to Cubbage, who was watching him closely, carefully.

''I was gone for almost five years. . . .''

The knife was in the desk drawer.

Pick pulled open the drawer a bit, only the tiniest crack. Now he could look down and see the smooth silvery white of the handle.

Simply taking it out of the hall closet had been exciting. Now, with this man here, talking—the knife so close—it was *wonderful*.

Pick asked him questions . . . and made him talk about the pain.

A lot of people were trying to get the hell out of the city. Friedman cursed himself for taking the Deegan Expressway, where traffic was barely crawling.

''I should have taken the damn West Side Highway,'' he said aloud.

CBS Radio 88 was on. News and weather until you explode. Already they were getting wild about a coming storm. Batten down the hatches. Hide in the cellar. *It's the blizzard of the century.*

Except usually the blizzard petered out into a dusting, and the weathermen went into hiding for a few days.

Friedman crawled past Yankee Stadium. He could see what was slowing down the traffic. A jackknifed trailer truck had closed two of the lanes heading north. Friedman looked up at the stadium, the renovated house that Ruth built.

Thanks to All Our Fans!

Friedman's knee was throbbing. It didn't do well when he sat in one position for a long time. Now, sitting in the car, his bad knee felt as if it had a needle stuck in it.

I'm not going anywhere here. Shit. He looked at his watch. It was near two. He wanted to see Pick and then get to Cubbage before dark, but at this speed, it might be dark before he even got to Pick.

He looked at the map. He had circled Ossining in red ink. The halfway house was on Broadway, right on Route 9, the main drag.

He had drawn another circle around the college, on 117, near Pleasantville. He saw the name in tiny letters on the map: Hudson College. He couldn't read them now. They were much too small. But he knew they were there.

Damn, if I can get moving, Pleasantville is only forty, maybe fifty minutes away.

He dug out a piece of gum. He felt his small spiral notebook in his coat pocket. It was chock full of questions for Pick.

Like—why did you come to New York? And did you know Mary Nova? And how come you have a chunk of steel in your pecker?

Cubbage could help. He might know the story on Pick. How fucked up was he? Could he be the Meatman?

Or am I spinning my wheels here . . . wasting time?

Friedman popped his gum.

There was some movement ahead.

A single lane of traffic inched forward with a kind of sluggish inevitability. Sure, makes sense, Friedman thought. That's the way this whole thing feels.

Inevitable . . .

The psychologist took a breath. It seemed odd to Simon, the funny way the man breathed, looking right at him. Then the psychologist asked, "What did they say to you, Simon?"

Simon nodded. He wants me to help him. Is this real, he wondered, being in this stuffy room, with the pale light from the windows, the sick, washed-out gray light? Is it real?

"Simon, what did they say to you? What did your captors do to you?"

Simon turned and looked at the doctor. He doesn't fit in this house, Simon thought. Right now he's smiling as if I'm some kind of crazy person.

Simon felt like standing up and yelling: I'm not crazy! Do you hear me? I'm not crazy. I've been through this experience, that's all.

The psychologist smiled. "It will help if I know what they did to you. You were in their power for a long time. They tried to"— the man looked up to the mustard-colored ceiling and plucked a word—"*shape* your image of yourself. To make you into a prisoner. To make you feel guilty." The smile faded. *"What did they do?"*

Simon took a breath. He spoke quietly; the words brought the memories. It was so hot in here; the air felt dead. Simon looked out the window. He wanted to get up, to walk around the block, to get in the car, to go away, out of here.

"They kicked me. Sometimes they beat me. They jumped on

my legs. They'd laugh and jump on my legs. It was like a game. Once . . . once they wrapped me in old smelly cloth—I don't know. They were wrappings of some kind. They wrapped me, and I couldn't breathe.''

Simon gasped. For a second he felt no air in his lungs.

Stop, he thought. Please, no more questions.

''What are some of the other things they did, Simon? Tell me what else they did.''

Simon shook his head. He won't stop, and I can't leave. Because if I leave, I'll lose them. Lizbeth. Erin. *They'll be gone.*

''What else?''

''Once they put a gun to my head. They said I was worthless. I was garbage. Nobody wanted me. Nobody would pay for me. So they were going to kill me. I was blindfolded. Always blindfolded. They made me kneel. They—they put the gun to my head. I felt the barrel. I smelled the gun. The powder, the oil. I could smell it. I heard a sound. They were pulling back the hammer.''

Simon looked up at the doctor. He's watching me, Simon thought, just listening. How will this help me get better?

I don't want to remember any of this. I want to forget.

''Go on.''

''They laughed. Then the man holding the gun squeezed the trigger. The hammer hit. But nothing happened. They did it again. I wet myself. And after they were done, they made me lie there, chained to the radiator. Chained in my own mess.''

Simon felt the tears, and God, how he fought those tears. But he couldn't win, no matter how many times he blinked, no matter how big a breath he took—and held it. He couldn't stop the sobbing.

He heard a sound. The psychologist ripped a tissue out of a box.

''Here, Simon. That's good. Here you go.''

Simon reached out for the tissue. His fingers brushed the man's hand.

And . . . there was something odd about the contact, some bit of information, some important information. There was *something* in that touch. . . .

Cubbage waited and then said, ''Your last weeks, before you escaped—were there any *special* horrors that you saw, anything that might have given you an extra drive to escape?''

Simon held a crumpled tissue tight in his hand. ''Yes. There was this man down there, with me. They hanged him, they cut off his hand, his fingers.''

The psychologist's eyes went wide. Simon heard the desk rattle. "Oh? How do you know that?"

Simon shook his head. No more questions, he thought. He looked out the windows, through the thick gauze of the curtains, the dirty gauze, like the material of his blindfold.

He wants it all, Simon thought. All the horrors.

So he told him. . . .

Next to the knife were the small pieces of newspaper, the photograph cut into so many pieces, almost to the size of confetti.

Pick slid open the drawer. He rested his hand on the knife.

He could picture everything Simon Farrell was telling him *so* clearly. At the same time, the fantasies were flying through his head.

He imagined tying this man up. He couldn't fight much, not with the bad leg and a broken hand. That would be easy.

Pick slid his fingers over the smooth plastic knife handle. His thumb played with the blade.

The hostage squirmed in his seat.

He's *my* prisoner now, Pick thought.

Friedman cruised up the Thruway, taking it slow. Puffy flakes were falling, and the road had started to look icy. He kept the radio off, the better to deal with his thoughts.

He saw a ramp leading from the Thruway to the Saw Mill River Parkway. The driver ahead of him slowed down and put his blinkers on as if he was going to get off. The guy slowed some more, lost, confused, and then quickly zipped to his left, back onto the Thruway.

Asshole, Friedman thought.

Friedman took the ramp leading to the highway.

The Saw Mill River Parkway was dark. Friedman saw unfamiliar signs.

He knew that he'd have to thread his way through suburbia to get down to the Hudson River, to the house where Pick was staying.

"Do you think . . ."

The psychologist waited until Simon looked up. He wants my attention, thought Simon. This is no different than the other places I've been. I have to do what I'm told.

"Do you think your wife was unfaithful, Simon?"

Simon shook his head. The man repeated the question, louder, walking close to him.

"Well, do you?"

"I don't know."

"Yes, you do. Of course you do. Now, answer the question. I can't help you unless you answer the questions."

"Yes. I think there was someone else."

"Was?"

"Look, I don't see how this can help me."

The psychologist smiled. "You have to understand what you're coming home *to*. Don't you see? You have to understand how you fit in."

The man paused, and Simon could sense the unspoken thought. *If* I fit in . . .

The psychologist walked to the windows and pushed aside the curtains. The phone rang, as it had before. Cubbage never answered it.

"I want to see your family. I want to talk to them, to explain to your wife and your daughter what you're going through."

Simon shook his head. "I don't think that's—"

"Your wife wanted my help. I have to talk to her, to all of you."

Simon had to get out of there, to feel the cold air, to limp down the wood stairs to the cold walkway.

If all I have to do is give him my address and let him talk to Lizbeth, I'll do it.

Simon said, "Come after dinner. My daughter's sick."

"No matter."

"I live at thirty-two Gaheney Drive."

Simon watched the man write down the address, and then directions, on his pad.

Friedman rang the bell of the halfway house. The curtains were drawn, and it looked as though company was certainly not welcome. He heard nothing, and rang the bell again.

Then the door opened, and he heard a woman muttering in the shadows. The puffy snowflakes stuck to Friedman's coat.

The black woman muttered to herself. "Goddamn. What the—"

Friedman showed her his badge. "Mrs. Williamson?" He had seen her name on the sign outside.

She scratched her head. It looked as if she had two bathrobes on, and her dark, chubby face seemed scrunched up from an afternoon nap.

"What d'you want?"

"Could I come in?"

She shrugged disgustedly and held open the door. Entering, Friedman smelled dinner cooking. Something with cabbage and potatoes. It didn't smell bad.

She stood in the hall, holding her two robes across her ample chest, arms folded. "Well, what is it?"

"You have someone staying here. His name is Donald Pick. I'd like to—"

Already the woman was shaking her head. "No. He's not here. I mean, the man paid for the room for two weeks, but he ain't been here but the first day. I hope he hasn't gone and moved and taken my damn key."

Friedman felt a sudden chill. He took a breath. Okay, he thought. That's no big deal. Ex-cons moved from one place to another, stopping at joints like this until they found their bearings and got used to not looking at the world through bars. That was no big deal.

He could have gone somewhere else. If he'd told his parole officer, it would be okay. Pick should have called in.

Friedman would check on that.

And what if he'd jumped?

Ex-cons jumped parole all the time. Some of them seemed to have a death wish. It was as if they wanted to get their butts back in jail. Three square meals and all that security.

"Could I see his room?"

Again Williamson shrugged, turning to the stair. "Sure, I don't care. He's not here. He's got my key. You're the policeman. I don't care."

I get the feeling that she doesn't care, Friedman thought.

He followed her up the stairs. The carpeting on the steps was threadbare, with loose threads exposing wood underneath.

She went to the first door and opened it.

"G'on," she said. "Take a look."

Friedman walked into the room. . . .

Lizbeth sat down on Erin's bed and watched her sleep fitfully. Erin's breathing was ragged and raspy. The dark room hid the girl's color, but Lizbeth knew . . .

She's washed out, a pale alabaster doll.

She felt Erin's brow. It was still warm, still cooking away. Soon she'd have to wake her. Give her some Tylenol, a spoon of amoxicillin, the pink goo that would chase away the infections . . . if that was what she had.

Lizbeth had to take her temperature rectally. Erin would cry, saying that she just wanted to sleep.

"Watch the temperature," Dr. Heinemann had said. Watch the temperature. Cool her down if you have to, put her in a tub of tepid water. Keep her cool.

Now Lizbeth sat on the edge of the bed, listening to her breathing, smelling the curried chicken cooking downstairs.

Simon should be back, she thought. He's out there somewhere, driving around. He should be back by now.

Lizbeth waited in the dark for Erin to wake up and for her husband to come home. . . .

Pick's room was empty. There was nothing here. No clothes, nothing from the hospital.

There was no sign that Pick had ever stayed in the room.

"You're sure this is his room?" Friedman asked.

"Damn," the woman said, sounding annoyed. "'Course I am."

He's gone, thought Friedman. Donald Pick is gone. Then he shook his head. No. From the looks of things, Pick had never even stayed here.

And if he never stayed here, then where the hell did he go?

Like a pebble in a quiet pond, a sleeping pond. Pick is gone. Plop goes the pebble.

Mrs. Williamson walked Friedman to the front door.

45

Finally she arrived at Dr. Cubbage's apartment. Karin Ostrom didn't like cleaning there. These days it was always dark when she arrived. But his was the last apartment, and she'd be free when it was done.

She used her keys to open the door. Immediately she smelled something. Cubbage was always cooking strange things. He fancied himself a chef, she knew.

She stepped into the apartment and turned on the lights. The masks were waiting, their elongated heads looking weird.

She reluctantly shut the door behind her.

She'd vacuum first. Get that over with. Dr. Cubbage was a meticulous man; his bathroom was easy to clean.

The smell in the apartment was strong, rank.

Whatever he had been cooking, Karin Ostrom was sure that *she'd* never eat it.

They were talking snow on the radio, always snow in the mountains. The roads would all go to shit, and who the hell knew *when* they'd start plowing.

Ink looked out at the window, at the sky turning dark and mean. Maybe I'll build a fire, Ink thought. I'll do something to get the chill out of this place.

He thought of that kid in the gorge in New York State.

Bet he felt cold, Ink thought. Bet he froze his ass off down there while he was getting cut, while he watched.

Ink turned and looked at his phone. Suppose I call . . . Yeah, suppose I call and the cops don't catch him. And suppose he figures out that I'm the one who called them, 'cause—like, Christ, who else would know? Suppose he comes after me. . . .

Ink licked his lips. He couldn't take that, couldn't stand the pain.

But Ink knew what he had to do. The kid in New York was young, but they would get even younger. How am I going to feel then? Yeah, how will I feel when they start showing pictures on TV of little kids?

The last time, something had stopped the killer. Somehow he had disappeared. But now he was back. And this time, Ink thought, this time I have to do something.

He picked up the phone. He had called New York information; he had the number.

I won't give my name, Ink thought. No name . . . no number. None of that shit.

He rehearsed it inside his head, preparing himself.

A voice answered.

"State Police, Putnam County," the voice said. "Sergeant Scotto speaking."

"Sergeant," Ink said, feeling the wind cut through his drafty windows, listening to the small shrill whistle. Ink cleared his throat. "There was this kid killed, and—" Ink felt his mouth go dry.

"Yeah, go on."

Ink imagined the sergeant waving his hand, telling someone to trace this call, to find him, to get to the nut who was calling in. Ink hurried.

"He cut up this kid just like he did years ago. He was called the Meatman. It's the same guy; it's gotta be the same guy. His name is Donald Pick. *You got that?* He's Donald Pick."

"Hold on. Wait a minute. How do you know this? Where are you calling from?"

"Pick," Ink screamed. "That's all you need to know. You got to find him and stop him."

"But—"

Ink hung up. The kitchen was cold, cut by the tiny stream of icy air from the drafty window. Ink stood there shaking.

This time I did it, Ink thought. This time I did something.

He stood there a long time, shaking from fear, thinking that he actually *did something*.

Friedman stopped at a pay phone and tried calling Cubbage's number again. He let it ring seven times. Damn, maybe it was the wrong number.

Already bulletins were going out requesting the detention of one Donald Pick for parole violation. Friedman had added a note that Pick was also wanted for questioning in regard to homicide.

But what are the odds? he thought. What are the odds that someone will stop him, maybe in a stolen car or for running a light?

The odds are nil.

I'll go up there, he thought. I'll go to the college, see Cubbage. Ask him if this Pick character has any possibilities . . . ask him what are we dealing with here.

The streets were white, and the gray sky was turning an inky black.

Erin looked out the window. Her bare toes were touching the wood floor. Her mother's car backed out of the driveway. Erin watched the car stop at the street.

Mom said that real bad snow was coming. So she wanted to get milk and some other things.

"I'll be gone just a few minutes, sprout," she said.

Her dad hadn't come back from his meeting yet. Erin thought that maybe her mom was worried. Maybe she thought he wasn't going to come back.

Erin said it was okay, that she didn't mind being alone.

Erin waved. Then she coughed.

She didn't like being sick, and she didn't really like being alone.

But her mother's car hurried away, a big puff of smoke shooting from the back. There was no wave. She watched her mother drive away. The street was empty, the dark road the same color as the clouds, everything looking so gray, so unfriendly.

Through the icy coating on the window she looked across the street.

She saw someone over there, standing across the street. Funny, she thought. Where in the world had that man come from?

She grabbed the sleeve of her pajamas and wiped at the window. She coughed as she rubbed.

When she looked again the man was gone.

I saw someone. Over there behind that tree, right in front of the Hills' house. And now he's not there.

Erin's pajama sleeve was wet with flakes of ice.

I don't like being alone, she thought.

Erin put her face right up to the window.

He was watching us. He was watching our house.

Why would anyone watch our house?

And then—so quietly—Erin's door opened.

Karin Ostrom shut off the Electrolux. It took a few seconds for the powerful motor to come to a quiet stop.

It's definitely worse! Ostrom thought. The living room smelled real bad. And there was a big stain on the carpet. Did Dr. Cubbage have a party? Did someone spill something?

The smell was dizzying. But even at that—familiar.

There was carpet cleaner in the kitchen. Though the reddish-brown stain seemed to be ground in, she had to try to get some of it off.

She walked into the kitchen and switched on the light. She had hoped to clean the apartment up fast, a two-hour quickie, and now there was *this*.

She searched under the sink for the foamy carpet cleaner. She pulled it out.

She looked at the sink.

There was a stain there, too, a bit brighter, a bit less brown . . . a bit more red.

The sink was bone dry. Cubbage had been gone a week.

Her mouth went dry. She wanted something cool to drink—a soda, some juice. . . .

She opened the refrigerator. It was filled with heavy green plastic bags. Something sloshed out from the bottom, some red liquid.

She looked at the shelves, each filled with a plastic bag. Except . . .

One apparently had a leak. Because something was dripping from one of the bags.

She stepped back. She looked at the shelves, and she knew what was inside the plastic, what was making the smell, what was dripping onto the bottom of the refrigerator and running out onto the floor.

Because there was a hole. Something stuck out, gray-white. She saw a fingernail. She screamed and screamed, running out into the hall, past the masks looking glumly down at her.

Erin turned around quickly.

Her father was there. He stood at the doorway.

"How are you feeling?"

Erin walked away from the window. It was okay, she thought now. It's okay, my dad's here.

He'll watch out for me. . . .

She didn't look good. Simon took a step into the room, seeing Erin's dolls, her Barbies on her bed, and on the wall a poster of bears sitting around drinking tea.

I've lost so much, he thought. All those years, the things she learned, the times like this, when she was sick and wanted someone close by.

She came close to him.

"Shouldn't you be in bed? It's cold."

Erin looked back to the window as if she wanted to say something about it.

But then she turned back and smiled. The smile changed into a cough, and she hacked at the air.

"C'mon," Simon said. "Into bed." With his good hand, he pulled back the covers. One of the Barbies rolled over, falling onto Ken in a compromising way.

Erin snuggled into the bed and pushed her feet down.

"Daddy, sometimes I used to dream about you." Simon smiled. "I used to dream about what was happening to you. They weren't nice dreams."

Simon sat on the bed and brushed her hair off her forehead. She still felt warm.

"That's over, sweetheart. That's all over."

She smiled. "I'm glad. And I'm glad you're back."

Now it was Simon's turn to smile. He didn't tell her that he was going to leave, that he needed to leave.

He couldn't tell her.

Instead, he kissed her brow and then went out of the room.

Friedman got back onto the Saw Mill River Parkway. The traffic moved sluggishly as the falling snow stubbornly stuck. He felt the wheels of his car grow more wobbly by the second.

He was glad to get off the parkway at Route 117. Hudson College was only minutes away. The roads were dark because the streetlights hadn't flickered to life yet, as if they didn't know it was winter. It was already dark by 4:00 P.M.

A large truck, dwarfing the two-lane highway, barreled past Friedman. In the truck's headlights Friedman saw the swirling snow turning icy on the road—a trap waiting for a bald tire or someone gunning a car too much.

Clumps of older, dirty snow caught the scant light, more slippery smears of ice. It was so damn dark, hard to see. . . .

I'm getting old. Bad night vision. He felt so damn tired. . . .

He reached the gate to the college. Twin concrete slabs stood on either side of the entrance. Big block letters announced Hudson College. There was a security guard, his little hut just to the side, next to a speed bump.

A black sports car came out, flashing its headlights at Friedman, and then roared away. Friday night. Party time, except for the gigundo storm.

Friedman pulled into the entrance as big clumps of snow fought his windshield wipers.

Bethany Clarke waved the donut in the air. She felt a light dusting of white sugar on her lips and swiped at it with her tongue, tasting the sweetness, laughing, telling a story to the other women.

"So he's kneeling, naked as a jaybird, like he's presenting the crown jewels or some shit." She laughed along with the other girls. "And he inches closer on the bed, his eyes all hot and dark and steamed up. Whew, was he steamed up! And he came closer, holding himself in his hand like he's going to write his name with his dick or something."

More laughter. The cafeteria was nearly deserted. People who lived out of the city had left already, but Clarke just lived a subway ride away. She was enjoying her last coffee break before the weekend.

"And my mouth is open because I'm *laughing* at this big dude. And I say to him, 'Get that thing out of my face.'"

Her voice was loud; she didn't care who heard her story. "Get it the *fuck* out of my face. If you're going to do anything with it, mister, you're going to stick it where it belongs or get the *fuck* off my bed!"

Jasmine, her girlfriend, a keyboardist from the fourth floor, was doubled over.

Bethany liked telling stories.

"Too much, babe. You're too much," Jasmine said.

Clarke looked at the clock. The break had already gone on for too long, not that anyone was watching. Not that anyone gave a damn.

"Got to split, girls." Bethany got up from the table, carrying

her tray with the empty coffee cup and donut wrapper over to the
cubicle where the Latino kitchen staff lived.

They made sounds at her. She was twice as tall as any of them,
and these little runty guys with thin mustaches made lip-smacking
noises.

Shit, she thought. I could do some dwarf tossing with them.

She took the elevator up to the third floor and walked to the
office, past rows of computers. Some people were gone, and
others were taking it easy, talking, letting the minutes slip by.

She sat down. You weren't supposed to smoke here. There were
signs: No Smoking Except in Designated Areas. But Clarke pulled
out a tinfoil ashtray and a pack of Merits. She tapped out a
cigarette. Who the hell would know?

She put the cigarette in her mouth and lit it. Through the bluish
haze, she saw a small box flashing on her CRT screen.

A message was coming in from one of the networks. Usually
they just got dumped in with the day's E-Mail for sorting and
delivering. It was no big deal.

Unless it was flagged. Unless whoever put it out, in whatever
network it was on, flagged it, like this one.

Important.

Needing immediate attention.

It didn't happen all that often. She hit the F9 key. And the
message appeared. . . .

46

Lizbeth came in carrying a brown bag. She shifted the groceries in her arms. She looked up and saw Simon walking downstairs.

"Where were you?" he said.

"I needed to get some things. There's a storm coming."

She watched him pass her and walk to the hall closet.

"How did it go? Your meeting with the psychologist."

Simon turned and smiled. "Just great. He said it sounded like I had a *wonderful* time over there." He got out his coat and put it on.

"What are you doing? Where are you going?"

Lizbeth still held the groceries, still clung to the bag, to the normalcy of picking up some milk and eggs.

"He wants to speak with you. You and Erin. I—I don't think I should be here when he arrives." He looked at her then. "I'm going to go someplace."

Lizbeth shook her head. "No. Simon, it's getting bad out. Please . . . don't go."

He walked to the door. "He's coming here later." Simon opened the door and walked out.

"Simon," she called.

He shut the door behind him.

Lizbeth stood there, holding the groceries, listening for the sound of the car and, from upstairs, the sound of Erin coughing and calling for her.

"I wish I could help you." The security guard had the fake-fur collar of his jacket pulled up against the cold. He had a small black-and-white TV in his cubicle. Friedman felt the warmth of a space heater jacked up high.

He had hoped that the guard could direct him to the house that Cubbage was using.

"We get lots of visitors, a lot of lecturers at the college. Yes, sir, and there are a lot of guesthouses."

A red Ford pulled up to the speed bump, braking noisily. The car passed the guard, eased over the bumps, and gunned away.

"Lots of visitors come here. I can't tell you about this fellow, though, this Dr.—"

"Cubbage."

The guard shrugged. "Could be he's here. I mean, you say he's here and all. So he could be. But I don't recall the name. I suggest you try the registrar's office on Monday. They're all closed down now, with the storm watch and all. Everyone's heading home."

The flakes had gained strength. Friedman put his windshield wipers on high to push away the heavy snow.

Damn, maybe this was going to be a real storm. And won't that make getting back to Brooklyn a lot of fun? "I can't wait until Monday."

The guard backed away. "Sorry." He shrugged, dismissing Friedman. "Nothing more I can tell you."

Friedman got out of the warm car. His ears tingled from the cold.

"Hey, you can't leave your car here, buddy!"

Friedman came close to the burly guard. He held the folders tight in his ice-chilled fingers. He had the dean's name in here somewhere. With his other hand he pulled out his badge.

The guard looked at it.

"New York City?" the guard said. "You've come a long way."

Friedman spoke quietly. "I need your help. Will you help me?"

"But I've already told you. I don't know where Dr. Cubbage is staying."

Friedman tried to dig out the dean's name. He couldn't find the paper. Shit. Now what the hell do I do? I'm so tired I can barely stand. Cold, tired. Beat.

The folder fell from his hands. The folder, the notes, the pile of photos, all tumbled down to the white ground, snow quickly covering them.

The guard bent down to help him gather the odd pieces of paper and collect the photos.

The guard stood up. "Hey. Wait a sec. Yeah."

Friedman looked at the guard. He was holding some pages and a photo. "Hey, I know this guy." The guard tapped the photo. "Sure, I remember him. He was a real friendly guy. He was looking for one of the guesthouses too."

Friedman stopped, felt a chill, an icy breeze cut through his coat; What is this? What the hell?

I'm looking for Cubbage, and now . . .

The guard handed him the photo. "Sure, I've seen this guy here."

Friedman took back the photo of Donald Pick.

He took a breath, and he asked a question. "You know where he is?"

What did Pick come here for? To do what? Friedman wondered. To find Cubbage? To find the little psychologist and do what?

The guard smiled. "Sure do. Gave him directions myself the other day, like I said, to one of the houses."

Erin came downstairs for dinner.

She looked better, Lizbeth thought. Despite the cough, the horrible hacking that made her whole body spasm, she looked better.

I have to explain. I have to tell her that a man is coming who will help Daddy, help us.

Erin picked at her ravioli. "I'm not hungry," she said, looking up at her mother. "Where's Daddy? Where did he go?"

Lizbeth poured Erin some more milk. "He went out for a while, honey. Just a bit. He'll be back." Lizbeth made herself smile. "But a man is coming to talk to me . . . and you."

Erin's face scrunched up. "What does he want to talk to me for?"

Lizbeth took a breath. "To explain how your daddy feels, how we can help him."

"You mean I'm not helping him?"

Lizbeth shook her head. "Oh, honey, we're doing fine. This man will just—I don't know—talk to us."

Erin looked away. "I wish Daddy was here," Erin said. "I want him to stay here."

"Yes," Lizbeth said. She was about to say something else when the doorbell rang. . . .

* * *

Clarke read the message again and then printed it out. It was short, only one page long. Friedman has to see this, she thought. Shit, Friedman has *got* to see this. I can't just leave it here.

It was five o'clock, quitting time. The office was almost deserted. Big fluffy snowflakes swirled past her window, catching the light.

She called Communications, and they put her through to his car radio. She waited for Friedman to answer. Goddamn, she thought, pick up your radio.

She lit another cigarette, waiting to speak with Friedman.

He looked at the house, such a strange-looking ranch house, with a stone foundation and brownish-black logs.

There were no lights on.

Was Cubbage in there? Had Pick found him? Or was Cubbage safe at home in the city.

Friedman got out of the car and looked at the house again, the empty house. No lights on anywhere. So no one was home, right?

Not necessarily. He started up the walkway, his feet crunching on the snow, dry now, piling up. . . .

And what do we have here? he thought. The snow stuck to Friedman's coat, dusted his hair. He took a step toward the house, another. What the hell do we have here?

Friedman walked up the steps to the wooden porch. He rang the bell, waited, and then knocked.

Not a creature stirring, he thought. He walked to one side of the porch and pressed his face against the window, almost expecting a strange face to whip away the curtains and say boo!—nose to nose with him.

"Hello? Dr. Cubbage?" Friedman whispered.

Then he sang out the words. Abbott and Costello meet the Killer.

"Anybody home?" Anybody the fuck home? Well, boys and girls, I guess there's no one home. I guess the manse is empty. Friedman walked to the front door. He looked over his shoulder. For a second he thought someone was watching him.

But the nearest house was a couple of hundred yards away, shielded by somber pine trees quickly turning white.

Friedman looked at the lock, then dug out his wallet. Might as well use the Visa card, he thought. I've reached my credit limit, so it'll be a bit of useless plastic for a while.

He wedged the card between the door and the frame. He fiddled with the plastic card, his fingers cold, cramped. He looked over his shoulder again.

A truck roared past. Big headlights sent shadows scurrying across the lawn. Friedman froze for a second. I don't want the truck driver stopping, wondering, Hey, bub, what the hell are you doing?

He acted as if he was fumbling for his key. Yup, just going to let myself in here. Gotta find my damn key.

The truck passed. The card slid in another half inch. Friedman levered it to the left and heard a click.

And the front door was unlocked.

He was inside. Behind him, the sound of his car radio was muffled by the closed doors and the blanket of snow.

47

The inside of this guesthouse owned by Hudson College was, if anything, even gloomier than its exterior. Friedman didn't turn on any lights.

Let's not advertise that I'm here. He took a penlight out of his coat pocket. It wasn't much, but it would help him explore.

He heard a clock tick. A big thunk, and another minute sludged by, inside this cheery house. *Do I have time?* he wondered. *What's the time situation here?*

He turned on the penlight, but instead of a sharp, thin stream of light, there was a dull yellow glow, growing weaker by the second.

Maybe time was running out.

He started his tour by turning right, with his tiny light, laughable amid so much bleakness. He walked into a room that looked like an office. There was a desk, some chairs, a bookcase, a wall of empty shelves. The desk top was clean, Spartan.

Not exactly loaded with clues.

Thunk! Another minute plodded by. He walked to the desk. His penlight was little better than the ambient light. Only if he held real close to something did it do anything at all.

He opened a side drawer. There were yellow pads, a scattering of pens. The drawer below it held a phone directory. He opened the center drawer.

There was a notepad. Friedman put down the penlight and flipped through the pages, all of them blank.

He felt the top of the pad for an impression, the residue of a message, a phone number, an address. . . . *Something to tell me where the hell you are, Cubbage.*

It was perfectly smooth.

That leaves upstairs, he thought. For me and my little penlight. Maybe I'll get lucky. . . .

Simon drove around the town. He felt the car going sloppy, drunkenly sliding on the slippery roads.

He thought of a newspaper headline: "Ex-hostage Killed in Car Crash. Family Better Off."

He drove down Main Street in Harley. The Christmas lights still dangled from one street lamp to the next, bright white lights that made the falling snow look unreal, like a stage effect.

He slowed for a light and felt the Taurus skid to the right. I'm out of practice, Simon thought. I'm out of practice with a lot of things, with being a husband, with being a father. Maybe it's not like riding a bike. Maybe you can't just get back on and do it again.

He looked to his left and saw a bar. There were shiny foil letters on the window: Merry Xmas.

The holiday from hell, all the talk about Baby Jesus, the music, the sentimental movies.

It's a Wonderful Life. Now there's a dad who lost it. He left his family, didn't he?

But he got it back.

He got it back.

Someone came out of the bar, starting the weekend early, stumbling, slipping in the snow, on the sidewalk that seemed to angle down, straight to the river.

The light changed. Simon watched the man. Thinking about him and about Jimmy Stewart standing on a bridge, looking into the icy water, wanting to jump from the bridge, needing to jump, until an angel showed him that he was needed . . . that he was important.

Simon was crying.

There's no angel to do that for me, he thought. No one—

A horn blasted behind him. He took his foot off the brake.

Shit . . .

Bethany Clarke stubbed her cigarette out in the yellow foil ashtray. She heard someone vacuuming the next office.

She had to tell Friedman what they'd found in Cubbage's apartment.

What they'd found in the refrigerator, in the freezer. The clumps of hair in the bathtub. The stains on the rug, on the wood floor, even on the masks.

One of the cops at the scene had freaked. He said the apartment looked like a butcher shop.

It was getting dark. There was a blizzard outside. Bethany wanted to go home. She wanted to get away from the office, from the murder.

But Friedman wasn't answering his radio.

Clarke dug out another cigarette and waited.

Friedman went up the stairs. The carpet, once thick and luxurious, seemed to tug at his feet with loose threads. Every step was a thrill for his bad knee. Each step turned up the juice a bit more.

I should call the locals in, Friedman thought. Let them know I'm here. Let them know that Donald Pick, recently of Sing Sing, has been looking for his old psychologist.

And you don't want Donald Pick looking for you.

It took forever to reach the top of the stairs. There was absolutely no light. He thought about finding a switch. *I've got to see. . . .*

He took a few more steps. The smell was musty, a smell of old wood, old people.

There was a door to his left; he could make out its outline. He hoped no one was on the other side.

He grabbed the doorknob and twisted it.

Lucky me, he thought. It's unlocked.

He walked in. There was a bit more light in this room. The whitish glow of a street lamp was able to sneak through the curtains. He saw a rumpled bed. A small suitcase. A shirt on a chair. It looked dirty.

There were blackish stains on it.

There were some papers on a small end table. Friedman walked to the table and sat down on the bed. His penlight showed signs that it was dying. The light started to fade completely. Friedman gave it a vicious shake.

"That'll teach you," he said. He hoped speaking would take away some of the eeriness, the feeling that this was a house of ghouls about to come to life and drag him down to some cannibalistic feast in the basement.

Mrs. Bates's meat pies . . .

The penlight struggled to stay on. He held it close to the papers.

There were gasoline receipts, all signed by Cubbage. A business card—Dr. Lane Cubbage, Psychologist, Ph.D., A.P.A., and—

Friedman stopped. He heard something downstairs. He touched his gun, a reflex. It felt safe and warm there, under his arm. Yeah, and it makes *me* feel safe and warm.

He pushed the business card away. There was a small pad beneath it. He picked it up. His trusty penlight, the sickening little flashlight, so close to the card, almost kissing it, caught *something*.

On the pad. There were bumps, lines . . . an impression. Friedman picked up the pad. He tilted it one way, the other, trying to make out the words.

He took a pencil from his pocket. It had only a blunt stub of a point, and he rubbed the dull side of the point on the pad, back and forth, back and forth. . . .

The penlight caught the letters as they appeared.

A street address: Gaheney Road. And directions. There was another sound from below. The click of the boiler going on, the sudden whoosh of heat.

He had the address. Maybe Cubbage went there . . . unless Pick got him . . . unless the Meatman got him first.

Friedman dropped his light. He bent slowly and picked it up. There was nothing he could do to get it to go on again.

Dead is dead, he thought. . . .

Lizbeth opened the door. The man who stood there, under the white light, was not at all what she'd expected. He was younger and taller, with shaggy sandy colored hair and a bright smile.

"Mrs. Farrell?" he said. "I'm Lane Cubbage."

"Yes, come in," she said. "My husband said you'd be coming."

The man passed her, and Lizbeth looked out at the snow, so thick now, big dry flakes piling up.

"My husband . . ." She turned, but the psychologist had already moved into the house. Almost too freely, she thought, the way he walked up the steps to the landing, right next to the kitchen and the living room.

Lizbeth hurried to follow him.

Erin still sat at the kitchen table, her plate of ravioli in front of her, ignored.

"This must be Erin," the man said, turning to Lizbeth. "Your daughter."

The man seemed pleased to see Erin. His voice sounded—what? Happy, she thought. She watched him looking around.

"Your house is . . ." His eyes locked on the Christmas tree. The lights were off. He stopped and stared at the tree.

Lizbeth waited. She heard him take a deep breath, like a man with a lot to say . . . or a lot to do. . . .

The joy, the intense pleasure, vanished.

Just like *that*. Pick had felt the excitement, and then he saw the tree, the goddamn tree.

Memories were bad things. He couldn't really enjoy the Work if he was preoccupied with bad things, *old* things. He chewed at his cheeks, sucking in the skin and biting down. Only a bit, only enough to cause a little feeling—*there*. . . .

The tree was skeletal, with some stupid lopsided ornaments hanging from its branches.

Christmas. That was when it had happened. She'd started in on Patty, with the clothespins, pinning them on her body, saying she had to be punished. She was a bad little girl, and bad girls needed to be punished.

His mother went and got things. Donny stood by his little sister. She was crying, frozen by fear. He listened for his mother. She got things out of drawers.

Patty had broken some ornaments on the tree. She had to be punished.

Donny saw something gleam in his mother's hand when she came back. Not for me, he thought. God, please—that's not for me.

But she grabbed Donny by his hair and then seized Patty. She grabbed them both in the back. Had it been snowing that night? Or was there just old snow on the ground?

They had been in their underwear.

She threw them both outside.

She shut the door and screamed at them: "It's locked. You'll never come back. I don't want you."

He cried, and Patty came close to him, shivering. It was so cold. His mother watched them from a window.

He didn't notice, till then, that his mother had given him something shiny. A knife. Patty shivered.

They huddled together, trying to keep away the cold.

And Donny had a shiny knife.

• • •

"My husband . . . I'm sorry, but Simon isn't here."

The psychologist turned around as if her words had pulled him away from something. He looked angry. "I wanted to see all of you together. That was the idea."

Lizbeth nodded. "I know. But he's very upset. Couldn't you just talk with Erin and me?"

He looked away, from the dining room to the living room, to the tree. . . .

"Yes," he said, "but please, not here. In the living room . . . by the tree. We'll be more comfortable there."

Lizbeth called to her daughter.

48

"Please," he said. "Please, sit."

Dr. Cubbage sat close to Erin. He patted the child's knee and smiled at her.

He makes himself at home, Lizbeth thought. What a strange man, to sit there, looking so relaxed.

"I'm worried about my husband."

The psychologist nodded and smiled. "I'm sure he's fine. Don't you think so?"

What an odd question, she thought. Of course I don't. "No. I'm worried about him. Can you tell me what's going through his mind?"

Then she saw the man turn very slowly from her to Erin. He looked at Erin. He spoke to Erin.

"He's very sad. He's very confused." He snapped his eyes back to Lizbeth. "You'll have to help him, you know. Both of you."

"Mommy," Erin said. Her voice was hoarse and raspy. "My throat hurts."

Lizbeth sat down next to her, touched her cheek. "I'll get you some Tylenol."

The psychologist touched Lizbeth's hand. His hand was big—a strong hand, more like a laborer's hand, than a head doctor's.

"Yes, do that," he said. "And then—"he smiled at Lizbeth—"would you leave me alone with Erin for a few minutes?"

Lizbeth shook her head. "Alone? Why do you—"

"Just for a few minutes. It will help me—to hear what she thinks, what she might be scared of. . . ."

Lizbeth chewed her lip. She nodded and got up to get the medicine.

Clarke was breathless, her voice high-pitched, excited, over the top.

Friedman listened.

She described what the police had found in Cubbage's apartment, and Friedman could imagine what the place looked like, all covered with blood, the kitchen stained, the refrigerator filled with plastic bags, one holding Cubbage's head, another a chunky leg.

Friedman stopped her.

"I'm going to this address." He gave her the Gaheney Drive address. "Maybe Pick is staying there. Or maybe someone else. It might be nothing, but get the local cops there as soon as you can."

Maybe they'll beat me there, he thought. He signed off on the radio and started the car.

He followed the directions, down Route 134 to the suburban cul-de-sac. When he got there, he didn't see any police cars.

I'm all alone, he thought. . . .

Lizbeth gave Erin the Tylenol and a sip of orange juice. Cubbage smiled at her, then nodded, indicating that she should slip away, upstairs.

Lizbeth went to her bedroom. She sat on the edge of the bed watching a game show, watching someone spin a big wheel and pick letters.

Suddenly she heard a scream, shrill, unreal. Erin screamed for her.

"Mommy!"

Lizbeth stood up, and a dozen possibilities went rushing through her head, all these *possibilities*.

Erin fell, she skinned her knee, she dropped her juice, something scared her on TV.

But other possibilities occurred to Lizbeth as she stepped to the door, opened it, hurried down the hall.

She thought of this man, and she recalled the stories on the news of people who did bad things, monsters who get families and children.

She hurried along the hall, running, calling Erin's name, yelling it. "Erin!"

She'd forgotten about the bat she kept by the bed to protect her daughter.

She ran down the stairs . . .

And stopped.

"Mommy!" Erin screeched. She was in a chair, and the man had bound her body with silver tape, around and around, pinning her to the chair.

The phone. *Jesus, the phone,* she thought. So close. I can get to the kitchen, pick it up, hit 911.

She took a step.

"Don't," he said.

She was still moving, still heading toward the kitchen and the blue wall phone—the same phone she used to check on a Brownie meeting, to ask about ballet class, to call the school nurse. So close, and the man said, "Don't."

Lizbeth turned and saw that the man had a knife in his hand. He held it against Erin's neck.

"Oh, God . . ."

He spoke quietly, still the psychologist, so thoughtful and quiet. "Another step, and I will have to cut her."

His words implied that there was a chance that he wouldn't cut her. If she didn't go to the phone, he wouldn't cut Erin.

She stopped moving.

Erin was crying, screaming. Perhaps someone would hear.

But it was winter, and the house was shut tight. . . .

Friedman had trouble seeing the numbers of the houses on Gaheney Drive. The numbers on the mailboxes seemed to jump by tens, from 21 to 31. He didn't see 32 anywhere.

The houses all looked the same, low-slung ranches, a few lights on in each.

Probably nothing here, he thought. Probably only an address left over from someone who stayed at the house before, or someone who was invited over for dinner.

Friedman looked left and right, and saw a house with a driveway leading to a garage. He saw the number on the front door, number 32.

There was a car in the driveway, and there were lights on.

Friedman slowed, listening for sirens. It had only been minutes, and he expected the police to be here. He stopped his car and opened his door.

He didn't hear sirens. He heard something else.

There was a chair facing Erin's chair. The man pointed to it. The blue phone seemed miles away now.

"Sit down," he said quietly. "If you sit down—"

"Mommeee!"

"Nothing will happen to either of you."

Lizbeth shook her head. "Please don't do anything to my little girl. Please. I can give you money, anything—"

But she knew that this man didn't want money. Erin's screams were like ice picks in Lizbeth's brain, goading her to do *something*. Then Erin started coughing and her screaming stopped.

"Sit *down*," he said.

Lizbeth sat down. She searched for a way out, a way to end this. There was only one way.

Simon will come back. Simon, with his bad leg, and his busted hand, and . . .

Oh, sweet God.

"Close your eyes."

Lizbeth shook her head. No, I can't close my eyes. I can't, I can't.

He pressed the blade to Erin's neck.

"Ow," her baby cried. And then, without a word of warning, without saying anything, the man moved his wrist. A tiny red line appeared on Erin's neck.

"No!" Lizbeth howled, and the man smiled. He liked that sound. Lizbeth stood up, shouting, crying, thinking, My baby, *my baby*.

"Sit down," he said, ordering her.

Lizbeth froze. It was only a thin cut, a warning, she told herself. Just a warning. I can't scream again. I can't—

Erin sobbed, begging, "Mommy, please, Mommy, help me."

"Close your eyes," the man said.

Lizbeth took a breath and shut her eyes. Her lids fluttered, letting in a little light. "Don't cut her again, please. Whatever—"

She heard steps. The man had moved away from Erin, closer to Lizbeth. She heard the tearing sound of tape, the silver tape.

He's going to kill us, Lizbeth knew.

She opened her eyes. The man held the blade and the tape end in one hand and was pressing close to her.

Lizbeth stood up. She pushed at him.

But that was silly, he was so strong. She felt his muscles. His body unmovable.

He dropped the tape to the floor. "You bitch," he said. "You stupid bitch."

Lizbeth felt something warm in her midsection, a sting, like a paper cut, and warmth there, wet and—

She took a step. She fell, groaning, grunting, to the floor. Erin was still screaming.

Lizbeth's hands went to her midsection, fluttered over the wound, taking its measure, assessing the damage, feeling the river of blood flow out of her.

Friedman heard something from inside the house.

The TV is on, he thought. Some movie. That's all. Screaming and—

He got out of the car. He patted his gun. He limped up the walkway. He saw a yellow ribbon on a tree.

He took another ungainly step.

For Desert Storm, he thought. The ribbon was kind of old.

Another step, and he heard a new sound, a new scream.

Lizbeth screamed as loud as she could, even though it made the pain much worse.

"Help. Somebody, help!"

The man turned to her. Her yells didn't seem to upset him. He seemed relaxed, calm. He had done this before. He knew what he was doing, and he had no reason to worry, none at all.

He took a step toward her. He crouched down close.

He shook his head. "No. You have to watch. Don't make so much noise. Just watch."

He brought the knife around in front of him. Lizbeth went cross-eyed looking at it, looking at the blade stained with her blood, with Erin's blood.

She shook her head and tried to speak. She didn't want to die. But even more than that, more than anything, she didn't want Erin to die . . . to feel any pain.

"No noise," he said. And he stuck the blade in Lizbeth's mouth. She tasted the blood. Her tongue recoiled from the razor-sharp blade. But the man quickly jerked the knife left and right, cutting her lips, cutting into the muscles.

The pain made Lizbeth choke. Her mouth filled with blood. She spit it out, and the man stood up.

She watched him, shaking her head, trying to get the blood out of her mouth.

Now when she tried to beg, to scream, all she did was sputter. "Mnn . . . mmmm . . ."

She thought, *My baby. My girl.*

He stood by Erin. He held the blade against her face. He giggled. He laughed.

In slow motion he rested the blade against Erin's cheek. The man turned, making sure that Lizbeth was watching. That was important, making sure . . .

He pressed down. . . .

The Work was here, and everything was so bright. Everything was filled with a wonderful warmth and brightness. It's not only the blood, Pick thought. It's where I take them. We journey together, past the limits of human senses.

Mary taught me that. She showed me where we could go.

We become lovers.

We become family.

The little girl sang her song of pain. Pick cut slowly while the woman, the mother bubbled next to him, little red foamy bubbles popping out of her mouth.

He thought of the pattern he'd use, of a design, something to express the beauty of the Work.

Perhaps, he thought, I can cut around the child's face, then peel the skin away while the girl screams.

Perhaps . . .

Lizbeth saw the cut on Erin's face. Her eyes were locked on her daughter's eyes, locked in this horror. Sick moans belched forth from Lizbeth.

She was trying to say the word, to comfort Erin.

My baby, she was trying to say.

But all she could do was watch.

49

Friedman stood by the door. The screams had stopped. The windows were high and covered with curtains.

I can wait, I can wait for the town police to show up, he thought. He looked at his watch. Four minutes. It hasn't been so long, only—

He heard another scream.

His breath stopped. That's not TV, he thought. He reached out and tried the door knob. It turned a bit and then stopped, locked.

The scream, a child's voice.

"Oh, God," Friedman said. He pulled out his gun and fired at the lock, then kicked open the door and hurried into the house as best he could.

Maybe I'll get blown away again, he thought. Maybe this is another stupid move.

But there, above him, in the living room, he saw a little girl, and he heard something bubbling.

The little girl was bleeding. She'd been cut. Her eyes were wide, and she was saying something to Friedman.

What is she trying to say? Friedman thought, hurrying up the steps to her. He saw a woman on the floor facing the girl in the chair. Her face and body were a mess of blood. "Oh, God."

The girl was still yelling, but he couldn't really understand her. But then he heard.

"No . . . noooo. Be—be—be—"

"I'll get you out," Friedman said. While he thought, *Be . . . be . . . behind—*

He turned around, and there was Donald Pick.

• • •

Pick had expected Simon. He had checked out the window when he heard the car pull up to the house.

That would have been good.

But this wasn't good. He slashed at the man with the gun, cutting his hand, his wrist. Then another slash, coming back, and this time he dug the blade into the cop's gut, twisting it.

The cop's gun flew into space.

The man fell to the floor.

Now, Pick thought, now there would be others.

He turned to the girl.

Friedman tried to get to his knees, but something kept pulling him back to the floor. He started gagging, then heaving, though nothing came out.

He heard a cutting noise. He looked up, expecting to see the little girl being cut, quickly, while Pick hurried.

Instead he saw Pick cutting the tape away, ripping it roughly off the hysterical girl.

He looked for his gun. It had slid away . . . so far away. Sirens, thought Friedman. Where the hell are the local cops?

"The police are coming," Friedman said. "You won't get away."

He saw the woman, the little girl's mother, looking at him. Her mouth was a red bloom. Flaps of skin hung loose, leeching out of her mouth.

Her eyes spoke to Friedman, begging. . . .

"You won't get away," Friedman said again.

Pick ignored him. Grunting, he pulled off the last of the tape and grabbed the girl. He picked up Friedman's gun from the floor and started for the front door.

Friedman heard them then, the sirens, sounding faint, in the distance.

C'mon, Friedman thought. C'mon!

Pick stopped and turned to look down at the door leading to the backyard.

Friedman tried to stand again, and once more he fell to the floor, only feet away from the woman.

They looked at each other. Then the woman looked away.

Lizbeth took a labored breath. She blinked and wondered how much time had gone by.

She could turn her head. The hooks were quiet, the thousand hooks in her stomach. If she didn't move, they were quiet.

She turned her head and looked to her left. The man held Erin like a piece of lumber. She saw the man's hands in plastic gloves, holding her tight, moving down to the den.

He's taking her out in back, she thought. He's taking her out to the woods and the lake.

She heard the sirens.

Lizbeth tried to move. She tried to push herself up. How does it go? Push up with your arms. Your knees. Get into a crouch.

She couldn't move. She couldn't even feel her arms.

But she tried to move her lips.

''My baby, my baby, my baby.''

There were woods in the back, and a lake. I can cut across the lake, Pick thought. I can disappear.

The little girl kicked, and Pick squeezed her tight, squeezing the air out of her. She groaned like a sick animal.

Pick ran through the den, pushed open the sliding door to the backyard, and then ran toward the woods and the frozen lake.

Lizbeth forced her eyes open. The detective's eyes were shut. Maybe he's dead, she thought.

She felt sleepy, as if she had the flu, as if she wanted to crawl into bed, curl up under the covers, and sleep forever . . . to make this nightmare go away.

She opened her eyes because someone was standing there. The sirens still sounded so far away. . . .

She raised her head. The blood in her mouth was gummy, like phlegm. She tried to spit it out.

She craned her head up.

Lizbeth saw Simon.

50

She saw horror on Simon's face. It's me, she felt she should say. It's *me*—Lizbeth.

She spit, and stuff dripped from her lip. The hooks pulled at her insides. How much blood can you lose? How much?

"Heg rook . . . genin." The words didn't make it.

She tried again, opening her sliced mouth wider, trying to shape the words with her tongue.

Simon's face filled with horror. Is this worse than being a hostage? Please. Run after Erin. Please. I need you. If it hasn't been hours since he left, if it's not—

Then—miraculously—there was a gift. A gift, undeserved, surely, undeserved. Simon crouched down close, close to her. He touched her cheek. "I'll get help," he said. "An ambulance, and—"

She shook her head violently. She felt great rips bloom in her middle. The pain, a white light, exploded in front of her eyeballs, white, searing. "No," she said, the word almost clear. She spit as she talked, and something dripped out her mouth. "Heg . . . he's . . . ga . . . ga . . . got . . . her."

Simon didn't move. There was no reaction. God, don't make me say it again. I can't, I can't. Then, slowly, looking at him, she said, "Er-in."

Simon stood up.

Lizbeth was dying.

That was how people looked when they died. The eyes went dull. There was so much blood. A hellhole. Someone had turned Simon's home into a hellhole.

He had left this, escaped this—and someone had brought it here.

He went outside and down the stairs, feeling the cold air, frigid, frosty, already seeing clouds of water vapor erupting from his mouth. He hurried, running, ignoring the pain.

He tripped on the metal guide rail of the sliding doors, and he banged down hard. His knees smashed to the tiny cement patio outside the doors, the patio covered by a thin layer of ice.

When he looked up, he saw them. A man carrying his little girl out to the lake.

On the other side of the lake Simon saw the black hills, a forest, filled with places to hide. Black hills, all those dark trees over there, with places to hide.

That's what he's thinking.

But they'll never reach it.

Never . . .

Some of the little girl's blood dripped into his hand. The ice groaned, and Pick lost his footing. His left leg slipped.

When he turned, he saw someone following, someone who was having trouble walking.

The girl kicked at him. More blood dripped onto his hand.

Pick sucked in the cold air, so cold. . . .

It had been cold the night he and Patty huddled together. Pick had held the cold knife in his hand. His mother looked out the window at them, scowling.

There was a frost on the uncut lawn, and his sister had screamed while their mother watched, mad, shrieking.

"You did this," Donny said to his sister, and he touched Patty's skin with the point of the knife. "You did this," he said.

You did this!

Donny Pick had felt warmth, a funny kind of warmth, while Patty tried to squirm away, screaming now, kicking and pulling away.

But Donny held her, making the blade touch her tiny T-shirt, cutting through, to the skin. Warm, warmer, and . . . he felt close to his mother then.

They were together in this.

When she finally let them in, Patty had only a few cuts on her. Nothing major . . . no big deal.

And who could the little girl tell? Who could she complain to?

In six months she was dead, her intestine perforated by a wire scrubbing brush.

And that, that they had done together. . . .

Simon saw them on the ice.

He pushed past the naked branches of the pine trees. His foot smashed against rocks hidden by a frosty dusting of icy snow.

Simon reached the edge.

The ice is going to open up and swallow them. And there's no way I can catch him.

He stepped on the ice, and his foot slipped. He hurried, ignoring the sick way his leg wobbled.

Got to keep taking steps without falling.

The ice made a sound underneath him, a slow, low note. It can't hold, he thought. It's going to eat them up.

Simon yelled her name, his voice hoarse. "Erin!"

The ice isn't strong enough. He took more steps, and each one was answered with new groans. And then, on one step, there was a crack, a voice protesting his trespassing.

He ignored it.

He didn't have gloves on, and his good hand was curled, frozen. But he kept moving toward the two blackish shapes.

The little girl didn't have a coat on.

Her body felt so tiny, so small. Pick squeezed her hard, real hard, to make sure that she didn't slip away, that he didn't lose this treasure.

We're nearly halfway across the lake, he thought. Halfway.

The police were probably at the house, looking around, busy.

This is better.

We can get lost in the woods, in the trails. I'm good at that. . . .

After I've finished with her.

He looked over his shoulder and saw that someone was still following. Maybe it's him, Pick thought. Maybe it's *Daddy.*

He ignored the groans, the creaks, of the ice.

The cracking noises. . . .

Please, Simon prayed. The ice moaned, a living thing bellowing out an ancient warning: *Stop. Don't go any farther.*

"Erin!" He thought he saw her turn her head, he thought. He

saw her pull against the arm that held her. He hurried, panting, gulping the icy air.

Then there was a crack, clear, like a rifle shot, the sound of ice breaking. . . .

The man and the child disappeared as the lake swallowed them.

51

The ice was deserted, as if the vision of Erin and the man had been a dream, now faded, leaving only Simon.

He kept moving. Please, God. Please let me get there in time.

He saw the black hole and arms popping up. The ice below his own feet grumbled at his steps.

An airplane passed overhead. A jet flying high, the giant engines whispering above the sound of the wind. He heard the hum of traffic, the cars on 9A.

"Erin!"

There was no answer at first. But then he heard her cry out, such a sweet noise. A cry, a scream. Closer now, Simon saw the dark shapes bobbing around in the just-opened hole.

Simon kicked at the ice, and slid, stumbling. He unbuttoned his coat. It will eat me too, he thought. The lake will swallow me. . . .

Closer, and he saw Erin grab the jagged lip of the hole. But the man pulled her away and pushed her under the water. He was holding her under.

Simon inched forward. "Let her go! God, please, let her go."

I'm begging again. Always begging . . .

Erin popped up, sputtering, her eyes closed. She was freezing, dying.

Simon stepped forward, getting his coat ready to throw to Erin. Closer . . . The ice creaked and then, with horrible suddenness, cracked, and Simon slid into the water, next to his little girl, next to the man.

The freezing water squeezed the air out of his body.

I know pain. There's nothing new here.

He grabbed Erin while he kicked at the water, trying to stay afloat. He pushed her close to the edge of the large hole.

He whispered to her, not even sure that she could hear. "I'm going to lift you up and"—the last word caught in his chest—"ou-out."

But he felt a hand on his shoulder, pushing him down, and he had to let go of Erin.

A foot kicked at him, forcing more air out, and he sucked in some of the water, tasting it, cold and foul.

He bobbed up again.

Erin's head was dipping under the water. Simon moved next to her. He felt the deadweight of his shoes, his wet clothes.

He grabbed her hair and yanked her head up. Erin's mouth opened as soon as she was above the water. Simon hurried. He got his good hand under her while digging his broken claw into the ice at the edge. He pushed up. Erin's body surged up, nearly out, but then she slid back in.

Simon felt hands on him again, pulling him away.

"No!" he yelled, and he brought a leg up and kicked back at the man.

He pushed Erin up, and it was hard.

Hard, as it was hard to crawl out of his hole, his dungeon, all the pain, forcing the window open, getting his body up.

He watched Erin's body sail up onto the ice. He pushed her across the ice. . . .

He got to see her take a breath, lying there. Erin's chest rose, God, her chest rose.

The man grabbed him.

And the two of them slid under the water.

He was strong. His hands closed around Simon's neck. They popped up to the surface, but there was ice above them, blocking the air.

We've slid under the ice.

The man's hands closed Simon's windpipe.

It was black, an underwater blackness, a perfect night.

Simon reached out and locked his hand around the man's neck. He felt his lungs burn, demanding air. His head bounced against the icy roof.

The man tried to shake off Simon's hand, but Simon held on.

I held on this far, he thought. I held on this far, and I can hold on *forever*.

Erin took a breath. *I saw that.* I saw that, he thought.

He *had* to open his mouth, his hand locked on the man's throat. And he felt the man, too, gulping the water, forcing the water into his lungs.

The freezing water filled Simon's mouth. It coursed down his throat. He gasped as he gulped water into his burning lungs.

Then it was even blacker.

EPILOGUE

Friedman had spent two weeks in Phelps Memorial Hospital. He'd read all the newspapers. A young D.A. from White Plains had laid the whole story out for Friedman. It was big news—the death of the Meatman, the story of the heroic father, the hostage who had saved his daughter, the father.

The dead father.

Friedman worried about Lizbeth Farrell and her daughter. When he asked about them, he was told that the little girl was doing *real well.* The mother needed facial surgery, and she was still mending inside.

Friedman asked to see them.

But he'd had to wait until he could sit up and move around.

For his first visit with Lizbeth Farrell he limped into her room.

The last time we saw each other, he thought, *we were both lying on the floor, bleeding.*

Embarrassed, Friedman introduced himself.

When he told her how sorry he was—the words sounding stupid—Lizbeth shook her head.

She started crying, the tears falling into the heavy bandages around her jaw, and he apologized again and backed away.

His own bandages pulled against his stitches when he walked.

But he kept coming back, never talking about what had happened, simply asking how she was being treated by the D.A.'s office, the police, the New York detectives.

She smiled and said that she was fine and everyone was kind to her.

Friedman asked her if he could visit her daughter.

Lizbeth agreed.

He brought Erin a large, floppy stuffed dog, black and white with big blue eyes. Erin smiled when she saw it. The girl was going to have two scars, a long thin scar on her face and another on her neck. The doctors told Friedman that, with cosmetic surgery, the scars would virtually disappear by the time she was an adult.

Friedman was glad of that.

He asked Erin if she was looking forward to getting back to school.

He asked her how the food was. He talked about the cartoon show blaring on the mini-TV hanging over her bed. He ordered her a dish of ice cream.

Then he asked her if he could come and visit her again.

She nodded.

Finally, one day it felt like spring, even though it was just a warm day in March, a day promising things to come. Friedman went to see them in their house.

It had been cleaned from top to bottom by a professional service. There had been no trace left, he had been told.

No blood anywhere.

No, thought Friedman, there will always be a trace. He knew that he would do all he could to get Lizbeth and Erin out of that house, moved into someplace else.

Erin smiled when she saw him.

He asked her how school was. He touched her cheek, feeling the line, the place where she had been cut.

He sat in the living room, and Lizbeth fixed him a cup of tea.

He wondered how many times Lizbeth had seen the videotape of the two bodies being hoisted out of the water, their hands locked on each other.

It was on TV a lot. There were a lot of specials on serial killers. Serial killers were hot.

Lizbeth's mouth was still lopsided where the muscles had been cut. The stitches were gone, but a lot of reconstructive surgery remained to be done.

Friedman would make sure she had it done.

She brought him the tea, and Erin went outside to play.

When Erin was gone, Friedman said to Lizbeth, "She seems better."

Lizbeth nodded. "Sometimes. Sometimes she's almost happy. Then—I don't know. It's like a cloud passes over her."

Friedman looked at Lizbeth. "And you? How are you doing?"

She smiled, and her face looked all askew, the muscles not right, the scar tissue pulled funny. She didn't question his interest in Erin, in her.

"I guess—I guess that sometimes I'm okay, too."

Friedman waited. He knew that he'd wait until it was time to come out.

He heard Erin outside playing. Lizbeth looked at him. "More tea?" she said, starting to stand up.

Friedman shook his head. I could have retired, he thought. And then what would have happened to them, to this family?

"I thought—" Friedman cleared his throat. "I'd like to take Erin to the Mets' opening game." He smiled. "Maybe you'd like to come too?"

She nodded, but her eyes had a faraway look, glazed, staring into forever. She turned back to Friedman. "Simon loved baseball," she said. "When—when he came back, he said to me once, 'I'll get to see'"—she took a breath—"'I'll get to see a game again.'" She shook her head. "But he never did."

It was time.

Lizbeth looked away, her eyes wet. "I don't understand. What was the point? Can you tell me that? He went through all that pain. He fought his way back"—her voice rose, shaking—"to get away, to escape, to—oh, God—to get *here,* to get home." She stopped. She took a breath. Friedman had to sit and watch the tears fall from her eyes. "Just to die," she said. A whisper, a fall wind blowing skeletal leaves.

Just to die . . .

Friedman stood up, a task more difficult than ever. He had his own kids. They were married. They were far away. . . .

I'm not here to replace them, or Simon, he knew. This was something more than that. We're all tied together in this now. Simon, Lizbeth, Erin, me . . . and Pick.

He sat down on the couch next to her.

"It's so terribly sad," she said.

He shook his head. He had waited. Now it was time.

"You were alone with Erin," Friedman said, "and then Simon came back. He came back . . . and he saved Erin."

Lizbeth shook her head, still turned away.

Friedman heard Erin's voice, the sounds as she came into the house.

"Let me tell you what I believe. . . ." Friedman took her chin, felt her scars. He turned her face to look at him. He stared at her wet eyes. "He got away, Lizbeth. Simon escaped; he got out of his hell. He came back. He came back to you, but more than that he came back to his daughter." He took a breath. Lizbeth was sobbing now.

"When you needed him, when God himself seemed to have deserted you, when you needed him like you've never needed anyone, he was here. He came *home.*"

Friedman patted her hand. He smiled, hoping she'd see it, that she'd believe it.

"It's what he came home to do. Don't you see that? No one knew it. But it's what he was here for, to be there that night. To save his daughter."

Footsteps on the stairs, Erin hurrying into the living room.

Lizbeth was crying openly. She quickly rubbed her eyes. "Oh, God. Oh, Jesus, I don't want her to see. I cry so much. She's seen so many tears." Lizbeth looked away.

Friedman leaned close and whispered. "He came home to save his little girl."

Then she was there. Erin, her cheeks flushed from the wind and the still-cool air.

"I'm hungry," she said, with a wonderful directness. "Is it lunchtime yet?"

She hadn't noticed that her mother was turned away, rubbing at her eyes, or if she had noticed, she didn't pay it any attention.

Lizbeth took a breath. When she finally turned to look at Friedman and Erin, she smiled. She *smiled.* . . .

"Okay, sweetheart. I'll fix something now," she said.

She turned back to Friedman, her hand closing on his. "And you'll stay, won't you?" she said.

Friedman nodded . . . because he had no intention of leaving.